PRAYER OF THE DRAGON

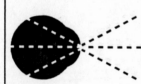

This Large Print Book carries the
Seal of Approval of N.A.V.H.

PRAYER OF THE DRAGON

ELIOT PATTISON

WHEELER PUBLISHING
A part of Gale, Cengage Learning

GALE
CENGAGE Learning·

Detroit • New York • San Francisco • New Haven, Conn • Waterville, Maine • London

Lg Pt
Pat

Copyright © 2007 by Eliot Pattison.
First published in the German language in 2007 as *Der Berg du toten Tibeter.*
Shan Series.
Wheeler Publishing, a part of Gale, Cengage Learning.

LIBRARY OF CONGRESS CATALOGING-IN-PUBLICATION DATA

Pattison, Eliot.
  Prayer of the Dragon / by Eliot Pattison.
    p. cm.
    ISBN-13: 978-1-59722-787-2 (pbk. : alk. paper)
    ISBN-10: 1-59722-787-0 (pbk. : alk. paper)
    1. Shan, Tao Yun (Fictitious character) — Fiction. 2. Ex-police
officers — Fiction. 3. Buddhist monks — Fiction. 4. Navajo
Indians — Fiction 5. Murder — Fiction. 6. Tibet (China) —
Fiction. 7. Large type books. I. Title.
PS3566.A82497P73 2008
813'.54—dc22   2008013163

Published in 2008 by arrangement with Writer's House LLC.

Printed in the United States of America
1 2 3 4 5 6 7 12 11 10 09 08

This book is dedicated to the Tibetan and Navajo peoples, who keep the mysteries of the human spirit alive.

Special thanks to Matthew Woolford Pattison.

CHAPTER ONE

Before being condemned to the Tibetan gulag, Shan Tao Yun had never known there were so many ways of dying, so many words for death, had never considered how the wonder of death could be as great as the wonder of birth. Tibet was a land steeped in riddles, and, for Shan, none was greater than how, in a place where living was so difficult, dying could be so perfect.

For more than five days now, the elderly man on the pallet in front of him had been sitting cross-legged in the lotus position. Shan's former cellmate, Lokesh, now his friend, had told him this upon Shan's recent arrival. Though death hovered nearby, something in the elderly man's spirit kept it at bay. He was in a place few attained. After the first two days, the people of the remote village had replaced the death-rite objects at his side with offerings of fruit and small butter sculptures. Some believed that if a patch of his skin was peeled away there would be only blinding light beneath.

Gendun, the aged red-robed lama who sat at the head of the pallet, intoned an unfamiliar mantra, invoking a deity Shan did not recognize. Lokesh had accompanied Gendun from their illegal, secret monastery to this remote village when summoned. Shan, who had been away at the time, had been sent for when they realized the nature of the problem. Now Lokesh settled beside Shan and rubbed his grizzled jaw. A woman waved a stick of incense over the inert form on the pallet. "They say he is in a state of spiritual perfection," Lokesh declared in a flat voice.

Shan studied his two friends. Gendun, his face as worn as a river stone, acknowledged Shan with a nod, not breaking the rhythm of his prayer. Lokesh, gazing at the peaceful countenance of the man on the pallet, squeezed the prayer beads in his hand so tightly his knuckles were white. Shan knew he had not been urgently summoned over nearly a hundred miles of treacherous mountain trails to witness an unknown farmer's miracle.

"Except?" he asked.

Lokesh cupped his hands around his beads and stared into the hollow they made.

His whisper combined wonder and melancholy. "Except he is a murderer."

Shan sank back against the wall, his eyes now locked on Gendun. If the old lama, abbot of the outlawed monks Shan had lived with since leaving his gulag prison, had sat with the man for so many days, by now he would understand things about the stranger no one else could, in ways no one else would, though he would never express them in words. Gendun, like many of the old Buddhists, distrusted words, considering them only awkward, incomplete links between humans. He would not speak directly about the peculiar mix of fear and awe that seemed to hold the village in its grip. But Shan knew his teacher well and had seen the moment's hesitation in his nod. He surveyed the villagers sitting along the wall of the smoky dirt-floored chamber who were anxiously watching the man on the pallet. Gendun and Lokesh weren't engaged in this uneasy vigil because of a killing but because these impoverished farmers were trembling in their souls. They depended on Shan to cope with the murder — his province, not theirs.

Shan's senses had been dulled by fatigue when he had reached the village. He had rushed through the mountains, barely keeping up with the taciturn young shepherds who had come for him, frantic with fear that disaster had befallen the two men who had become like family to him. Seeing they were safe, he had relaxed, closing his eyes for a few minutes, listening, letting Gendun's soft, resonant words pour into him. Lokesh's announcement burned away the remnants of his fatigue and, alert and alarmed, he studied the old stable as he would have when he had been a Beijing special investigator. An oxlike man stood guarding the door. A cracked plank lying near the foot of the comatose man's pallet held several charred sticks, the remains of incense. In front of the incense sticks stood a row of small *torma,* sculptures molded of butter and barley flour, images of sacred signs, one of them artfully worked into a goddess with graceful bent arms. On a nearby wall were smudges of chalk. Shan studied the faint marks. Someone had chalked in the *mani* mantra, the prayer for the Compassionate Buddha. Someone else had rubbed it away.

A sturdy woman in a black dress stooped in front of Shan, extending a bowl of the buttered tea that was a fixture of Tibetan hospitality. His nod of gratitude froze as his gaze met hers. Her forced smile did nothing to conceal the grief etched on her features.

The thin layer of soot on her face, common to those who illuminated their homes with butter lamps, was streaked with the tracks of tears.

The man on the pallet was tall and lean, his ragged black hair tinged with gray. He shared the weathered skin, the hard, muscular hands, the worn clothes of those sitting along the walls. He wore a soiled fleece vest that matched those of several of the farmers. Had the villagers preparing the man for the death rites bared his feet for washing, Shan would have assumed he was one of them. But now Shan saw his heavy cleated leather boots with finely worked metal fittings that reached past his ankles. They would have cost half the annual income of any family in the village. The man before them, perched like a god on an altar, came from somewhere else, from down in the world. Perhaps from Lhasa?

A dozen questions sprang to Shan's mind about the stranger on the pallet, but the deepest mystery was that of his own friends' actions. The man was wedged against the back wall, loose blankets at either side arranged to hide other, rolled blankets that held his legs in the meditation position. Yet Gendun and Lokesh must know that the man was unconscious, not meditating.

Shan sat, studying Gendun and the stranger on the pallet, watching the nervous way the villagers approached when the lamps had to be replenished, not missing the wary looks they cast toward Gendun. Few of them, he suspected, had seen a real monk in years, the younger ones perhaps never. Beijing had scoured the land so harshly it was difficult for new growth to find a hold.

He leaned toward his old friend. "Who rises?" he asked in a whisper, knowing Lokesh would understand.

"Red Tara," came the hesitant reply. The mantra Gendun recited was an invocation of a fierce form of the Tibetan mother deity, called upon to fight demons and obstacles to compassion. Shan again gazed at the faces of those gathered in the stable. The lama's mantra was not for the man on the pallet, but for the villagers.

Lokesh was strangely restless, leaving Shan's side to help with the lamps, taking a seat away from Shan near the door, then rising to stand in the doorway and look outside, sitting again to work his *mala,* his prayer beads. Shan had seldom seen his friend so unsettled. The one time he returned Shan's gaze there was something Shan had never seen before in his eyes, not even in their gulag days — a terrible desperation, an anguished helplessness.

When Lokesh stepped outside, Shan rose to follow but halted, retreating into the shadows. A new figure had appeared, a stocky man in a black sweatshirt with its hood pulled low over his face. He angrily pushed past the guard and marched toward the pallet. Shan sprang forward but he was too late. The intruder raised his hand and slapped the face of the unconscious man. The woman in the black dress moaned. An old man beside Gendun cried out in alarm but as he tried to grab the intruder's arm he was knocked to the ground. An instant later the guard and another burly farmer each seized one of the intruder's arms, pulling him backward.

"Stickman!" The intruder spat the word as if it were the name of a devil as he wrestled his arms free. "We know the face of death on this mountain!" The guard picked up a short, stout plank and threatened the man with it. The intruder responded with a sneer. "Bloodwalker!" he snarled, then reached into his pocket, threw something at the man on the pallet, and turned toward the door. But before he reached it, he halted, darted to the torma offerings, bent over them, and tossed something else at the pallet. The men dragged him outside.

The woman who had offered Shan tea rushed forward and lifted something from the end of the pallet. She hid the objects in her dress, but not before Shan recognized them. They were from the little goddess sculpted in butter, which was now mutilated. The intruder had ripped the arms off the image and thrown them at the man on the pallet.

Gendun had paid no heed to the intrusion, continuing his mantra. His soft tones calmed them, and soon it seemed as if the intrusion had never taken place. No one seemed to notice when Shan bent to retrieve the little bundle that had bounced off the comatose man's chest. It was composed of four straight twigs, their bark peeled, each twig bearing three thin stripes near the top, one blue, then two red. *Bloodwalker.* The word tugged at his memory, as if he should recognize it.

Shan stuffed the sticks into his pocket. Lifting his tattered hat from the peg where he had left it, he went outside. The brilliant late-afternoon sunlight exploded against his retinas. He jerked his hat down and staggered, nearly falling as a rush of small hooves surrounded him. By the time he

14

recovered his balance, the sheep had sped by, led toward the grassy slope above by a herder. Neither Lokesh nor the intruder could be seen.

The village was called Drango, Tibetan for Head of the Rock. It consisted of perhaps forty structures, most of them built in the traditional fashion — compact two-story houses with quarters for livestock below and humans above, each with a rear courtyard defined by crumbling rock walls, many of which contained goats cropping at weeds. The whitewash on most of the houses was faded, their maroon trim bleached to pinkish gray. Two round stone granaries for storing barley stood near the paths to the fields. Beyond the houses lay the stone foundations of a much larger building inside of which vegetable gardens had been laid out, a familiar sight in the mountains. The Chinese army, deeming such places too remote for infantry, had allocated enough aerial bombs to such hamlets to ensure that each local temple was destroyed.

Shan wandered along the paths between the buildings, admiring the lotus blossoms carved on a roof beam, the small richly colored rug hanging half completed on a well-used loom, the stack of handmade baskets awaiting the grain harvest. No mo-

15

tor vehicle could reach closer than fifty miles, and taking goods to market would mean a backbreaking trek with yak and mule. The village must feed and clothe itself, as it had for centuries. He followed a small maze of winding walls past a forge, an oven, storage bays for dung and wood, and rows of large clay jars holding pickled vegetables. The pungent scent of yak milk being churned floated in the cool late-summer air, intermingled with the earthy scents of soil, dung, and tea.

Drango village was remarkable for what he saw and for what he did not see. It was frozen in time — a proud, peaceful community little changed in fifty years. But the only evidences of Buddhist tradition were a small strand of tattered prayer flags flapping from a rock cairn above the village, faded emblems painted beside half a dozen doorways, decrepit wooden altars at the rear of a few houses, and a huge pile of dried juniper, the fragrant wood burned to attract deities, at the end of the only street. There were none of the prayer flags that often hung between buildings in such hamlets, no prayer wheels, no effort to rebuild what the Chinese army had destroyed when it invaded Tibet decades earlier. With increasing foreboding he paced around the back of the village, studying the wide circle of packed earth at the end of the street, devoid of rocks and barley. It could have been a place for winnowing grain. It could have been a helicopter landing pad. He felt an uninvited twitch, the stirring of the old instincts that refused to die, honed by twenty years as special investigator for the inner circle of Beijing's top officials.

From the shadows he studied each of the houses. At first glance he had seen a dozen empty poles from which prayer flags would have traditionally hung. But then he saw that the pole beside the largest, best maintained of the houses had a radio antenna strapped to its side. He continued to wander among buildings until he encountered two boys of perhaps four years of age playing on the stone step of a house. His stomach went cold, and he retreated. They were playing with small clay figures of Buddhist saints, lifting them one at a time and pressing them with their thumbs until the heads popped off, erupting with laughter each time. The headless bodies were lined up on the step.

Shan found Lokesh sitting cross-legged on a long, flat rock fifty yards up the slope, a perch that offered not only a view of the entire village, its fields, and the stream that flowed past them, but also of the lower

eam of wood that encircled his

e," Lokesh explained. "I have not
a collar since I was a boy. Until
han has stayed on the slope above
large brown dog, one of the
sed to guard the sheep, appeared
nd the canque-bearer, gazed at
Lokesh, then toward a small flock
pe above, before settling beside

ad never seen such a device but
of it in the tales prisoners in their
told on long winter nights. Old
d had no prisons, and almost no
s. When punishment had been
it varied according to local prac-
sser criminals were sometimes
nto such devices, then released, to
eir prison with them. "Surely," Shan
can't be . . ." His question died on
gue. Can't be real? But he saw it,
nessing the ordeal the man faced to
tarving. Can't be permitted? The
ment paid little attention to such
communities.
ne is rare in Drango," Lokesh said.
hen a crime is committed, the head-
ecides on the punishment. He has an
ok he consults. Thieves are sentenced

mountain ranges that cascaded toward the south and west. Shan paced around the rock as he reached Lokesh, taking in the long view before turning toward the huge rugged peak that towered over them, the highest point for dozens of miles.

Lokesh seemed to read his mind. "They call it the Sleeping Dragon. It is a sacred peak," he declared in a tired voice, "home to a powerful land spirit. Some of the villagers say it is why they are so blessed." It was the kind of announcement that Lokesh normally would have offered with great excitement. The last time he and Shan had visited such a mountain they had spent a day climbing toward the top, making rock-cairn shrines along the way, then meditating near the summit as the moon rose. But the children of this mountain laughed as they snapped off the heads of saints.

"They were surprised to see us when we arrived," Lokesh said abruptly. "Chodron, the headman, said no one had sent for us. He was angry when an old woman declared it was destined we should be there and led us into the stable. Since then, Gendun has left his vigil only for a few hours' sleep while I stayed to continue reciting the mantras. Whenever I go outside, the villagers follow me with tea and *tsampa,* as if to tempt me

away from som
of what happen
men are dead a
in the stable. Ch
his sight. He has
stable door to wa

"But someone
stated. He had b
tion and had retur
tain hermitage t
gone. Later, two
rived, panting from
ranges, with an urge
for Shan to acco
Drango.

Shan sat beside hi
the weakness in Loke
he might be ill. He f
along the rock wall th
est field. Nearly two
where the wall turned
windblown juniper, wa
took a long moment f
hend it.

A woman in a traditi
was feeding a man of
tiently placing small mo
pieces of fruit perhaps, or
The man was incapable
because his arms were c

foot-long b
neck.

"A *canqu*
seen such
now that n
town." A
mastiffs u
from behi
Shan and
on the sl
the man.

Shan h
had heard
gulag ha
Tibet ha
crimina
necessar
tice. L
locked i
carry th
said, "it
his ton
was wit
avoid s
govern
remote

"Cri
"But v
man d
old bo

to the collar."

Shan was beginning to understand his friend's anguish. "And killers?"

"There has never been a murder in anyone's lifetime. They consulted their book. They are not fully decided but they are making preparations."

"Preparations?"

"They have resolved that if the stranger dies or continues in his blissful state it will prove he is joined with the gods. If he awakens . . ." Lokesh looked toward the shadows behind the nearest house, where a man bent over a grinding stone. His voice cracked as he explained. "They are sharpening spoons."

"Spoons?"

"If he awakens they will either throw him from the cliff or gouge out his eyes."

A chill ran down Shan's spine. He stared around the quiet little village. "That is why you have not tried to heal him," he concluded.

"If I wake him, I condemn him to their punishment."

The air itself seemed to have grown colder. Shan pulled the collar of his quilted jacket more tightly around his neck. "What is known of the ones who died?"

"Two men from away, they say," Lokesh

told him. "Some villagers found the man who is in the stable up on the mountain, propped against a rock as if meditating. He was sitting close to the bodies. An image of a sacred vase was drawn beside him." It was what a hermit might do — sit at the base of a high rock with the drawing of a sacred image nearby on which to focus his meditation.

"No writing?"

"Only the vase, and another sign they could not understand. It was drawn in blood. Chodron says the killer drew it to show remorse, that it is as good as a confession. His fingers were covered with blood, and there was a hammer at his feet."

"A hammer? Were the corpses bludgeoned to death?"

"They will not show me the bodies," was Lokesh's reply. He explored his pockets and extracted a withered apple, stood, and ventured toward the pair at the end of the rock wall. The woman leaped up, tipping walnuts from her apron. She grabbed one of the straps of the man's collar, urging him to his feet. He heard Lokesh offer the apple as he might to a skittish horse, speaking in a gentle tone about a large boulder above the pasture that, he suggested, had the appearance of an earth spirit's habitation.

With what appeared to be a well-practiced motion, the man twisted the collar, breaking the woman's grip, and turned toward Lokesh with a friendly expression, nodding toward the boulder, speaking in a voice too low for Shan to hear. The woman gathered the spilled nuts in her apron and scurried away. The dog advanced, sniffed Lokesh, wagged its tail, and settled between the two men as they sat in the shade of the solitary tree.

Shan pulled the bundle of sticks that the intruder had hurled at the unconscious man from his pocket. *Stickman.* And another name had been spat out by the intruder. *Bloodwalker.* The thing that had been burned in his memory surfaced. Years earlier, when he had shuttled through prisons in western China, before being finally transported to Tibet, that epithet was used by hard-core gulag criminals to describe assassins within their ranks. With new foreboding, he rose.

Lokesh and the canque-bearer were so deeply engaged in conversation that neither took notice when he sat beside them. The man seemed to have discovered that Lokesh had a healer's knowledge, and was discussing the herbs used to strengthen orphaned lambs. Shan noticed a pot and a fire pit with a small pile of twigs and dried yak dung for fuel nearby. In the shadow of the wall was a rolled blanket and a stout stick, two feet long, peeled of its bark and carved with lotus blossoms. A slab of wood had been wedged into the stones halfway up the wall, and on it lay several hollow reeds. On the grass beneath the slab was a large, flat stone on which lay a rectangular sheet of paper weighed down with pebbles, a sheet from a *peche,* a traditional unbound Tibetan book.

Shan realized that the two men had stopped speaking. He met the silent gaze of the villager. "I did not mean to invite myself into your home," he apologized.

The man's eyes smiled as the fingers of one hand gestured toward the objects by the wall. " 'This fine stone mansion of meditation was built by me, a beggar.' " He was reciting from Milarepa, Tibet's great hermit poet. " 'When the wind blows, my students, the sheep, offer me their fleece blankets,' " he added amiably. Before Shan could reply, he added, "And you are the Chinese wizard who dissolves prison bars and reaps truth from crow-picked fields."

Shan searched the man's face, expecting but not finding signs of mockery. "My father always said I was burdened by too much curiosity," he offered. "When I was a boy I was given a small clock. By the next day I had unfastened every screw, every pin, every spring to discover the magic that made it work."

"At an early age breaking through the illusions of time and reality," the man in the collar observed.

"At an early age," Shan corrected, "never being trusted with another timepiece."

The man's laughter was subdued, and Shan did not miss the wary way he glanced toward the buildings.

"I am named Yangke," he offered. "Poet shepherd of Drango." He studied Shan a moment, leaning forward to look under the brim of his hat. "Once I, too, aspired to be a monk. I had heard of the old one with the joyful eyes who helps the hidden lamas," he said, "and of the elusive lama who is seen in the moonlight above Lhadrung Valley with a phantom from the gulag at his side. Even of the exiled Chinese inspector who sometimes does impossible things to help Tibetans. But I did not realize the phantom and the exile were the same. The herders sent by your friend to Lhadrung thought they were fetching one more outlawed lama, which terrified them. But a former investigator from Beijing, that scared them even more. You are from a different place altogether," the man observed. "I have read about oracles from other worlds who walk among us to explain things the rest of us cannot fully comprehend."

"I have heard much about oracles, too," Shan said. "They are melancholy, sickly souls whose heads are filled with too many voices. They are consumed by the miracles they reveal."

Yangke made a motion with his shoulders, curtailed by the canque, that Shan took to be a shrug. "But unlike the inhabitants of Drango, you will not shy away from miracles," he said.

As Shan and Lokesh exchanged a glance, images flashed through Shan's mind. Aged lamas, imprisoned most of their lives, nursing Shan's broken mind and body back to health after he had been discarded, sent to the gulag. A Tibetan in their prison losing his foot after leaping into the path of a truck to save an injured bird. Gendun and his outlawed monks secretly working in their caves to illuminate prayer books for future generations, risking imprisonment or worse, when they could be safe in India. "Ever since I arrived in Tibet," Shan rejoined, "I have lived from one miracle to the next."

"*Lha gyal lo,* Victory to the gods," Lokesh whispered, his habitual exclamation of joy.

The old Tibetan extracted a small worn pocketknife from his pocket and began slicing pieces of the apple to feed to Yangke. As he worked, a little girl appeared, stepping sideways to keep Lokesh and Shan in front of her, and set a bowl of buttered tea on the slab of wood that was anchored to the wall. She placed one of the hollow reeds in it, then backed away before scampering off. Yangke looked uncertainly at his guests. At an encouraging gesture from Lokesh, he hobbled to the tray on his knees and began drinking through the reed straw.

"Tell us of the miracles of Drango village," Shan said when he had drained the bowl.

"A sturdy, shining ferry across the ocean of existence," Yangke declared. His playfulness was genuine but so too was the melancholy that hung over him. "The biggest miracle is our abandonment," he continued. "Everywhere people try to forget the world but seldom does the world forget a people. We have lost all our chains."

"Not every chain," Shan observed.

Yangke grinned. "My imprisonment has released me. I have become a tree, and the tree has become rooted in the teachings. I watch the sheep and memorize sacred texts. On the day I am able to prostrate myself again, my body will open up like a ripened fruit and a ball of fire will shoot out."

Shan gestured toward the shabby little village. "The temple where you acquired your learning is well hidden."

"My temple and I," Yangke replied acidly, "had no further use for each other."

And that, Shan suspected, was the closest to the mark any of their arrows had landed. Although Beijing was allowing Tibet to slowly rebuild a few monasteries, one of the ways it kept control was by periodically purging the ranks of monks who threatened dissent.

"This paradise of yours had no need of a lama until a murderer struck?" Shan asked.

"This paradise I returned to," Yangke corrected, "can barely grasp the notion of one man killing another, let alone the horrible thing that they discovered. These are things not of our making but they will be our unmaking. For all its many faults, Drango is worth preserving."

"Just as Gendun is," Shan declared. "We must get him away from here." Perhaps Drango might be worth preserving but it felt like a trap to Shan.

Yangke looked toward the stable. "I have known of him for years. They call him the Pure Water Lama because he was ordained before the Dalai Lama left."

"He is unregistered," Shan said, "like Lokesh and me. But as a senior lama, defying the government, he is in greatest danger. A bounty has been placed on him," Shan added with a guilty glance toward Lokesh. The only time Gendun ever chastised Shan was when Shan expressed concern for him. Before Shan had introduced him to the mysteries, and suffering, of the outside world, Gendun had not left his hidden complex of caves where he was safe. "He will not leave here of his own will now, and when Public Security comes they will seize him and make him disappear forever."

Yangke's face sagged.

"None of us know anyone here," Shan continued. "Why did someone send for Gendun and Lokesh?"

"You just said it. He is an outlaw." Yangke turned to Lokesh, who was stroking the dog's back. "For Drango it is only safe to deal with outlaws. Is it not true that in the old days the monasteries had their own police and judges who dealt with monks who performed criminal acts?"

Lokesh leaned forward, suddenly very interested. "Senior lamas, sometimes abbots, would sentence sinners among them to penance," he confirmed.

"The ones who died so terribly last week,

29

they were like holy men. And they too were outlaws. Just like the one in the stable."

The big dog rose, growling. Yangke glanced back toward the village, his muscles tensing.

"Apricots!" an eager voice called. "Fresh from the orchard!" A compact man in a tattered fox cap jogged toward them, shouting as if trying to drown out anything Yangke might be saying.

"Chodron," Lokesh muttered. It was the *genpo,* the village headman, carrying a small basket.

Yangke struggled to his feet and turned his back on the approaching man. "Forgive me for what I have done to you," he said to Shan and Lokesh. "And all I am going to do. Lha gyal lo," Yangke added. Then, the dog at his side, he hurried toward the grazing sheep, staggering as he tried to keep his heavy collar balanced.

The jovial air of the headman seemed to increase when he learned Shan's name. He pushed his square, fleshy face under the brim of Shan's ragged hat as if to confirm that there were indeed Chinese features in its shadow. Forcing some of the fruit into Shan's hands, gesturing for Lokesh to follow, he escorted them down, into a small shed behind the main street where three

30

pallets were arranged on the rough plank floor. Beside Shan's frayed backpack rested a familiar canvas sack embroidered with sacred signs that Lokesh used for journeys, and the tattered work boots Gendun wore under his robe when traveling.

"There is another house that would be better for you," the headman said to Shan. "Bigger. You would be more comfortable there. Dolma, the widow who lives there, will see to your needs."

"We need only a floor for our blankets," Shan said. At his first encounters with Tibetans, Shan was often feared, sometimes reviled. But the rare occasions when he was doted upon because he was Chinese made him much more uncomfortable.

"I insist," pressed the genpo.

"Only if my friends can join me," Shan replied.

"Of course," Chodron agreed hesitantly. "It's the house next to the stable. I will see that your bags are moved."

Outside, a woman worked at the loom Shan had admired earlier, and a man had begun applying new whitewash to the walls fronting the street. "Are you preparing for a festival?" Shan asked, gesturing toward the pile of juniper wood.

"Two great events at once," Chodron

confirmed. "First the barley harvest, then the First of August," he said. "There will be singing all night. And many jars of *chang,*" he added, the Tibetan barley ale. For the first time Shan saw several men by the granaries, working with stones on steel, sharpening sickles. Soon they would work in the fields, loading sheaves onto carts pulled by broad-backed yaks. Against the granary walls were stacked wooden flails and the wide, flat baskets that would be used to thresh and winnow the grain. To a village like Drango nothing was more important than the harvest, nothing more dangerous than a bonfire while the paper-dry barley still stood in the fields.

As Shan followed the genpo toward the largest of the structures along the short, dusty street, he glanced at Lokesh, seeing in his friend's troubled eyes confirmation that he had heard correctly. August the First. The little village, so remote it seemed to have escaped the notice of the government since the day it was bombed from the air, was preparing to celebrate one of Beijing's most patriotic holidays, the day set aside for praise of China's military.

In the sparsely furnished sitting room on the second floor of his house, Chodron's wife silently served them more buttered tea

32

while the headman boasted of the accomplishments of his village. Most of the families had lived in Drango for eight or more generations, he explained. Once they had been renowned for their finely woven carpets like the one that adorned the room they sat in. Shan's gaze drifted over the headman's shoulder to a shelf heavy with books, all hardbound printed books, all in Chinese, then finally to a framed photo on the wall of a much younger Chodron in the uniform of the People's Liberation Army.

As they walked back outside, a bell rang somewhere. Lokesh smiled. It was a way of summoning deities, a way of accompanying the rhythm of mantras. But these peals quickly became frantic, and from the slopes men began shouting. Sweet, acrid smoke wafted around the houses. The headman gasped and darted toward the street, Shan a step behind him. Someone had set the pile of juniper wood alight.

The village exploded with activity, some villagers running to the stream with buckets, others toward the fields with brooms and blankets. Every flying spark threatened their precious harvest. Shan ran with them toward the thick column of smoke, then saw Lokesh headed for the stable at the other end of the settlement. Shan paused only long enough to see the headman confer with the big farmer who had been guarding the stable door. The man began to run up a track along the stream at the side of the fields, pausing only to lift a heavy harvest knife from a bench by a granary.

A minute later, Shan was at his friend's side. The guard at the door was gone, the chamber emptied of everyone but Gendun and his charge. Lokesh approached the pallet and lifted the man's hand, taking his pulse at his wrist, then his neck, and temple. Shan brought tea from the kettle by the door.

Lokesh raised a hand. "It might revive him. Water, not tea. I have given him water every few hours."

Lokesh tipped the man's head back as Shan filled a ladle from a bucket and began dripping water into his mouth. Long bony fingers reached out and closed around the man's lifeless hand. Gendun had stopped his mantra. Lokesh straightened the man's legs and began massaging the limbs, pausing twice to press his ear to the stranger's chest and check his pulse. "His flesh cannot endure without nourishment," Lokesh declared in a worried tone.

"This particular life," came a voice like rustling grass, "is not rounded."

Lokesh and Shan looked up. Except for his prayers, these were the first words Gendun had spoken since Shan's arrival. Gendun's words were used between monks of their hermitage or by the monks of Shan's former prison to describe a strong stumbling spirit that had failed to resolve itself before death.

"The mountain," Lokesh said. "He may have come to learn from the mountain."

"A pilgrimage," Shan added, completing the thought. Devout Tibetans sometimes made secret pilgrimages to remote shrines, to give thanks to a deity, seek absolution, be cured, or fulfill a promise to a loved one. To wear down the rough edges that cut at a troubled soul.

"Lha gyal lo!" Lokesh exclaimed. He'd seen the man's tongue appear between his lips in response to the trickle of moisture. As Shan cradled the man in his arms, Lokesh stroked the stranger's throat. He swallowed. They gave him half a ladle more of water mixed with honey from a jar by the door, a few drops at a time, then returned him to the pallet. Shan went to the door. The villagers had extinguished the fire by pulling the logs from the pile and soaking them, and were now beating out small patches of flame in the fields. They'd saved nearly all their crop.

"Someone is asking for help," Lokesh declared when he returned to the pallet. He saw the confusion on Shan's face. "Don't you see? It is like a desperate prayer. Someone is willing to lose the crop in order to summon the deities."

Perhaps his friend was right, Shan thought, though the fire could just as easily have been a distraction, even a warning.

He checked the invalid's pockets and found them empty except for a few Chinese coins and a stick as thick as his index finger and half as long. The bark had recently been peeled from the little piece of wood and it had been carved at one end, with three holes cut into the rounded surface, arranged like two eyes and a mouth. The other end, where its waist and legs should have been, was broken off. He stared at the stick on his palm for a moment, then slipped it into his own pocket. The man wore no ring, no watch, no amulet, no adornment of any kind except for a very strange tattoo on his forearm, a thick blue line that extended nearly from his wrist to his elbow, the body of a stick figure with a rectangular head, arms and legs made of jagged lines like lightning bolts, and a long triangle arranged like a skirt low down.

Shan, like his friends, cocked his head at the image. *Stickman.* The intruder had pronounced the name like a curse. The tattooed image was unfamiliar, as was, for most Tibetans, the concept of the decoration of the skin with ink. The stranger was not just from down in the world but from far away. Shan probed the man's clothing, running a fingertip over the fabric, pausing over each button, each stain. He said nothing about the thin line of tiny rust brown spots across the front of his shirt or the fanlike pattern of similar spots on his denim trousers that ran from the knee up his thigh, or the faint line of spots along his chest. They were dried blood that had sprayed onto his clothing from a severed blood vessel less than an arm's length away.

He gazed a moment at the man's unseeing face, then ran his finger over the inside of his vest, looking for a hidden pocket. "Something is sewn inside," he announced, trying to make sense of the three shapes he felt. Neither Lokesh, massaging the man's legs, nor Gendun, still holding one of his hands but reciting his prayers again, took notice. Shan rose, darted out the door, and returned with a small wooden tube retrieved from his pack. He extracted the cork from the top and withdrew a long needle and thread, then with his knife opened the seam of the vest's lining. Tucked into small, tight pockets, expertly sewn, were the feather of a large bird, a small leather pouch bound by a drawstring, and a long plastic vial of yellow powder.

They stared at the unexpected, inexplicable objects in silence, the pace of Gendun's recitation slowing as the lama reached out, one thin finger touching not the objects but the space just above them. Lokesh's jaw opened and shut silently. When the old Tibetan looked up at Shan he knew his friend too was recalling Yangke's description of the comatose man and his dead companions.

"What kind of holy man is this?" Lokesh asked at last.

What kind of bloodwalker is this? Shan almost added.

A shout from somewhere within the village broke the spell. Lokesh rose and stood at the door, watching the street, while Shan refastened the lining with hasty stitches.

The villagers returned to their vigil in twos and threes, their chatter fading as they approached the stable, new, excited whispers rising as they saw that their would-be saint had moved.

The guard appeared, followed a moment

later by Chodron. "What have you done?" the genpo demanded as he neared the form now outstretched on the pallet. "He awakened! I must speak with him." He kneeled and poked the man's arm.

Shan asked in a loud, slow voice, "How often have you seen such a great column of juniper smoke?"

The headman stared at Shan, his brows knitted. The villagers leaned forward.

"The juniper smoke touched the sky," Shan explained, fixing Chodron with a level stare. "And then he moved without waking." A murmur of wonder rippled through the onlookers.

"The deities arrived!" a woman exclaimed. "And they lifted him!"

The headman glared at Shan. Then, with a wary glance at the onlookers, he went to the wooden bowl holding incense sticks, lit one from a lamp, and placed it in the cracked plank that held the others. Chodron settled against the wall, studying Shan with intense curiosity, then after several minutes, rose and left.

As the purple light of sunset filtered over the horizon the three friends shared tsampa and *momo,* Tibetan dumplings, with a score of villagers around a fire pit behind the headman's house. The villagers listened with rapt attention as Lokesh spoke of his many travels around the fringes of modern Tibet, even touching, ever so tentatively, upon his years, decades earlier, as an official in the Dalai Lama's government.

At last there was no one left but the headman and three gray-haired villagers, introduced as the village elders, two men and the woman in the black dress who had first given Shan tea. Although Chodron fastidiously performed his obligations as host, filling their cups one more time, all warmth had left his face. "Seldom do we receive visitors," the headman said. "You have honored us. But as you see, we are beginning our harvest. Every hand must be lifted to the work." He was inviting them to leave.

"Then it is fortunate my friends and I are here, so we can care for the stranger in the stable, freeing others for their tasks," Shan replied impassively.

"You mean the murderer in our jail." The deference Chodron had previously shown Shan was gone.

The elders said nothing. One stared into his bowl of tea. The woman, her hands clasped in her lap, chewed absently on a piece of dried cheese, glancing repeatedly at Shan before looking away.

"It is a terrible responsibility, to sit in

judgment of others," Shan said.

"I will not flee from my duty," Chodron shot back.

"He is ill. When he awakens he may not be able to speak for himself."

Chodron silently rose, entered the rear door of his house, and returned a moment later with a small wooden chest that he set on the ground by the fire. The headman extracted a cloth bundle from within, then unfolded it on the ground in front of Shan. "We already know the blackness of his deeds."

He displayed a hammer, a modern rock hammer, one end blunt and square, the other extending in a long, slightly curving claw. There was still enough light for Shan to see the dried blood and small gray flecks on the claw. "His hands were covered with the blood of those he killed," the headman explained. "He finished one of them with a blow from that claw to the back of the head." Chodron tapped the handle of the hammer with his boot, revealing a second object underneath. "No one wants to even think about what he did with his other weapon."

It was a slender rod of stainless steel that rose into a curved sharp hook at one end. It was so out of context that it took Shan a moment to recognize it as a dental pick. The tip was covered in blood.

The woman shuddered and looked away. The other two elders stared into the fire, carefully avoiding looking at the objects.

"The people of the town say there are no witnesses," Lokesh reminded them.

"My people are like children when it comes to things of the outside world," Chodron said. "They must be taught right from wrong."

"And you will do so by killing this stranger?" Shan asked.

"If the deities wish to prevent it, they can take him before he awakes. Otherwise," Chodron said in a brittle tone, "those of us responsible for the village know our obligations. We will have a town assembly. We will speak of what happened, of why we must do what we have to do. I have been rereading the old records with the elders. Perhaps it will be enough to take something of his body, perhaps only one eye. In the old days they sometimes just took an eye. We are taught to be compassionate."

"Compassion in Drango," Lokesh observed in a haunted tone, "has a flavor all its own."

The old woman tightened her hands. They covered something inside her blouse. She

42

was wearing a *gau* around her neck, Shan realized, a prayer box, the only one he had seen among the villagers.

Chodron ignored Lokesh. "The punishment will be carried out according to our custom. If he is still alive afterward he will be taken to the nearest road. For as long as the village has been here it has punished its own wrongdoers. The true test of a leader, like that of a barn beam, is when a storm wind blows. I will not retreat from my duty."

"We have seen what you do with beams in Drango," Shan said.

Chodron clenched his jaw. "I caught Yangke stealing from my house. He confessed in front of the village and I read out the traditional punishment. Some argued that he should be taken to the county seat, to Tashtul, that he was not subject to our decision because he had lived so long away from the village. I gave him the choice. I said I would write a report and send him with it to Public Security, which already has a file on him. I reminded him there were many prisons ready for people like him — new prisons are being built all the time. The next morning he asked me to put the wooden collar on him. As for this stranger, how do you think they would deal with a double murderer down in the world? Do you truly wish me to summon the authorities? They will send a helicopter, with soldiers carrying machine guns. If you continue you give me no choice."

Shan's mouth went dry. "Continue? I just arrived."

"Your presence and that of your two friends has caused people to speak behind my back. Many who were weaned of their prayer beads years ago secretly ask your lama for blessings. Half my people realize that this man is a murderer but the others call him a saint. We had plenty of lamps in that stable already but the day after your lama arrived, people insisted there be one hundred eight," Chodron said with scorn. That was the sacred number, the number of prayer beads on a string and the number of lamps traditionally placed on altars for special ceremonies. "My people speak to perfect strangers about our private affairs. My authority is in question. Our village's progress is in jeopardy."

"Do you know who Gendun is?" Shan asked.

"I have heard of someone called the Pure Water Lama who wanders the hills like some lonely old goat. I have no idea what he does."

"What he does," Lokesh said, "is collect

44

delicate blossoms in old cracked jars."

The words elicited a hungry gaze from one of the old men.

Chodron ignored the comment. "I have heard of this lama. I have also heard of talking yaks and mountains that fly."

"Gendun is here," Lokesh said, "because these people need him. If he had been aware of what was happening here he would have come long ago."

Chodron glared at Lokesh. "Do you truly believe you can descend upon our village and destroy all we have struggled to build?" Anger flared in his eyes. "I know now why you sent for this man Shan behind my back. You thought having a Chinese with you would change everything. You thought our people would be so scared of a Chinese that you could simply order us to release that killer."

"The village needs to understand what took place," Lokesh protested. "It needs to stop fearing —"

"I am not frightened," Chodron interrupted. "I know your dishonorable kind. One of his arms will show what he is."

Lokesh slipped his prayer beads from his wrist and extended them toward the genpo. "Take these to understand *our kind.*"

Shan put his hand on his friend's arm to

quiet him. He rolled up his sleeve and turned the inside of his forearm into the light of the fire. One of the old men moaned. The old woman covered her mouth with her hand. The elders might know little of the outside world but they knew enough to recognize the row of numbers tattooed on his skin. Shan understood why Chodron's demeanor toward him had changed. The herders who had traveled with Shan and seen him roll up his sleeves at mountain streams must have disclosed that he was tattooed with a number.

"Tell me this, prisoner," Chodron asked triumphantly. "Do you have your release papers?"

The question hung in the air for a long time. Somewhere a dog barked. A lamb bleated.

"No," Shan admitted. He had not escaped but his release had been unofficial.

He was vaguely aware of movement at his side but did not see what Lokesh was doing until the old Tibetan had thrust his own bared arm into the firelight, displaying a similar line of numbers.

"Shan is the reason I did not die in prison. He forced my jailers to release me," Lokesh explained. "From the hour he was thrown past the barbed wire into our camp Shan

46

has helped Tibetans."

"You are welcome to join him," Chodron replied in a chilly voice. "You can help each other back to the hole you slithered out of."

"Or else?" Shan asked, repressing his anger as he struggled to understand the strange power Chodron held over the village.

Chodron's thin lips curled into a smile. "Or else it will be like old times when the headman presented proof of the crime, then exacted the punishment with the blessing of our abbot. You will cure my people of this reactionary notion that saints may walk among them. You will restore my people's confidence by giving me the proof I need to demonstrate my authority."

"We will not lie," Shan stated.

"Only affirm the truth," Chodron replied. "Stand with your lama tomorrow morning and declare that man is a killer and all three of you can be twenty miles away by sunset. You are the ones who created our problem. You are the ones to correct it."

"The Tibetans I know do not gouge out eyes or throw men from cliffs."

"Those *you* know!" Chodron spat. "You are an outsider. A criminal. Do not presume to instruct us in our traditions."

In the silence that followed, the wind

surged for a moment, fanning the flames, tossing open the back door of Chodron's house. Shan saw a blush of color in the dim light, red with dabs of yellow. An altar? The pattern of color coalesced. Chodron had hung the flag of Beijing at the rear entry.

Shan studied the elders for a moment. "Where are the children?" he asked abruptly.

"Children?" Chodron shot a wary glance toward the elders. The old woman cupped her hands and stared into them. The oldest — a frail man with a white, wispy beard — cast an empty, longing look at Shan. The genpo rose and stood between Shan and the elders.

"I have seen none between the ages of perhaps five and eighteen," Shan continued. "Tell us where you've sent them."

"Away," Chodron muttered.

"Chinese school," Lokesh said, grasping Shan's meaning. "Where they lose their Tibetan names. Where they are forced to speak only Chinese and sing the songs of Beijing. Where they are taught the Dalai Lama is a criminal."

Chodron offered no denial.

"How many times have *you* gone to school, Chodron?" Shan asked. At schools for municipal leaders, the curriculum was established by senior Party members. Chodron spoke and dressed like a farmer but at his temple the lamas were Party bosses.

"Who are you?" Chodron snarled. "Why were you in prison?"

Shan ignored his question. "What bargains have you made in order to keep Drango the way it is?"

Lokesh extracted a cone of incense from a pocket and dropped it into the embers at the edge of the fire. The man with the white beard stared at the thin plume of smoke, absently extending his fingers into it.

Chodron's countenance grew rigid. "You shall give the village the affirmation it needs," he declared. "The headman always carried out severe punishments with a lama at his side. Your lama will stand with me when the sentence is executed, to give me his blessing. Meanwhile, we keep your lama. If he does not restore order by joining me at the appointed time, then I will speak to Public Security about outlaws in robes. Our herders now know where you hide."

The gray-haired woman set her bowl down and turned her face away.

Chodron added as he took a step toward his house, "But *if* the deities are truly on your side, they will take the killer into their embrace and never let him wake."

"So the way he proves his innocence," Shan said, "is by dying?"

Chodron rejoined in a mocking tone, "Death is but a reward to the virtuous, isn't that what you teach? But if he awakes . . . We will deal with him after the harvest. Before our festival. You have seven days."

"Please understand," came a voice as dry as straw. The gray-haired woman finally spoke. "Look at our village. We live on a diet of promises and fear. Chodron has preserved our ways the best he knows how. All we want for Drango is justice, our own justice. You must give us justice."

Lokesh and Shan exchanged a melancholy glance. Justice. It was a topic they had long ago worn out, a word that had acquired a strange, alien ring to Shan's ears. He had once thought he could obtain justice for Tibetans. But Lokesh had taught him better, shown him that the government cared little about crimes committed among such remote people. For such Tibetans there was only truth, and the terrible consequences of truth.

CHAPTER TWO

Shan left in the gray light before dawn after glancing through the cracked stable door and over the shoulder of a guard slumped against the inside wall, to confirm that Gendun still maintained his vigil. It was the kind of morning when he and his friends would often slip away to greet the sun, sometimes sprinkling a few kernels of barley for the birds. But the feeling of foreboding that gripped Shan made him wonder if he would ever find such peace of mind again.

A pebble bounced onto the bare earth in front of him, then another. He paused, expecting to spot a sheep on the shadowed slope above, but he saw nothing. Another pebble flew over his shoulder. He heard soft, hurried footfalls on the trail behind him before he could make out the figure hurrying toward him.

"You are not the only one who needs a morning blessing," Lokesh said when he

51

reached Shan's side. The first rays of the sun were considered by some of the old Tibetans to be a special gift of the earth deities.

"At the end of this particular trail will be no blessing," Shan warned.

"The only answer we have found so far is that there are no answers to be found in the village," Lokesh replied and raced ahead, disappearing around a high rock outcropping.

By the time Shan reached him, Lokesh, who was more than half again Shan's age, was seated on a high, flat ledge, legs folded into each other, staring at the ragged silhouettes of the eastern ranges as he told his beads in a whisper. Nearby, half a dozen sheep stared at the horizon as intently as did Lokesh himself.

Shan lowered himself onto a slab of rock ten feet away, not wishing to disturb his friend. He knew what to expect, having seen Lokesh in the predawn light with the same joyful expectation on his countenance scores of times before, and though his anxiety at the events of the day before robbed him of his own tranquillity, he drew strength from watching his friend and waiting for the inevitable moment to come.

Lokesh would recite his mantra as the

darkness faded, then just before the first rays of light he would abruptly cease, catch his breath and hold it, not inhaling again until the sun appeared. Shan had never seen him fail, never seen him have to draw in another quick breath before the brilliant rays of light appeared. At first he had tried to decipher the strange calculation that Lokesh surely must be doing, then eventually decided there was no calculation, that Lokesh was connected to the natural world in a way he would never experience. Once, coming from a twenty-four-hour meditation, deprived of sleep, Shan had found himself watching Lokesh, not the sun, and for a moment had been overcome with panic that Lokesh would forget to inhale, and the sun would not come up.

Shan was close enough to see Lokesh's chest freeze and found that he too was holding his breath, watching until a blinding seed of energy materialized on the rim of the mountains. Lokesh acknowledged Shan with his uneven smile, made crooked by the boot of a prison guard years before, then finished his rosary before rising and continuing up the trail. It was one of the many little rituals that defined the lives of the old Tibetans.

They had walked perhaps a mile when

they saw a second group of sheep, a dozen rugged, long-haired creatures that sat in the lee of an outcropping above a stream, all intently watching something below. Shan saw the familiar brown mastiff first, on the slope a hundred feet away, as curious as the sheep at the strange sight on the bank of the stream. The figure at the water's edge was readily recognizable, though the actions of the man in the canque were not.

Yangke was performing what appeared to be a dance, jumping in the air, then kicking out with one foot. His hands were no longer bound by the fittings of the canque, though he was forced to keep a grip on it with one hand to maintain his balance. As they watched, he kicked several times, the last so violently the weight of the collar threw him backward onto the ground. Rising, he made a long sweeping arc with the end of the beam, seeming to scrape the earth, then moved fifty feet downstream and repeated the motions.

"I do not know this ritual," Lokesh declared in a puzzled tone.

This time Yangke executed a more delicate step, using his toes to separate rocks in a small pile at his feet and coax them along the bank before swatting them into the fast water.

"He practices one of those games people play with sticks and balls," Lokesh suggested.

"What he practices," Shan said as he watched Yangke, "is anger."

The former monk did not turn immediately when his dog barked, but walked a few more feet up the stream, then gave a high-pitched cry, one of the calls used to summon wandering sheep.

As the dog bounded toward them with a wagging tail, Shan bent to pick up a stick lying near the first place they had seen Yangke kicking at the earth. The wood, two feet long and over an inch thick, had been stripped of bark and painted with three thin rings near the top, two red with one yellow between. Shan pulled out the little sticks that had been tossed down by the angry intruder in the stable. The markings were similar but the colors did not match.

"The sheep are apt to roam far this time of year," Yangke explained as he turned with a show of surprise and greeted the two men.

Shan went to the second place they had seen Yangke perform his strange dance and retrieved a second stick from under some stones that had been kicked on top of it. It bore the same red and yellow colored rings as the first. He held the sticks, tapping the painted ends in his palm as he approached the young Tibetan. "Or perhaps it troubles them to see their shepherd become so upset over a few sticks," Shan observed.

Yangke walked up the slope to where his dog sat and eased himself down beside the animal, resting one end of his heavy collar on a nearby rock. The dog licked his face and Yangke began stroking its back. "Cho-dron allows me the use of my hands when I am working with the herds, as long as I work my hands back into the bindings when I go near the village. For him," the former monk added, "that is compassion."

Shan lowered himself onto the grass beside Yangke and surveyed the landscape. He saw another painted stake on the far side of the stream, then another a hundred feet upstream. "I met an old lama in prison," Shan said after a moment, "who always laughed when he heard about Chinese buying plots of land on sacred mountains. He asked who signed the papers for the land deity." As they watched, Lokesh waded across the shallow, ankle-deep stream and collected the sticks that were still standing.

Yangke kept patting the dog, which watched attentively as Lokesh gleaned a piece of rope, then a ragged piece of canvas from the rocks beside the water. "When I was a boy we would come up the mountain on festival days, with my uncles and aunts and cousins. The children would collect the pretty yellow rocks in the streams and put them inside cairns with prayer flags and mani stones arranged about them," Yangke explained, referring to the stones that bore inscribed prayers left by the devout at sacred sites. "Each visit we would build one cairn, to honor the golden earth deity that resides in the mountain. Sometimes it would be six or eight feet high." He paused and gazed into the clear cobalt sky. "After I went down to the world my surviving aunt wrote me letters. When she described how men came and tore down all the cairns, I didn't really understand. When she said they had changed the course of some of the streams and stopped a waterfall I used to play in, I thought she was making some sort of strange joke."

Shan watched a soaring bird, a huge lammergeier, as he pondered Yangke's words, then surveyed the long, wide slope before them. Scattered along the stream were piles of rocks, not the carefully stacked cairns of the devout but what could have been the ruins of cairns. "I don't understand," he said. "Gold mining requires roads and enormous machines." He glanced up at the bird circling overhead. The feather in the vest of the stranger in the stable had come from such a large bird of prey.

"Suppose a mountain was so remote that Chinese survey crews ignored it when they cataloged mineral resources decades ago," Yangke said. "Suppose a secret base happened to be built on the far side of the mountain that discouraged anyone from venturing too close. Suppose, eventually, a few Chinese discovered streams with nuggets and gold dust, even veins of gold in the rocks, but they knew the army would never permit legitimate mining operations because the secret base was so close. Suppose it became something of a hobby for some of them, a pastime, to sneak across the mountain after the snow melted and extract a few ounces of gold. It wouldn't take too many years before word would spread and others arrived, who took their work more seriously."

"Outlaw miners," Shan ventured. He had heard of such men elsewhere in Tibet, prospectors who operated far from the reach of government taxes and mining regulations. The mountains are high, and the emperor is far away, ran the age-old saying.

"It's been a closely guarded secret, confined to criminals mostly, men with little to lose, with good reasons to keep out of the government's sight. They used to hide, from the rest of us and from each other. But they grow bolder every year. Some work the streams with pans. Some use dynamite to open the veins. They arrive after the snow melts and leave in September. Like migrating geese. Except these geese eat the land itself."

"Why would they bother to stake claims?"

"They respect each other's workings. They've begun to organize themselves, enacting rules for peaceful coexistence with each other and with Drango village."

"But someone in Drango could inform the government."

"And what then? The slopes would be crawling with troops. Public Security would ask questions about Drango that no one would want to answer. The Bureau of Mining would descend on us. Municipal administration bureaus. The Bureau of Religious Affairs," he added with a shudder.

"But you said the two murdered men were holy men," Shan reminded him.

"I crept as close to their campsite as I dared with this tree about my neck. They had rebuilt a cairn near their camp. These men ignored the streams. They wrote in books and cleaned old paintings. They had started making a *kyilkhor* when they were killed."

"A sandpainting?"

Yangke nodded. "But maybe they were miners as well. They dug into the rocks and crawled into small caves. But I think they were scared of the others. The other miners camp in the open, to warn competitors off. But the ones who died, they camped in out-of-the-way places, hidden places."

Miners and monks. It seemed to Shan an impossible combination. "Were these sticks used by the dead men?"

"No. They never used claim stakes. These are new. No one has ever staked a claim so close to Drango before. Some of the miners say the village sits on the richest vein of all. Once I had a nightmare in which they blew the village off the side of the mountain to get at the gold."

Yangke followed Shan's gaze up the slope. "You'll just make more trouble," he said. "Chodron has forbidden anyone to go up there. He warned the villagers against disturbing the deities."

"Do you and Chodron share the same deities?" Shan asked, immediately shamed by the harshness of his words. He'd felt an unfamiliar surge of anger at the mention of the headman's name. In the same perverse way that he invoked the old traditions, Chodron was seeking to use Gendun as his minion, to turn the lama's compassion into something dark and ugly.

Yangke contemplated Shan's question. "What Chodron and I share is the will to survive."

"For some, the most difficult thing in life is knowing what they are surviving for," Shan said, pausing over the mystery not of the killings but of Yangke. He had been born in the village and left it for a monastery, then knowingly returned to Chodron's peculiar brand of despotism.

Yangke did not reply.

They watched the sheep spread out over the broad, rolling slope, the early sun washing over them, the light breeze bringing a scent of mountain flowers. Shan was falling into a languid doze when thunder suddenly boomed and the earth seemed to tremble. Several sheep bleated and trotted toward Yangke, who pointed to a plume of dust perhaps two miles away. It was not thunder that they had heard.

As Shan watched the settling dust a new sound rose, an alien, crackling whirling that he could not identify. Yangke shouted out in warning. Sheep bleated in alarm. As Shan spun about, a man in a tattered green quilted jacket and a soldier's helmet painted with black and yellow stripes burst around a rock on the trail, riding a bicycle. The sheep scattered in terror. Shan dove into the grass as the man sped by, laughing, waving a bundle of claim stakes over his head.

Yangke bent and launched a well-aimed stone. Though the rider was already some distance away, it bounced off his back, raising another laugh from the man before he disappeared around an outcropping.

"Something else new this year," Yangke said in a low, angry voice. "They brought in two or three of those mountain bikes. After so many centuries the sheep trails crisscross the mountain like highways, worn smooth enough for those heavy bikes. The sheep hate them. I hate them."

Only Lokesh seemed unaffected by the sudden intrusion, and the shadow that settled onto Yangke's face gradually lifted as he watched the old Tibetan. Lokesh had rearranged the stakes, placing them in a long line perpendicular to the stream, anchoring them with small cairns built around each base, then stringing rope from one to another. He had torn small pieces of canvas from the abandoned tarpaulin and was tying them to the rope. A grin appeared on

Yangke's face and he struggled to his feet, then went to the remains of an old campfire near the stream. Shan was at his side a moment later and saved him the trouble of bending by handing him a stub of charred wood.

Lokesh had begun writing a series of familiar Tibetan words on the cloth scraps. He was turning the miners' equipment into a battery of prayer flags, erected in a defensive line between the miners and Drango village.

"Lha gyal lo," Shan said.

The young Tibetan silently opened and shut his mouth, as though trying to remember how to speak the words. "Lha gyal lo," he finally repeated in a voice that cracked with emotion, then stumbled down the slope to help inscribe more flags.

An hour later Yangke led them onto a long, wide shelf, one of the many tiers that rose like irregular steps for several miles before ending at the base of the jagged summit.

"One of the other shepherds discovered the bodies," Yangke explained. "They had made camp by the trees," he said, indicating several gnarled junipers and pines that grew by a small spring, beside a series of high outcroppings that would have shielded them from anyone higher up on the slope. "He did not know about one camp but one of the dogs started growling as if a wolf was near and then he saw a backpack lying out in the open. He was going to skirt the camp but the dog went in and wouldn't return."

"Where is their equipment and bedding?" Shan asked as they approached the grove of trees. There was no sign that anyone had been there except for compacted soil under the trees.

"Gone. I came here two days later, as soon as I could without Chodron's men seeing me. I found the cold ashes of a small campfire. Lots of dried blood. Boot marks all over. The miners watch each other. If one dies, any equipment that is not looted immediately is gathered up and auctioned to the others. They are like vultures."

Shan paused and looked back at Yangke. "Do you mean miners have been killed too?"

"It's a dangerous job," Yangke said. "And the miners like to take care of their own problems. I hear things from the other shepherds. There was talk about a miner killed last year, another found dead last month. But the miners and I, we stay away from each other." Exhausted from climbing while burdened by his canque, Yangke settled between two boulders, resting one end of the beam on each. He raised a weary arm to gesture toward a small mound of rocks not far from the trees. "Their campfire was there."

Someone had tried to obscure the fire pit by stacking rocks over it to make it look like the base of one more cairn. Shan kneeled and rolled away the rocks, then examined the ashes, trying to recognize the mélange of scents released when he stirred them. He closed his eyes to focus on the smells. Burned feathers. Burned plastic. Rice and wild onions, scorched in a pot. Singed butter. Sifting the ashes, he produced a lump of hard blue material, three inches long, then another similar piece. The remains of water bottles or plastic cups or even remnants of a small nylon pack? The ashes yielded nothing else but pebbles, dozens of small gray pebbles. He sifted several onto his palm. They were identical, each less than half an inch long, with a dimple on one side and a corresponding convex curvature on the opposite side. He retrieved more of the little shards, placed one on a flat stone and smashed it with a larger rock. It dented but did not break. The pebbles were made of plastic.

At his side another hand reached into the pit and began retrieving more of them. Lokesh scooped them into a pile as Shan, still perplexed, tossed one in his palm and began pacing in ever-widening circles around the fire pit. The scavengers had been thorough. But on his first circuit he found the stub of a pencil, on his second a little red feather, and, pushed into the dirt by a heavy boot, a silver instrument, eight inches long, as thin as a pencil but ending in sharp curved points at the end. Another dental probe. On the third and fourth, a dozen slivers of wood, all tapered, all a uniform length. Toothpicks. He stepped under the trees, noting the pattern of the pressed earth and pine needles, the imprint of a sleeping bag. The soil beneath the trees was dry and loose. He raked his fingertips through the earth at the edge of the imprint. Pebbles turned up in the little furrows, then a white nugget, as hard as a pebble. Dried cheese, a traditional Tibetan food that, like buttered tea, appealed to few outsiders. But an outsider might have politely accepted the cheese and then discreetly buried it so as not to offend. He tried again, turning up a small stick, bits of quartz, a shard of old bone. It was a camp that had, no doubt, been used before. He rose then paused to pick up a little stick. Its bark had been peeled, a shallow groove cut in one end as if to indicate legs. He extracted the piece he had taken from the comatose stranger in the stable. The two pieces fit together, forming a crude figure that reminded him of the little clay images of saints traditional Tibetans used. This one, like those in the village, had had its body broken, perhaps by the killer.

Shan gripped the little figure, studying the ground, seeing no more signs, then sniffed at it. It had been cut only days earlier. He walked around each of the half dozen trees, and found four stubs oozing sap, then held the stick close to one of the stubs. It was a match, or close enough. Had there been four stick figures? But there had been only three people in the camp. Pocketing the sticks, he took a step, then looked back at the trees. There were many branches that might have served the purpose, but all of the sticks had been cut from the east side of the trees.

When he looked back he saw that Lokesh had laid the plastic pebbles in a row and was counting them in a low voice. As Shan approached he reached one hundred eight.

"Not for a rosary," Shan said to his old friend. "Not for praying." He picked up a handful and with a tentative expression began a second line parallel to the first. He laid out the double line for eighteen inches then held up two of the pebbles and showed Lokesh how each curvature fit into the dimple of the next. "A zipper," he explained.

Lokesh gestured to the pile of gray shards. "But it would be four or five feet long."

"Do you smell the ashes? A sleeping bag was burned. Nylon and feathers would be easily consumed by the flames. Though why someone would burn something so useful in the mountains I cannot say."

Shan left the old Tibetan wearing a puzzled expression, continuing to assemble the charred teeth in tandem lines. He paced about the campsite again, noting now the broken twigs of several nearby bushes. He kneeled to study the way the slanting rays of the sun played on the ground. A vague line of shadow, the barest smudge of gray, ran from near the fire, around the outcropping, and up the slope. It was the vestige of a very old path, unused for many decades.

Two other paths were betrayed only by crushed plants and a few boot prints, recently made, going toward separate clusters of large boulders spaced a few hundred feet apart. Shan followed each, confirming that they led to makeshift latrines: two of them.

Finally he found a third path, or rather a track, where, judging from the bent stems, something heavy had been dragged. It led to a cluster of high boulders a hundred feet away.

Yangke rose and walked unsteadily toward Lokesh as Shan reached the entrance to the cluster of outcroppings, a narrow passage between two eight-foot-high flat-faced boulders. With a glance toward his companions Shan stepped between the rocks, then froze. Rope was strung waist-high around most of the small clearing, with squares of white paper taped to it at intervals. The papers held Chinese ideograms, inscribed with a ballpoint pen.

"What sort of prayer flags are these?" a raspy voice asked over his shoulder.

"Not prayer flags, Lokesh," Shan said in a worried tone as he approached the rope. "Warnings." As he read the words on the flags he shuddered. *Keep out,* the first said. *Danger,* said the second. *Special Police* and *Murder Crime,* read two more. Then, *Night Lab Squad.*

Feet shuffled in the dirt behind them and Yangke appeared, squeezing sideways through the boulders. "Is this where . . . ," he began.

There was no need to announce that this was where the two bodies had been discovered. On the ground before them, inside the rope, were white silhouettes. Two of them were ovals, three feet long. Another, wider, was nearly four feet long. A circle was less than two feet wide, beside a long irregular outline with two appendages that must have been legs, the shape of a human body sprawled on its side. Shan stepped over the rope and knelt at the first outline, the largest oval, rubbing a finger on the white powdery line. He touched it to his tongue. Flour. The discovery caused him to again gaze uneasily at the warning flags. Whoever had strung up the flags was from a place far away from the mountain. Someone who used bleached flour to draw on the earth came from a different world.

Still kneeling, he surveyed the bizarre scene, beginning to grasp that it was not one mystery he faced but several. Layers of riddles that began not with the killings but with the unknown identity of the victims and ended with the unknown hand that had created the facsimile of a criminal investigation scene. Patches of flour dotted the adjoining rocks. Four pieces of wadded-up tape lay scattered about the clearing, the nearest two feet from his knee. He unfolded it. The backing was covered with flour smudged with lines and grit from the rocks. Someone had been playacting, someone who did not fully understand forensic technique, did not know such rough stone was unlikely to give meaningful fingerprints but who knew enough to go through the motions of a forensic investigation.

But the bronze stains on the ground and patterns of stains on the rocks told Shan there had been nothing contrived about the objects outlined in flour. Someone dead, or dying, had been dragged into the little clearing. Someone else had died there, among the rocks, blood spurting in a fan pattern from at least two savage, puncturing blows. He glanced back at Lokesh, hoping that the old Tibetan did not grasp the truth that lay before them. Four silhouettes, two bodies. At least one of the victims had been dismembered.

"There were some vultures," Yangke said. "I could smell the . . . I could smell what the vultures smelled."

"Where did the bodies go?"

"I don't know. The vultures frightened me. I didn't know this was where . . ."

"Vultures don't eat clothing. Vultures don't eat bones."

"Who would touch them?" Yangke asked. "Who would want to move bodies?"

It was, Shan realized, one more layer of mystery. "Are there *ragyapa* nearby?" he asked, referring to the fleshcutters who traditionally disposed of the Tibetan dead through sky burial.

"Not for thirty miles."

"What happens when people die in the village?"

"The old ones want their bodies taken to the ragyapa. The bodies of the others are burned. We have lots of firewood. It's a more efficient use of resources to burn them, Chodron says."

Shan turned to Lokesh, recognizing the forlorn expression on his old friend's gentle countenance. Those who died a violent death were seldom prepared, seldom in the peaceful, focused state of mind that would allow them to make the difficult transition to the next life. In Tibetan tradition such victims of murder often became angry ghosts who destroyed the harmony of the land they occupied.

Yangke seemed to sense something wrong with Lokesh and touched his elbow, gesturing back, toward the opening. The old Tibetan silently retreated.

"Why would they burn a sleeping bag?"

Yangke asked as he followed Lokesh.

"Because it was soaked in blood. One of them was attacked in his sleep, then dragged here inside his bag."

Shan watched his companions retreat with an unexpected ache in his heart. Then he went to work in the little clearing. He examined the bloodstains, tight patterns projecting from a broad, flat rock that had been laid close to a corner of the little alcove. The sprays of droplets had been made by limbs that still had blood pulsing in them. Soon he had collected eight more pieces of wadded tape. The tape itself had fine fibers woven into it, and had none of the blotchy adhesive or chemical smell of the cheap product sold in Tibetan markets. Along the rock walls were tracks with the patterns of expensive boots like those he had seen on the man in the stable. He stood and studied the little clearing, trying to reconstruct the events of the past few days. First had come the killer and his victims, later someone else who, in his own awkward way, seemed to be seeking the truth. What had that visitor learned? Had he taken away evidence? On a rock face on the opposite side Shan noticed strangely raised marks, partial fingerprints in a hard gray substance that seemed to have been extruded from the surface. Two feet away was a narrow V-shaped opening where two of the boulders came together. He probed it with his fingers, pulling out two long cotton swabs, a bent, exhausted tube of industrial glue, and a half-used tube of lip balm. Sexy Sheen, read the label in English and Chinese. He examined the swabs. They were on eight-inch-long sticks, the kind found in a well-stocked medical lab, something seldom seen in Tibetan towns.

When he finished, and emerged from the murder site, Lokesh was handing three sticks to Yangke, who had three more in his hand, all identical, all painted with three bands at the top, one blue then two red.

"I thought you said these people were not miners," Shan said.

"These have been put here since I visited last. Lokesh found them, arranged to lay claim to this whole campsite and beyond."

"Do you recognize the colors? Which miner's are they?"

Yangke's only reply was to insert the stakes into one of the iron hand straps of his collar, and snap them in half. He opened a small trough in the ground with his heel. Lokesh silently helped him bury the broken claim stakes.

Shan gestured toward the high spine of

rock that rose toward the summit, dividing the mountain into eastern and western halves. "I know how hard it is to reach this side of the mountain from below," Shan said. "But what about from the east side?"

"Toward the summit it gets very dangerous," Yangke explained. "Lightning frequently strikes there without warning."

"Lightning?" Lokesh asked, suddenly interested. Earth deities often expressed themselves through lightning.

"In the spring and summer, if there is storm anywhere near, lightning will strike there. Sometimes lightning strikes the summit even without a storm."

"It's the tallest mountain for dozens of miles," Shan pointed out. Neither of the Tibetans responded. "Are there farms on the other side?"

"Just that Chinese place, miles away."

"You called it a secret base."

"It has a high wire fence around it. Some white buildings. Very quiet. Few are aware of its existence. Even in Beijing it's a secret, they say."

"Not an army base?"

"When I was young I used to slip over the top to look around. My aunts said it was a Chinese base, full of death. The headman said it was full of poison."

"Chodron?"

"No, that was his father. I would sit in a shadow on the eastern slope for hours, watching. There were a few soldiers. I would hear them singing sometimes. I wanted to speak with them, maybe get some medicine for my mother, who was sick. The soldiers put grain out for some wild yaks. Wild yaks are close to the deities, our old ones said. I knew they must be kind if they fed the wild yaks. Each day I drew a little closer, like the yaks."

"They weren't helping the yaks," Shan suggested in a tight voice, having often seen what Chinese soldiers did to Tibet's wild animals.

"No," Yangke said, looking into the water. "The day I determined to go speak with them, a beautiful white yak approached the grain. I watched since everyone knows that white yaks are especially sacred, an omen of great things to come. At that time I had never seen a gun except the old muskets of our hunters. I had never heard a machine."

"But they had a machine gun," Shan ventured.

Yangke nodded.

"How do I get there?"

"There is no way, not anymore. Maybe they saw me or some of the other herders.

76

There was only one gap like a narrow gate in a high wall. Soldiers put bombs in the gap and brought the rocks down. The two sides of the mountain can no longer meet. They haven't for years."

Lokesh had wandered up the trail to the second set of rock outcroppings. As Shan watched, the old Tibetan tilted his head one way then another, then made a series of hand gestures, ritual *mudras,* beginning with his hands pressed together, pointing outward, the thumbs and forefingers folded inward. It was the sign for water for the face. He was making the mudras for what the devout called the Eight Outer Offerings.

As Shan approached he found his friend at a long, flat ledge, perhaps five feet high, leaning over a rust brown image. To his right was another image, the familiar tapered egg shape of the ritual treasure flask, often depicted in the hands of painted deities.

But Shan had never seen the image on the left before.

"It is lightning," Lokesh said, "yet not."

The zigzag line drawn in blood did indeed look like a thunderbolt. Except that at its top, at its thickest part, was a triangular head with two eyes. "Or a snake," Shan ventured. "Except," he added, pointing to the two pairs of bent lines near top and bottom, "what serpent has arms and legs?"

"A dragon," Lokesh concluded in a tone of somber discovery. "A thunder dragon." He had followed a particularly Tibetan logic. The mountain was famed for lightning. Lightning was born of thunder and, as the older Tibetans knew, thunder came from the throats of dragons. And here they were on the mountain called Sleeping Dragon. Shan found himself gazing toward the summit. More than a few Tibetans believed dragons existed, though, like lamas, they were not faring well in the modern world. Shan had accompanied Lokesh on a race through the mountains the year before after a report of a sighting of one of the sacred creatures.

Shan left his friend's side to search the ground where the man who was either a saint or a murderer had been found, his fingers bloodstained, with a bloody hammer. He stepped over dried, curled leaves to take in the scene more completely, then walked back and forth. Here there were none of the broken stems he had found elsewhere, no sign that anyone had been dragged, but likewise no sign of the cleated boots the comatose man had been wearing. He examined the small cracks between rocks and the gaps between boulders for a hundred-foot radius, pausing at a flattened circle of earth that showed particles of colored sand. There had been a sandpainting, Yangke had said. From a shadowed crack halfway between the charnel ground and the place where the stranger had been found, he pulled a toothbrush, its bristles stained red-brown. So the saint had not painted the images with his fingertips. It seemed unlikely that he was the one who had painted them.

Something nudged his senses, and he paced along the wall again. The dried leaves caught in the grass. There were none anywhere else, only near the painted images of the flash and the dragon. He bent and gathered several, then sat and probed one. It was not a leaf, it was a flower, one of the dried trumpet flowers that bloomed on the slopes, though the nearest plants were some distance away on the far side of the stream.

"It was an altar," Lokesh declared. He retrieved some of the flower heads closest to the rock and held them toward Shan. They too were stained with blood.

It took a moment for Shan to grasp his meaning. The body of the stranger had been arranged beneath the painted images, along with the flowers, a traditional altar offering. Or perhaps an atonement. But the bloody hammer did not fit. Had two different people played a part in the killings? The saint had been carried to his place beneath the altar, which would have required two men. One had been devout, in his own strange way. But the other — the cool, calculating one — had dropped the hammer there to implicate the stranger in two murders.

When they neared Drango village they found men with heavy staffs stationed at the outer edge of the fields. They did not greet Shan and Lokesh, did not even acknowledge them as they stepped onto the path that wound down through the barley fields to the village proper. Shan paused and gazed back up the mountain. What were the men watching for?

The young children in the village fled when they saw Shan and Lokesh. A woman churning butter leaped up and darted into her house, dragging her churn inside with her. A small white dog barked at them. Shan approached the stable and froze. The door guard was gone. But a bar had been placed across the door, locking any occupant inside. He lifted the bar and used it to wedge the door open. Inside, only a few pots of butter remained lit, enough to show the man lying exactly as Shan had last seen him.

But he was alone. The villagers who had maintained a vigil were gone. Gendun was gone.

Lokesh and Shan exchanged alarmed glances. Lokesh approached the pallet and sank to the floor beside the comatose man. "Go," he said to a Shan in a hollow, frightened voice. "Find him."

Shan ran to the house they had slept in. They had never seen its owner, but the night before they had found blankets in the corner of the stable below the living quarters, on rough straw and canvas pallets. Their three pallets were now rolled up against the wall. A shadow moved at the top of the ladder leading to the second floor. When Shan followed, he saw the woman of the house standing at the only window, staring out through the battered pane of sooty, cracked glass.

"At times like this Gendun will forget to eat or drink unless we remind him," he said to her back. "There are stories of lamas in meditation rising up as if sleepwalking and stepping off cliffs."

The woman didn't respond. Finally, she said, without turning, "When the wind blows just right, I can hear the whirling of the prayer wheels on the porch of the old temple."

"If you are one of the few who can remember the temple perhaps you also remember compassion." He could not understand the strange breed of people that inhabited Drango village. Why did these Tibetans, alone among all those he had encountered, make him feel so resentful? He recognized her as he came closer. She was the elder from the night before. Chodron had given a name to the widow who owned the house. Dolma.

"I need to talk to one of the men who found the bodies," he said to her back.

When the widow did not reply he left her staring out the window and began to search the town, trotting up the street, then back, and around the houses on each side, pausing to gaze into the stone-fenced yards behind each. No one protested as he searched for Gendun but no one offered any help. Some yelled at him. One man threw a stone toward him. Most glanced at him and looked away, as if they might will him to leave.

After a fruitless search, he reached the rear door of Chodron's house. He knocked, then tried the latch. The door opened and he found himself in the lower chamber, facing the Chinese flag. To the left was a heavy plank door, padlocked shut. To the right, the door to the rest of the house was also locked. Shan tapped, then pounded on it, calling first the name of the headman, then that of the lama. He paced around the entry chamber, pausing at a small table beneath the red flag. On it lay stacks of brochures. *Scientific Principles of Village Management,* one was captioned. *The Power of Community Socialism,* read another. They were all in Chinese, though he doubted more than a handful of the villagers read the language. Beside the brochures was a little copper bust of Mao Tse-tung. Chodron had an altar after all.

As he left the building he glimpsed a child, the girl who had brought food to Yangke, standing by the nearest stone granary, peering inside. When she discovered Shan at her side the girl gave a yelp of fear and scampered away.

"Gendun!" he cried as he opened the door wider. The lama sat in the middle of the stone floor, a solitary lamp flickering at his knee. His arms were bound behind him, wrapped around the heavy center post. He acknowledged Shan with a weak smile.

"What have they done?" Shan groaned. Across the lama's cheek was a discolored line of little drops of dried blood. Across the back of his right hand was a similar mark. Gendun had been caned.

"He raised a hand and spoke words I could not understand," the lama said hoarsely as Shan knelt behind him, untying the ropes.

"Did the man on the pallet strike you?"

Gendun cast a perplexed glance at Shan. It was as if he was unaware that he had been beaten. "His words had the sound of a prayer. I think he spoke one of the old tongues." There were dialects in parts of Tibet that were nearly lost, that dated back to the centuries before history.

Shan's heart leaped into his throat as he saw the bent fingers of Gendun's left hand. They were twitching, curled like claws. "Noooo!" he gasped, and quickly pushed up the lama's sleeve. A terrible dark panic swept over him as the saw the twin sets of bruises and burns. "Who did this? Why?"

"That one is confused about the way of things. He seemed to think he could inflict pain to show me a new truth."

They were no longer talking of the man on the pallet. "Chodron? But why? What did he want?"

"He said I must tell the people the beetle had to be returned to the mountain deity."

"What beetle?"

"A yellow beetle. I said it belongs to no

deity I know. He laughed and had men put me in here, and they did those things to me. He said no food and water for a day and night would change my mind." Gendun stood and stretched, rubbing his discolored wrists, staggered, then nodded vaguely. "The one in the stable is not ready to be alone," the lama declared, and without another word he left the granary.

Shan quickly found what he was looking for, in a corner behind the door. His hand had closed around his own upper arm without his knowledge. That was where a similar device had been used on him years earlier. A heavy truck battery, with spring clamp cables. In the doorway Shan almost collided with the old widow. Dolma's eyes welled with tears as she watched Gendun hobble toward the stable. Concealed by the blanket she had thrown over her shoulders was a small wooden pail, holding a jar of water and several cold dumplings. "Lha gyal lo," she whispered to Gendun's back.

"Why is Chodron so concerned about a yellow beetle?" Shan demanded.

"It wasn't always like this," Dolma said. "The Drango I grew up in would never have permitted harm to befall a lama."

Shan realized he had asked the wrong question of the woman. "What happened to

Drango?"

"What happened to Tibet?" the woman rejoined warily.

"Terrible things happened to Tibet," Shan admitted. "But what happened here is different. The things done to Tibetans here are done by Tibetans."

Dolma stepped inside the stone granary and set down her pail. She began smoothing the dirt around the center post, as if to eliminate all signs Gendun had been there. "It was done to save us," she asserted. "We heard stories of villages that disappeared in clouds of smoke, or had their people relocated to cities. A village on the far side of the mountain was wiped away by big machines. In another village all the men and boys were lined up and shot because one had thrown a stone at a soldier. Our headman was very clever to have saved us."

"Chodron?"

"His father."

"How?"

"Gold." The woman spoke with a strange mix of pride and melancholy. "Our gold has always been our great protector."

The words hung in the air. It was like a village prayer. Drango sat on a gold mountain watched over by a golden deity. It had been preserved not because of the virtue of its inhabitants but, he was beginning to suspect, because of greed.

Shan found Gendun seated in the stable as if he had never left, his legs crossed under him, his eyes focused on the stranger's face, his fingers on the prayer beads in his hand, Lokesh on the other side of the man. As Shan lowered himself to the floor beside Lokesh, he saw the discolored flesh on Gendun's arm again. His mouth went dry. The wave of emotion that surged through him almost made him physically sick. He clamped his hands together, staring into them, forcing himself to focus, to find the calm within, as Gendun would want. Anything to keep his mind away from the catastrophe ahead.

Gendun did not seem to notice when Shan lifted the stranger's wrist. The man's pulse seemed stronger. Shan immersed his fingers in a bowl of water beside Lokesh, then held them over the man's mouth, letting the water drop onto his open lips. The man's tongue slowly reacted, seeking the liquid. Shan immersed his fingers again. He continued the process for some time, pausing when he caught himself staring at the marks on the lama's arm.

A voice abruptly spoke behind him, "Yangke is being punished. You may not use him as your servant."

"My servant?" Shan asked Chodron.

"You forced him to guide you to the scene of the crime."

Shan faced the angry headman. "I envy Yangke. It must be a relief to know so exactly the dimension of one's burdens."

"You are closer to that luxury than you think, Prisoner Shan." Two sturdy farmers stood in the shadows behind Chodron, one holding a length of rope similar to that which had bound Gendun.

"Have you ever visited a hard-labor prison camp?" Shan asked.

"I had the honor once of attending a camp for May Day events," Chodron replied. "I remember a banner. KNEEL TO THE ALL-POWERFUL PARTY."

"You date yourself," Shan said, shuddering. He recalled sitting under such a banner, many years earlier, as one of the privileged guests watching a prison parade outside Beijing. "The verses are more subtle today. Think of advertising slogans for some global enterprise. PERSIST FOR PROGRESS. BILLIONS SERVED."

Chodron's eyes narrowed. "Yangke defies me. You are making matters worse."

"You don't understand Gendun."

"I understand he is made of flesh and bone."

"There's your mistake. After my first year in prison with Tibetan lamas," Shan related, "I realized many of them did not really see their guards. It was as if they were undergoing a long meditation in which constant suffering was a method for focusing the mind. What they expected of a man like you was little different from what they expected from the natural elements. A beating was like sitting in a hailstorm. A bullet in the head," he said, trying to keep the sorrow out of his voice, "like a bolt of lighting."

"What a pathetic creature you are, Shan. Enslaved by worthless old men who live in the past. A trained dog for a crew of scarecrows."

"If you mean Gendun, I can only aspire to be his dog."

Chodron muttered something over his shoulder in a low voice. The men behind him laughed. "Where is Yangke?" the headman demanded.

"He is attached to his sheep almost as closely as to his collar."

Shan saw a flash of nervousness in the headman's eye and replayed in his mind's eye his last minutes with Yangke. He had been sitting with the sheep scattered on the slope above. But he had been gazing at a trail that wound through the flock and continued higher.

Chodron glared at Shan a moment, then motioned with his hand. The two men stepped forward, one holding a short stave that looked like an ax handle. They moved behind Shan.

"What is the yellow beetle?" Shan asked Chodron.

"He must declare that it should go back to the mountain god."

"Where is it now?"

For a moment Chodron studied Shan, then gestured toward an inverted bowl lying on a plank. Shan warily stepped past the two farmers, then kneeled and lifted the bowl.

The two-inch-long object inside was unmistakably an insect, an exquisitely worked image of a long scarab. Its bent legs glittered brightly, and the shifting flames of the lamps gave them an illusion of motion. The head was smooth, the thorax dimpled, its eyes made of polished turquoise. He lifted it, feeling the weight of solid gold. Two jointed antennae folded back along the carapace. It was beautiful. It had a look of great age. It was not Tibetan.

"Why must this leave the village?"

"People are saying it protects the killer. It encourages dangerous speculation."

Shan glanced at Lokesh, who gazed at the beetle with wonder in his eyes. "You mean you originally found the beetle at the murder site?"

"One of my men tried to move it. Your lama put a hand on his arm to stop him. By protecting it, your lama protects the killer."

Shan met Chodron's icy gaze. "Gendun is not your puppet."

Chodron seemed to welcome the comment. "He is an old man, exhausted from lack of sleep and food. But, more important, he is an outlaw, in need of an active *tamzing.* Surely one with your experience in the world understands this. We gave him just a taste of the main event." The headman leaned forward, lowering his voice. "I need to know I have your undivided attention."

Shan fought down a shudder. Tamzing. Though it sounded like one of the demon names Tibetans are loath to utter, it was entirely a creation of Beijing. It was a ritual of another generation, a favorite tool of the dreaded Red Guard, in which many innocents had died. A tamzing was a struggle session, where correct socialist thought was pounded into the unreformed, usually with words but sometimes, Shan well knew, with batons, boots, hammers, or lead pipes. An unfamiliar fog seemed to envelope him for a moment. He found himself between Gendun and Chodron.

"You were about to say something?" Chodron chided.

Shan gazed forlornly at the floor, gradually becoming aware of the headman and his bullies staring expectantly at him. It had taken his prison commanders months to discover what Lokesh called his flaw, the weakness the officers had learned to use against him. Chodron had grasped it in a day. Shan would not lie, would not let himself be used, would not jump at the bidding of men like Chodron, except to protect the old Tibetans.

"The beetle must be returned to the god of the mountain," Shan whispered in Chinese.

"I can't hear. We must all hear what the lama says, so the rest of the villagers can be told by each of us. In Tibetan."

"The lama says this jewel of the mountain deity does not belong here, that it must be returned." Shan felt his lips move but the thin hollow voice that spoke the words seemed to come from far away.

"And the lama says this unconscious man may be the killer," Chodron added.

Shan looked at the dirt floor. "And the lama says this man may be the killer," he repeated.

Chodron, a victorious gleam in his eyes, flicked his wrist and one of the men grabbed the beetle and dropped it into the bowl, then covered it with the overturned bowl as if it might fly away. Chodron muttered something, his men laughed again, and the trio left the stable.

Shan looked at the empty door, looked at the lamps, looked at the comatose man, looked everywhere but at Gendun's face. He knelt and extended his fingers into the water bowl again, then quickly withdrew them. They were trembling. When he glanced at Lokesh, his old friend wore an expression Shan had never seen before. He would never openly reprimand Shan but Lokesh could not hide the look of betrayal in his eyes.

Shan left the building, quickly walking beyond the end of the village to the edge of the high cliff. The wind rushed against him as he tried to lose himself in the emptiness that stretched below. Chodron did not begin to fathom the nightmare he was creating for Shan. To stop the headman's torment of Gendun and the comatose stranger it might be necessary to use outright violence. But if

Shan lifted a hand against Chodron to save Gendun, Shan would never be able to sit at the old lama's side again. Already Shan had been forced to lie in Gendun's name, in front of him, to save him from Chodron's cruelty. He had left that morning desperate to find an answer to the murders. Now all he wanted was to save Gendun and Lokesh. Drango village was not the rustic enclave it had first appeared to be. It was a strange gray place in which the worst of both worlds was combined.

When he turned back, he went straight to the granary where Gendun had been imprisoned, then he returned to the cliff, bent under the weight of the heavy battery. It flew in a low arc as he heaved it over the edge, like a small boulder ejected by the quaking of the mountain.

Dolma was standing in the entry of her house when he left the cliff. She beckoned him as she glanced nervously up the street. So as not to be noticed he circled behind the buildings, approaching indirectly. By the time he reached the door she had disappeared. When he climbed up the ladder stair, her quarters were empty. He quickly surveyed the modest room. It was simple and tidy, all of wood, lit only by its solitary window. Feeling like an intruder, he had started to descend when he noticed how uneven the shadows on the far wall were. He hesitantly approached it, finding a large piece of black felt suspended from wooden pegs. He lifted the felt. Behind it was a *tangka,* a very old painting on cloth of a deity, richly colored, under which was a small incense burner. The widow, who as an elder supported Chodron in his campaign to deny the village its traditions, actively prayed to Tara, the mother protectress of Tibet.

He was about to descend when muffled voices rose from below. The big man, the first guard in the stable, appeared on the stairs, his beefy face apprehensive. He glared at Shan, who backed away. Then two more figures rose behind him: the elder with the wispy white beard and Dolma, who hustled her two companions forward like an impatient shepherd. She positioned herself like a sentry at the head of the stair.

"The investigator desires to know about the bodies," Dolma declared.

"He's a convict," the big man spat. "He deceived us."

"He's the answer to our problems," Dolma replied with strained patience.

The big man looked at the elderly man. Then he uttered a low curse and began speaking, looking at Dolma, not Shan. "We were moving a flock of sheep up the mountain to a new pasture. The dog found the one in the stable first. He was all bloody, with those signs near him. The other two were inside a circle of tall rocks, what was left of them."

"What was left?" Dolma repeated in a quivering voice.

"Their hands were gone, chopped off. We ran and sent for Chodron."

A chill settled along Shan's spine. He had seen the evidence, but having the butchery described aloud was still unsettling. "The camp," he said after a moment, his tongue dry as tinder. "What did you see in the camp, by the trees?"

"Blood. Ashes. Some equipment, though it was gone when we went back. Pots and pans. A blue pack. A red pack with a rising sun on its flap. Sleeping bags."

"Could vultures have taken the hands?"

"No. It was too early for vultures. They come when the stench starts."

The old man started to sway. Dolma helped him to a chair and fetched him a cup of tea.

"Where did you take the bodies?"

"Tibetans know what to do with bodies." Resentment was building in the big man and his voice betrayed it. "There are the

96

fleshcutters. . . ."

"Where did you take the bodies?" Dolma repeated reproachfully. "You did not take them to the ragyapa. That would have meant at least a three-day trip."

The elder with the beard looked at the man again. "We never touched the bodies," he admitted. "They were there the first day and gone when we returned the next. Only white lines were on the ground where they had been. Someone said that the lightning had taken them, leaving only the white dust of their bones. Chodron said not to tell anyone."

"What about the colored sand," Shan asked, "the mandala?"

The man looked up in surprise. "There was something like that, I almost forgot. It was there the first day. I only glanced at it. We were scared. It was gone the next. Like the bodies."

Shan studied the man. If that was true, he now knew something about the killer's priorities. Taking the hands had come first. Then the removal of the bodies and the obliteration of the mandala. "Can you describe what was drawn in the sand?"

The man knitted his brow, then shook his head. "You are speaking of old things. We are forbidden to learn those things."

"Could you draw it?"

"I don't think so."

"Did you recognize the dead men?"

The man gazed into his hands. His hesitation brought Dolma's head up. "Who were they?" she demanded. "Chodron said they were strangers. Tell Trinle. Tell your father and me the truth."

"Strange people in a strange place," the man said. Then, with a single bound, he leaped into the stair hole and was gone.

Dolma and the old man named Trinle exchanged a silent worried glance.

"Who is missing from the village?" Shan asked.

"No one," Dolma replied, puzzled.

When Shan returned to the stable, Dolma followed with a bucket of water. Neither Gendun nor Lokesh acknowledged him. As he settled to the earthen floor Dolma handed him a moist cloth, and together they began washing the comatose stranger's arms. Shan let himself be drawn into the silent rhythm of the task, sometimes washing the man himself, sometimes wringing out the cloth for the Tibetan woman, aware that what they were doing was usually done for the dead. He paused only once, to check under the overturned bowl. The beetle was gone.

They worked in silence. Then Dolma, distracted, failed to grasp the cloth Shan extended toward her. He followed her gaze. The stranger's hand had closed around her arm.

"Lha gyal lo!" Lokesh whispered in joy.

"Lha gyal lo," the old woman repeated and began stroking the man's hand. They watched as the man's other hand was slowly lifted. Its fingers started moving, pointing into the shadows as if through his eyelids he sensed things they could not see, pointing here, pausing, pointing there. No, not pausing, Shan decided. Drawing. He was drawing something in the air. When the hand finally settled back onto his chest, the man sighed deeply. And whispered something.

Shan leaned forward, cradling the man's head now, desperately trying to understand the words.

"Dsilyi neyani. Dsil banaca."

The words meant nothing to Shan. They were not Tibetan, not Mandarin, Cantonese, neither English, Russian, nor any of the dozen other languages Shan thought he could recognize.

The words continued, still whispered, though in a stronger, even an urgent tone. *"Tsilke nacani! Nigel icla, nace hila!"*

Dolma and Shan exchanged a confused

99

look. Gendun had reminded him that there were obscure ancient dialects still alive in remote areas of the mountains. Dolma cupped her other hand around the man's, cradling it the way a mother might that of a sleeping child.

The man's eyes opened. Shan feared he was blind for they seemed dull and unfocused. Then they settled on the worn, kind countenance that hovered above him, mouthing prayers. The stranger's eyes grew round and he hastened his strange, urgent chant, twisting about to face Gendun, a hand reaching out as if to touch the lama. Then it stopped as if he was afraid to test whether Gendun was flesh and blood.

"Qojoni qasle, quojoni qasle!" he whispered, fear in his voice as he bowed to Gendun. *"Qojoni qasle,"* he repeated weakly, then collapsed, dropping back on the pallet, unconscious again.

When Shan turned the man over, his unseeing eyes were filled with tears.

CHAPTER THREE

Shan leafed through the wondrous parchment book the now-conscious man had given him, trying to make sense of the stick figures that matched the one on the man's arm, the ancient poems written in Chinese, the prayers in Tibetan, trying to grasp why it displayed a photograph of a young Shan standing proudly in a tight-collared Mao jacket with his newly graduated class of investigators. Why did his foot itch so terribly? he wondered. The man sat across from him, smiling serenely, counting Tibetan beads in one hand, holding a bloody rock hammer in the other.

"Take the book with you," the man said in a voice that matched Gendun's for its quiet gentleness. "You will need it where you are going."

Shan shook his head. "I am not leaving."

"It is you they have come for. On this mountain your life will end. Tell me this —

do you prefer we leave your corpse for the birds or shall we use fire?" There was snow in the saint's hair, mixed with yellow powder. Behind him in the shadows, two other men appeared, wearing red robes, waving the stumps of arms without hands. As they advanced he saw their faces — Lokesh and Gendun.

The itching in his foot became a terrible burning. Shan pulled up his trouser leg. There was nothing but bone below the knee. A swarm of golden beetles was devouring his flesh.

He awoke gasping for breath, his heart pounding, not aware he had leaped up from his pallet and dashed outside until he stumbled on a rock in the yard behind Dolma's house. It took him several minutes to recover from his nightmare. He steadied himself by holding onto the flat stones that formed the top of the rear wall. The sky shimmered with stars, lending an eerie glow to the pale houses. A nightjar called. The bleat of a lonely lamb echoed off the slope. All else was as still as death. Shan retrieved his boots from the doorway, and began walking.

Though it was well after midnight, the gibbous moon and the light of a thousand stars illuminated the path. He paused on a ledge overlooking the slumbering village. Only one structure showed any life — the stable where Lokesh had relit the one hundred eight butter lamps whose light leaked between the wind-withered boards. The old Tibetan would not follow him this time. When Shan had left the stable the night before, the door had been barred from the outside by Chodron, locking in Lokesh, Gendun, and Dolma. And a guard had been posted by the entry as well.

Shan walked through the barley fields, the grain a rustling silver lake in the moonlight. He soon found the compacted trail that traversed the slope and fell into the slow, steady jog that some Tibetans used when traveling long distances in the mountains. When, much later, he reached the clearing where the murders had occurred, he lowered himself onto a flat boulder. Something on four legs, a wild dog or wolf, drank at the stream, then lifted its head in Shan's direction and bolted. Two small animals scurried along the base of the rocks. One of the little owls that frequented the slopes uttered a short, sharp screech.

Not only wildlife seemed to revisit the campsite. After the killer, the shepherds of Drango had come, then Yangke, then the person who had left the crude warning signs and clumsily sought fingerprints, then someone — the killer again? — had returned for the bodies and obliterated a sandpainting. A miner had staked a claim to the site. Someone, either the killer or the miner, had looted the equipment. Holy men, Yangke had called the dead men. Holy men with modern camping equipment. Holy men with crude wooden effigies. What message had they placed in their sandpainting that required their killer to destroy it?

Shan slowly approached the moonlit campsite, reminding himself that this was the way the killer had approached, before dawn, as the owls called. Smoke had probably been rising from the smoldering fire.

What had the dead men said to one another before falling asleep? As great as the mystery of the killer's identity was the mystery of the victims'. Lokesh would insist that the spirits of the dead, like those of all murdered men, still lurked nearby. Shan found himself scanning the darkened slope. He would have welcomed a conversation with a ghost. His first question would be the one that had gnawed at him since visiting the death site the first time, when he'd seen the lightning snake and a portion of a little wooden figure. Why were these Tibetan things being done in non-Tibetan ways?

He looked back at the grove of trees where the two men had lain before dying. Had they exchanged pleasantries, spoken of family, exclaimed about the endless night sky? Had they, as some old Tibetans believed, seen a meteor just before their deaths? He entered the grove and almost stumbled on a low mound of dirt. Someone had been digging. He dropped to one knee, studying the moon shadows. At least a dozen small holes had been dug since he had been there — dug, then filled in.

He paced in front of the circle of tall rocks where the bodies had been found, surprised at the fear that kept him from walking into the shadows. He jogged past, on unfamiliar ground now, at each moonlit fork taking whichever path went higher. By dawn he was still far from the summit but had reached the last of the long shelves of land below the high, jagged peak. The windswept, barren place was separated from the far side of the mountain by a forbidding fifty-foot escarpment, the stony spine that divided east and west. While studying the escarpment, he drank from a brook and chewed on a piece of hard dried cheese he had saved from the evening meal Dolma had brought them in the stable. Yangke had been right in saying that the worlds of the two sides were separate. This natural barrier was far more effective than any razor wire the army might use. He could see half a dozen spots where the wall had split apart, though from a distance each appeared to be filled with boulders or great slabs of rock that had fallen.

It took him an hour to explore the first three clefts, struggling up the jumble of rocks that filled each, until he was forced to retreat by massive blocks of stone that could not be climbed without ropes. He was about to enter the fourth cleft when he spotted movement half a mile away. A mountain goat had materialized as if out of the wall itself, one of the nimble white creatures native to the ranges. Shan eased into the shadow of a boulder and watched as another shaggy goat appeared, then three young kids and another adult. As the small flock wandered down the slope, languidly nibbling at the lichen-covered slabs, he slipped along the wall. Had he not fixed the point in his mind he could easily have missed the goat's portal, for it was not one of the clefts he had seen but a narrow shadow behind an outcropping that folded out, parallel to the wall.

The twisting trail was sometimes so narrow both shoulders brushed against stone, sometimes so low between overhanging slabs he had to crouch to continue. After two hundred yards the trail was blocked by a huge mound of rubble that seemed impassable. But then he noticed scattered piles of goat droppings on several boulders and pulled himself up onto the first of the massive rocks. More than once Lokesh had joked with him that those who lived on the fringes of Tibet, as they did, had to be half goat to survive.

He paused after several minutes' hard climbing to study the scratches and gouges that began to appear on the stones underfoot. Someone had worked with chisels and levers, prying up rocks, levering them this way and that, clearing if not a path then at least a course that could be attempted by creatures less nimble than a goat. Near the crest, at the center of the wide escarpment, two huge fallen slabs created a treacherous pit at least twenty feet deep. A goat might have tried the tiny five-inch lip of rock that followed the side wall but for humans someone had laid a makeshift bridge of juniper poles and twine, constructed like a ladder, with narrow cross pieces every two feet.

The jumble of rocks grew more treacherous, with sharp jagged stones, some scorched by explosives, jutting upward, threatening injury. A huge bird of prey, another lammergeier, soared overhead, interested not in Shan but in the small furry rock pikas that scurried in front of him. He tried to visualize the high-walled path that had once existed underneath him. The dark winding passage would have made a natural *kora,* a pilgrim's path, which the lamas of earlier centuries laid out not simply to lead to the homes of deities but also to teach the pilgrim something about hardship and humility.

Shan and Lokesh had visited a pilgrim's shrine on another mountainside earlier that year, reached through a much shorter passage whose walls had been painted with guardian demons. It was to have been the last day of that painted rock shrine. The government was about to destroy it in order to erect a radio transmission tower. Although the engineers agreed to move the painted rock, Lokesh had settled onto the ground as the bulldozer advanced.

"That rock picture is just a bunch of old peeling paint, abandoned by its deity years ago. They don't understand. Here is what is important," the old Tibetan had said, patting the path, compacted from centuries of pilgrim's prostrations. "Here is the sacred thing." He had not resisted when the machine's operators lifted him bodily and set him on the ground fifty feet away, then continued ripping up the old path. But he had carried a little sack of the compacted earth with him ever since.

On the far side of the ruined trail he was traveling now, Shan found proof of his speculation that inhabitants of the eastern slopes were aware of the passage. On one side of the entrance to the cleft was an image in faded paint of Tara, the mother protector. Opposite the Tara was an image painted by another kind of pilgrim. In fresh, bright colors, someone had portrayed a four-foot-high Buddha sitting, like a cartoon character, in a miniature convertible car, cigarette dangling from his mouth, sunglasses covering his eyes. He had reached the real world.

The landscape on the eastern side of the mountain was gentle, the slope sweeping outward for miles, interrupted by occasional outcroppings and a few low ridges that jutted like fingers from the main peak, joining with the matching slope of the neighboring mountain to create a wide, lush, and empty valley. Almost empty. In the distance, perhaps five miles away, was a small compound of white buildings, surrounded by half a dozen antenna masts and three huge white saucers that seemed to have been tipped by the wind. Satellite reception dishes.

Much closer to Shan, half a mile away, was the only other visible structure, an old *dzong,* one of the small mountain fortresses that had once dotted the Tibetan countryside. Centuries earlier, its builders had chosen its location well, laying its stonework at the end of one of the long, jutting ridges, where the finger of rock and grass abruptly plunged two hundred feet to the valley floor. Its crumbling five-story stone tower would once have been manned for signal fires. The narrow windows had been designed for archers. Later, after Tibet's warring kings had been replaced by Buddhist leaders, many such dzongs had become monasteries or hermitages. Now, if Shan could safely enter the ruins, it would be a perfect perch for studying the land beyond.

He hurried across the high meadows, wherever possible using outcroppings to block the line of sight to the distant compound below, knowing that its sentinels could use powerful lenses to scan the landscape. He paused for a moment, ambushed by his emotions again, a voice within shouting that he had to return to the village. He would find Gendun beaten unconscious. He would find Lokesh lashed to a canque. He would reach the stable and find nothing but bloody spoons on the floor. The waking nightmares would not leave him, distracting him so completely he did not realize something vital about it until he was only fifty yards away from the dzong.

The building was inhabited. The narrow windows were glazed. The structure at the base of the tower was new, though built of stone in the traditional boxy, tapered wall style of the original dzongs. Flowers were planted along the walls. Prayer flags flapped in the shadows behind the tower. Not prayer flags, he realized as he ran toward the shadow of another outcropping. Laundry.

"You're not a soldier," a voice behind him suddenly declared. "You're not a scientist. You don't look prosperous enough for one of those damned miners." The voice was oddly whimsical. "If I shot you right now, we could call it a socialist experiment and devise a sad, politically correct story of the path that led such an antisocial creature to his inevitable death by a bullet." The words were spoken in fluid Mandarin, tinged with a Beijing accent.

Shan replied in a level voice as he turned to face the speaker, hands open at his side.

111

"The particular experiment I represent was declared a failure years ago. What is left was considered not worth the price of a bullet."

He was prepared to confront a soldier, an angry bureaucrat, anything but the figure in front of him. The man was a head taller than Shan, well groomed and athletic, with long blond hair going to gray that covered his ears. Resting in the crook of one arm was a high-powered rifle and a case for a compact set of binoculars hung from the belt that held up his khaki trousers. A brown cashmere scarf was tucked under the collar of his leather jacket, which covered most of a black T-shirt bearing the image of a red dragon over the legend, in English, BORN TO BE WILD.

"Then how do I classify you?" the stranger asked. "Animal, mineral, or vegetable?"

"Perhaps you believe in ghosts?" Shan ventured. He remained still as the stranger circled him, examining him from head to toe.

The man seemed to appreciate Shan's wit. "I think," the man said with a grin, "we will just call you the most interesting luncheon guest we have had in weeks." He gestured Shan toward the dzong.

It was the most extraordinary new construction Shan had seen in Tibet. On the outside great care had been taken to keep the structure's sixteenth-century appearance, right down to the small mound of mani stones near the door. But inside were touches that spanned the five centuries since. The entryway was flanked by two long portrait scrolls of Chinese emperors, hung over a beige fabric wall covering. Bamboo stalks grew out of an elegant willow green celadon pot. As the stranger left his rifle by the door, Shan leaned over the nearest painting of one of the early Ching emperors wearing a fur cap and yellow brocaded gown embroidered with dragons. It was not a reproduction. From a speaker somewhere behind the planter came the soft, hollow music of a wooden flute.

Shan followed his escort up two flagstone steps into a large room lined with a huge carpet in which were woven traditional Tibetan symbols. The left wall was covered, floor to ceiling, with shelves of books and that to the right with paintings, dramatic mountain landscapes, and maritime scenes, all in Western style. In the center of the floor was a huge overstuffed U-shaped sofa, arranged to give the occupants a view out a long row of windows in the far wall. As his escort paused, gazing toward a half-closed door by the paintings, Shan took tentative steps toward the windows, his eyes on a powerful telescope that stood on a tripod.

He paused and placed a hand on the sofa, pressing his fingers into the soft fabric. It wasn't real. It couldn't be real. The house was impossible. It belonged in the Swiss Alps or the mountains of North America. Except for the homes of senior Party officials he had never seen such a residence in China, let alone on a remote mountain in Tibet.

"You may sit," his companion said, still in perfect Mandarin. "The doctor does not begin dissections until after his morning refreshment."

Shan did not sit but walked past the sofa, watching the westerner, glancing at the three doors that led out of the large, comfortable chamber, mentally tracking the distance to the entrance behind him, his instincts shouting out warnings. Soldiers must be near. Any moment he would be seized.

The blond man lounged on the sofa, hands behind his head, an amused grin on his face as he watched Shan. The closest of the three doors leading out of the room was open, revealing a sunlit chamber containing a large wooden desk. The shelves built into the wall behind it held three-ring binders and notebooks, dozens of them, with carefully printed labels too small for Shan to read from where he stood.

"I was not aware there were still palaces left in these mountains," Shan remarked.

The westerner's grin was honest, almost friendly. "Dr. Gao and I long ago decided the only good place of comfort is a hidden place of comfort."

Shan lingered another moment at the office door. On the wall behind the desk were at least thirty photographs, in identical gold frames, most in black and white. Some were posed portraits of distinguished gatherings, many were of men shaking hands with victorious smiles, three were of a man standing beside models of rockets. One showed an actual rocket sprouting out of a cloud of smoke. A chill crept down Shan's spine. Even from that distance he could recognize several of the men in the pictures. At least two were former general secretaries of the Party and three were past commanders of the People's Liberation Army.

Sounds behind the door on the opposite side of the room drew his escort's attention. Shan stepped to the second door, which led to a short flight of stone steps, beyond which he could see a chamber furnished only with a bamboo mat on the floor, three of its walls lined with the fragrant wood used in temples, the fourth consisting entirely of glass, opening toward the long fertile valley below. A Chinese man with close-cropped graying hair stood facing the window, both arms raised parallel to the ground, right arm bent backward, left slowly moving forward, in one of the traditional postures of Tai Chi, called Bending the Bow.

The man was clad in a short white robe and loose white pants, his feet bare. Below the window five granite spheres of different sizes rested on a bed of white sand. The sounds of the wooden flute came from concealed speakers. Shan warily stepped to the side of the doorway, pushed a hand into his pocket, and pinched his thigh. He needed to awaken from this strange dream.

Something touched his arm. He spun around. The blond stranger was extending a glass of iced water. Shan accepted the glass, then caught himself staring at it and looked up self-consciously.

"It's just water," the man explained, lifting an identical glass to his lips.

"It's the ice," Shan said. "I can't remember the last time I had a drink with ice cubes." The world Shan lived in now did not avail itself of refrigerators, televisions, telephones, or any other machines.

"You don't get out much."

"I am out," Shan said, still wary, "all the time."

The westerner grinned again. "We've got tons of it. The army first used this as a barracks for guards, a patrol base. There's a walk-in freezer downstairs that once supplied twenty men. We only need to be resupplied four times a year. When I get lonely for home I walk inside and slide around the floor."

"Ah. I grew up in the north as well," Shan said. "I used to look at photographs of skaters when I was a child. One year I greased blocks of wood and tied them to my feet."

"We used to skate for miles down a river, almost to the Baltic Sea. There were kiosks on the ice that sold little sausages on sticks and sugared tea."

"Poland?" Shan queried, and dared a long swallow.

"The German Democratic Republic. Its athletes were so good the rest of the world had to make it disappear. My name is Heinz Kohler."

Shan shook the hand that was offered but did not reply. He drained his glass and stepped to the telescope, half expecting Kohler to stop him when he pressed his eye to the tube. He pulled back in surprise at the image that leapt to view, glanced at the bemused German, and looked again. In a great nest on a cliff nearly half a mile away he could see three young birds of prey, their beaks uplifted, opening and shutting. The home, no doubt, of the lammergeier he had seen.

"Karl, Friedrich, and Albert," Kohler declared.

"Marx," Shan ventured after a moment, "Engels, and Einstein."

Kohler's blue eyes went round for an instant and he nodded respectfully. "Dr. Gao is on a first-name basis with all the great ones."

Shan ran his hand down the sleek, powerful instrument. The telescope had been imported long ago, probably from Kohler's native country, but the squat tripod was homemade. A small metal plate, painted over but still legible, declared it to be the property of the People's Liberation Army.

"I should be leaving," Shan said with a glance toward the entrance.

"That would be ungrateful." Kohler settled into a wooden chair by the entry as if assuming the role of sentry and gestured Shan toward the sofa. On the low table in front of it were magazines, in Chinese, English, and German, all at least two months old, devoted to science and engineering, fashion and gardening. None were newsmagazines.

For ten uneasy minutes Shan listened to the muffled clink of dishes and to footfalls passing the one doorway he had not been able to explore. For a moment he heard the dim, urgent beat of rock and roll. He paced the width of the room, studying it again, listening to the creaks of the floorboards, seeing now that although the furnishings were elegant, their construction was rougher than he had first realized. Finely trimmed boards had been fastened over crude planks. It had been built as a barracks, not a palace. But someone accustomed to palatial comforts, with palatial possessions, was living in it. He stepped to the window, fighting the urge to train the telescope on the distant installation below. It was not large enough for an infantry garrison and had none of the repetitive white ground hatches and mobile cranes that would indicate a missile base.

He became aware of Kohler standing expectantly at the far door, which now stood open. Shan stepped past him into a small, elegant dining chamber. The walls were of white plaster, and the paintings displayed on them of bamboo and snow and birds.

119

On the table were four porcelain bowls of traditional Tibetan soup with noodles. Behind the door was a large framed work of calligraphy, one of the slogans handwritten by Chairman Mao, copies of which had once been framed and hung in every government office. STRIVE FOR THE PEOPLE, it proclaimed. It was, he suspected, also an original.

"I should wash," Shan said.

Kohler tossed him one of the linen napkins from the table.

A youth burst through the swinging door bearing a bowl of steaming rice and vegetables. He was Chinese, perhaps twenty years of age. His long hair had a narrow blond stripe bleached along the left temple. His clothes were all black. Muffled music came from a pair of earphones hanging around his neck, connected to something small in his pocket. The boy paused, studying Shan for a moment, taking in his ragged clothes. A restrained laugh escaped his lips. He turned to Kohler, extended a finger to his brass-studded ear, and pulled the trigger of an imaginary pistol.

A moment later, the man Shan had seen doing meditation exercises entered, now wearing a neatly pressed white shirt and khaki pants. The youth stiffened, quickly removed his headphones, and disappeared into the kitchen. The man greeted Shan with a nod, his eyes showing not the contempt Shan expected but curiosity. Shan's tattered work shirt was hard to miss, but he was looking at Shan the way Shan would examine a stranger, taking in the small scars on his hands, evidence of his years of manual labor, the freshly split fingernails that spoke of recent rock climbing, the small round nub of scar on his neck that, to the experienced eye, suggested the hospitality of the Public Security Bureau.

"I am Gao Hu Bo," his host offered, gesturing for Shan to sit as he took his place at the head of the table. "Please," Gao said, pushing the bowl of rice toward Shan. "You are no doubt hungry from your morning exertions. Few goats are up to that passage."

"I was seeking a few other goats," Shan said in a level voice.

Gao's steady gaze did not drop but a thin smile formed on his lips. "Officially this entire valley is a military reservation. Officially, Heinz and I are supposed to call friends below should intruders appear. Their response time averages eleven minutes. They would convey you to a rather unpleasant place."

"Of course," Kohler interjected, amused

by the conversation, "what is unpleasant to one man may be mere routine to another."

The youth in black reappeared, carrying a teapot, and slid into the last empty chair.

"Officially," Shan said, every nerve alert, acutely aware of the treacherous ground he trod on, "this would not be an approved place for a general to retire to." For Gendun's sake, he could not afford to be arrested.

The youth choked back a laugh. Then, eyes lowered, he began to noisily consume his soup.

"Since you are as yet unacquainted with us," Dr. Gao replied in his smooth, refined voice, "we will not take that as an insult. Generals are seldom invited to this table."

"Still," Shan said, "I can't help but wonder if your invitation to lunch means I am to be the main course."

Gao's laugh was genuine. He rose and extended his hand. "I like you, comrade. When I saw you coming down the slope in the open sunlight I said, there is a man without fear, the rarest of creatures."

Shan hesitantly took the man's hand. "I am called Shan," he said, "and in the world I inhabit fear is as common as salt."

Gao held his hand for a moment as he gazed at the row of numbers tattooed on

Shan's forearm. Shan mentally raced through the possible explanations for his host's presence there. One moment Gao seemed like a monk, the next a gloating bureaucrat. Gao was not a soldier. Senior politicians were sometimes disciplined with internal exile, but never in such comfort.

"My nephew, Feng Xi, is visiting from Beijing," Gao explained as he sat again and began to eat. "Summer vacation from his labors at the university."

The youth acknowledged Shan with a disinterested nod. "Thomas," he interjected. "My name is Thomas." Even before Shan had been sent into exile, to the gulag in Tibet, it had become popular among certain of China's globally connected youth to adopt Western names.

Gao offered the boy a patient smile and spent several minutes describing the nest of lammergeiers they had been observing. Kohler took over the conversation, speaking about the weather, recent news reports describing the cloning of a dog, the announcement of a new Chinese space mission, and even, to Shan's mute surprise, a new movie about invaders from outer space.

"Of course, if it were true, the aliens would have had to travel thousands of years to get here," Thomas interjected.

"Hardly seems worth the trouble," Kohler rejoined.

"It is impossible to travel faster than the speed of light," the youth added with a hint of pride. "We've done the calculations."

"Nearly as difficult," Shan offered, "as trying to bridge the worlds on the two sides of this mountain."

"We know of no one else who has traversed the old pass, if that is what you seek to learn. No one crosses without our knowledge since, as you see, we are situated like a gate across the path."

"There are miners."

"The miners are the perfect buffers for us. They may be terrified of us but everyone else is terrified of them."

Shan declined a serving of what the boy described, in English, as French fried potatoes. "I know that for some men, forbidding them something only makes it more desirable."

Kohler set his utensils down. "At our table, we are the ones allowed to prod and pry. Why are you here?" he asked.

"Because two men were murdered on the other side."

"And are you playing policeman?"

"A man may be punished although there is no proof of his guilt. A lama is being

124

punished for not condemning the man."

"Rapaki?" Kohler asked. "Who would want to hurt a crazy hermit? Good court jesters are hard to come by."

Shan did not correct him. The conversation was beginning to get interesting. It was the first time he had heard that name.

Gao proclaimed in a contemplative voice, "Proof is a dangerous concept. The essence of science is showing that most truth is opinion."

"A dangerous proposition," Shan said, "when your government is dedicated to the opposite."

Gao lowered his cup. "I'm sorry?"

"You've lived in Beijing. The stronger the opinion, the greater the truth."

Kohler glanced at the doors — a habit, Shan suspected, from a career spent worried about who might be listening. "Truth is what the people need," the German said in a pious tone. It was an old slogan, one blazoned on public walls.

"Who *are* you?" Gao's question, though whispered, was as sharp as a blade. The promised dissection had begun.

"Just someone else who has difficulty adjusting to the rest of the world."

Kohler gazed at Shan as if trying to decide whether to take offense. "*We* conquered the rest of the world," Kohler declared, "and are enjoying the fruit of our labors."

Gao, still staring at Shan, seemed not to hear the German. As a female appeared and began removing dishes, the older man rose and silently followed her into the kitchen.

Thomas's silence was one of amusement, but Kohler's was becoming one of unease. He seemed to have seen something in Gao that disturbed him. Down in the valley, beyond the small white buildings, a squall brewed.

"How many years have you and Dr. Gao been in Tibet?" Shan inquired.

"Draw a radius of five hundred miles and we have spent almost our entire careers inside it," Kohler said.

"Which makes you very good at doing something the government finds important," Shan observed. The circle Kohler described included most of China's key nuclear weapon research and missile establishments.

"The ruler who brings a nation's enemies to their knees is beloved of his people," Kohler replied, "but the men who give that ruler the means to do so are beloved of the ruler. Gao was never interested in public displays of affection."

"Beloved enough to dictate the terms of his retirement."

"A small price. An infinitesimal price."

Shan gathered up several dishes and darted into the kitchen, before Kohler could protest. Gao was nowhere to be seen.

"Tashi delay," he greeted the housekeeper in Tibetan. She replied in kind with a polite smile.

He asked her if she was from Drango village. She did not answer and hurried away as Kohler appeared to herd Shan back to the dining room. The youth was at the window, watching the storm below. He hesitantly answered Shan's questions, explaining that he had lived in Shanghai until his uncle had arranged for him to study astrophysics at Beijing University.

"Perhaps you can compare notes about the faculty," a cool voice interjected. Gao had returned, and fixed Shan with an analytical stare. "Or perhaps," he said to his nephew, "you should start by asking our guest what kind of fool rejects the offer of a senior Party status sponsored by a minister of state."

Shan's gut began to knot.

Gao came closer. "You netted a unique specimen, Heinz," he observed. "A special investigator for the Ministry of Economy, in charge of secret cases for the State Council. Cases of great importance. Once an official

Hero Worker, privy to the most confidential matters of state."

Gao had focused on Shan's tattoo for no more than five seconds, yet he had not only memorized the numbers but in the span of a few minutes been able to reach one of the very few cadres left in Beijing who knew how to locate Shan's file.

"A highly strung pedigreed hunting dog who turned on his handlers," Gao continued, studying Shan suspiciously. "After a few years of hard labor he was let loose in the Tibetan wilderness by a colonel he did a favor for. He defies the laws of physics. In an age when scientists can turn dirty rocks into diamonds, he is the diamond who became a dirty rock."

"In Beijing there are so many diamonds their radiance was blinding," Shan replied. He eyed the exits, mentally gauging how quickly he could make it to the pass, comparing that to the response time of Gao's soldiers, and wondering how good a shot Kohler might be when his target was moving.

"You thought you could send one of the most powerful ministers in Beijing to the gulag. A personal friend of the Great Helmsman."

"I started tracking the dollars he had sent

to secret accounts in Switzerland. I lost count after twenty million."

"Where is he today?"

"He died in office and was given a hero's funeral while I was in prison."

Kohler laughed first, but Gao soon joined in, followed by young Thomas. Shan stared out the window. His gaze settled on the lammergeiers' nest. The predators on top of the food chain on this particular mountain liked to consume their prey while it still breathed.

Eventually he became aware that the others had left the room. When he tried to follow he found that the doors were locked. He pressed his ear against each door, but no sound betrayed his captor's activities. He paced around the table, then slipped his shoes off and sat, lotus style, atop the bare table, his eyes on the mountain across the valley, his hands folded into a mudra. His fingers were intertwined, the index fingers raised and pressed together like a steeple. It was called Diamond of the Mind, for keeping focus.

He wasn't aware of the door opening, only of Thomas appearing in the chair nearest him, holding two bottles of water. The youth, new excitement in his eyes, handed Shan a bottle, a peace offering.

"How many criminals have you killed?" Gao's nephew asked.

Shan shuddered. "I never carried a gun," he finally replied.

Thomas seemed disappointed.

"But my investigations sent over a dozen men to firing squads," he offered.

Thomas brightened. "I have told my father and uncles that I plan to enter the Academy for Forensic Science."

"I once taught there," Shan said, slipping off the table to sit close to the youth, eye to eye. "A guest lecturer."

Thomas saluted Shan with his bottle. "My uncles tell me I am destined for great things. They want me to become an astronomer, for when China has its own space station. Uncle Heinz calls me the first citizen of the new world. He says they can get me into the astronaut corps when I finish university. But when I arrived here this summer I told them I wanted to enroll in the forensic academy, because that is where science and real life come together. They laughed at me." He took a swallow from his bottle. "But they're wrong. I saw the head of a murder investigation squad in Beijing, driving a Mercedes. In America they have red convertibles."

A dozen rejoinders came to mind, but as

Shan sifted them, realization burst upon him. "Give me your opinion of the murders."

Thomas glanced nervously toward the closed doors.

Shan said in a quiet, conspiratorial tone, "Surely there is only one other person on this mountain who knows how to treat a murder scene. The trick with the glue, that shows great resourcefulness. Did you use a spoon and match?" It was an improvisation Shan himself had used more than once in his prior life. The isocyanate of the industrial glue adhered to the oils in fingerprints, producing a print of gray raised ridges.

Thomas flushed. Then he admitted, "I took photographs. I took fingerprints. Everything. I put particles of bone in plastic bags. I am making a special portfolio for my academy application, to guarantee my admission."

"Everything?"

"You know. Tissue samples, for DNA. Blood samples. The dirt from their boots. I recorded the direction of the wind, the time of sunrise, air temperature. The entry wound to the back of Victim One was inflicted by a heavy-edged weapon and probably severed the spinal cord. The puncture wound in the skull of Victim Two could have been from a large-caliber bullet."

"I think the killer stood right beside his victims," Shan explained. "I doubt if he used a gun. Did you see any stippling on the skin around the hole? When a gun is fired at close range particles of burning gunpowder leave traces."

Thomas's eyes widened. He pulled a piece of paper from a pocket and scribbled a quick note, then began to brag again. "I took a fly larvae out of the flesh and froze it. We can correlate the life-stage development of the larvae with other indicia, to confirm my finding of the time of death."

"And how exactly did you make your finding?"

"Rigor mortis. The hardening of the skeletal muscles begins within two to three hours and begins to dissipate within twenty-four hours. When I found the bodies in the morning the stiffness was just disappearing."

"It may be dangerous to rely on such criteria when the limbs have been severed."

"The hands. Only the hands were cut off at first. I do wish I had the hands." Thomas fixed Shan with a meaningful gaze. "Even if the flesh of the fingertips was deteriorating we could inject them with saline solution to raise the ridges enough for prints, right? And I could probably match the hands to the bodies from my photographs and even draw inferences about their professions."

Shan went very still. "Are you saying you have photographs?"

Without another word the boy leapt up and shot out the door. He returned panting, extending a small silver digital camera. "I haven't printed anything out, but you can view them right here. The hands were gone when I discovered the bodies. When I returned with my equipment the bodies had been dismembered and some of the limbs were missing."

His camera held a dozen photos, and though the small screen did not display much detail, there was enough. Shan had to calm himself before taking a second look. Unfortunately, Thomas had taken pictures only of the small clearing where the bodies had been, not of the campsite itself, and none of the two men's faces. Their clothes were blood drenched. The shirt on one of the bodies also bore soil stains showing its wearer had been dragged. One appeared to be younger; on his back was a long wound, as Thomas had described. The flat rock in the center of the little clearing still had one arm stretched across it, in the direction of the low sprays of blood. Shan pointed to the puncture wound on the older man's skull. "The edges are not uniform enough for a bullet entry."

Thomas nodded. "And there was no stippling. You have changed my theory of the case."

"You have a theory?"

Thomas nodded again. "I have to have a case theory, a hypothesis, for my project. The criminals were runaway soldiers, that was my first idea, deserters turned bandits. But if there was no gun, then I will say the culprits were Tibetans, a gang of hooligans with axes and hammers." He looked up, his eyes brighter. "Ragyapa! It could be a gang of criminal fleshcutters. This could be a movie script!"

"Ragyapa remove the clothes from corpses before cutting them up," Shan pointed out. "And they don't take away body parts. They leave them all at the scene. And they crush the bones."

Thomas frowned. "Reactionary Tibetans then. The first victim lingered. A cloth was stuffed in his mouth to silence him."

Shan nodded solemnly, wondering about the boy who coldly took photos of dismembered men for a school project. "What exactly did you do," he asked, "after your first visit?"

"I went back for one of Heinz's guns. When I returned there were dogs circling about the rocks. I fired the rifle and they ran."

Shan stared at the boy in disbelief. "Another approach," he observed in a steady voice, "might have been to wait in hiding with your camera, in case the murderer returned to dispose of the bodies." If Thomas had scared away the dogs, then certainly he would have spooked the murderer.

"But then my portfolio would have been incomplete," Thomas pointed out. "I still had to lift the fingerprints and evaluate the angle and force of the cutting instrument. The dogs would have destroyed evidence and contaminated the crime scene."

"And your conclusion about the instrument used to cut off the hands?"

"It had to go through bone and ligament. A surgical bone saw would fit."

It wasn't so much an investigation, Shan told himself, as a word game. *Sound bites from famous detective shows I have watched.* "I'm old-fashioned," he said. "How about something that fits the context, like a small ax? It would account for the wound in the back and the severed hands."

Thomas nodded, making more notes.

There were four more photos of the dead men. The young one had worn denim pants and a sweatshirt; the older man, a T-shirt and sweatpants. The other eight photos were all of bloodstain patterns.

"Why were you really imprisoned?" Thomas asked. "I saw a movie once where an investigator was sent to prison to infiltrate a criminal ring. Did you kill anyone in prison? A good policeman doesn't need a gun. I have a book about the ten ways to kill with your hands."

Shan clenched his jaw. As unlikely an ally as Thomas might seem, Shan needed the boy. "I saw many people die in prison."

Thomas hesitated, then nodded. "Of course, if it was true, you would deny it. The best ones never break their cover."

"I can see you have a brilliant career ahead of you in Beijing."

"Would you write a letter of recommendation for me?"

The charade was getting out of hand. "Your family has imprisoned me," Shan pointed out.

"But I unlocked the door," Thomas declared.

Shan pushed open the door to the large sitting room with a finger. He stepped into the empty room, then eyed the door that led outside. He returned to Thomas and leaned on the table beside him. "Where is your evidence? Your samples?"

"I sent them to Beijing, to a friend in a lab."

Shan paced around the room. The adjoining office was empty. "Why did you cross to the other side of the mountain? Why go to the trouble, when you have all this?"

"This is my uncles' stuff. I'm my own man. I do my own thing. They wouldn't approve but I've made friends of some of the miners. They are always looking to trade things."

"What do they have that you could want?"

"Gold, of course. I can get them little comforts. A can of peaches, a bag of raisins, a toothbrush, a razor. Vodka and brandy. The closest store is fifty miles away. Everyone is in business, right? Uncle Heinz says we all participate in the global economy, no matter where we live."

Thomas's particular home in the global economy, Shan realized, was a storehouse replenished regularly by the People's Liberation Army. "How often do you go to Drango village?"

"That dump where the farmers live? Never."

"Then how often do you see Chodron?"

"That old yak? He stays in his wallow on the far side."

Shan considered the boy's words. He said he never went to the village but he had admitted that he knew who Chodron was. Shan picked up the camera and asked Thomas to show him how to scroll through the photos, pausing at the last, a tiny one of the man sometimes called the saint, sitting between the blood-drawn images. He leaned over the boy, speaking in a low, urgent voice, Thomas nodding assent to his secret assignment. When they finished, Shan scrolled through the photos one more time. "Did you look for identification on the bodies?"

"Everything was covered in blood. I brought plastic gloves when I returned but —"

His answer was cut off by an angry exclamation from the dining room. Kohler stood near the door, glaring. Thomas colored, then without another word trotted toward Kohler, who led him into the kitchen.

Shan darted toward the entry, then hesitated and slipped into Gao's office instead. He spent a moment surveying the framed photos, ashamed at the quiver of fear that some of the familiar faces sent down his spine. Lingering at the back of several photos, looking like a tourist who had wandered into the scene, was a younger Kohler.

On the desk were recent letters, most sent by fax, from addresses in Beijing. He glanced at the small gray fax machine at the side of the desk that had received the letters. It meant there was a telephone wire strung from the base below, but it also might mean there was no reliable electronic mail connecting Gao's little palace to the outside world. He quickly scanned the faxed messages for their originators. The Academy of Scientists, arranging a speaking date for a conference in January. The Special Science Section of the State Council, one of the unofficial, private little committees that advised Beijing's top echelon. The director of civilian personnel for regional military bases, asking for staffing recommendations. The Party Council on Scientific Policy, seeking review of a secret research paper.

Beside the correspondence was a rolled-up newspaper. On closer examination Shan saw that it was not simply rolled but taped tightly to form a cylindrical package. One end had been sealed with tape, the other was cut open. Shan upended the tube, dumping out a hard object wrapped in the coarse toilet tissue used in most Tibetan homes. A second later he held it in his hand. Despite Gao's assurance to the contrary, someone had come from the other side, from Drango. The gold beetle glistened more brightly in the sunlight shining through Gao's office window than it had in the light of the butter lamps in the stable. He recalled Gendun's punishment and Chodron's obsession with sending the beetle back to where it belonged. Shan looked up at the nearest photo of Gao, a portrait in which his breast gleamed with the medals bestowed on civilians who performed vital services for the state. Shan had found the home of the mountain deity.

He pushed the golden beetle back into the tube and headed for the door to the outside. With a surge of relief he felt the knob turn. The door opened. But as he stepped outside Kohler looked up from a nearby rock where he sat smoking a cigarette.

"Do you have any notion how quickly our garbage disposal system works?" he asked. "One call, and a squad of soldiers appear. Then our garbage disappears forever."

Shan looked longingly at the cliffs above, the route back to his world. "But you and Dr. Gao don't like to reduce yourselves to that level."

Kohler grinned. "Something like that. And

you present such an interesting opportunity for us."

"If you are looking for kitchen help, I am always dropping things."

"Comrade, you are going to have Gao rolling on the floor," Kohler said and gestured Shan back into the house.

Four hours later he sat with Kohler on the square stone-walled roof of the high tower. The room under the roof in which Kohler had locked him was the most agreeable of prisons. Though a windowless chamber, it contained an actual bed and linens. Before locking him in, the German had explained that he and Thomas had similar rooms on the levels below.

Kohler had invited Shan to the roof to watch the sunset with a bottle and two glasses, and was now holding the fifth glass of pepper vodka he had consumed. Shan had sipped from the first glass of the pungent liquid when Kohler pressed it on him, then clandestinely tipped the contents over the side, only to have the glass refilled.

"We're all outlaws of a sort," Kohler said, his eyes reflecting the purple light of the dusk. "How could any sane man not be, in this world we have created?"

"Have you been away from home long?" Shan probed.

"Home? What's home? My homeland was declared redundant. Mergers and acquisitions, they call it. Someone in Bonn or maybe Washington decided to make a takeover offer so good it couldn't be refused. Presto, no country. Just a bunch of branch offices reporting to what had once been our biggest competitor. Entire towns were discontinued. I got a letter from my sister, who once headed a school. She scrubs floors in Frankfurt now. But she has her own car and a mountain of debt so she is happy as a pig in mud." He saluted the sunset with his vodka glass. "Lha fucking gyal lo.

"I never really had a home there anyway. I came to Beijing as a doctoral student on a special exchange program for physicists. Dr. Gao took me on as a special assistant. The first year we communicated by drawing equations on chalkboards. By the time I understood Mandarin I was already living in a spare room of his house, though we spent damned little time sleeping in those days. I could go home and be a cog in a wheel of Moscow's science machine or stay and live out every scientist's fantasy. Unlimited resources. Billions and billions. Unlimited glory."

"At least within certain bureaus in Beijing," Shan submitted.

Kohler saluted him with a clumsy sweep of his glass. "Once wars were won by the side that could best afford to keep sending men to the slaughter, which for centuries made China the mightiest nation on earth. Every man with a beard who rode out of the West was smothered by a hundred Chinese. "Now it's a game of cards. Small men at a big table play guessing games about what equations the other side's big men have written on secret chalkboards." Kohler burst into laughter, then drained his glass again.

"If you have a chalkboard," Shan said, "I would guess it's full of questions about two murders that took place on the western side of the mountain. You betray your concern by holding me."

"What we worry about is the inexplicable. Death happens all the time on the other side of the mountain, it's to be expected. It's like the Wild West over there. You know, American cowboys," he said, using the English words. "But you, Inspector Shan, are inexplicable. Why do you appear at this moment? That worries us. We had another escaped prisoner once. He was found looking in the windows. He begged us not to call the army. He offered to be our slave, offered to go back over to the other side and bring us gold. Thomas guessed you must be a secret agent of some kind. I laughed." Kohler examined Shan for a moment. "What explains a man like you?"

Shan became aware of music rising from below, a confused mixture of sounds that he eventually distilled into muted rock and roll overlaying the more distant tones of Beethoven. "That other prisoner. What happened to him?"

"He was annoying. Too nervous. Too talkative. I arranged for him to disappear." Kohler poured himself another glass of his medicine. "But you, you are like a monk. You are focused, quiet. You have secrets. We have learned to be very careful about gray men with secrets."

"I am nothing but what you see before you. My gray clothes are rags."

Kohler drained his glass again.

The sun had disappeared over the ridge. The purple sky became streaked with silver. The narrow cleft had long since disappeared into shadow but not before Shan had fixed in his mind's eye its location and a line of outcroppings that led straight to it.

"This Rapaki you spoke of earlier. Does he live in a cave?" Shan asked abruptly.

"Who?"

"The hermit no one wishes to discuss."

"He's harmless. Forget him. He's just a goat with a robe. You might glimpse him in the distance before he scampers away."

"Forgetting things. That seems to be the house specialty here."

Shan refilled the two glasses, toasted the German, stealthily dumped his over the side, and refilled Kohler's again. Kohler held the glass under his nostrils for a moment. "A good retirement requires discarding the last moment and living in the next."

"Sounds lonely."

"Sounds painless," Kohler retorted. His head began to roll. He had to exert himself to keep it upright.

"I'm sorry we won't have more time to get better acquainted," Shan said. Kohler did not protest when Shan took the glass from his hand and set it on the wall.

"I have hidden the fucking key," the German mumbled, though he seemed unable to move. "You will stay until the dragon decides to eat you." Then he passed out.

Shan arranged Kohler as comfortably as possible, taking the precaution of removing the man's shoelaces and using them to tie his hands to the arms of his chair before Shan descended to his bedroom. Kohler had proudly pointed out the nearby linen closet. Shan did a quick calculation, then removed ten sheets from the closet, quickly returned to the roof, and began knotting them together. One of the many things his years in Tibet had cured him of was his fear of heights.

Chapter Four

Shan was nearly in sight of Drango village the next morning when he heard an angry shout. He flattened against an outcropping, wondering if, against all odds, Kohler had had him followed by a squad of soldiers. He bore the bruises of a night passage through the ravine, having crossed the flimsy ladder bridge just before the moon hid behind clouds and then spent a restless few hours in a hole in the jumbled rocks, certain every tumbling stone was the sound of pursuing boots.

A string of curses in Mandarin erupted from the far side of the outcropping. He studied the trail behind him, then cautiously stepped around the rock, freezing momentarily before his foot came down on a freshly erected cairn. Eight inches high, it had been carefully constructed inside one of the pans used by miners for working streams, a sprig of fresh heather inserted in its center. It still smelled. It had been made of manure dropped from a mule or horse, and carefully placed in the middle of the trail above Drango. Peering around the rock Shan saw a middle-aged Chinese man berating a mule stacked high with cargo, trying to coerce it to turn down a fork in the trail. He grabbed a handful of the sweetgrass that grew in the cracks in the rocks at his feet and stepped around the far end of the outcropping. The animal's head snapped up and the mule leaned toward the grass in Shan's hand.

"It's *my* beast," the man growled. He raised his makeshift staff, a crooked but sturdy juniper limb, as if to hit Shan.

"But it's Tibetan," Shan said. "Tibetans have a custom of sharing part of the load when they travel."

A pick and shovel were lashed to the top of the mule's panniers. The man's hand went to a knife in his belt. His grin was aimed past Shan's shoulder. The hairs on the back of Shan's neck rose as he slowly turned. A large dog sat on a slab of rock six feet away, fangs bared, ready to pounce.

"No bark," the miner declared, showing his own yellowed teeth. "All bite."

Shan let the mule eat the grass, then kneeled, facing the dog. "Why do you leave the mountain halfway through the season?"

he asked the miner, who did not reply.

Shan spoke to the dog in Tibetan, as Lokesh did when meeting an unfamiliar animal, asking it how it felt, praising its obvious strength. A belief in reincarnation made for interesting relationships with animals. The dog's fangs disappeared. It cocked its head and stepped forward, tentatively licking Shan's hand.

"You're no miner," the stranger said. "And you're not one of those damned farmers either."

Shan pulled up his sleeve and displayed his tattoo. After so many years he had learned that though for many it was a cause for alarm, for others it was an icebreaker.

The tautness left the man's face. He studied Shan, then extracted a small gleaming nugget from a pouch at his belt. "This is yours if you help me down the mountain to the road. Three days' work. I've twisted my ankle."

"I can't," Shan replied. "But I can wrap your ankle if you have some cloth so it will be easier for you to walk on it."

"Under the shovel," the miner said. "There's an old piece of canvas."

Shan did not miss the worried glance the man cast up the trail. Was he being followed? "Sit and unlace the boot," Shan advised as he pointed to a nearby rock, then he retrieved the cloth. In five minutes he was expertly wrapping the swollen ankle. When he finished the man uttered a satisfied grunt and extracted a much smaller piece of gold.

Shan raised his palm to decline payment. "Just tell me what has frightened you."

"I don't fear a damned thing. It's the way of things this summer. My old grandmother knew, after all the famines and wars she saw. Sometimes death stalks a land, she said, and there's nothing man can do to stop it. If you aren't smart enough to come in out of a hailstorm, don't complain when your skull gets cracked. They closed my factory. Everyone says move to a big city to make money. I don't want a big city." The miner shrugged, watched a passing cloud for a moment. "I've got family I want to see again."

The man lit a cigarette. "Two years ago an old friend from the army shows up. He asks me to hide him from the police for a few days while he waits for a ride to Hong Kong. In return he tells me the biggest secret in Tibet. After the snow melts, he says, load up a mule with supplies and follow this secret map to a place called Sleeping Dragon Mountain. Pick up gold from the ground and it's yours. Last year I came, and it was good. I got enough to pay off my debts. This year started the same but then it got ugly. My camp was looted, half the gear stolen. A miner not far from me woke up in the night to find all the trees in his camp on fire. Another miner's mule was killed by a painted stick stuffed down its throat."

Shan looked up with sudden interest.

"Two weeks ago someone killed my other dog and stuffed a claim stick in its mouth." The miner blew a plume of smoke toward the sky.

"Why? What do they want?"

"No one ever sees who does it. When it happens to you, you move your claim and they leave you alone."

"Then they take over the claim?"

"No one takes it."

Shan considered the reply a moment. "It's as if you were just getting too close to something they don't want you to see."

"That's what I thought. But they've all been in different places. Once up against the wall that divides the mountain. Once in a small grove of trees by an old painted rock. Once at the edge of a cliff. There's enough gold, enough room, so it's not worth it to try to oppose whoever is doing it."

"But then those two men died."

The man inhaled deeply on his cigarette,

studying Shan. "A day after the murders I was on a high trail, walking along the top of a slope almost as steep as a cliff, when I saw two men above me, maybe three hundred yards higher up. I ducked into the shadows and didn't think they noticed me. They were carrying heavy loads wrapped in cloth, on shoulder poles. One of them dropped something that rolled down the trail toward me. Round as a ball, in a burlap sack. It rolled almost to me before it fell off the trail and bounced into the gully far below. Some use twine to mark out their claims. I figured it was a ball of twine until it fell out of its sack. . . ."

"But it wasn't twine," Shan said as he gently eased the man's foot back into his boot, lacing it loosely. He lifted the man's staff and began working on it with his pocketknife.

"It wasn't anything I ever want to see again. It had been pounded by the rocks, as if someone had played soccer with it. I looked up and one of the men was studying me with binoculars. I leaped up and ran down the slope like some damned fool. That's when I twisted my foot."

"The head in the bag," Shan said. "Young or old?"

"It's not like I had time to study it. But I

saw some gray hair."

So two men had been involved in the killings, and they had cut the bodies up to dispose of them. "Where would you go, if you had something like that to get rid of?"

"Right about where they were. There's a crack in the cliff that goes down deeper than anyone can see."

"The cliff where a miner was chased away from his claim?"

The man thought for a moment. "Now that you mention it, yes, it was the same place."

"Did you recognize the men?"

"They were too far away. But they had binoculars. They saw me."

Shan kept whittling on the staff. "Were you here last year when a man was killed?"

"That's over and done with."

"What do you mean?"

"The son of a bitch was a claim jumper. We found claim sticks taken from four of us at his camp. No one was sorry to see him disappear. But it spooked us."

"You mean because of the way he died?"

"Because he was found in front of one of those paintings of demons, the one of the blue bull, and there was fresh blood on the painting, as if the demon had come to life. Because his hands were cut off. But that's ancient history. Captain Bing proved who the killer was and chased him off."

It was Shan's turn to look up the trail in alarm. "Captain? You mean the army was involved?"

The miner offered a sour grin. "Call it the miners' militia. Bing discovered that the man's own partner had killed the claim-jumping bastard. Later, the dead man took care of things."

"The dead man?"

"We buried him in a shallow grave under a mound of heavy rocks. Two weeks later a skeleton appeared, draped over the grave. Some said the dead man rose up from the grave, that he was too angry to stay buried before obtaining vengeance. But then we saw the skeleton's fingers."

"The fingers?"

"One of them held his partner's ring," the man said with a shudder. "The skeleton was that of the dead man's partner, who'd killed him. I saw it with my own eyes. The dead man did rise up and take revenge. No one goes near there anymore. We know better than to interfere with the business of the dead."

"Where exactly is this no-man's-land?"

"The grave is on a long black ridge that juts out to the west. About a mile north of

Little Moscow." The man saw the confusion on Shan's face. "And if you don't know about that already, you don't want to know. They don't take to strangers. Captain Bing organized things last year after those killings."

Little Moscow. Captain Bing. The lonely mountain was becoming more crowded all the time.

"Don't mess with Bing. He'll chew you up and spit out your bones."

"So at least one man was killed last year. And two men were murdered last week. Was there anyone else?"

"Why do you care?"

"I collect stories about the dead. Something I started in prison."

The miner contemplated the point for a moment, glanced at his expertly bound ankle, and nodded. "A young miner, a newcomer barely out of his teens, was killed in front of a painting of a blue bull demon. The body disappeared so fast no one knows for certain what happened. Only one other miner saw it before it was carried away. Ugly business. He said at first he thought the boy was just lying down, smoking a cigar."

"A cigar?"

"But when he came close he saw it was a small stick, jammed into the boy's dead mouth. Not a claim stick. It had eyes carved into it. It scared everyone, because of all the other things that happen on this mountain."

"You mean the skeletons."

"Skeletons. Ghosts. Those damned paintings. People say this is where all the old demons come, to hide from the rest of the world, that the demons in the paintings come to life at night."

Shan handed the man the staff he had been working on. He had cut off some of the stubs protruding from the juniper limb and turned the top joint into a smooth, curving cradle. The staff had become a crutch.

The man accepted it with an approving nod, then rummaged among the packs on the mule. "If you don't take something it'll jinx me." He extracted a small blue nylon pouch tied with a drawstring, hesitated, then tossed it to Shan. "Take it. Not my kind of trinkets." He avoided Shan's gaze now, tending to his packs, talking soothingly to his animals. He seemed grateful to be rid of the little blue sack.

"After this fork in the trail," Shan said, "the quickest way down is straight, past Drango. It is why your mule stopped here. It knows the way."

"Not today," the man said, with a wary

glance in the direction of the village. "If you see that prick Chodron, give him a message," the miner said as he rose. "Tell him I left his payment on the trail." He hobbled away, using more of the grass to coax his mule onto the side trail.

Shan waited until the man was fifty yards away before sitting and emptying the sack onto the ground. In it was a small plastic thermometer with a ring by which it could be attached to a lanyard and a small stack of papers bound with a rubber band. Each was covered with little round discs with adhesive backing, in half a dozen colors. A small pencil sharpener. Three identical screwtop brown plastic containers. The first contained matches, the second a variety of medicinal tablets, and the third was apparently empty. He laid his discoveries on a rock, studying them, trying to understand what he saw. At last he picked up the thermometer and read it. The degrees were marked in Fahrenheit, only in Fahrenheit. It had belonged to someone from America.

Nothing appeared to have changed when he entered the village. But when the guard at the stable door hesitantly lifted the bar for Shan something seemed to be blocking the door from the inside. "One moment," he heard Lokesh say, and seconds later the door opened and his old friend motioned him inside. The stranger lay flat. Gendun, at his head, looked frail. The lama's arm trembled where the electrodes had been attached. But Gendun was steadily murmuring his prayers. Dolma, nearby, worked a small wooden churn.

At the sound of the bar dropping into place Dolma stopped and Lokesh bent to a cluster of butter lamps he was using to heat a tin kettle. Dolma extended a hand and the stranger grasped it, pulling himself up as he fixed Shan with bright, intelligent eyes.

"Tashi delay," Shan ventured, offering the traditional greeting.

"He doesn't understand us," Lokesh said. "He speaks one of the ancient tongues."

"Ni hao," Shan tried, switching to Chinese.

"Ya'atay," the stranger said. It was neither Tibetan nor Chinese, nor any language Shan knew.

"I am called Shan," he continued in Chinese, pointing to himself.

"Ni . . . hao," the stranger offered in a slow, uncertain voice, then switched to his strange tongue. "Hostene," he said, pushing a thumb toward his chin. Dolma busied herself at the little churn and soon handed the stranger a cup of buttered tea, which he eagerly raised to his lips and tilted down his throat. A moment later he gagged, coughed, and set the cup down, holding his belly. This Tibetan who spoke the ancient Tibetan tongue was not familiar with the traditional Tibetan drink.

Shan studied the bench where Dolma had churned the tea, then chipped off a corner of the brick of black tea she had used, dropped it into another cup, and filled it from the kettle without adding butter or salt. He extended the cup to the man, who hesitantly accepted it, sniffed the contents, and tested it with a cautious sip.

"*A'hayhee*," the man said. The gratitude in his tone needed no translation. He drained the cup, then became aware of Gendun's eyes fixed on him. The lama, Shan saw, was seized with intense curiosity, a mix of confusion and fascination. The stranger awkwardly pressed his palms together, fingers extended, the traditional offering of respect.

Gendun cocked his head first to one side then the other. "If the gods are trying to take us to a new place," he said in a quizzical, excited tone, "why would they use our old words?"

Shan watched in mute confusion as the lama reached inside his sleeve and produced the stub of a pencil. On one of the smooth planks leaning against the wall he drew something, then set it in front of the stranger. Surprisingly, it was a fish. Not any fish, but the traditional image of the leaping golden fish, representing spiritual liberation, one of the Eight Auspicious Signs sacred to the Tibetans.

The stranger rubbed his head a moment, gazing uncertainly at his companions, then accepted the pencil offered by Gendun and ran his fingertip over the image in the same way Lokesh did with unfamiliar images. The silence was that of a teaching, when novices waited for the slow word of an old lama. At last he lifted the pencil and drew an object opposite the fish on the plank, something that might have been a stalk of corn.

Gendun ran his own fingertips over the new image, then drew another of the sacred symbols. A lotus flower, sign of purity. The stranger made another. A bundle of arrows.

A sigh of wonder escaped Lokesh's lips. Gendun sketched still another of the eight sacred signs. A treasure vase, repository of the jewels of enlightenment. The stranger sketched. A rainbow. Gendun drew again. A wheel of dharma. With a somber gaze the stranger once more bent over the plank. When he had finished Shan saw Lokesh's eyes grow round. The man had drawn the zigzag snake, the thunderbolt serpent that they had seen drawn in blood. "The gods are making a proposal," the old Tibetan exclaimed, then his face sagged. "But I don't know what it is."

As his friends bent over the sketch, Shan stepped to a corner, where sunlight leaked through cracks in the plank wall. He pulled from his belt the pouch given him by the fleeing miner, kneeled, and extracted the brown plastic jars, realizing he had not opened the one he had assumed to be empty. He had been wrong. It was filled with small colorful feathers. He unscrewed the container with the medicine. It contained two types of pills, neither of them the small white tablets strangers often brought to Tibet for altitude sickness. He discovered a slip of paper tucked so tightly around the inside of the jar that he had not noticed it on his first examination. With a finger he pried at it, discovering there were in fact two slips, both drug prescriptions. One was for methotrexate, the other for leucovorin calcium. Along the top of each slip ran a legend in ornate silver letters. Monument Pharmacy, Shiprock, New Mexico.

For several minutes Shan continued to watch the silent, energetic exchange between his two Tibetan friends and the

161

stranger, his mind racing. The riddles of Sleeping Dragon Mountain never generated answers, only more riddles. Finally he poured another cup of black tea and squatted by the trio.

Shan said in English as he extended the cup to the man, "I hear there are more Tibetan scholars in America than in China."

At the sound of the English words the stranger's jaw dropped. His reply came out in a dry and cracked voice, but it was understandable. "I have never met a Tibetan who spoke English."

"I am Chinese," Shan said, returning the man's grin.

"I am called Hostene, Hostene Natay." The man looked about, studying each of them in turn. "I guess you saved my life."

"Lha gyal lo," Lokesh whispered, the words echoed by Dolma a moment later. Gendun, his hand pressed to his side as if he was in pain, offered a serene smile, then gazed at the plank with the drawings.

They spoke rapidly for a quarter hour, Shan pausing to translate for his friends until Hostene discovered both Gendun and Lokesh spoke Chinese. In slow, clumsy Mandarin, with many apologies for not having kept it polished since learning it in the US Army many years earlier, he explained

162

that he was a retired judge from New Mexico in the southwestern United States. Lokesh gave Shan no chance to ask Hostene about the murders, instead peppering him with questions about the stick figure, the lightning bolts, and the dialogue in symbols he had carried on with Gendun.

"It is why we are here," Hostene explained. "To unlock the links between the Tibetans and my people."

"Your people?" Shan asked.

"The Dine. The Navajo."

Shan had a vague recollection of the term. "You mean Native Americans?"

"There are many names for the tribes that first inhabited North America. First Nations. Original Peoples." Hostene pressed his hand to his temple. "The people to whom the gods entrusted the continent." His wry tone did little to conceal his obvious pain. "My tribe is the Navajo."

He closed his eyes a moment. "I don't remember how I got here. I was sleeping. Someone walked through the trees and stepped on a branch. I rolled over and something hit me on the head."

Shan asked, dreading the answer, "Who else was with you?"

"A retired professor from Beijing, Professor Ma Hopeng, and a young Tibetan guide.

We met in Chamdo." Hostene paused, looking toward the door with anxious eyes. "Where are they?" he asked urgently. "I must see them."

Shan and Lokesh exchanged a glance.

Hostene struggled to rise, then slumped forward. He seemed to be losing consciousness again. "The boy is covered in blood!" he groaned. "Warn her, up on the mountain!" His eyelids fluttered and shut, and he dropped back onto the pallet.

"The mountain deity," Lokesh concluded. "He wants to warn the mountain deity."

As they rolled him onto his back, Hostene came to life again, resisting their efforts, trying to get to his feet. He was perhaps fifteen years older than Shan but, at least for the moment, seemed to have the strength of a man in his prime.

"They are beyond our help," Shan told him. "There are words you might wish to say for them. Gendun has been offering prayers for them."

Hostene looked at Shan, seeking comprehension. Shan caught him as he sagged and lowered him back to the pallet.

"Something happened that night," Shan said. "You were found covered with blood, sitting against a rock. You are the only survivor."

Hostene lowered his head into his hands. No one spoke. Dolma lit another stick of incense.

"I was in my sleeping bag," the Navajo finally whispered. "The sun had not yet risen. I turned and . . . that's all I can recall. Who?" he asked. "Why?"

"We don't know," Shan admitted.

"The police?"

"No government reaches here."

Time passed. "She said she was going to close the circle between two peoples," Hostene finally said in a grief-stricken voice. "She was so excited about her discoveries. So full of life. I used to say she was like one of the wild mustangs we sometimes glimpsed in the arroyos."

Shan could not make sense of the Navajo's words.

When Hostene looked up, tears were streaming down his cheeks. "What will I tell my sister when I see her in the night?"

"Your sister?"

"Abigail was my niece. Her friends begged her not to try this, not to come so far. I told her that if she insisted I would accompany her, to watch over her. And now I've let her be killed."

"But only two bodies were found," Shan said in confusion. "Neither was that of a woman."

Hostene grabbed Shan's wrist. "Abigail! Where is she then?" He had realized that his niece might be alive, alone on the mountain where a murderer was at large.

The door opened. Shan crossed the floor an instant too late. The guard took one look at Hostene, gasped, and with a swift, panicked motion tapped the side of the Navajo's head with his club. Hostene collapsed to the floor.

"Gasoline." It was Chodron's only greeting when he finally opened his back door to Shan an hour after dawn the next day. The headman, wearing a sleeping robe, handed Shan an empty gas can and pointed to a small lean-to shed built against the house. Inside the shed was a barrel with a hand pump screwed into the top.

Hostene's scalp had been cut open by the guard's club. He had drifted in and out of consciousness most of the night, nursed by Dolma and by Lokesh, who mixed healing teas from the little bag of herbs he kept on his belt. At times Hostene seemed to have the same ageless vitality as his two Tibetan friends, at others his body was as weak as an infant's.

"He may die," Shan said as he handed the

filled gas can to Chodron, who now wore a blue dress shirt and black trousers, as if he were attending a Party meeting.

Chodron passed Shan and went to an object at the foot of the wall. Tossing off the felt blanket that covered it, he revealed a small generator, connected to wires that led into the house. Shan gazed at three villagers who stood silently at the garden wall. They winced as the generator sputtered and sprang to life with a low hum.

The headman seemed to expect Shan to follow him through the inner door. Chodron gestured him toward a chair in front of the table that served as his desk. He did not offer Shan the black tea that he poured from a porcelain pot into a tall mug.

"I remember going to the circus as a boy," Shan recounted after a long pause, "and exclaiming to my father that the most amazing men alive must be the jugglers. He said, 'Look closely. None of the jugglers are old because eventually they begin dropping pins. Then no one remembers all the great magic they once made, only the dropped pins.' "

"I have no time for your idle banter. Yesterday you proved I cannot trust you up on the mountain. I want you to write out your explanation for the murders. Today."

Chodron flipped on the switch of a goose-neck lamp and began sifting through papers.

"It may become difficult for you to keep control of both the villagers and the miners," said Shan. "Perhaps you only need show your authority to rule the particular type of villagers bred in Drango. But you'll have to produce value for the miners."

"It is well documented that former hard-labor prisoners suffer from a variety of mental ailments."

"There is only one plausible explanation as to why the miners remain undisturbed by the government. You protect them. In most years such a service must be quite valuable, considering all the taxes and regulations they avoid."

"You haven't got a shred of evidence. You are playing with your life, prisoner."

"With such a difficult juggling act to perform perhaps you have not had time to catch up on Chinese history," Shan continued. "A pity, as you would soon learn that for centuries the most serious crime in China has been corruption. Murderers simply had their heads cut off. Sometimes they might even be allowed to buy their freedom. But those who stole from the emperor were always condemned to death by a thousand slices. Sometimes the criminals were paraded around entire counties and at each town pieces were removed from their bodies. Today, entire offices of the Public Security Bureau are dedicated to searching out corruption. It is such a problem that every lead is energetically followed. The PSB compiles the proof. They only need someone to point them in the right direction."

Chodron sipped his tea, looking bored.

"You lost a miner yesterday," Shan continued. "He followed a different trail down. It was longer than the regular trail but it kept him out of view of Drango village. He said to tell you he left your tribute on the trail. Still steaming, courtesy of his mule."

The grin that had begun to form on Chodron's face slowly faded and was replaced by a resentful glare.

"Why should the miners keep paying you tribute if you can't stop a murderer?"

Chodron set down his tea and picked up a pamphlet on his desk. "This begins to sound like a negotiation," the headman grunted.

"I want the stranger freed to go up the mountain with me. I want Yangke freed of his collar and allowed openly to assist me."

"Impossible."

"You fail to appreciate that your survival

depends upon a delicate balance. You are not the only one who can call in troops."

"You wouldn't dare. You'd be back in prison in six hours. It would be my word against a felon's."

"I meant Dr. Gao. The true king of the mountain."

Chodron grew very still.

"What if Dr. Gao thought the peace of his retreat was being disturbed?" Shan asked.

"You know nothing about Gao except what some miner told you."

"I was his guest yesterday. His photo gallery is much more impressive than yours. I noticed his beetle collection."

"You? He would have you thrown out with his rubbish."

"In the past we knew many of the same people in Beijing. Only in our retirement years have our paths diverged."

"Yangke's punishment was fixed. The lesson is lost if I relent."

"August 1," Shan suggested. "You are preparing for the national holiday. There is a long tradition of granting amnesty to prisoners to honor our noble founders."

Chodron stared into his mug. "You can't wander into my town and give me orders."

"I prefer to think of it as giving sound political advice."

Chodron tossed the pamphlet toward Shan, leaned back, and flipped a switch on a box. Dials and needles, lit from within, sprang to life.

"Drango village calling," he said into the peglike microphone in front of the box, after reciting a series of numbers.

Shan began to understand the expressions on the faces of the villagers. They were afraid of the generator, they feared the radio. It wasn't guns, tanks, or helicopters that were Beijing's most potent tools in occupied Tibet. It was little black boxes like these, hundreds of them scattered across the far-flung land.

"*Wei,*" a woman's voice said, in the universal telephonic greeting. "Municipal Affairs. Uncle Chodron, is it you? How is my favorite drunkard? When will you bring us some of those delicious apricots?"

For a moment Shan was deaf to the banter that followed. The pamphlet, entitled *Ax to Root* for internal distribution among Party members in Tibet, announced a political campaign. *The time has come to destroy the persistent roots in the countryside that are pulling the people back into the old traditions of despotism and servitude,* it read. This was Party code for the old monks and lamas who wandered the countryside. *Old men and women being given shelter in the mountains and farming villages, soliciting money for temple construction, tempting children to become hooligan monks are violating the decrees of the Bureau of Religious Affairs.* The government was about to pursue a zero-tolerance policy. All such individuals were to be identified and surrendered to Public Security.

"Ax to Root," Shan heard Chodron say, and listened as the woman on the other end uttered a happy exclamation, then transferred him to another office. "I caught scent of some old cultists." The headman stared at Shan as he spoke.

The understated energy in the authoritative voice at the other end disturbed Shan as much as the ice in Chodron's eyes. It was, unmistakably, the voice of the Public Security Bureau. "Lhasa has been assigned a quota," the man said. "Major Ren is coming soon."

Shan did not miss Chodron's reaction at the mention of the officer. "How soon?" the headman asked.

"Not for a few days. Let me arrange a helicopter today and I can offer the cultists to him. We like to feed our jackals well when they go hunting."

Chodron smiled as he covered the microphone with his hand. "Your lama stays with me," he told Shan. "You report to me what you find, only me. If you go up the mountain and don't report back within, say, three days I will give him up to Public Security. Try to get Gao involved and he goes to Public Security. Embarrass me in front of my village again and he goes to Public Security."

Shan looked down at the floor. "If you hurt him —"

"You'll what, prisoner?" Chodron hissed. "Send a letter to the Party chairman? The lama is mine. And the stranger remains in the stable with him." Chodron lifted his hand and laughed into the microphone. "Slow down, comrade. I don't have them in custody yet. We don't want to spook them into hiding. I know how to smoke out such creatures. Leave them to me."

"Watch your back," the officer replied. "Those old ones can turn themselves into dragons."

The grin on the headman's face as he shut off the receiver revealed a row of uneven teeth. "Major Ren. Biggest shark in our sea full of sharks. He's not as subtle as I am. If I use one battery for tamzing, he uses three. Where I might hit you with a baton while you stand, he would first strap you to a table and then use a lead pipe. Perhaps you are acquainted with the type."

When Shan did not reply Chodron grinned again. As he gestured Shan toward the door a woman outside shouted in alarm, and someone else uttered an anguished cry. Shan ran. Chodron reached the villagers gathered at the base of the sloping fields half a step behind him.

A man was being carried by two of the shepherds. Or what was left of a man. The body was strung from a pole, suspended like fresh game. The two men seemed weary beyond words as they reached the village, but few words were needed. The corpse was that of a farmer. His left temple was soft and pulpy. It had been crushed by a violent blow.

A woman collapsed over the body, sobbing.

"Murdered!" shouted another, fixing Chodron with an angry gaze.

"Another murder!" The fearful cry swept through the crowd.

Several of the villagers, Shan realized, were looking at him. As he stepped forward the crowd wordlessly parted. He knelt as the weeping woman was pulled away from the corpse, quickly examining the man's pupils, touching the spongy flesh around the wound, confirming that the hands were intact, noting the discoloration on the man's fingertips, then checking his clothes, pausing for a moment over his strangely misshapen belt buckle. Even Chodron stood silently by as Shan unbuttoned the man's shirt to look at his skin. A dim red pattern showed on the skin of his left shoulder. One of the farmers helped Shan ease the man onto a blanket that had been spread at his side.

"Ay yi!" came a frightened cry as Shan pulled away the shirt, exposing the man's back. The pattern continued from the shoulder down the dead man's back. It was as if a long red fern leaf had been etched onto his skin, radiating upward from the spine just below his heart.

"The gods!" came another alarmed cry as the villagers shrank away. "The deities have touched him!"

"The gods took him!" moaned an old woman. Several villagers murmured nervous agreement.

"Get the lama!" a forlorn voice called.

But the young shepherd who broke away in the direction of the stable was seized and shoved to the ground before he could get very far. "Murder!" shouted Chodron as he stood over the man. "Anyone can see it's murder," declared the headman in a loud voice. "Another hammer blow to the skull." A hesitant expression twisted his face a moment later. He glared at Shan. Chodron recognized his dilemma. The headman could not tolerate the suggestion that a god had marked the man but if, as he had just declared, someone had murdered him with a hammer, the killer could not have been Hostene. The headman barked out orders for the body to be taken to the victim's home, then summoned Shan to the shadow of the nearest granary.

It took three hours for them — Shan, Yangke, and Hostene — to reach Hostene's campsite. Although Yangke was carrying a pack containing food for three days, he leaped over rocks, apparently feeling only a slender connection to gravity now that he had been freed of his imprisoning beam. Hostene, having eaten a huge meal in Dolma's house, likewise seemed a new man. He often paused to ask Yangke questions about why certain boulders were painted red or why mani stones had been left beside one boulder and not another. He stood attentively as Yangke drew in the dirt the bizarre image that had appeared on the dead farmer's back. When Hostene suggested that it must have been some kind of decoration painted on the man's body, Yangke insisted it was exactly as he had drawn it, the perfect image of a fern leaf etched into the man's skin like a tattoo, where no mark had existed the day before. The two men looked at Shan as if for an answer, but Shan kept on walking up the trail.

Lokesh had had his own theory when Yangke had described the mark in the stable. He thought the image was of the spire of a *chorten,* a sacred reliquary shrine. Shan had not replied, only held Gendun's hand a moment, for the old abbot had grown faint again.

"See that he eats," Shan had said. The memory of the lies he had been forced to tell in front of his friends was like an open wound.

"Dolma will do that. I am going with you," Lokesh had replied.

"No. You must not." Shan could not recall ever before arguing with his friend but he was not going to expose him to the dangers on the mountain. He knew from experience to trust the deep feeling of foreboding that had been rising within him. "You must stay to help Gendun."

"You are mistaken, Shan," Lokesh had

said. It was as if the mountain itself were coming between them. "You don't understand this mountain. Dolma says its deity has been growing weaker and weaker. What you intend could kill it."

It was the blackest thing the gentle old man had ever said to him. From the way the words had been uttered it seemed they tortured Lokesh's soul.

Shan did not know how to reply. They were speaking of things for which words were useless. It was possible that Lokesh knew something of Shan's intentions that he himself did not know. There might have been things about the mountain that Lokesh and Gendun could not explain to him. But there were certainly things Shan had seen on it that they could never grasp, and if the old Tibetans did touch them they would be like moths to a flame. They had sat silently as Hostene had readied himself. Then, leaving Lokesh gazing into Gendun's nearly unconscious face, Shan had left the stable and barred the door.

During the second half of their trek, Shan and Hostene, aided by a new staff cut for him by Yangke, walked side by side. Shan pieced together the journey Hostene and his niece had made to Sleeping Dragon

Mountain. They had landed in Beijing a month earlier, where they were joined by Professor Ma, who had been a colleague of Abigail's when she had done a six-month exchange tour teaching Eastern religions at Beijing University. Professor Ma had spent several summers studying ruins fifty miles to the south, where he had met the Tibetan guide who had brought them to the mountain.

Abigail Natay was a thirty-four-year-old woman who had spent her childhood in the Navajo lands but had fled to California as soon as she was old enough to leave home, distancing herself from everything tribal as she pursued an academic career.

"Five years ago her father died, then, soon after, her mother, my sister," Hostene explained. "Before her father's passing Abigail had refused to go to a ceremony for him. Toward the end, before my sister died, there was a healing ceremony that she made Abigail promise to attend. Abigail resented it but did so, every hour of it. Then she left without a word. But at a later healing ritual for a cousin, there she was, and then at another."

His sister was dead, but Hostene had mentioned speaking with her at night. With a stab of pain Shan thought of Lokesh, who not infrequently carried on conversations with his long-dead mother. And Lokesh was the only person alive who knew that Shan sometimes sought advice from his father, who had been killed in the Cultural Revolution decades earlier.

"A year later," Hostene continued, "I discovered she was teaching a course on Navajo culture at a big university on the East Coast. A year after that she took a job at the University of New Mexico. I told her she should get married but she said she was too busy writing a book about the ceremonials of our people. She was offered a job at Harvard and turned it down because she had to be close to the old ones who were her sources."

Shan paused and picked up a round rock. "Here," he said, pointing to a spot a third of the way down, "is New Mexico. And here," he moved his finger to the opposite side, "is where we are standing. Her sense of geography is peculiar."

Hostene said, "She calls her project the crown jewel of her career. Every professor dreams of rewriting history." Then the Navajo said, after pausing as if to gauge Shan's reaction, "She is proving that the Tibetan and Navajo people are fruits of the same tree. Long-lost cousins."

It started, Hostene explained, in a Santa Fe gallery that sold antique art from around the world. "She saw an old blanket there. Abigail was sketching its faded symbols for her work on Tibetan Buddhism when the shopkeeper told her it was actually Navajo, from a very early period. When she argued with him, he urged her to check it out at the Navajo college. I knew many of the professors so I drove her there. It took us half an hour to get past the entrance gate, where there was a map of the college, which had been built in a series of interrelated circles to reflect traditional beliefs about our peoples' relationship with the holy ones. She photographed the map, saying it matched the structure of a monastery she knew in Tibet and the structure used in many Tibetan mandalas. Six months later she was in Lhasa, learning the language, studying the temples there. That was nearly three years ago, about the time I retired.

"She started with what she termed the empirical data. Scientific studies of linguistic patterns, DNA strains, dental patterns, earwax, geologic evidence from the ice ages."

"Earwax?"

Hostene grinned. "I've heard it all so many times I could recite it in my sleep.

181

There are two types of earwax, wet and dry. Europeans and Africans almost always have the wet type. People with dry wax are found in pockets all over Asia, especially in cold climates. You can trace population drift by following the groups of peoples with dry earwax in North America."

"Including the Navajo," Shan suggested.

"Including all Native Americans. That's what she calls the macro evidence. The same patterns exist for sweat glands. Tibetans and Navajos sweat far less than the average person of European descent."

Shan found himself liking the old Navajo, whose quiet yet energetic demeanor reminded him of Lokesh. "So she persuaded you and won you over to her theory?"

"Not at first. When she mentioned things like sweat glands I reminded her it was just another Asian versus European thing, and almost everyone agrees that the American Indians came across the Bering Strait from Asia. No, at first it had more to do with my promise to my sister on her deathbed to watch over Abigail. I know no one who is smarter than Abigail about the things you can learn in libraries. But she is not always so street-smart — about people, about bureaucrats, about the real world. And she has the spirit of a lion. She will never wade first, she always jumps into the deepest water."

As they finally approached the murder scene Hostene grew quiet. He squatted by the fire pit just as Shan had done earlier, fingering the plastic rubble left from the burnt sleeping bag, then with a grim expression paced along the brown-stained grass.

"We had a tent," he said, "but we slept in the open most nights. We would talk about the stars."

"She was with you that night?"

Hostene nodded. "But she was restless. When the moon was bright she would go off and sit on a high ledge, sometimes all night long. Or she would leave before dawn to get the best light to photograph a painting up on the slope. She was troubled about the mountain, she was worried she wouldn't be able to unlock its secrets before we had to leave."

"Why this mountain?" Shan asked. "What made it worth the risk?"

Neither man had mentioned the gap in Hostene's story. No westerner would ever have been granted a travel permit to the region, and no American would ever have been given official permission to conduct research that validated the ethnic or genetic identity of Tibetans as independent of the

Han Chinese. His presence was surely as illegal as that of the miners.

Hostene was silent so long that Shan decided he had not heard the question.

"She spent months demonstrating similarities between the root words of the Athabascan language that Navajo is based on and the Tibetan language, even recording native Tibetans and Navajos reading the same passages. She confirmed that the timing of migrations across the Bering Strait were consistent with evidence of dispersions of people from central Asia. Then suddenly it was all about religion." He paused, squatted, and with a finger drew a figure in the dirt, a three-part line, with an arm extending to the right at the top and to the left at the bottom, with a matching line set perpendicular to it. "Centuries before Hitler perverted the sign, my people were using this in religious ceremonies, in what we call dry paintings, sacred sandpaintings."

Shan, on one knee, felt someone hovering behind him.

"And for centuries," a weary but excited voice observed, "the Tibetans have used such a sign."

Lokesh had followed them. He knelt and drew an identical swastika beside Hostene's. "In sandpaintings, and elsewhere. It is a symbol for eternity, a sign used for good fortune." He did not look at Shan.

Hostene responded with a solemn nod. "So we learned. We have sacred mountains that are home to our Holy People. Tibetans have mountains that are the residence of deities. She says the land gods are the oldest, because people who live in high mountain lands have to explain lightning and thunder. The structure of beliefs around the oldest deities would have the best chances of showing connections between our peoples, Abigail decided. And those beliefs far predated the Buddhist's arrival in Tibet."

Hostene put a finger in the dirt below the swastikas they had drawn. "Many of my people today draw this shape as we have done. But Abigail traced the earliest references, on old pots and on old petroglyphs. She thinks our people used to draw it this way." He drew another swatiska, this one left facing, turning counterclockwise.

"That," Lokesh declared, a sense of wonder in his voice, "is the way the oldest ones drew it in Tibet. The Bon people." He was referring to people with an animist religion who had lived in Tibet long before Buddhism was brought to Tibet from India.

Hostene, nodding, continued. "The paths to our sacred mountains have markings and signs that have been there for centuries, and she wanted to look for parallel markings in Tibet and connect the myths that accompanied them, to trace them back to some common origin. But all the signs she could find had been defaced or destroyed. Sometimes the mountains themselves had been leveled. Then Professor Ma told us he had heard of a place that had never been touched, with very old deity paintings, on a mountain sacred to the Bon." The Navajo's gaze drifted toward Lokesh, who was staring at the summit of the mountain.

After a moment Hostene edged around the little grove, then asked Yangke to tell him where he had been found unconscious. He was kneeling at the rock wall when Shan reached him, studying the paintings drawn in blood.

"We stayed up late that night watching a meteor shower," the Navajo explained in a sorrowful tone. "Our guide showed us a constellation that he said was the Mother Protector of his people. He said when she saw stars shoot out of the constellation his mother always cried out in joy, then quickly recited a mantra."

"Tashi," came a mournful whisper behind them. "Tashi the shepherd."

"Tashi the guide and camp cook," Hostene said. "Tashi the truck driver. You knew him?" he asked Yangke.

Yangke caught Shan's accusing gaze and quickly looked away, his face reddening. "It didn't seem important that you knew," he said.

"He was originally from Drango," Shan suggested.

"I told you, I didn't see the bodies," Yangke said. "I wasn't sure he was one of the victims. Until now."

This was why the shepherd in Dolma's house had been so nervous about who had died, Shan realized. One of those who had been murdered had been *of* the village, but not *from* the village.

"But you acted as if you didn't know who was camped here, or what they were doing," Shan pointed out, speaking Tibetan now.

"I didn't," Yangke rejoined. "Not exactly. Tashi would not let me get close to the camp. He wouldn't tell what his customers were doing."

"He called them customers?"

Yangke nodded. "He told me they were professors, interested in old things."

"You said they were holy men. You said they made a sandpainting."

"They did. They cleaned shrines and

187

made sandpaintings. What was I to think? All the professors in Tibet once were lamas." The young Tibetan looked away. "I didn't send for Lokesh and Gendun because of Tashi. I sent for them because of what Chodron says he is going to do to Hostene. I'm not sure the village could survive if he ever . . ." His voice trailed off without finishing the sentence.

"*You* sent for them?" Shan clarified.

Yangke nodded.

"He was lying beside me on top of his sleeping bag that night," Hostene continued, bracing himself against the rock face. "I do remember something else. Just before I passed out, he groaned. I think he tried to speak but his mouth seemed to be full of water."

Shan saw Thomas's photographs in his mind's eye. A blade had sliced into the younger victim's back. His lungs had probably filled with blood. He asked Yangke, "Why would Chodron hide Tashi's identity? Why would he keep it from the villagers?"

"Because of Dolma, Tashi's aunt. My great aunt."

A melancholy sigh escaped Lokesh's lips. "Dolma," he declared.

Yangke gazed at the ground. "I was hoping he had just run away. There were two bodies." He cast a guilty glance toward Hostene. "It didn't necessarily mean one was Tashi. I don't know how I will tell her."

Hostene's sad gaze drifted along the horizon. "As I fell asleep Tashi was talking about how some of the old ones in his village felt this was the most important mountain in all the world. He just knew bits and pieces of the tale. He said no one still alive knew the whole truth. He said dragons and gods, like lamas, were becoming extinct and this was where they were making their last stand. He said if we were lucky we might meet the gods. I think he was a little drunk. But when I awoke, in that stable, with Gendun bending over me and my head still swimming, I thought that's where I was, in the gods' hidden home."

"The words you spoke then to Gendun, what were they?"

"They just came out. I didn't think them first, if you know what I mean. It was an old prayer to a Navajo mountain god."

They walked together around the site, staying away from the outcropping where the mutilated bodies had been found. "Did you ever encounter the miners?" Shan asked.

"Never up close. We tried to stay away from them, though I often felt we were being watched. Tashi spoke with them and made sure they knew we meant them no harm. He warned us before we arrived that we would have to avoid them at all costs. He spoke of them as if they were some kind of wild animals that only he could tame."

Shan extracted the pieces of the carved stick figure from his pocket and handed them to Hostene. The Navajo nodded somberly, as he fit the two pieces together. "It's called a *ketaan*," he explained, his voice filling with emotion, dropping to a near whisper. "An offering figure, always made of wood from the east side of the tree. Used in some of my people's ceremonies. Abigail would leave them at the base of the old paintings, as a token, as a way of thanking the deities for letting her study them. She asked me to make four the night before, one for each of us, for protection."

"I don't understand," Shan said. "A professor compiling a scientific report doesn't stop to thank the gods."

"We started out to make a scientific investigation," Hostene said. "We never spoke of how that changed after we arrived. One day I started carving a ketaan, the way my father had shown me many years ago. That night, Abigail said if the key to her work was in the ways of reverence then she

190

would never find it without reverence."

Shan left Hostene staring at the little broken figure. He paced slowly through the camp again, stopping after every two or three steps, examining the slope above and the grass below as he considered Hostene's words. What had he missed? He wandered toward the stream. He had examined everything, everything but the one surviving stone cairn on the far side of the stream, the only intact one he had seen. Stepping across the narrow waterway, he circled the cairn. It was old, yet not old. The rocks were all lichen covered, but only on the bottom tiers had the lichen grown together, binding the stones. The upper stones showed ragged pieces of lichen that had been pulled apart. With a guilty glance toward his companions Shan begin dismantling the cairn.

He had removed nearly every stone except the old ones at the base when he discovered a piece of folded felt that showed no signs of age. He gingerly extracted it, laid it on the ground, and began unfolding it. It had been carefully arranged, with multiple folds, to hold multiple objects. After unfolding three layers, pieces of parchment appeared, eight in all, each in a separate fold, each inscribed with a prayer. In the final fold were eight small nuggets of gold.

"We didn't like to take the cairns apart," Hostene said over his shoulder. "When we did it felt as if we were opening an old tomb. The hidden fabric usually fell apart in our hands, so we always put in new cloth before restoring the cairn."

Shan considered Hostene's words a moment. "You mean you opened cairns in order to examine the old prayers inside?"

The Navajo, kneeling beside him, nodded. "Professor Ma and Abigail were making records of old prayers, some of them centuries old by her calculations. She said if we weren't going to meet any of the old gods, this would be the next best thing. Excavating the deities, she called it. She took photos of the prayers. It felt like we were intruding, but she said it had to be done, it was vital to her work. Some bore symbols. Some bore left-turning swastikas." He stretched the felt out on the grass. "Tashi said it was all right as long as we respected the old prayers. And Abigail said we must never betray any interest in the gold."

"But you weren't looking for gold."

"Not exactly," Hostene said. "But Tashi said up here, you can't separate the gods from the gold." Shan searched his face for an explanation, but the Navajo was finished.

The others arrived. Lokesh reverently

straightened out each prayer in its fold of cloth. Yangke picked up an exposed nugget of gold, then quickly put it down, surveying the slope with nervous eyes. They watched in silence as Lokesh refolded the cloth, then all four joined in rebuilding the cairn around it.

"Did you have a hammer?" Shan asked. "A rock hammer?"

Hostene nodded. "Somewhere in the camp. We had used it that day." He looked up at Shan in alarm. "The corpse they found today. He was killed with a hammer."

"No, he wasn't," Shan said. "That farmer's head was struck after he was dead. And not with a hammer. A rock was probably used."

Beside them, Lokesh was drawing in the dirt again, a sketch of the fern pattern on the man's back. "Is this a Bon thing?" he asked no one in particular.

"What it is," Shan finally explained, "is proof that the man was killed by lightning. It doesn't happen often, even when lightning strikes, but nothing else causes it. It's called a Lichtenberg figure, something I studied years ago. If anyone had bothered to look, they would have seen that his belt buckle was partially melted. When the farmer left the village he was carrying a heavy iron blade."

"But you . . . ," Yangke began, but seemed uncertain how to end his sentence.

"Didn't tell anyone? If I had, Hostene would still be imprisoned in the stable. And we may learn more if we keep the riddle to ourselves."

"The riddle?" Hostene asked.

Shan lifted the last rock onto the reconstructed cairn, "After three murders already this summer, why would someone fake another one?" He did not give voice to the new question that had begun to trouble him — why had the gold hidden in this cairn survived when miners had been dismantling cairns for years? "How long had you been camped here?" he asked Hostene instead.

"A week. Abigail was photographing the old rock writings, so they could be translated back home."

"Old writings?"

Hostene led them up the grassy slope to another outcropping, a short distance above the camp. Behind it he pointed out a natural wind-carved formation that extended above a small ledge. It had a curving, tapering shape, with a vaguely spherical top like a head, an oval center, and two folds of rock at the base that could, with a little imagination, be seen as crossed legs. Lokesh uttered a cry of delight. It was what the Tibetans called a self-actuating deity, a natural formation that approximated the appearance of a sacred figure. The belly of the figure and the slab below it had been adorned with sacred emblems and several lines of a mantra. Dim outlines of painted lotus buds ran in a line below, as they might on an altar. Strands of yak hair, some sections encased in lichen, were wrapped around the neck — all that was left of what many years before had been a necklace.

"The Tara goddess," Hostene said. "Abigail said the words were a prayer to Tara in her green form. She found several old paintings of the Green Tara on the slopes."

Lokesh reverently placed some of the small flowers that grew nearby on the goddess's shoulders, then ran his fingers over the words. They had, until recently, been covered with lichen.

"You cleared away the lichen?" he asked Hostene.

The Navajo nodded. "With toothpicks. And dental probes."

Shan studied the scene. The dry, dusty earth below the rock showed the indentations where a tripod had stood. "What other equipment did she use?" he asked Hostene.

"A still camera, a video camera, a laptop

computer with a solar recharger." As he spoke, Hostene's expression grew excited, as if he had just remembered something. He took a step toward the upper slope.

"Was the equipment all in your camp that night?" Shan called to his back.

Hostene's only reply was a quick gesture to follow. In less than a minute they were at the mouth of a shallow cave. "She worried about storms," the Navajo explained. "She wanted to be sure everything was kept dry, since it couldn't be replaced out here."

The equipment he had described lay there, exactly as the small party had left it the night before the murders. A silver video camera lay seemingly undisturbed on a flat rock. Each camera was enclosed inside a clear plastic bag. The computer was in a blue nylon carrying case, and a blue nylon backpack stood on the cave floor. Their value would have been far greater than the camp equipment stolen below.

Shan glanced back at Lokesh, who had lingered at the cave entrance to study the self-actuated Tara. He stepped into the shadows as Hostene opened a pack to check its contents, lifting out a plastic bag of toiletries, then a small blue folder, then a pair of denim trousers. "Clean clothes," he declared. He extracted and donned a soft hat with a wide brim. As he bent to loop the backpack strap over his shoulder Yangke interceded, taking the pack on his own back. Hostene seemed about to protest but then he scanned the ground behind the young Tibetan.

"Abby's pack!" he exclaimed. "It's gone. And her digital camera."

The Navajo darted to the entrance as if he might catch a glimpse of his niece. When Shan reached them Lokesh had his head cocked, listening to what sounded like a clap of thunder. Yet the sky overhead was clear. The thunder turned into a low, rolling rumble.

Shan stepped outside and glanced at the slope above uncertainly. His heart lurched into his throat. "Avalanche!" he shouted, and grabbed Hostene's arm. If they did not outrun the tons of rock hurtling toward them it would mean certain death.

Shan pushed the Navajo toward a small ravine a hundred feet away and darted toward Lokesh as Yangke ran past them. Small rocks were already hurtling through the air around them. Shan reached Lokesh, seized his shirt with one hand, and half dragged his friend toward the ravine.

They had nearly reached the shelter of the gully when Shan fell and lost his grip on

Lokesh. He half crawled, half rolled into the gully, realizing they had escaped death by a split second.

But Lokesh had stopped a few feet from the shelter and was standing, extending an arm toward the old Tara, as if to beckon her to safety. A moment later a rock smashed the head of the goddess. A stone slammed into Lokesh's open hand, another struck his arm, and an instant later one the size of a melon hit his shoulder, knocking him off his feet. Rocks exploded against other rocks, propelling sharp shards into the air about them. Shan launched himself toward Lokesh. A small boulder glanced off his thigh, knocking him back. The last thing he saw was his old friend, unconscious, being buried alive.

CHAPTER FIVE

The nightmare came in glimpses, bringing terror such as he had not felt since his early days in the gulag. Lokesh's belly was awash with blood. A familiar hand, spotted with age, lay lifeless twenty feet from Shan, a splinter of rock piercing its palm. One arm was twisted and thrown backward in an impossible position for the living. Blood-specked stones occupied the space where his legs should be.

Shan's world was turning red. This was the way the universe looked to the dying, draped in a veil of blood.

"No!" Something flashed inside Shan and with a stab of pain he pushed himself up. "Lokesh!" he cried, wiping his temple on his sleeve, realizing the veil of blood was dripping off his own forehead.

Yangke and Hostene were already trying to clear the rocks away, uncovering Lokesh's head, bending over him, pulling the stones off him. They carried him inside their shelter.

The old Tibetan coughed. His eyes flickered open but he did not seem to see. "The Tara!" Lokesh's plea came in a hoarse croak. "Save the goddess!"

Hostene began rummaging in his pack as Yangke placed a rock under Lokesh's head to elevate it. The Navajo produced a shirt that he began ripping up for bandages. Then he extracted a small metal flask.

Shan took Lokesh's injured hand, opening the bent fingers, cradling it in his own before, with one swift motion, Yangke extracted the shard of stone. Hostene quickly poured some of the flask's contents on the wound and they sat for a long, agonizing moment, letting the blood ooze onto the palm before Yangke began wrapping it with the makeshift bandages.

Shan had seen Lokesh pummeled by guards in prison and by hail in the mountains, seen him with the skin flayed from his leg after he'd fallen down a steep scree but had never seen the desperate agony that now radiated from his eyes. As he cradled his friend's wounded hand he felt numb. It was the same paralysis he had felt forty years earlier holding the hand of his dying father, who had been fatally beaten by the

Red Guard. The hard words they had exchanged in the stable echoed in his head.

He was vaguely aware of movement around him, of Hostene examining Lokesh, then gesturing to Yangke, asking him to brace the old Tibetan, of the Navajo removing his belt and wrapping it around Lokesh's other wrist. There was a sudden jerk, a whimper of pain from the gentle old Tibetan, then Lokesh's head rolled toward Shan, fixing him with a small forced grin. "The goddess," he groaned again before he passed out. But the goddess was dead.

Shan became aware that Hostene was trying to pry away his fingers from Lokesh's arm. "He's going to be all right, Shan," the Navajo declared. "No broken bones. Just bad bruises and that hand. His eyes are clear, no serious concussion. His shoulder was dislocated, that's what hurt him so much. I put it back. An old trick from my horse-riding days."

As the words sank in, Shan's paralysis melted away. He began to study his surroundings. They were trapped in the little gully by a wall of loose rocks nearly ten feet high. Yangke, climbing the wall, began to clear away the stones at the top.

"No!" Shan cried, jumping up to tug at the young Tibetan's leg. "We're dead! Make them think we're dead!"

Yangke descended but gave no sign of understanding.

"Before the roar of the rocks," Shan explained, "there was another sound, an explosion. The avalanche was no accident. It was aimed at us."

For a moment Hostene and Yangke stared in confusion, then they grasped Shan's meaning. The avalanche had been an act of murder.

"But they will have seen us escape," Hostene pointed out.

"No. Whoever did this would not have risked being anywhere below when the explosive detonated. The dust from the avalanche will have obscured the view from above. He must believe we are still in that cave. The explosion was timed to trap us there, or kill us coming out. It would have been successful if Lokesh had not remained outside."

"So what would you have us do?" Hostene asked.

Shan bent over his old friend. "Sit. Wait. Don't speak above a whisper. If he was conscious, Lokesh would be praying for the goddess that was destroyed." He entwined Lokesh's beads around his limp fingers. As he did so his friend awoke for a moment and beckoned Shan with his head. "The kora," he whispered, then he lost consciousness again.

Ten feet away Hostene sat with the blue pack between his legs, fidgeting with the small video camera from the cave. They watched the small rectangular screen as a young woman with long black hair gathered at the back in a knot conferred with a thin Chinese man with graying hair beside the Tara that had just been obliterated.

"She always complained when I used the camera for casual shots. We are not tourists, she would say. She only brought it to obtain footage she could use in class," Hostene explained. He turned toward Lokesh. "What did he mean, before he passed out?"

A kora. Lokesh had disagreed with Shan's approach to finding the killer, to applying logic and deduction to the mountain, because he thought such tools useless, even misleading. He had his own way of understanding the mountain. "The statue and painted words were once part of a pilgrim's path." The little shrine would have been a way stop, probably a place of vigil for pilgrims, a rest station for those following a path laid out by lamas or saints in another century.

"Is that important?"

The words of the fleeing miner came back to Shan. The man murdered earlier that summer had been found in front of an old painting, as had the miner the year before. "It links all the murders."

"Have there been others?" Hostene asked.

Shan explained. "Four people have been killed. All on the kora, the pilgrim's path. All have had their hands severed."

Hostene's face darkened. He gazed at Lokesh again, then turned back to the camera and adjusted the volume so they could dimly hear a rich, energetic woman's voice point out the features of the sacred rock. The Navajo's eyes watched the little screen with affection, pride, and reverence. Once the woman's head jerked to the left and anger flashed in her dark eyes. Someone off-screen apologized in Tibetan.

"Every day she was here she gained energy," Hostene said. "She was making a great discovery. Professor Ma wasn't sure what she meant. Something very old was here, she said. She told us it would be clearer to us in a week or two."

"Where would she have gone?" Shan asked. "The night of the killings."

Hostene stared at the screen as if he were watching a ghost. "The moon was bright. That night as it rose she said there was a reason why many of the Navajo ceremonials are performed only at night. She was still there, by our fire, when I climbed into my sleeping bag." He looked up at Shan. "If she thought we had all died, she might still be working, finishing her research."

"Surely she would go home. Or at least go down the mountain, to notify the police," Yangke interjected.

"Not Abigail. Not this mountain," the Navajo replied cryptically. "Not this summer. She knew Tibet better than I do. She would have known there were no police who could help. She would continue working, thinking she could evade the killer. Her research was too important to her."

"But she left all her equipment in the cave," Shan pointed out.

"Not all of it," Hostene said. "A digital camera with a small tripod is missing. She likes to travel light. Tashi and I usually carried the other equipment."

"And she took her backpack," pointed out Yangke.

"But may not have done so voluntarily," Shan reminded them. He saw the anxiety in Hostene's face and tried to force hope into his voice. "We need to keep all possibilities in mind."

After a moment Hostene said, "The killer

doesn't have her, he can't have her. She must have been sure we'd all died and so she kept working. It's her way. She would have returned to the camp, been terrified by all the blood, and run to hide somewhere for a day or two. If she went back and found no sign of us, she knows what Tibetans do with bodies. She also knows she'll never have another chance to complete her work. She knows what I would want."

"Then the question is where is she working?" Shan replied.

They continued to watch the video with new, intense interest. Abigail Natay, even in miniature, was an impressive woman. Like her uncle, she had a quiet strength about her. Shan could sense her confidence, see the fire in her eyes, as she was buoyed on a flood of exuberant commentary. Though the Tibetans had had the technology of the wheel for centuries, they used it primarily for prayer wheels, she explained. They chose to muster armies of monks instead of armies of warriors. Near the end of the scene she seemed to catch herself, glanced at the camera, and self-consciously brushed back a long black lock that had drifted across one high cheekbone.

Shan said, "You mentioned before that Tashi got drunk. Surely you didn't bring bottles of liquor with you."

"Just the brandy in my flask," Hostene replied. "It was the miners. I never actually saw him drinking but twice I saw him come back to camp when he thought we were sleeping, and he was staggering."

In the next video Abby stood before another smooth rock face, but this one was adorned only with barely legible words.

Yangke leaned forward, studying the image intently. "I've roamed this mountain for years," he said. "But I have never seen this place."

"You said nothing about a pilgrim path," Shan said.

The Tibetan's face clouded. "It's not well known."

"You mean the people of the mountain try to keep it a secret. Why?"

Yangke gazed toward the summit. "It's from another time, another world."

"Why?" Shan repeated.

"In the country we live in, when Tibetans reveal that something is important to them, those who watch us will destroy it. Besides," he added after a moment, "the path is lost to us. It disappears into the grass a few miles up the slope. No one has ever found the rest of it. All those who knew its course died when our temple was destroyed fifty years ago."

"Abby and Tashi would take the camera and disappear for hours," Hostene said. "She was making new discoveries every day, finding Buddhist things, Bon things, ancient things." The three men did not need to articulate the question that hung in the air. Had Abigail discovered the route of the ancient pilgrim path?

Hostene checked the bandage on Lokesh's hand. Shan continued to watch the screen. "I thought you said no one was looking for gold," he said after a moment. Abigail stood in front of a tunnel framed by old timbers. The camera panned, showing old metal implements, rusting to dust, and an old iron-framed chest whose boards were nearly rotted away.

"I said 'not exactly,' " the Navajo replied. "Some of the very old prayers spoke about mining gold for the gods." He paused, cocked his head, and looked out over the pile of rocks.

Shan thought he heard an insect at first, singing in the languid heat. Then, for a moment, he thought it was something on the tape. He touched the power button of the recorder. The sound came from just over the high rim of the rocks that had trapped them and grew louder as they listened, resolving into a familiar pattern. Someone was energetically reciting a mantra.

Moments later a scalp of shaggy black hair appeared, then a small surprised face, then shoulders draped in reddish rags. The chant faltered as the man peered at them over the edge, then ducked down. He repeated the motion several times, bobbing up and down, disappearing then returning, as if to get a better idea of the creatures trapped below. He disappeared and the mantra picked up again, this time with the rhythm of a cheerful song.

"Rapaki!" Yangke exclaimed. "Stay here or you'll frighten him away," he warned, then began scaling the loose, treacherous pile of rubble.

Shan and Hostene, sitting beside Lokesh's prostrate form, waited as Yangke spoke in encouraging tones, gesturing as if to a skittish dog. When his words had no effect on the singsong mantra, he began pulling rocks from the top. They would have to clear a path if they were to carry Lokesh safely over the rubble.

After several minutes the strange ragged figure reappeared, veering in and out of view as he lifted and moved stones, gradually approaching Yangke, still chanting, until finally the two men were working side by side. He had the wild appearance of one who lived exposed to the elements, his skin leathery, his hair long and uneven. The rags on his back had once been a robe, though it now bore so many patches of different colors and fabrics that it appeared as if he had tied a quilt around himself.

When Rapaki finally noticed that Shan was slowly advancing toward him, he ducked behind Yangke, then tilted his head to peek around Yangke's back, grinning, his eyes wide. He ducked in and out as before, using Yangke as his shield. Then he froze, his carefree expression becoming solemn. He had seen Lokesh. He advanced without fear, seeming not to notice Shan, until he stood before Lokesh, studying him, his head tilting one way then the other. Then he spun about and disappeared behind the rocks.

Yangke gazed after him, then with one hand made a corkscrew motion next to his temple. "Totally crazy. I guess we'd be like that too if we'd lived in a cave for nearly forty years."

But the action of the hermit was not crazy at all. Yangke and Shan were still clearing rocks when Rapaki returned, clutching the stems of a plant that he crushed and placed under Lokesh's nose. The old Tibetan sneezed, snorted, and woke up. His eyes lit with pleasure at the sight of the ragged figure before him. Rapaki was a figure directly out of the old tales, the hermit beggar with brambles in his hair.

"Rapaki, Rapaki, Rapaki," the hermit said as Lokesh was propped against the rock wall. Rapaki paused, gazing at Hostene as though for the first time, then abruptly he jammed a finger into Hostene's chest, repeating his own name again several times, as if it were a protective mantra. He then studied Shan with the same intense gaze, jumped toward him, jammed a finger into Shan's chest, jumped back to Lokesh, and began whispering something very quickly under his breath. He rose warily as Yangke approached.

"What is he saying?" Hostene asked.

Shan paused for a moment, confused. Yangke was trying to question the hermit about the avalanche, about whether he had seen anyone on the slope above but Rapaki seemed unable to hear him. "He seems only to speak in song and mantra," said Yangke.

Soon they had cleared a path sufficiently that they could carry Lokesh across the rubble.

"He has to be taken back to the village, to Gendun and Dolma," Shan told Yangke.

"We can make a litter, with poles and

shirts, then the four of us can carry him."

"No. Hostene and I must remain here. The murderer must be up here. And his niece, too."

"It will take all day," Yangke said with a sigh.

Rapaki materialized at Shan's side and put his hand on Shan's arm as he pointed in the opposite direction from the village. Lokesh looked up. Shan recognized the words the hermit now sang, in ever-louder tones, as he pointed with increasing vigor up the slope. It was a healing mantra. Rapaki might have lost all capacity for human conversation but he knew how to convey his meaning to the deities.

Rapaki had not been the first to use the cave they reached an hour later. The soot of butter lamps was heavy on the ten-foot ceiling and stained the upper half of a vast mural on one wall portraying protector demons. They were in an ancient shrine, intended for more than a hermit's dwelling. Despite his injuries, Lokesh would not settle onto the pallet offered by Rapaki. First he hobbled along the walls, greeting with low exclamations of delight the small statues standing in niches carved in the living rock and the altar made of a heavy beam set on rock pedestals.

"It's Bon," Lokesh declared as he gazed at the once-vivid painting. "Very old. For the mountain deity. I do not even recognize some of the demons," he added as he gazed in confusion at one in the corner. He had once been a monk official in the Dalai Lama's government and was as intimate with the pantheon of Tibetan deities as any lama. He might not be able to name the crimson-faced deity but Shan had seen it before, on one of the open-air rock faces in Abigail Natay's video. Below the painting, on a rough-hewn block of juniper, was an unbound book, a peche. Loose pages were strewn on the floor around it. Shan kneeled to study the pages. They were old, illuminated in still-brilliant colors.

It was not the old but the new that Shan was seeking. He had begun to wonder how the hermit survived. In the summer, the slopes might be full of berries, even wild grains, but winter in such a place would be brutal. He supposed that like the yaks and goats the hermit must migrate in the winter to a lower altitude. Then he saw a sliver of shadow in a corner. As Rapaki and the others helped Lokesh onto his pallet he picked up a butter lamp and slipped into the narrow opening.

The chamber beyond, adorned with more

dim paintings on the walls, had once held butter, barley, and water in orderly arranged ceramic pots, the shards of which could be seen along the far wall. Rapaki's arrangement was much more modern, and chaotic. The floor was littered with empty cans of beans, fruit, and soup, as well as empty sacks of plastic and muslin. Along one wall were unopened cans, and sacks of rice, not stacked but carelessly tossed in a pile, on top of which was a small round tin. Shan lifted the tin and opened it. It had once held hard candy and was edged with little yellow flowers. Lemon Freshies, it said in English.

There was crumpled paper in the trash heap, thirty or forty pieces, most of them labels from cans, most of those with writing on the white reverse side. Shan flattened one across his knee. At first he thought it was a sketch for a tangka, a sacred painting, for there were figures of deities and sacred symbols along the edges. But most of the paper was taken up by Tibetan words. He struggled through the first half, some of which was crossed out. He could not read all the cramped words but many phrases were familiar. It was a letter addressed to Tara, signed *your secret Rapaki.* Or more exactly, it was a draft of a letter to the deity. He unfolded five more of the labels. They were all similar to the first with minor changes. Some of them, he judged, were many years old.

"I always wondered how he fed himself," a voice said from the shadows. "He's gone," Yangke added. "He took a bag and ran as if he were leaving for good. He suddenly seemed to be afraid of us."

"Did these supplies come from Chodron?"

"Not a chance. Chodron hates him and would be pleased if he starved to death. He is a symbol of all that Chodron cannot abide."

"It would not be difficult for a man like Chodron to get rid of him."

"Not as simple as you may think. You don't understand how small our village is. Rapaki is Dolma's first son. She only sees him every couple of years, but she won't let Chodron forget the relationship."

Shan sifted through some of the empty cans. Most were small, containing simple, basic fare, but several newer ones contained more expensive items like lychee nuts and pickled onions. Nearest the door were plastic bags whose labels indicated they had held salted sunflower seeds. A small foil pouch had contained chewing gum. Some of the labels were worn, as if having rubbed together in a pack.

"Why would the miners give him sup-plies?" Shan asked.

"I didn't know that they do. But to some he's like a mascot, a good-luck charm. And at the end of the summer some of them don't want to carry extra supplies out." Yangke squatted before the pile of cans, probing them. "If they left food behind, he would know how to find it."

Shan lifted the lamp and went to the far end of the chamber, where he saw newer supplies. An unused pad of paper. A cotton quilt with a pattern of pandas frolicking among clouds. A sealed pack of sweet biscuits. These were not the abandoned sup-plies of miners.

"There were stories in the village when I was younger, about Rapaki's grandfather," Yangke said as Shan moved back to his side. "He came back from his flock one day very excited about the paradise he would soon live in. Next morning he took a pack of food and left, never to be seen again. People said he had stolen gold from the gods and gone down in the world to spend it."

"What," Shan asked, "was the name of his grandfather?"

"Lobsang."

Shan picked up one of the letters and

extended it to Yangke, holding the lamp close. Rapaki had mostly written to the gods. But at least one letter, which appeared newer than the rest, had been addressed to his grandfather.

"Impossible," Yangke said in a troubled tone. "Even if he survived to a great age the man would have died decades ago."

"One of the great advantages of being Rapaki," Shan observed as he rose to check on Lokesh, "is that you are not constrained by the possible."

Shan let Hostene lead the way as the two of them climbed the slope an hour later. The Navajo had been about to leave the cave to search for his niece by himself when Shan had stopped him, explaining that Yangke would stay with Lokesh. There was no clear path through the complex network of ravines, high meadows, ice-fed springs, and long fields of wind-carved outcroppings, and soon they realized that the best clues to Abigail's trail lay within the little silver video camera.

"Can you find these places?" Shan asked as they watched the first few scenes on the tape again. "Sometimes the same painting appears in more than one scene, as if she were revisiting them."

"New theories occurred to her, and new

interpretations. Sometimes she would be in the middle of studying one painting and find she had to go back to another she had visited two days before. I always offered to accompany her, but sometimes she refused. She said she would have to jog to cover the distance and didn't want me to risk twisting an ankle. She didn't think I shared her fervor for her work," he said remorsefully. "When you spend your life behind a blanket I guess it's hard to drop it, even to those who come back to the family."

"A blanket?" Shan repeated.

"My wife used to say that in the last years before she died. There were many like me, like Abigail, who lived with the old ways when we were young and then went into the world to pursue careers outside the tribe. We chose other ways to live. On the map I didn't go far, just a couple hundred miles, but it may as well have been ten thousand. Law school, prosecutor's office, the state court. An entirely different universe from the one I grew up in. You learn not to speak with anyone about the sacred ways, the old ways, partly because they are secret, but also because they are mocked, because other people want to turn them into trinkets to use in schemes to make money. You learn to pull the Navajo blanket up and never speak about those things. If someone wants to discuss the Navajo you speak about the artists who make the blankets and pots, no more. I had two chants but I didn't use them for nearly thirty years, except behind my own closed doors, to keep them alive."

"Chants?"

Hostene, fixing his leathery face on the distant clouds, was silent so long Shan thought he would not reply.

"It is the way we speak with our holy ones. Something like a prayer, something like a song. One can last for days. The chanter recites from memory. The chants are handed down from one generation to the next, taught in quiet, dark places. Abigail said the Tibetans do the same thing. It has a very old feel to it, the learning of such things. I used to get shivers walking into the hogan, the house, of my teacher."

"You mean you were a priest?"

"We have no priests. We have our chanters, the singers. If you need healing for a sickness caused by witches you go to the chanter of the Ghostway. If you want to protect your crop against frost you find the singer of the Starway. You always start with the Blessingway, to open the door to the holy ones." He glanced self-consciously at Shan, as if surprised by his own words. They were not speaking only of blankets and pottery now.

"This was what Gendun was doing in that stable," Shan observed. "For many days, he invoked the gods on your behalf, almost without stopping, every line he spoke different, every line from memory."

Hostene scooped up a handful of loose earth and tossed some into the wind. *"Kac tcike eigini eigini qayikalgo."* His voice was a whisper, his words aimed at the clouds. He caught himself and looked at Shan. "It is one of the phrases from my second chant. The Mountainway. Holy Young Woman sought the gods and found them, it says. On the summits of the clouds she sought the gods and found them." His eyes welled with moisture and he looked away.

Shan said, after a moment, "Your niece was usually shown under trees in the videos, because the paintings were meant to be stops on the kora, resting places for pilgrims, offering water and shade. This high up on the mountain there aren't many groves."

But he had not realized how many there were until the two of them began seeking them out. They spent the rest of the daylight hours investigating a dozen groves scattered across the slope. Shan kept alert for signs of miners. They were approaching the mysterious place called Little Moscow that Yangke had mentioned to him. In late afternoon they paused in the shade of an outcropping to study the videos again, rewinding, fast-forwarding, noting a distinctive rock formation here, a gnarled stump there. A butterfly materialized before them, its scarlet and yellow wings quivering as it alighted on the camera. The Navajo froze. There was sadness in his gaze, as if the creature reminded him of the missing woman, but his eyes were also suffused with the same gentle childlike wonder Shan often saw on Lokesh's face.

Shan did what he could to explain the images he recognized on the little screen, although often the Navajo woman on the tape explained them just as quickly. Fierce protector demons dominated many of the rock paintings. Four-armed Mahakala, Shrivi mounted on a horse, Rahula with a bow, dressed in human skins. Devotional images of the early Tibetan kings were depicted. Abigail had learned her icons well, accurately pointing out the details of the ritual hand gesture — a downturned hand in the earth-touching mudra — made by one ancient king, the gesture called Turning the Wheel of Law made by a blue-skinned saint. At several points she paused and drew Navajo images, discussing the similarities between the fierce deities embraced by both peoples and the taboos that had grown out of their beliefs.

It was midafternoon when Hostene touched Shan's shoulder, then silently directed him down a nearby side path, into a rough gully that was devoid of any paintings, then into a maze of twisting, overgrown paths marked with inconspicuous chalk marks, low to the ground, at each turn, and finally through a narrow slit in two rock walls, onto what looked like a goat path. They emerged into a natural bowl abutting the rock spine that divided the mountain. At the base of the spine was a high pile of jagged stones, recently splintered, some blackened. They were at the old mine, or what was left of it.

"We could have been killed when the bolt of lightning struck," Hostene said.

Thirty feet in front of them was the twisted, scorched iron frame of an old chest. On a rock wall opposite the debris was a large faded painting of a fierce protector demon riding a blue wolf, painted so its eyes seemed to follow the observer as he walked around the bowl's circumference.

Shan studied the pile of rocks, the twisted iron, the splinters of old beams thrown across the clearing. "I have never seen lightning do such a thing."

"We had nearly finished our work here and were examining a painting of a blue bull god some distance away. Professor Ma said he had left a set of cleaning brushes here. He retrieved the brushes, and when he returned he asked who had moved the equipment. Someone had taken all the old iron pieces, the trunk, straps for a forge, an anvil, old chisels and pry rods and piled them up in front of the tunnel, then added iron pry rods at the top of the pile, strapping three together like a flagpole."

"Or, more likely, a lightning rod," Shan said. He bent and scrutinized one of the scorched rocks, holding it under his nose. "Someone put explosives under the pile and used the lightning as a detonator. Whenever it went off whoever did this would be far away and could have an alibi. And they didn't care who was nearby when it exploded."

Hostene went to the far side of the pile and squatted, pulling away stones frantically, as if something had told him his niece might be underneath. Then, abruptly, he stopped, shuddering, gazing with a weary expression at the destruction.

"What had you found here?" Shan asked.

"Words painted on tunnel walls. Tashi and Abigail translated them but I never asked what they said. We had seen so many old writings already."

"And gold?" Shan suggested.

"Not much. Just little nuggets here and there that seemed to have fallen in cracks or behind rocks and been forgotten. Abigail became very angry the first time Tashi touched one."

"But he did take some — eight nuggets for the cairn by your camp."

Hostene nodded. "Tashi changed her mind. He said it was the right thing to do, that it was what the old monk miners intended. He said it was how you recharged the prayers. That's the word he used, 'recharged.' "

"How much gold did you take?"

"Enough for four or five cairns, I guess. It wasn't our gold, we all agreed we had no claim on it, that it would be wrong to do anything else with it. It wasn't stealing. It was in line with what Abigail called the reverence of her work."

Shan asked for the camera again, and found a scene of Abigail in front of the mine, speaking of Tibetan artisans who rendered exquisite goddesses out of gold, then of the Tibetan and Navajo shared reverence for turquoise, which they incorporated into both jewelry and holy images. The demon represented in the sole painting at the site was stated to be the main guardian of the powerful land deity that inhabited the mountain. Hostene lingered only a moment after handing the camera to Shan, then went to the head of the trail, impatient for Shan to finish.

But Shan kept watching. The scene at the mine ended, the screen turned blue for a moment. Then he saw the image of a lichen-covered rock and what might have been a shadowed painting beyond.

"The camera lesson is done. Stop playing and listen to me," a female voice declared in English. It was Abigail Natay, but not the careful, patient Abigail. This was an urgent, insistent voice. The camera had been set down but it had not been shut off.

"This has to be done tonight," Abigail said. "I finished most of it this afternoon. You know what to do, where to put it?"

"Yes, if I must," came a whispered, fearful reply. The man sounded young. He spoke in slow but confident English. He had pulled the camera closer. Abigail appeared, sitting on the rock, her shoulder and one side of her face visible. Long shadows fell across her arm and the rock-strewn ground beside her.

"Take this," Abigail said, almost apologetically. As she turned to lift something from behind her Shan glimpsed her front pocket. He pushed the rewind button and found the moment when she turned, then froze the image, staring at it in confusion. Pinned to her shirt pocket was a paper talisman, in Chinese, reminiscent of a charm to guard against evil spirits. It brought the superstitions of his childhood back to him. He studied the ideograph on the paper. It was not a protective charm, he realized. It was a prayer for the soul of one who has been killed by violence, to help it avoid one of the many hells that such victims were susceptible to.

It made no sense. Hostene had said Abigail could not speak Chinese. She was not there to study Chinese traditions. But then, as he studied the rest of the scenes, nothing made sense. Nothing happened that could be explained by anything he had learned thus far on the mountain. Abigail began extending things toward her invisible companion. First, she handed a small nugget of gold to the man who remained offscreen. Then, from the shadows on her opposite side, she lifted four more items, which she dangled in front of her unknown companion with an expression that chilled Shan. Two sets of bones, two humerus bones fastened to two ulnas, then two femurs fastened to two tibias, each set connected with what appeared to be shoelaces through holes bored at the ends of each bone. Two arms, two legs, as if she were constructing a skeleton.

"I can't," the man moaned.

"You will," Abigail insisted. "We have to do this together or all is lost. There is a war on this mountain and you have to choose sides."

After a long pause, the man said, "First tell me how many sides there are."

Abigail offered a sympathetic smile but did not reply. "Think of your family. Think of the old ones," she said. Then, impossibly, "Think of Eight Treasures in a Winter Melon." Surely he had heard wrong. The words described a traditional dish favored by China's gourmets, eight special ingredients cooked in broth, then poured into a hollowed melon.

"They've starting putting out other things, on sticks. The blood drips down into pools," the man said.

Shan's mouth went dry. He replayed and replayed the exchange again. The sound from the tiny speaker was poor but he dared not raise the volume while Hostene was nearby.

That was the end of it. Abigail moved off-screen. Shan saw nothing but rocks and dirt and then, as the shadows shifted, the sandal-clad foot of a deity. He fast-forwarded the tape. There was nothing but empty blueness, until the tape ran out. He stared at the blank screen, shut off the camera, and silently returned it to Hostene before gesturing him toward the gully.

They had just turned onto the main trail when a high-pitched cry brought them to an abrupt halt. A figure on a red bike hurtled around a rock. The hood of a black sweatshirt covering his face, one hand was on the handlebars, the other swung a five-foot-long pole.

In an instant, the faceless man was aiming at Hostene's head. The Navajo twisted and leaped. The club landed a glancing blow on his shoulder as he dropped to the ground. Shan stumbled as he ran to help Hostene, and with a kind of war cry the man struck Shan's knee with his front tire, barely missing Hostene's head with the pole. Shan pulled the Navajo up, shoving him toward rocky ground where the bicycle could not follow, then grabbed a short stick from the ground. He waited for the rider, feinted one way, ducked to avoid the savage swing of the pole, then shoved the stick into the rear wheel as the man passed.

The effect was exactly as he had hoped. The stick caught in the spokes, stopping the bike so abruptly the rider flew over the handlebars.

"*Cao ni ma!* Fuck your mother!" the man spat in Chinese as he hit the ground. Seeing that his prey had left the trail, he lifted the bike in two hands and threw it toward them before fumbling for something in his pocket.

Shan did not linger to see what sort of weapon he had. He grabbed Hostene and dashed behind a boulder, watching as the man recovered his bicycle and rode away.

As they waited to be sure their attacker was gone, Hostene replaced the videotape with another from his pack and they sat by a bubbling spring, watching a second tape on the camera. On it Abigail described how sacred mountains anchored the Tibetan gods, much as they did in the Navajo belief system. After several minutes the screen abruptly went black. Hostene looked as if he had been struck. He had lost Abigail for a second time. "Battery," he muttered, and silently stowed the camera in his pack.

The sun was nearly gone, and Shan was fixing the location of the next grove of trees in his mind so they might reach it in the dark, when a sleek gray shape swooped across their path. He paused a moment to admire the creature and walked on, before realizing that Hostene was not following.

"What is it?" he asked.

"The owl. It's an omen. We must make camp."

"I can find the way to the next grove," Shan countered. "I can . . ." But seeing the way Hostene stared at the patch of sky where the owl had disappeared, he silently began to gather fuel for a fire.

As they arranged their blankets under an overhanging ledge, Shan asked why the American military had taught Hostene Mandarin. His companion explained that the Navajo were often considered linguists because usually they were raised speaking two languages, that sometimes, as in World War II, the army still assigned the Navajo to speak their native tongue in combat zones in lieu of a code. But Hostene had gone to language school during the Vietnam War to enable him to serve on planes that took off from the United States, refueled in Guam, and patrolled the Chinese coast, monitoring Chinese radio broadcasts.

"You must think me an old fool," Hostene said as they lit their fire. "A lawyer and a judge, frightened by a little gray owl."

Shan said, as he pulled out some of the cold mutton dumplings Dolma had packed, "The only fools are those who do not obey what their hearts tell them. I often made camp with Lokesh because he thought he saw a face in a rock or believed a pika was trying to tell him something."

"It's not exactly that I" — Hostene struggled for words — "I never . . . it's just that here we are on the sacred mountain with my niece trying to connect with the sacred things and . . ." He shrugged. "To our old ones, an owl was a harbinger of death."

"Whether we do it for the old ones or for Abigail or for the owl or because my legs ache," Shan replied, "this is where we will make camp."

Hostene smiled gratefully. "We don't do well with death, my people. For centuries we lived in hogans, round houses made of logs and earth. If someone died in a house it was abandoned and a new hogan built. Ghosts were to be avoided at all costs. My father would undergo a purification rite whenever an owl flew close to him. He said otherwise someone in the family would die.

"When my sister was dying, she talked to Abigail about her birth, things that her mother said she must know. Abigail wasn't born in a hospital like she'd always thought, but in a hogan. They never mentioned it before because when she was a teenager, they realized she would have been embarrassed. An old singer was there to bless her first breath. The first thing she tasted was corn pollen mixed with water, to make sure the holy people were aware of her and blessed her too. They used a special cradleboard for her, one that had been in our family for ten generations. Then, when she laughed, we had a welcoming ceremony."

"Laughed?"

"It is our old way. You know a baby is truly a human, and that it will live, when it laughs out loud. A feast is held and gifts are given by the parents to all their friends, especially rock salt, to honor Salt Woman, one of our Holy People. Special amulets were given to Abigail as an infant, which she was to keep all her life. A small pouch with soil from each of our sacred mountains, small stones from secret places, other things no one may speak about."

Hostene searched the dark sky and shivered, pulled his blanket over his shoulders. "But when she was young, maybe five or six, a terrible thing happened. Her family was visiting that same old singer, the *hataali*.

When they were outside she found his sacred objects used in the ceremonies. She put his ceremonial basket over her head and broke open a pouch of sacred pollen. They say such a sin will affect the child who commits it later in life. Her parents asked for a chant, a purification, but the next week the old man got sick and never recovered. Abigail was due to go away to the government boarding school. The rite was never performed. They tried to bring her back for it but the government teachers wouldn't permit it. They said that was exactly the kind of thing she had to stay away from. Later, we found out they had thrown away all her amulets.

"Abigail made light of it when she first heard the story, saying she would use it in her classes to illustrate the psychocultural elements of taboo. But it's been troubling her recently. One night after we arrived on the mountain, she admitted she was worried that what had happened when she was young might affect her work here, might blind her to important signs here on the mountain."

Shan said nothing. They retreated into their rock shelter. A cloud had passed in front of the rising moon. From somewhere higher on the mountain an owl called.

Hostene was awake at dawn. Shan had been tortured by nightmares, and been up for hours. Hostene declined the dried fruit Shan offered him for breakfast. They continued on to the next grove of trees, where they found only the remnants of dozens of small conifer cones consumed by the pikas. At a second grove there was only a ketaan stick jammed into a crack in a painting and broken off. Shan pointed to the many boot prints in the soil, and they each picked a set to follow. Shan went in the opposite direction from Hostene, after they'd arranged to meet back at the painting in ten minutes. But Shan's trail soon disappeared at a rock ledge. He stood, staring at the treacherous-looking summit, still covered with small patches of snow. He was about to go back when a shadow appeared on the rock beside him and he heard muffled murmuring. He lowered himself to the ground and began to whisper a mantra.

The shadow moved one way, then another. Up, then down. When the hermit finally showed himself he circled Shan, who maintained his recitation. Rapaki finally squatted in front of him.

"On the summit," Shan ventured, "wait the secrets of the Lord of the Mountain."

The hermit's eyes grew round. "At the top

crouches the great one," he said in the singsong rhythm he used for all his utterances. "His mane of turquoise flows everywhere. He spreads his claws upon the snow." Rapaki's head bobbed as he looked up and down the slope, as if searching for something.

"You are trying to reach him. I want to help too."

"When there was a fertile field, there was no master." Rapaki's voice was like a machine in need of oiling. "Now the master has come and it is overgrown with weeds."

The only intact book in the hermit's cave, Shan recalled, had been the *Song of Milarepa*, the teachings of the greatest of the Tibetan saints. He realized that every sentence Rapaki had just spoken was a verse from the sacred text.

"In strict seclusion without man or dog, you may have the torch to see the signs." Shan also knew some of the verses.

Rapaki responded with a rapid fire of words. Those that Shan made out seemed to be disconnected. *Honored by the waking dead,* he heard, *face like the circle of the autumn moon,* then finally, *raksa raksa svaha,* the ending of what was called the mantra for cheating death.

The hermit squinted at Shan as if to see him more clearly, then circled him again. As he completed the circuit he gasped and bent, pointing at Shan's arm. A tiny, brilliant reflection from a crystal in a nearby rock had appeared on the back of Shan's hand. Rapaki gazed intently at the silver patch of light. *"Ni shi sha gua!"* he exclaimed. *"Ni shi sha gua!"*

Shan was dumbfounded. It was not possible that the hermit knew Chinese. But he had perfectly pronounced four Mandarin syllables, an insult. Literally, it meant, *You stupid melon,* though it was commonly understood as *You retard, you idiot, you damned imbecile.*

Shan could see the white surrounding Rapaki's irises. The hermit seemed terrified. Something struck Shan's arm as the hermit backed away. He was throwing sharp-edged stones at Shan. Each connected painfully with Shan's arm or chest. Then the light shifted, the silvery reflection vanished, and Rapaki stopped. Shan raised his hands, palms outward.

"You may have the torch to see the signs," Shan repeated.

The hermit cocked his head, clutching the prayer amulet suspended from his neck, his frightened expression changing to one of confusion.

Hostene called. Shan glanced over his shoulder. When he turned back, Rapaki was gone.

He did not mention the hermit to the Navajo, who was waiting at the painting. As Hostene began to walk toward the next grove, a quarter mile away, Shan put a restraining hand on his arm.

"No more trees," Shan declared. "We must investigate elsewhere."

"But Abigail —," Hostene protested.

Shan countered, "Gendun is the reason you are alive. And last night I had nightmares about Gendun being tortured. When we catch the murderer, I think we will learn where your niece is. If we don't catch the murderer, she may be his next victim. But it is certain that when Chodron does not get what he needs, Gendun will pay. And then you."

Hostene gazed forlornly at the trees. For a moment Shan thought the Navajo was going to flee up the mountain alone.

"This mountain is more alive with activity than all the ranges around it," Shan said, surveying the slope again. "But all its people have become skittish and secretive. They are only active in the shadows, shy of the open. It's how you survive when predators lurk overhead. There is a nerve center here for the miners' operations called Little Moscow. It cannot be far from this place. We must go there now."

He pulled out the rough map Hostene kept in his pack, looking for somewhere central but hidden, where thirty or forty men might converge without being conspicuous, and focused on a shaded area low in the center of the slope, about three miles from where they sat.

"That's a maze of ravines," Hostene explained. "Tashi warned us to stay away because they were so dangerous."

They began a cautious descent to the labyrinth of gullies that stretched below them. As they proceeded, vague scents of roasting meat and wood smoke told them they had guessed correctly, but they could not tell where in the maze the miner's camp was located. Then Hostene pointed to a tiny blemish in the sky, a ragged thread of smoke rising from one of the ravines to the east.

They soon discovered a well-worn trail bearing the tracks of boots and bicycle tires that wandered around serpentine rock walls and spires and found themselves in the shadows at the edge of a wide clearing in the center of which was a smoldering fire. Huge rock slabs had split from the walls,

238

falling upon each other, forming natural lean-tos and shallow caves. Awnings of canvas had been added to some, several had photographs of family or makeshift mileage signs to Chinese cities at their entrance. The square fronts of the makeshift structures, the laundry hanging on poles from several, the scent of fried rice and wild onions coming from a nearby brazier, the wooden birdcage that incongruously hung from a pole before one abode, the two men playing mah-Jongg on upturned buckets with small piles of cash beside them all brought an uninvited pang of nostalgia to Shan. The scene reminded him of a *hotung* from the cities of his youth — an alleyway, teeming with life, which had defined the character of many Chinese neighborhoods before the government had replaced them with blocks of high-rise housing.

From the shadows Shan counted sixteen miners. They had the wild look of men who took every advantage of living outside the law. Half of them stood near the dying fire, cursing, gesturing threateningly toward a forlorn, frightened figure sprawled on a blanket.

Hostene hung back, pulling on Shan's arm. But when a tall lean man in a leather vest kicked the helpless figure on the blanket

Shan stepped into the open.

"No — you mustn't!" Hostene warned from the shadows.

"I have no choice," Shan said. "They have my assistant."

"Ta me da!" gasped the first miner who spotted him. He gave a loud whistle of alarm.

Within seconds more men emerged from the shelters, some brandishing shovels and picks like weapons. The rough faces that stared at Shan appeared to have come from all corners of China. Some bore the mixed Tibetan-Chinese features that were becoming common on many Tibetan streets. But the eyes of each were stone hard. As Shan passed them, the men closed in behind him, following him to the blanket before the central fire.

This village too had its own protocol. The miners formed an outer circle, leaving Shan and the tall man in the vest in the center beside the frightened figure on the blanket.

"Welcome to Little Moscow," the man in the vest declared. "I regret to announce that applications for residency are no longer being accepted." A murmur of laughter swept through his audience. "We operate a very exclusive resort."

Shan made a show of surveying the makeshift structures of the miners' town. "I was hoping for domed churches and caviar." Over the man's shoulder, Shan saw a fresco, one of the most detailed paintings he had yet seen on the mountain, of deities and ritual items painted in an unusual style with unusual patterns.

The tall Chinese said, "Moscow is where the proletariat learned it had nothing to lose but the chains of communism. Moscow has shown the rest of us what the new age means."

Shan said, "Spoken like a true citizen of the world."

Some of the miners were well educated, Yangke had told him. Some were even former college students who had decided to get a jump on the market economy. A wide plank hung from a peg that had been pounded into the fresco. It was painted with patterns of colored stripes leading to corresponding names. He realized it was a guide to the ownership of the claims. Beside it, leaning against the wall, were several wooden poles, straight limbs that appeared to have been cut and shaped for use as shovel handles.

"Bing," the man identified himself, with challenge in his eyes. "Mayor Bing. Managing Director Bing, if you prefer." There were names in China that immediately dated their holders. Bing, Chinese for soldier, had been popular four decades earlier.

Thomas Gao was the man sprawled on the blanket before the dying fire. He was bruised and bleeding from cuts on his chin and arm but not otherwise injured. He looked up with the expression of a pampered child caught pilfering sweets. Scattered over the blanket were canned goods, a package of batteries, a saltshaker, pencils, two slightly used Chinese paperback novels, four metal cups, several packs of cigarettes, half a dozen old magazines, a stick of deodorant, and a cigar in a plastic wrapper. He had set out his wares but his customers had other business in mind that day.

As Shan bent to help him up, Thomas pulled him closer and whispered in his ear. Shan went cold. Then one of the shovel handles was pressed against his shoulder, levering him backward, away from Thomas.

At the end of the handle was a short, wiry man wearing a green quilted jacket. "Captain Bing says no," he growled. A scar ran down one side of his face. He had the hardened look of a soldier.

Shan straightened, studying Bing again, considering his indifferent expression and the obsequious way the man with the shovel

242

handle looked at him. "Public Security pensions must be losing their value," he said.

The tall man laughed. "Public Security officers are turning into babysitters and computer specialists. Who can afford not to accept a position at the forefront of the new economy when it offers itself?"

Shan edged toward the mining claim chart. As he reached it, the scar-faced man grunted a curse and deftly pushed the end of his pole into Shan's shoulder, spinning him about and shoving him against the fresco. He had seen enough, however. The sticks with the two crimson stripes and one yellow belonged to Bing himself. The blue and red marks had one name beside them. The miner who had claimed Hostene's campsite, the scene of the murders, was named Hubei.

"Look what you've done," Bing mocked. "You've upset the gods."

Shan saw that a small piece of the fresco had crumbled away where he had brushed against it.

Bing studied Shan coolly, then spoke into the ear of the short man with the pole, who darted away and returned carrying a rough-hewn bench. He placed it by the blanket, then heaved Thomas onto it.

"His people will miss him," Shan warned.

"He's going nowhere," Bing growled. "We've no interest in being hacked to death in our sleep."

"But Thomas is only —," Shan began.

Bing interrupted by snatching up a black plastic bag lying on top of Thomas's pack and tossing it at Shan. "He kept a trinket from us today."

Shan's throat went dry as his fingers extracted the hard, dark thing. It was a small hand ax, with an old hand-forged head and a short, uneven, homemade handle, smoothed to a sheen from long use. The head and part of the handle were mottled with a brown stain. Shan did not need one of Thomas's tests to know it was blood.

"Four and a half inches," Thomas said to Shan in a thin, nervous voice. "I measured the edge. It matches the entry wound on the back of Victim One."

"Who but the murderer would carry such a thing?" Bing snapped.

"I told you, I am investigating," Thomas protested, then explained to Shan in a lower voice, "I stopped to get a drink at a spring off the trail this morning. When I returned to my pack this was on top. Someone who knew I was interested left it for me."

"One lie begets another," Bing shot back. "Everyone here knows there can be no investigation unless it's by the government. And the government here is me. Elected by the vote of every citizen. This whelp is no investigator."

Thomas's eyes went back and forth, from Bing to Shan. "I am helping Inspector Shan. He is a famous detective from Beijing."

The declaration was not welcomed by the miners. Two men guffawed, but four slipped away into the shadows. Others stared warily at Shan, tightening their grips around their shovels and picks.

"A disgraced detective!" Thomas quickly added. "A convict."

"Shan? You're Shan?" Bing asked skeptically. As he studied his tattered visitor his amusement grew. "Inspector Shan has unique credentials," Bing said to Thomas. "But you have none. Which means —" A cry of alarm interrupted Bing. Two men appeared from the shadows, dragging Hostene between them. Fearing he would resist, Shan pulled him away from his escorts and led him over to the blanket.

A satisfied smile appeared on Bing's face. He knocked Hostene's hat from his head. Murmurs of surprise, then anger, rippled through the crowd.

"We hereby declare you a Hero Worker for exceeding your production quota," Bing proclaimed to Shan. "You have delivered to us a surplus of murderers. I will send word to Chodron. He wishes some of us to attend the trial, next to you and your pet lama. Nothing validates the social order like taking the life of the disorderly."

Shan led Hostene to the bench, seating him beside Thomas. The Navajo stared at the gathered men in confusion and despair. Shan stepped in front of the bench, surveying the angry, hungry faces of the miners. Bing's lieutenant stood by the stack of poles as if ready to distribute them.

Shan went to the center of the circle. "These men are not murderers. They are scholars, each in his own way."

Bing's grin showed he was warming to the entertainment. "You are a newcomer to this mountain. You have no notion of what these men have done. This isn't some prosecution to be dressed up for the propagandists. We are practical men here, we deal with practical facts." He aimed something in his hand at Hostene's head. With a momentary stab of fear Shan saw a brilliant spot of red light appear on the Navajo's forehead. One of the mayor's tools for keeping social order was a laser pointer. "This one, Inspector, not only was found near the two murdered men, he steals gold from hard-working miners, creeping about in the night like some wild dog. I have sent this information to Chodron. No doubt he would have kept him chained in that stable had he known."

Hostene flushed and glanced up at Shan.

Bing directed the pointer at Thomas. "And this one treats us like laboratory rats, observing us when he thinks we don't know, playing the peddler so he can get acquainted with his victims. Sometimes" — Bing strolled along the front of his audience, pausing for effect — "sometimes the young ones like this kill because they have discovered they are incapable of being men. So they express their lust in another way." He paused again, smiling at Thomas's expression, raising his brows as he delivered his punch line. "He can't make his sword work, so he picks up an ax."

Hostility was growing on several of the faces before Shan. "This man, named Hostene," he said, indicating the Navajo, "was nearly killed by a blow to his head." Shan lifted Thomas's pack, opened the front zipper, and pulled out the photos he had asked the youth to print for him. Thomas's whispered news had been about the photos and also about the demons on the far side of the mountain. "Here Hostene is some time after the murders. The real killer put him there,

247

then painted signs on the rock with blood."

"You don't know that," Bing growled. "He could have been injured fighting his victims, then used their blood to paint those signs before he collapsed."

"I do know it," Shan said. "We all know it because the picture tells the truth." He walked along the ring of miners, holding the photo out to them at eye level. "Because the bloodstains on his shirt and the blood-stains on his boots run across onto the rock and the grass, in perfect alignment. He was unconscious while someone else painted the images in blood."

"Which means," Bing shot back, "that the boy did it. This young lunatic turned on his partner in crime. The boy was the one with the ax. Chodron knows what to do with lunatics. The sharpened spoon, but not for the eyes! You put it up the nose and twist." A man in the back burst out laughing. But not all the men agreed with Bing. Shan saw several studying the photo, looking worried.

"The boy did it," Bing insisted, "then murdered the other one, the farmer, yester-day. Once the killing sickness starts, it becomes like a beast that has to be regularly fed."

There was a kettle on a brazier at the edge of the fire ring. Shan picked up two cups from Thomas's blanket, filled them with lukewarm black tea, and handed them to Thomas and Hostene. He walked along the line of miners then lifted the ax from the blanket, handed it to Bing, and stepped out of the circle to a place where two large rock slabs had fallen, forming a right angle. He pointed to an eighteen-inch slab at the front of a nearby lean-to that was serving as a table. "Move that," he instructed Bing's deputy.

"Do it, Hubei," Bing said in an amused tone.

The man leapt to action, lifted the stone, and placed it where Shan directed, one foot from the wall.

Shan paused, studying the short man a moment. He was Bing's deputy and the one who had claimed Hostene's campsite. He pulled another photo from the stack in Thomas's pack and handed it to one of the miners, who looked it over and passed it around the circle. "You can see the slaughter ground where the two bodies were found. Two rock walls close together, just like here, a flat rock below." He asked Hubei to lie on the ground, then Shan lifted his arm. "It's just after dawn. I drag my victims in here. The young one, Tashi, is unconscious but alive. I have to remove his hands for some reason. I chop them off on this rock, in the left corner of the little chamber, just as the picture shows. See how the blood spurts onto the rock wall, but not onto the chopping slab."

Hubei emitted a nervous laugh as Shan pulled back his shirtsleeve and arranged his arm on the stone slab. "The arm was held down for the cutting stroke, right at the edge of the slab. Give the boy the ax," Shan instructed Bing. The mayor of Little Moscow silently complied, then pulled Thomas to his feet.

"Come, cut off his hand, Thomas," Shan invited. The man on the ground cursed and began to rise, but a moment later was pinned down by a pole in his ribs. Bing, at the other end of the pole, gestured for him to spread his arms again.

"Show us," Shan encouraged Thomas. The man on the ground squirmed, the color draining from his face. Bing pressed harder on his pole.

Thomas advanced reluctantly to the man on the ground, paused, began to kneel, and paused again as he bent. Then he straightened, tried to step over the man but stopped, realizing he could not fit into the small space between the stone and the rock wall. He looked up to Shan with a puzzled, pleading expression.

"He can't do it," Shan declared, "because he is right-handed." He bent, positioned the man's arm again, and demonstrated how the chopping blow was delivered. "The killer was left-handed. Neither Thomas nor Hostene is left-handed."

In the silence that followed, Shan paced along the row of miners again, stopping in front of one who wore a soiled wool cap. "How many murders have there been?" he asked abruptly.

The man glanced at Bing, then gazed at his feet without replying.

"How many murders?" Shan asked the next man.

"Some die," the man said, "some get rich."

The next, an older man, gazed at Shan uneasily. "Why the hands?" he asked in a hollow voice, as if Shan should know. "A man's hands are the proof of his life."

Shan turned back toward Bing. "Keep hiding the truth and someone else will die." He swept his arm along the line of miners. "Maybe one of you. There are three dead this year for certain. The young miner at the painting of a blue bull, then the two at Hostene's camp. There were two more last year. The farmer yesterday would make five. Between the first two murders it was, what, ten months? Then the killer took only a month to strike again. If we count the farmer yesterday, the interval was less than two weeks this time. If that's a pattern, then in five or six days there will be another murder. One of you may be next. Or perhaps it will be a woman who is missing."

Hostene did not appear to hear Shan's reference to his niece. He was staring at the rock slab on the ground where Shan had reconstructed the dismemberment of his friends.

Shan turned back to Bing. "Or is she dead already?"

Bing too seemed to be contemplating Shan's performance. "A woman," he muttered at last, "wandering alone isn't safe."

"Her uncle has to find her," Shan said. "We all need to find her, for she may have witnessed the murders of her two colleagues."

No one spoke. Shan studied the ragged group of miners again. Why weren't they out working their claims? They were worried, Shan realized, even frightened. It was indeed likely that one of them would be the next victim. But it might be as likely that one of them was involved in the killings. He reminded himself that someone had tried to destroy their little party only the day before with explosives. Every man in front of him was an expert with explosives.

"The best chance you have of solving these murders," Shan said, "is to let us go. And to help us find the woman. Do you have any idea what will happen if an American is reported missing on this mountain?"

"American?" It was one of the older miners who replied. "Impossible. Tibetan. Nepali, perhaps."

Shan leaned over Hostene, whispering in his ear. The Navajo unbuttoned his shirt pocket and handed Shan something blue and flat.

"She is a professor," Shan said in a loud voice. "She is famous." As he lifted the object in his hand, a nervous murmur swept through the crowd. The little blue object was like one of the old charms used in Tibet and China to cast a spell on those who beheld it — a United States passport.

"Shall we speak of what happens when it is discovered that this famous professor is missing? Have you ever wondered how many soldiers can fit in the belly of one of those big planes? Shall we guess how long your secrets will last?"

It was as if a festering sore had been lanced. There was no more resentment, only worry. He walked along the row of miners, catching bits of their conversations. A man with a shaved head spoke of satellite surveillance. Someone else mentioned a movie in which the sky had been darkened with American parachutes.

Bing, looking weary now, picked up the kettle and offered Hostene more tea.

Many years earlier Shan had visited Dunhuang, where mountains honeycombed with caves had once been home to scores of Buddhist teachers and hermits, in which they had sealed away treasures of ancient texts and paintings. The honeycombed caves of Little Moscow had been in use for what Shan guessed to be at least a dozen years and had their own artifacts and shrines. Shan wandered past the miners, who were conversing among themselves, and absorbed, then slipped down a long ravine to examine some of the town's shrines more closely. He passed a heap of rusty cans and broken tools near the mouth of the gully, under a stripped tree trunk from which dangling ropes and pulleys extended over the lip of the ravine — a boom for lowering heavy objects. He paused at a shelter marked with placards bearing curses, warnings to stay away. Then he peered inside it. A red bike was parked within. Beyond, the soft shale under several overhanging ledges had been chipped away, creating small caves with a domestic appearance. Several bore Chinese names painted on wooden slabs hanging from poles. One pole held a two-year-old calendar with the image of a naked blonde woman posing with auto tires. A wind-frayed photo, torn from a magazine, of a gleaming silver pickup truck, dangled from another. Still another held an advertisement for a casino in Macao. This was how a sacred mountain entered the new age.

Shan glanced back toward the town square, considering what Thomas had whispered to him on his arrival after telling him he had brought the photographs as Shan had requested. *If Shan were to set foot on the other side of the mountain, Gao had ordered him shot on sight.* There never seemed to be answers on Sleeping Dragon Mountain, only more fear, more riddles.

From the shadows he absently watched the two mah-Jongg players set up a new game, stacking small piles of cash before them. Cash. The miners couldn't turn their gold into cash until the end of the season, until they left the mountain for the year. He would have expected them to spend their money in the spring, on equipment and supplies. He watched how the other miners glanced jealously at the pair. These two had enough to gamble with, as if the end of the summer had come early for them.

He walked past a den with a canvas front decorated with images of the heads of tigers, then bent and picked up a pebble before studying the next piece of municipal art, a glossy advertising photo of a robot holding a tray of cocktails, pinned above a can full of cigarette butts. On a rock beside the can was an army helmet, painted black with yellow stripes.

A rough voice announced from the shadows within, "Captain Bing has a rule. Anyone caught in another man's cave is tied to a rock and caned."

Shan bent and squinted, meeting the gaze of the scarred man in the quilted jacket. "It is you I came looking for. I saw you slip down this alley. Hubei, is that what they call you? After the province?" He had known many criminals who took the name of their homes to hide their real names.

"You played me for a fool once today. Don't make the mistake of trying it a second time."

"I was only protecting the boy," Shan said as he began tossing the pebble from one hand to the other. "If I had seen your arm before, I would have used someone else. Were you imprisoned in Tibet?" Shan had noticed the tattoo on the man's exposed arm during his earlier demonstration.

"Military prison. Xinjiang," Hubei replied in a surly tone, referring to the vast area north of Tibet known for its deserts and massive prison camps. "Five years. The first month I was there I thought we would all die of the heat. But it was winter that did the government's work. In January and February we stacked bodies like firewood."

Shan rolled up his sleeve and revealed his own tattoo. "404th People's Construction Brigade," he explained. "Sometimes when men died, the guards made us bury them right in the roadbed. The bodies were usually still warm." He looked away for a moment, fighting a sudden ache in his heart. He had never really left the gulag. Unpredictably, abruptly, the tormenting memories resurfaced, so vivid it seemed he was there, the dusty wind in his face, old monks being beaten with batons for mouthing forbidden mantras.

The wiry miner was staring at him, perplexed, and Shan realized the man had been speaking. "I asked, why seek me out?"

Shan said, tossing the pebble again, "I need to know if you and Bing saw the American woman and what she was doing."

"No one takes gold out of the streams for us," the man complained. "We don't have time to wander about watching pretty butterflies."

"What did you observe?" Shan pressed. "Bing has seen her and I don't think he ventures far without you. You can cover a lot of ground on that bicycle. The sheep trails are your highways." He glanced at the helmet. "Every town should have a mounted police force."

One end of the man's mouth curled up as he stared at Shan. "They say you came up from some valley to the south. Go back. Up here, we boil a man like you for soup. You don't belong. You don't understand anything. And we don't need an outsider to tell us who the murderer is."

"If something happens to the missing woman," Shan said, "Public Security will need to blame someone. You and I both know they tend to favor former convicts. Makes for good reading in Beijing."

Hubei frowned. "At first we figured they were just trying to snatch a share of our gold without registering a claim with us. We don't like newcomers. Bing dealt with them. He warned them to stay out of our way, said he didn't want to see them again, said if they had to pray to do so secretly. The idiots. Collecting pretty rocks and flowers in a place like this."

"Pray?"

"That's what it looked like they were doing mostly, praying in front of those old rock paintings of gods and devils. Or else measuring eyeballs."

"I'm sorry?"

"I saw the woman again. East of here, up the slope, two days ago. She was alone, and frightened, on her knees, measuring parts of paintings with a small ruler. The eyeball of the demon, the width of his arm. When she saw me she pulled out a pocketknife. I tossed her an apple. She ate it as if she hadn't had a meal for days. When I took one step forward she pointed the knife at me. I left. None of my business."

Hubei retreated into the shadows. When he emerged a moment later a pack hung from his shoulder and a pair of battered binoculars was suspended from his neck. Shan tossed the pebble to him.

Hubei caught it and stared at his hand for a moment. "Fuck you," he snapped. "It doesn't mean anything."

"It proves you are left-handed. Do you have any notion how few Chinese are left-handed? It's against official educational policy. You're a former convict engaged in an illegal activity, and you're left-handed. The Public Security report on the murders would almost write itself." Shan stepped closer to the miner. "Who found that dead farmer?"

Hubei hurled the stone against the opposite wall. "Some of the men. When I saw he was one of theirs, I went to tell some shepherds."

"Where did you find him?"

"The body was at the base of a ridge that juts out from the mountain, a mile up the slope." Hubei picked up his helmet and fastened it to a strap on his pack.

"You mean he was on his way down the ridge when he was killed?"

"I mean that's where he was found. No one from Little Moscow goes up that ridge. I can't speak for fool farmers and their murderers. Not our concern. I just wanted to be rid of the body."

Suddenly Shan understood. "Do you mean the same ridge where the man was killed last year?"

"Where we buried him. And where his ghost took revenge on his murderer. It's haunted. Men saw a skeleton on his grave. Some say it walks up there in the moonlight. Some say they see it elsewhere, as if it's on patrol in the night. More and more miners come back here to sleep after their day's work."

Shan paused, trying to connect the words to the strange video in which Abigail had handled arm and leg bones. "The two that were killed last week," he said. "What happened to their bodies?"

"If you're talking about the flesh, I guess the birds took care of it."

"I don't understand."

"Last year, two days after those two died, two new skeletons appeared on that grave. It scared the hell out of everyone, believe me." Hubei grinned at Shan's confusion, then twisted past him. "Touch anything and you die," the man said in an oddly whimsical tone and went toward the town square.

"Where does one get cash in Little Moscow?" Shan called after him. "Up here I would think cash is scarcer than gold."

Hubei glanced back impatiently. "Banking is a government monopoly," he quipped, then lifted the helmet and trotted away.

Shan had found more riddles. But he had also confirmed that Abigail Natay was probably still alive. She had survived the attack and continued up the mountain as her uncle had guessed. She was pursuing her work despite the danger, even despite apparently having run out of food. It was as if her life depended on it.

He wandered about the miners' quarters then paused as he rounded the corner of the square to survey Bing's new-age community. Every man there, including Thomas, Hostene and himself, was a fugitive of a kind. You couldn't enter the new world without leaving the old behind.

As he watched, men began moving quickly, spreading an alarm, dispersing, some with packs on their backs, some holding old hunting rifles. Bing stood near Thomas, who had grown pale and was gazing at the ground with a look of shock on his face. The mayor of Little Moscow spoke with a man who kept pointing toward the east, replying to Bing in low, excited whispers. The Navajo was staring at the fleeing miners, at Bing and Thomas, in confusion.

As Shan approached, Thomas said in a grief-stricken tone, "You should be the one to speak. Give him more hot tea, then tell him."

"Tell him what?" Shan asked Bing.

"A miner ran into town," Bing reported. "Some mine works were sabotaged this morning, all the stakes removed and left burning in a pile."

"But the miners sometimes —," Shan began.

Bing interrupted. "Not this time. Whoever did it left something behind, as a warning. It was a woman's hand."

CHAPTER SIX

They ran at a frantic pace at first, following Bing up one ravine and down another, soon emerging onto a sunlit plateau. Bing raised his hand for them to stop as he gazed toward a heap of rock slabs in the near distance. Shan did not miss the instinctive movement of Bing's hand to his belt at the small of his back.

"Hubei!" Bing shouted. When his lieutenant did not appear Bing cursed, took a step forward, then halted again as a column of smoke began to rise from the heap of rocks. He called for Hubei again, then turned to his companions.

"Wait here," the former Public Security officer ordered before sprinting back toward Little Moscow. "Not a step farther until I bring help."

Shan studied the rock slabs. They stood at the base of a steep black ridge that jutted to the west. He glanced at Hostene and

Thomas and began to run.

He paused a hundred feet from the fire, crouching to study the scene. If what he had viewed earlier was the town square of the miners' world, this was its temple. The huge slabs had sheared off a stubby rock tower and fallen at angles against its base, creating the effect of a large irregular spire pointing toward heaven. Those who used it had even printed their particular scriptures onto the entrance rocks with black paint. REJOICE IN WORK, one mocked, a long-ago Party slogan. WAN SUI! proclaimed another rock face — Ten thousand years! — the old salute to the emperor's health. Then, beside it, FEAR EVERYTHING. Across the main entrance was a rope hung with empty beer cans and one more sign. TOWN HALL, it said.

Hostene caught up with Shan. "The boy's gone," the Navajo said.

Thomas was nowhere to be seen.

"He ran as soon as Bing was out of sight," Hostene explained. "He'd had a bad beating. I don't blame him."

Together, they approached the fire. Shan gestured to a boulder. "Wait here."

"You heard them. A hand was found."

"I also heard them say claim stakes had been burned."

The fire near the entrance appeared to have been fueled by blankets that were doused in kerosene. Half a dozen painted sticks, barely charred, lay on top. "But this fire was only lit moments ago."

Hostene's reply was to push Shan aside. He lowered his pack to the ground and walked past the fire into the shadowy entrance. Shan glanced back up the slope. Then, seeing nothing, he followed.

Inside was a long table of hewn logs bearing several candles set in empty beer bottles, two of which were lit. Heavy sheets of canvas hung from beams braced in the rock slabs, serving as room partitions. A noise rose from the farthest one, the sound of a clay pot smashing. Hostene pushed past Shan, thrusting aside the canvas. A single candle inside flickered in the breeze that came through a gap in the rear wall. It was a storeroom, lined with baskets, sacks of rice, and small barrels, on top of which lay shards where someone had smashed a ceramic butter lamp against the wall. To one side were two nylon sleeping bags, an assortment of pots and pans, and — something Shan had not seen in years — a small coffee pot. In the center of the floor were two packs, one blue, the other red, each with a rising sun on its flap.

"It's ours! Our equipment! Our packs!" Hostene exclaimed, then sobered as he saw a piece of dirty cloth on top of the red pack, folded over a lumpy object. He stared at it, suddenly frightened, and did not react when Shan pushed past and lifted a small piece of paper left on the cloth, covered with Chinese ideograms.

"What is it?" Hostene asked in a hoarse voice.

"A death charm," Shan explained. "Inscribed for the funeral of a family member." He placed the paper in his pocket, then reached for the cloth bundle and, with a shudder, opened it.

Hostene let out a surprised groan. They saw a woman's hand with long graceful fingers lifted in what Shan recognized as the wish-giving ritual sign, a mudra. But it was a two-dimensional representation, painted on a piece of plaster, a fragment of a long-faded fresco. In the center of the palm was a white eye. This time Tara, the goddess, had been dismembered.

In the goddess's hand, inserted near the tip of the fingers, was a small stick with eyes carved on its end.

As Hostene reached out and picked up the fragment, Shan grabbed the straps of both packs in one hand and pulled him back into the main chamber. Hostene paused as they passed the table, set down the plaster, and gestured for Shan to place the packs on the table. For the first time Shan noticed their disproportionate weight. The red was very light, the blue very heavy.

"I told you to stay put," an angry voice snapped as Shan reached into the blue pack. Bing was not alone anymore. Hubei and half a dozen miners armed with shovels and picks stood behind him.

"What have you stolen this time, old man?" Bing demanded of Hostene.

"It's mine!" the Navajo muttered. "You can't —"

Bing grabbed the red pack, upending it onto the table.

Hostene's protest choked in his throat. The miners, even Bing, retreated a step, revulsion in their faces. The pack contained the hands of as many as six skeletons.

Before Bing could react, Shan shoved Hostene toward the entrance and swung the blue pack, knocking Bing off balance.

"Don't look back!" Shan shouted to Hostene. "Run!" He reached into the blue pack, flung a handful of its contents at the miners, and ran, too. The miners halted as they saw what Shan had thrown at them. Gold. Someone had dropped dozens of small nuggets into the blue pack.

Only Bing and Hubei made an effort to chase them. Then Shan spun about and with a heave scattered the remaining contents of the open pack across the slope. The nuggets rattled onto the rocky terrain in a wide arc, bouncing, rolling, scattering across the mountainside.

"Nooooo!" Bing moaned and flung himself down the slope, trying to catch the nuggets as they bounced. Then he tripped and went rolling too.

Once, according to legend, there had been monks who ran as a meditation exercise. As he ran, Shan only meditated on death.

A quarter hour later, when Hostene raised his palms and bent, gasping, Shan gestured him into the shadow of a large boulder.

"Someone is still convinced you are the killer," Shan said.

"Someone? They are all convinced now. I had the hands. I was stealing their gold. We just gave them all the proof they needed." Hostene straightened and looked back in the direction they had come. "The killer could have been there."

"Not the killer necessarily," Shan replied. "But a brother." He extracted the death charm from his pocket and scrutinized it. "This is a charm to protect the spirit of a dead man. It refers to him as 'brother'. No name is given, though it says the victim was nineteen years old. And it asks that his ghost be allowed to punish his killer." Shan followed Hostene's worried gaze. They began walking up the slope.

"Had you seen it before?" Shan asked. "The hand with the eye?"

Hostene thought a moment. "There was a goddess with an eye on her hand. Beside a blue bull."

Shan said, "The blue bull painting is where the young miner died."

"Abigail kept returning to it," Hostene recalled suddenly.

"Why?"

"She never said. Sometimes she took Professor Ma with her. They would have made videotapes." He reflected. "But those tapes were not with the others. She must have taken them with her."

"Can you find the blue bull painting?"

Hostene turned to the south, rubbing his temple as he considered the landscape, then pointed to distant grove of trees. "We can't risk it. Too close to Little Moscow."

As he spoke they heard a booming sound on the slope below, and a red rocket shell burst in the sky. Bing was an efficient manager of his little community.

"What does that mean?" Hostene asked.

"Bing's civil alert system, I would guess. I think the best answer for Bing and Chodron is still for you to be the killer. They were shocked that you were an American, but that will soon wear off. They'll realize that's not really a problem so long as you and your niece never leave the mountain."

"Then we must leave. I should hide."

"We have to inspect that painting."

"It's too dangerous," Hostene protested.

Abigail kept returning to the blue bull image. I think the killer keeps returning to it too."

Hostene grimaced, but he led the way to a small clearing surrounded by trees. It took Shan only moments to realize he had seen this shrine before. It was the place on the video where Abigail had passed arm and leg bones to someone who spoke English. The painting was the biggest he had yet seen on the mountain, or would have been, had it not been systematically destroyed by the blows of a hammer. Circular indentations were still visible on several pieces of plaster that had resisted. The surviving fragments showed a graceful shoulder here, the eye of a bull there. But between these fragments something new had been revealed. The destruction of the fresco had exposed a much older painting on the rock beneath it, the faded image of a god with a dragon's head.

"Did she know about this older image underneath?" Shan wondered out loud.

"She couldn't have," Hostene said hesitantly. "In any case she would never have destroyed the fresco."

"But she kept coming back, as if the key to something was here," Shan reminded him. "Maybe the painting underneath the blue bull is the real key." He examined the small panels of robed men and demons wearing human skins that formed a frame around the central deity, the dragon-headed god.

"She sat here," Hostene said, indicating a flat rock, the one Shan had seen in the video. "Filming every detail of the fresco, that day we waited for Ma."

Shan looked up. "You came here, the day the mine blew up?"

"Yes. Why?"

"What did she do when Ma returned?"

"She became very quiet when he told her what happened. Then, suddenly, she put on her pack and told us to go back to camp and to stay there."

"Where did she go?"

"I watched. She went in a new direction,

272

where I had never been." He turned and gestured. "There." He was indicating the steep black ridge they had just run from. Shan had not forgotten the description he had heard from the fleeing miner. When the mine blew up, Abigail had gone to "the ridge of the ghosts".

Their troubled silence was interrupted a moment later by another of the spiraling red rockets. They turned and ran.

Several minutes later they peered over a shelf of rock at the lower slope. Men were jogging below them toward Little Moscow. It would be a perfect victory for Chodron if the miners took revenge on the two men the village headman most wanted out of his life.

Shan asked, "What do they call it in those American western movies when angry citizens trap a suspected criminal?"

"A lynch mob," Hostene replied grimly as he pointed out another set of miners working their way along the slope to the south. Shan pointed toward the summit and began climbing.

It was early evening when they reached his destination, the maze of shattered boulders and broken rock slabs that led to Gao's fortress. Hostene collapsed onto a rock, gulping from the water bottle he pulled from his pack. The Navajo, though in remarkable shape for his age, had reached his limit. "I thought we would take shelter in the hermit's cave," he said.

"We would have endangered Lokesh, Yangke, and the hermit," Shan said.

Hostene slowly nodded then gazed guiltily at the empty bottle in his hand. "Was that the last of the water?" In his frantic flight Shan had left his pack behind.

"No matter," Shan said. "There are springs nearby." But he had no idea when they would be able to walk safely out onto the slope again. On this side of the mountain a mob of angry miners was searching for them. A lynch mob. And despite their frantic hours since entering Little Moscow that morning Thomas's whispered warning had never totally left Shan's mind. If Shan ventured to the other side he was to be shot on sight.

Wearily they climbed through the maze, then crawled into the small gap under a stone slab that had tumbled from the top, finding a niche sheltered deep in the debris that afforded a clear view of the sky overhead. Shan helped Hostene arrange his blanket against the wall and, as the light faded, shared the only food they had left, half a dozen kernels of dried cheese.

"What Bing said about me wasn't exactly the way of it." Hostene's voice was aimed toward the stars. "I wasn't stealing. It was for Abigail." In a near whisper he explained that his niece had been convinced that the ancient mine they had discovered had to be kept secret from the miners. On an old stone altar near the entrance to the mine, under an overhanging rock, they had seen a copper statue of an old god. It had been hollow, in the traditional style, with offerings inside and what sounded like small stones when they'd picked it up.

"Gold," Shan suggested.

"Ma and Tashi were certain of it. The first day we were there they left a little offering on the altar. After that, we all did. But the copper statue was stolen one night."

"I thought the place was a secret."

"It was supposed to be. Tashi was very distressed. He emptied his pockets and put everything on the altar as if to appease the gods, then when the sun went down he took me to a miners' camp about a mile away. The miners were asleep. I turned on my flashlight and saw the old statue. When I dashed in to take it, one of the men woke up. He fired a pistol at me. I kept running. But when I reached a safe place and could look, I saw that the back of the statue had

275

been pried open with a chisel. It was empty. The old prayers that would have been inside must have been burned. I didn't steal any gold. But that's what they thought I was trying to do."

"How much later was the mine struck by lightning?"

"Two days later."

Hostene said no more as he moved about trying to find a comfortable sleeping position.

Bing. Bing was the one who had declared Hostene a thief, and Bing's hand had reflexively reached for a pistol in his belt. But why, after finding out about the old mine, would he destroy it? Why destroy a depleted mine?

When Shan leaned back, he meant to close his eyes for only a minute or two. But when he opened them it was night, and he could hear Hostene's heavy regular breathing. Pulling the blanket around the Navajo's shoulders, he crawled out of their shelter, quietly backtracked, then climbed up one of the leaning slabs to the top of the chasm wall, following its edge in the moonlight to where it opened onto the main slope. He dropped and crawled the last twenty feet then, lying on his belly.

A mile away, toward Little Moscow, lay

the long black hulk of the ridge that jutted to the west, the haunted ridge where skeletons gathered around a grave. That afternoon vultures had hung over the ridge. Two days before, a farmer had died there, struck by lightning. Why had he been there? He must have been following someone at Chodron's order, since no one went up there voluntarily because of the ghosts. No one but Abigail Natay.

It was the hour when Lokesh said the wind scoured the last light from the bowl of the sky, revealing with each gust another hundred stars. A thin silver ribbon, the closest stream, wound its way across the blackened slope a quarter mile away. A bright speck appeared near the horizon, a planet. And another on the ground, a fire. Half a mile below them, a camp had been laid out. The fire, rapidly growing, was much bigger than the miners would need for cooking. It was a warning. Or was it a distraction? Their pursuers sought to lull them into thinking they had stopped for the night but, as he watched, a pair of men were silhouetted against the silver reflection of the stream. Fortunately, they had none of the skills of the old Tibetan wolf hunters who could blend invisibly with the night shadows.

A goat bolted across the shadows, running hard from an outcropping, away from the pair of men Shan had seen. No doubt another pair of searchers lurked near the outcropping. The miners were systematically sweeping the slope above Little Moscow. If they found nothing they would begin searching the gullies in the morning, one by one, sealing each with a guard as they did so. Bing had learned well from his years in the Public Security Bureau.

Not fear but a deep melancholy grew within Shan, punctuated by waking visions of Gendun being tortured, being beaten in tamzing sessions to utter words he would never understand for reasons he could never comprehend. Shan had become the worm in the wood of Gendun's safe hermitage, the parasite that had edged into the lama's life. Through his own blind stupidity, through his naive assumption that he could become one of them, he had brought the horrors of the modern world to them.

He found another perch that offered a view of the summit and the quarter moon that illuminated it. His stomach growled, left unsatisfied by their sparse meal. He remembered that Dolma had given him a little pouch of rice. He reached into his pocket and held it in his palm.

It was an old prisoner's trick. Grains of

rice would fall from the sacks inmates were forced to haul into the guards' mess hall. A single grain on the tongue would swell up into a digestible morsel after several minutes, so that half a dozen grains almost seemed to be a meal. He measured out half the bag onto his palm, returned the pouch with Hostene's share to his pocket, then stared at the small mound in his hand as it glowed in the moonlight. His stomach growled again. It was the last of his food.

As he looked up at the moon, an owl hooted. He let the grains fall through his fingers onto the rock below, then swept them into a pile in front of him. Placing a single grain on his tongue, he counted out those that remained. Only sixty-three. He quickly, guiltily, pulled the grain from his mouth and placed it on the pile, then separated the grains into three smaller, uneven piles and began counting each of the piles. It was one of the ways he and his father had adapted the old stick-counting method for meditation on the Tao te Ching, one of the ways used by the devout in reeducation camps, where it was deemed a serious moral lapse to have traditional Tao throwing sticks.

Each round of counting yielded one of the lines of a tetragram, which he drew with a finger in the dusty soil at his side. When he had finished he had compiled a solid line over three lines of two segments each. It denoted Chapter Fourteen in a table his father had taught him. When they had first studied it together, his father had told him it was about the geometry of living correctly. Shan whispered the resulting verse to the moon:

The world is a mysterious instrument
Not made to be handled
Those who act on it, spoil it
Those who seize it, lose it

He sat motionless, sensing that a door was opening to a carefully guarded chamber in his mind. He heard the distant voice of his father, a whisper down a long corridor. He forgot his fear, forgot his helplessness, and listened with his heart. Eventually, he became aware of a faint smell, the scent of the ginger his father always carried in his pocket.

He did not know how long he immersed himself in his memories, but the moon was high in the sky before the hoot of another owl brought him back. Abruptly, he lost the sensation of his father's presence and the dim figures accompanying it who were the monks they had sat with when Shan was a child. He was alone again in the night on a cold, windswept perch, remembering the dangers that waited on either side of the mountain.

His stomach whined again, and he picked up several grains, ready to eat them, then looked at the moon and lowered his hand. He could not eat without reducing the number needed to cast. He tossed them down again to produce another tetragram. This time the pattern was a line broken in thirds over one broken in half, the pair repeated. It indicated Chapter Seventy-One, the verse that had seemed to come up more frequently than any other during his years in Tibet:

To know that you do not know is best
To not know of knowing is a disease
To be sick of the disease
Is the way to be free of the disease

The lives of everyone on the mountain who meant something to him, including the Navajo woman he had never met, hung in perilous balance, and it was impossible that all would escape unscathed unless Shan could solve the terrible riddles of the mountain. But all he knew now was that he did not know. And soon they had to choose between going west, to those who wanted to kill Hostene, or east, to those who wanted to kill Shan. The owl, Hostene's harbinger of death, landed thirty feet away and cocked its head, as if to remind Shan that he had known the answer to that particular riddle even before he had tallied the rice grains.

Even wolves halt to lick their paws. Well after midnight, as Shan watched from the rim again, figures appeared against the light of the bonfire, weary men who settled onto the rocks near the flames. He pushed back and found his way to the bottom of the chasm again and awakened Hostene with a brief touch on his leg. Without questioning Shan, the Navajo rolled up his blanket and followed. Shan handed him the full pouch of rice. "Keep this," Shan said. "Put a few grains on your tongue as you walk." He had returned his own sixty-four grains to the pouch. His hunger had disappeared during his final vigil with the owl.

When they stepped into the moonlight Shan explained his plan.

"But this side is where Abigail is," Hostene protested. "You say there are soldiers on the east side," he added in a plaintive tone. "If they arrest me they will deport me.

I will never see her again."

"We are doing this for two reasons. First, the miners are in a frenzy. They will execute you and march back to their camp, singing. Second, the key to finding Abigail is the hermit, who has fled from his cave."

"Rapaki? He doesn't even know her."

"There are two people on this mountain trying to unlock the mystery left by the old monks. The hermit knows more about the pilgrim stations than anyone else. I think Abigail and he do know each other. It seems impossible that they never encountered one another." Shan extracted the empty tin from his pocket. "I found this in Rapaki's cave."

The Navajo took the container, turning it over in his hand, holding it up to the moonlight. "Lemon Freshies," he said in a bewildered tone. "She brought three or four of these from home."

A bird flew up in the darkness overhead. Hostene put his hands up, palms out, to shield his face. The hands. It was, Shan abruptly realized, how Rapaki would have seen Shan the previous morning. As he walked, he replayed the encounter with the hermit in his mind. Rapaki's jumble of mantras had had a theme. *Honored by the waking dead* was part of the most common prayer to Tara. *Face like the circle of the autumn moon* was part of a ceremony for invoking the presence of Tara. Even the cheating-death mantra the hermit had used was one that invoked Tara. And though Shan had raised his hands to protect himself from the flying stones, he had not understood until now Rapaki's reaction. Shan's thumbs had been touching, palms flattened, turned outward. He had unconsciously made a mudra, one that was a special offering to the goddess, invoking the Laughing Tara. Shan and Hostene had been looking for Abigail. Rapaki had been looking for Tara.

Shan said, "In one of her photos, Abigail wore a short necklace with a large turquoise pendant. Did she wear it often?"

"It's one of her favorites. It was her mother's. Why?"

"We have to find Rapaki," Shan said urgently. "And the key to finding Rapaki is Thomas."

"That boy from the other side?"

"There were other things in Rapaki's cave — new pencils, a panda-printed quilt, clean paper. He didn't get them from the miners, he didn't get them from Yangke, and he certainly didn't get them all from Abigail."

Shan led them down the dark, treacherous path in short stages, stopping frequently to mentally revisit the terrain ahead, pain-fully aware of the jagged shards of stone, remnants of the earlier explosions, that waited below to impale them if they fell from the slippery rocks. Twice he lost his way and they had to backtrack. When they reached the makeshift ladder bridge Hos-tene balked. Shan waited for the moon to emerge from behind a cloud and, steeling himself, walked back and forth across it to reassure the old Navajo.

Much later, as they rested, looking at the stars, Hostene asked the question that had been often on Shan's mind. "Why the hands? Why does the killer cut off their hands? Why does he want hands?"

But Shan had no answer.

"What that old miner said," Hostene whispered later, "maybe he was right. About your hands being the proof of your life."

They finally reached the opening to the eastern slope an hour before dawn. Shan pointed out the vague shapes of the build-ings of Gao's compound, singling out the little stone hut that stood perhaps fifty yards from the main house, partially dug into the slope. "The road from the base ends there," Shan explained. "It was an old storage hut, a granary once. Now they keep supplies there."

"Once we reach it, what?"

"We hide there. Thomas comes and goes. We know he steals supplies, probably from the hut itself. We will find a way to speak with him." The long night with no more than an hour's rest had taken its toll on Shan. "At least we can sleep safely for a few hours," he said wearily.

After advancing on the hut in short bursts between taking cover behind rocks, Shan pressed a tentative hand against the plank door. Relief flooded him as it opened. He paused, noticing for the first time two small metal boxes sitting on the ground between the hut and Gao's darkened dzong, then stepped inside. He was caught in the beam of a flashlight. Behind him Hostene uttered a startled gasp. Shan had only a glimpse of the green-uniformed figure pinioning Hostene's arms before the butt of a rifle knocked him unconscious.

Of all the torments suffered by a gulag prisoner, the greatest was that once you entered, you never left. Long after their release, prisoners would cower in alleyways, flinch at the sight of a uniform, compulsively pace out the dimensions of their former cells within much larger chambers.

Since his first day of freedom Shan had

fought that compulsion. Now as he lay on a metal cot in the blackness, helplessness washed over him like some dark tide. It was pointless to resist. He was a prisoner again and would be for years to come. Even if he was eventually sent back to his former camp, where he might at least be reunited with his wayward son, there would be the inevitable softening up inflicted on repeat prisoners. His upper arm twitched where the battery cables would be clamped. His fingernails began to ache, as if they remembered what the Public Security soldiers, the knobs, had done.

No! a voice shouted in his head. He had to escape, whatever the cost. He would knock down the soldiers and run, dodging their bullets. He would leap out of the helicopter as it rose from the ground. He would dive out the door if they flew over a lake. There was a murderer on the mountain and Shan had to stop him. Gendun was in the clutches of Chodron, and had to be saved.

He rubbed the bump on his head where he had been struck, realizing in sudden panic that he had no way of knowing how long he had been unconscious. The cement floor and stone walls gave no clue as to where he was. He could have been drugged and transported miles away from the mountain. He searched his palate for the bitter tinge of the drugs that Public Security favored for prisoners. Nothing. Then a tiny vibration came through the ceiling, an intermittent, rhythmic rumbling. Rock and roll music.

A shadowy figure materialized at his cot without sound, holding a hand lantern, shaking him from a restless sleep. "They hit you too hard," came the soft words in Tibetan, and a porcelain cup of steaming tea was extended toward him. "They're just boys, most of those soldiers. Children with guns."

Gao's housekeeper helped him sit up and dabbed at his head with a damp cloth as he drank the strong brew. She answered his questions in quick whispers explaining that he had been brought here to the cellar of the tower by the soldiers, that he had been in the room for nearly half a day, that the other gentleman was being prepared, that a helicopter was coming that afternoon. Shan shot up and staggered to the door, where he clung to the frame a moment as his head cleared. Then he stepped into the hall.

Following a short corridor, he found himself in the austere chamber where he had seen Gao doing Tai Chi exercises. As he climbed the staircase to the sitting room, a figure in green fatigues leaped from a chair by the front door, hand on his pistol holster. Shan froze as he took in the unexpected scene. Thomas lounged in one of the over-stuffed chairs, reading a Western magazine. Kohler stood at the telescope, watching the nest of fledgling lammergeiers. At a small table set before the long row of windows, Gao and Hostene were playing chess. The muted music of a string orchestra emanated from the hidden speakers.

Gao caught the soldier's eye and raised a hand. The soldier frowned but retreated. When the guard reached the chair where he had been sitting, Gao made another gesture and he left the room.

"You missed lunch, Inspector," Kohler declared with amusement.

"The metal boxes," Shan said. "Some sort of surveillance device?"

"Motion detectors," Kohler confirmed. "We told the army we were having trouble with predators."

"Meaning that you want no more intruders from the other side," Shan offered.

Hostene rose and inspected the raw patch on Shan's temple, then nodded as if satisfied with what he saw. "It's OK," the Navajo said. "They know who I am."

"We understand you saved our new American friend," Gao said in perfect English.

"Again," Hostene added.

"For now," Shan replied, trying to eye the door inconspicuously. Thomas had said Gao wanted him to vanish, by means of a bullet if necessary.

"But he's free now," Gao said. "On this side of the mountain. His nightmare is over."

"We left" — Hostene seemed to search for a word — "someone. Shan and I must go back."

Gao sighed, a father losing patience with his children. "Surely you understand it is too dangerous."

Kohler appeared between Shan and Hostene, pacing slowly, playing with the end of the white cashmere scarf draped over his collar. He looked at them. "An illegal foreigner and an outlaw investigator. Perhaps they are trying to decide which side is most dangerous for them. Over there they merely have a crazed murderer to deal with."

"Heinz, perhaps you forget that Inspector Shan navigated the minefields of Beijing his entire career."

"Half a career," Shan inserted. "I prefer

to think of it as a rite of passage."

"What I don't forget," said Kohler, "is that he left us rather abruptly on his last visit."

"We won't be so careless this time," Gao observed. "We have summoned reinforcements from the base."

"I am going back," Hostene said. "The miners will cool off and then I must return. No one is going to stop me."

Gao shrugged. "I thought I mentioned the soldiers."

"They were already here," Hostene shot back. "You didn't summon them because of me."

Kohler rolled his eyes. Gao conceded the point with a nod.

"My niece is on the other side of the mountain. I will move heaven and earth to find her."

Gao shot a confused glance at Kohler. "Your niece? You let a young girl roam the mountain?"

"She is thirty-four years old and a professor of anthropology. We were together, a party of four, doing research."

Comprehension lit Gao's face. "The other two were the murder victims."

Hostene nodded soberly. "I think she believes that I am dead too. No one has seen her since the murders."

"I may have," Kohler declared. "Five days ago. With my binoculars."

Hostene stepped closer to Kohler, his eyes bright with excitement.

"You were on the other side?" Shan asked.

"Hunting wolves. Does she have long black braids? A gray sweatshirt? The woman I saw seemed to be taking measurements on a rock face. She kept stopping to look over her shoulder."

"But surely you went to investigate?" Hostene asked.

Kohler shrugged. "I was following a fresh trail. I planned to go back if I found the wolf or lost the trail. But I never saw him. And when I went back, she was nowhere to be seen. I'm sorry. I didn't know."

"Where was this?" Hostene asked.

Kohler withdrew a folded map from a bookshelf and laid it out on the dining table as Hostene and Shan pressed close. "Here." He pointed to a spot two miles above Little Moscow. "She didn't come down the slope or I would have seen her. And" — he gestured toward the set of undulating ridgelines, the steep terrain closer to the summit — "this is no man's land. She should have known better. I'm sorry," he added.

"What do you mean?"

"It's too dangerous up there. Wolves. And

the winds. Winds explode out of nowhere, strong enough to knock a man off a cliff. And as she goes higher, there is the lightning."

"Lightning?" Hostene asked. "Everyone makes so much of the lightning here. Surely it is no different from anywhere else."

"Wrong," Kohler rejoined. "Scientific fact. Some kind of geologic anomaly, probably related to all the iron in the mountain. We studied it before we set up the base below, to understand any possible effects on our radio telemetry. There are more lightning strikes here than on any mountain for hundreds of miles, maybe more than on any other mountain in all of China. Storms sweep over the Himalayas filled with water from the ocean. The moisture is dumped on the southern slopes, which is why Tibet stays so dry. But they still retain a lot of energy when they reach the northern side of the range. Sleeping Dragon Mountain is where they discharge it. The configuration of the ranges funnels storms to us. Metallic deposits at the top do the rest."

Hostene and Shan exchanged a worried glance. Lightning. Abigail was looking for the home of the mountain deity, the dragon that gave birth to lightning.

"I'm sorry," Kohler said in a sorrowful

tone. "I should have gone to save her."

"Save her?" Hostene asked, alarmed.

Kohler left the room for a few minutes, returning with a rag in his hand. "I did try to look for her later, and the next day as well. I think I may have seen her once more. I think it was her. A figure in the distance, standing on a high ledge, in an impossibly dangerous spot. A squall struck out of nowhere. The wind would have scoured that cliff of anything that wasn't tied down, even without the lightning. It was impossible to see what happened, with all the flashes. But afterward I went to the base of the cliff. I don't know who it was for certain. This is all I found."

Kohler tossed the rag onto the map. With a trembling hand, Hostene smoothed and straightened it. It was a piece of charred fabric from a gray sweatshirt. Despite several holes burned into it, the English words that encircled a small yellow sun rising over mountains were still legible. The surviving letters spelled The U ver ity of New Me ico.

Hostene buried his head in his hands.

"It could have been a miner," Kohler said. "I don't know. A miner could have found the shirt and worn it."

"It was a miner," came a voice from the

kitchen doorway. "It had to be." Thomas stood there, earphones around his neck.

"What haven't you told us?" Gao demanded.

Thomas sank into one of the chairs. "I thought I could find her. A day before the murders, I went past one of those old paintings that had been overgrown with brush, so you could hardly see it. Three days ago I went by it again and the painting had been uncovered. Someone had cut the brush down, and there were the fresh marks of a tripod in the soil."

Shan studied the boy as he spoke, remembering Thomas's warning that Gao intended to kill him if he crossed the mountain again. Had Thomas lied to him deliberately? Or had Gao changed his mind?

"Then yesterday I met a miner working by himself, singing a song. He had a new Swiss watch. A woman had given it to him, he said. She had traded it for his horse, asked him for directions to the nearest town, to Tashtul, and galloped off. She spoke Tibetan, but no Chinese."

Hostene hastened to Thomas and put a hand on his shoulder. "The watch, did you get a good look at it?"

"Silver. A red cross on the face. Little pieces of turquoise framed it."

"It's her! I gave her that watch! She finally realized her danger, and she left," Hostene said, relieved.

"Thank God," Kohler sighed. "I was going to town on business tomorrow," he announced. "I will leave today. If the army has a helicopter available I can be there before dark, probably before she gets there. Tashtul's a small town, and there's only one trail leading to it from here. An American woman on an exhausted horse shouldn't be hard to find."

It was the safest course, they quickly decided. Hostene would have difficulty navigating the long journey to the city alone, and Shan would not leave the mountain until Gendun and Lokesh were safe. But Hostene traveling with Kohler on a military aircraft might raise questions with Public Security that could not be conveniently answered. Kohler would have to make the trip alone.

Hostene visibly relaxed as Kohler reappeared, ready for travel, a pack on his back. The German shook the Navajo's hand energetically, assuring him his niece would be found safe. Then he took the trail that led to the base below.

The housekeeper brought bowls of soup. Shan and Hostene both consumed double servings before the Navajo accepted Gao's invitation to use a spare bedroom at the base of the tower, behind the kitchen.

"What am I going to do with you, Shan?" Gao asked as soon as they were alone.

"Help me find a murderer."

"No. That's not my job. And it's not yours either. Heinz is going to call Public Security when he reaches town. You haven't brought justice. You bring grief. You bring chaos. You bring crowds," he said. "You should leave the investigation to the authorities."

"That's what upsets you the most, isn't it? Being disturbed."

Gao's eyes narrowed. "I didn't pick this site by happenstance. I demanded anonymity. Secrecy. Privacy. A rather substantial investment has been to assure that I have it."

Privacy. It was, Shan well knew, the rarest treasure of all of China. "This is an elegant hermitage," he concluded. "Some make do with caves."

Gao ignored him. "The government can be tedious about protecting its investment."

Shan's stomach began tying itself into a knot. "What have you done?"

"I promised Kohler that you will dictate a transcript of what you know to Public Security when they arrive here tomorrow."

"And you worry about *me* disturbing the sanctity of your retreat? Wait until the Public Security knobs arrive. They will rip the mountain apart. Your little castle will be on the front page of American newspapers by the time they are done."

Gao studied Shan in silence, then frowned.

"Do you have any medical books?" Shan asked. "A dictionary of pharmaceuticals?"

Gao turned with a frosty gaze. "What do you wish to know?"

"Pencil and paper?"

Gao pointed to a drawer of the sideboard.

Shan quickly recorded the names of the medicines in Hostene's bag and handed the paper to Gao, who took it and went into his office. Shan stood to follow, thought better of the notion, then took more paper from the sideboard. He stared at the blank sheet for a long time, then wrote shorthand phrases describing events. A miner dies. Bing is elected to lead miners. Old mine destroyed. Abigail constructs a skeleton. Young miner killed at blue demon painting. Sandpainting destroyed. Professor Ma and Tashi, the guide, murdered. Camp equipment looted. Corpses mutilated and their hands taken away. Abigail's equipment removed from cave.

There were connections between each event he could not fathom. But did he even have the sequence properly? He studied the notes then added three more phrases. Yangke receives his canque. Hostene ventures into Bing's camp. Thomas, the fledgling entrepreneur, begins giving valuable goods to Rapaki, for which Rapaki cannot pay.

A thick reference book was slid across the table to him. Pages were marked with tabs of paper.

"Cancer," Gao declared. "These are drugs for someone who is in the advanced stages of cancer."

A new ache entered Shan's heart. He slowly opened the book and scanned the marked pages. "Could they be for something else?"

"No. They are highly specialized, very expensive. Not usually available in China," he added pointedly. "In this combination they have no other purpose. Drugs like these forestall the cancer from debilitating the body until it is in the final stage."

Shan stared without focusing, twisting the pencil that remained in his hand, reconsidering everything that had happened to Hostene: his coma, his fatigue, his having been passed over by the killer. The wise old

Navajo, who reminded him so much of Lokesh, was dying, and, worse, knew he was dying. Shan's confusion and sorrow took him to a dark, unfamiliar place, until suddenly the pencil broke and he snapped out of his trance.

"The motion detectors," he whispered at last, "how do they work?"

"Infrared heat signatures," Gao replied. "Solar powered cells with transmitters, all wireless."

"Where does the data go?"

"It is transmitted to the computer in my office and stored on the disc drive."

Five minutes later they sat at a small table in Gao's office, fast-forwarding through data from the prior twenty-four hours, watching the movement of vague yellow shapes across the screen as numbers indicating the time of transmission scrolled across the bottom left corner. The smallest blotches of color were the little creatures that nested on the rocky slope. Bigger patches of color were humans, although Gao had been warned by the soldiers to disregard patches that appeared at dawn and dusk in and out of certain rock formations, which represented groups of pikas entering and leaving their nests. "Sometimes false positives occur," he told Shan.

Gao pointed to a big shape moving up the slope from the house. "Kohler going hunting," he said, then indicated the two shapes that represented Shan and Hostene arriving that morning. They watched movements back and forth from the house. "Thomas helps the housekeeper bring in supplies. In the summer dry goods are kept in the old granary."

Shan noted the times of the movements to and from the little building. "Does Thomas go only around meal times?"

"Heinz and I made him responsible for keeping an inventory, a serious job since we can't run out to a shop when we're out of a necessity."

"You could always call Public Security for salt and rice," Shan observed. He was still resentful of what Gao was.

"The Party secretary would respond immediately," Gao replied in a stiff tone. "But regional commanders are not always as accommodating."

Shan stared at the screen as the display of the data entries finished, then asked Gao to run them again. He had missed the quick blurs of color on the upper left corner of the field on the first run-through but noted them on the second. He asked Gao for one more replay. A glow that,

301

though fleeting, indicated a human, re-appeared.

Gao took Shan to the main entrance and pointed out the location of the scanners. Shan noted blind spots; infrared light did not register through rocks. There were a lot of low spines of stone along which someone could have crawled undetected. Shan pointed out where the unknown intruder could have circled the house.

"Could it have been someone from the village?"

"No. They are not welcome here," Gao replied.

"But they do come. Bearing gifts."

"Nothing I ask for. That fool Chodron arrives every spring, kowtowing, bringing me tokens. I think he believes he keeps the soldiers away by doing so."

"But recently he sent you something else. A gold beetle."

"He sought my help in removing some intruders from the mountain," Gao said. "I declined to get involved." He studied the screen again.

"Could it be the guards?" Shan asked.

"No. They usually come twice a day, check the system, then walk around the perimeter of the house, and leave. I sent them away until tomorrow. If they knew a foreigner was here, so close to the base, it could be" — he paused to select a word — "problematic." Gao frowned, stared at the now blank screen, then walked to his office window. Someone seemed to be watching his house. Someone who, knowing that the scanners were operating, was using the cover of the rocks to come and go, leaving only the most slender traces.

"Why did this American come here if he is dying?" the physicist asked after a moment.

"Perhaps to prove he is still alive," Shan suggested.

But Gao answered his own question. "How many places on the planet are so completely removed from the eyes of any authority? Surely there are no more left in America."

"Hostene did not come to Tibet to commit a crime."

"We know he has already committed crimes. He achieved admission to the country under false pretenses, no doubt involving a lie on his visa application. He's trespassing in a restricted region. We know he is a criminal, even if we don't know the full list of his crimes."

"I trust him."

Gao stared at Shan, and shook his head in

disappointment. "You live in a fairy tale, Shan. You will have to grow out of it."

Shan searched Gao's face. Another time he might have taken the remark as a bitter joke. But now Shan saw no mockery in Gao's expression, which seemed to reflect his own sorrow.

"*You* live a fairy-tale life, Gao," he echoed. "A make-believe existence in a make-believe castle. You know you will have to grow out of it."

Shan had been slapped in the face by such men for much less. But Gao merely left the room. Shan stared at the screen again, glanced at the door, then quickly closed the program, and scanned the pile of papers in the tray beside the fax machine. Thomas had sent several messages to Beijing recently, each confirming that he had dispatched a new package of evidence — photos, fingerprints, and, later, fibers from the bloody cloth stuffed in the mouth of one of the victims.

Shan found Gao at the telescope, gazing at the distant nest of vultures. "I'm worried about Albert," Gao said. "He leans out of the nest too far. He does not have his flight feathers yet."

"Before you learn to fly," Shan observed, "you must learn to fear."

Gao continued to study the young birds of prey. "We can take a day or two and delay sending Hostene away," he said. "It would give me time to get a doctor to look at him. Neither of us wants him to die while he is on this mountain."

"If he dies on this mountain," Shan replied, "it will not be from cancer."

Gao shrugged and stepped toward his sand garden below. "For now we shall let sleeping Americans lie."

But Shan couldn't let things rest. He found the Navajo's pack and recharged the battery of the video camera. He had spent a quarter hour reviewing Abigail's videos when Thomas appeared from the kitchen, carrying an empty basket, wearing a black linen shirt. "Let's discuss the evidence," he said in a conspiratorial whisper. "After I finish my chores," he added.

Shan hurried to Hostene's side and shook him, gesturing for him to keep silent. He lifted the camera and pointed to a long silver object lying on a rock. "Whose is that?" he asked in a whisper.

"Tashi's," Hostene said with a yawn. "His pen case. He kept little drawings and things in it. You woke me up for that?"

"No," Shan replied. "You must come with me to the granary," he said urgently.

305

Hostene stretched. "That old stone ruin? Why?"

"Because of a ghost in the motion detectors," Shan said. "And because Thomas put on a clean shirt to go get groceries."

CHAPTER SEVEN

They approached the granary as they had before, running together from rock to rock, using the shadows for cover until they reached the plank door of the low stone structure. If Gao happened to open the monitoring program, he might assume the movement on the screen was caused by Thomas. Shan glanced at the padlock that hung open from the door's hasp and peered inside. He saw a second door beyond a stack of rice and onion sacks, on top of which sat a small lantern. There was no sign of Thomas. He withdrew, whispered to Hostene, then both men slipped around the side of the structure.

Thomas emerged fifteen minutes later, setting his basket, now filled with foodstuffs, on a rock in front of the door before he turned to fasten the padlock.

"Did you know the miners tried to kill us yesterday?" Shan asked as he came around the corner.

For a moment Thomas looked as if he was going to attack Shan. Then he shrugged. "That Bing," the youth said, "he tells people that they should still consider him to be Public Security, but without all the red tape."

"They're not hard to beat, Thomas," Shan observed, pointing to the nearest motion detector. "By shifting each a quarter turn you could create a corridor where they are blind. Or if you set a lighted candle in front of one, you blind that sensor."

Thomas cast an uncertain glance toward Shan. Then, acting on Shan's suggestion, he began turning the little metal box. Shan sensed Hostene behind him, going inside. Thomas paused, as if he too had sensed something. They heard a low moan from within the building.

Thomas sagged, and for a moment looked as if he was about to flee. "You tricked me," he said, wounded.

The sounds from inside turned to muffled cries of joy, then a low, feminine sobbing.

Thomas lowered himself onto a rock. "You wouldn't believe what she knows about rock and roll," he said. "She drives a car with satellite radio. It receives two hundred fifty stations. She says when I finish in Beijing she'll help me gain admission to a graduate program in America."

Shan gave Hostene five more minutes. Inside, Abigail Natay was crying on her uncle's shoulder. She scrubbed away her tears with the sleeve of her denim shirt and extended a hand to Shan, shyly smiling. "Some of the old Tibetans have told me there are things too important to be put into mere words," she said in a voice husky with emotion. "I guess one of those would be how I feel about your bringing my uncle back from the dead."

A remarkable opening from a stranger, Shan thought. But she wasn't a stranger, he reminded himself. She was the familiar image on the video camera screen. He self-consciously accepted her hand. "The old Tibetans would say he still has a destiny in this incarnation," he said.

Abigail replied, "Your mountain is the most beautiful and terrifying place I have ever known."

"One thing I have not been able to figure out," Shan replied, "is just whose mountain this is." He almost added that sometimes it seemed that if he could only solve that mystery all the others would fall into place.

Hostene and his niece began speaking, sometimes reverting to their native tongue.

Abigail showed her uncle the cozy nest of blankets among the stores of supplies where Thomas had hidden her in the inner chamber. A blue nylon backpack lying open near the door revealed a small digital camera, a plastic bag of toiletries, and half a dozen ketaan sticks.

Thomas, downcast and silent, ventured into the granary and settled onto a wooden crate near Shan. "You tricked me," he repeated.

"*You* tricked all of us," Shan rejoined.

Thomas clasped his hands together and stared at them.

Strangely, Shan felt sorry for the youth. "I still need to review your investigation notes," he ventured, "and I still need to hear how you met her, and when. Was it with Rapaki?"

"I take things to him. Uncle Heinz thinks he's a good-luck charm, like when a singing bird nests in your eaves. We communicate in pantomime, since I know no Tibetan."

Shan paused. "But you speak English with Abigail?"

"Sure. Anyway, I saw him a month ago and pulled out a box of sweet biscuits to give him. He started waving in another direction, singing one of his songs. He was showing me Abigail coming up the trail.

Like some kind of goddess. Who would have thought of seeing someone like her on this mountain?"

"Then you'd met her before the murders?"

Thomas nodded. "But she won't speak about them. Maybe knowing her uncle is alive will make a difference."

Shan asked, "Did you see her this morning?"

"Early this morning, on the way to Little Moscow."

"You ran away from there to warn her?"

The youth nodded again. "You made sure all of the miners knew she was still alive," Thomas pointed out.

Shan studied him, worried now. "You mean you're convinced the killer was there, among the miners?"

"He must be," Thomas said. "At least that's my hypothesis. I need a credible theory or my project is a failure."

Tears started flowing down Abigail's cheek as she uttered two names: Tashi and Dr. Ma. She leaned against Hostene's shoulder again, then gasped as she gazed past Shan.

A figure had materialized in the doorway. Kohler's hunting rifle was cradled in one of Gao's arms, and he held one of the small radio units he used to summon soldiers from below. His face, which had at first displayed a mixture of emotions, now showed cold anger. As he neared his nephew, Abigail stepped between Gao and Thomas. "I asked him to hide me," she said in a level voice in English. "He said he had a safe place where I could rest for a while. I said I would go only if I could remain invisible. He was trying to help me, to protect me."

Gao studied the Navajo woman in silence, taking in her heavy hiking boots, her scuffed blue jeans, the belt pack from which ink pens protruded, the turquoise pendant hanging from her neck on a silver chain, her long braided hair, her dark, intelligent eyes, full of challenge. "Invisible?"

"I have to finish my work, for which I must stay on the western slope without being noticed."

Gao looked past the American woman to his nephew. "You deceived us, Thomas," he said. "You have stolen from me and from the government, which pays for everything here. For what, to be a black marketeer? To disgrace us and never be allowed back to the university?"

Abigail looked from Gao to Thomas, her quick, bright eyes taking everything in. "It was for me," she declared. "The murderer took all my food supplies. I will gladly pay you back."

Gao's steady gaze shifted from his nephew to Abigail. "You misunderstand me. I refer to the goods he has been *selling* on the other side," he said. Thomas cast a confused glance at Shan then, understanding, shut his eyes. There was only one way Gao could have found this out. Thomas's other uncle had told him. Gao, still gazing at the Navajo woman, suddenly became self-conscious about the rifle. He lowered it, putting it behind him. "We have not been properly introduced, Miss Natay."

"You are Gao Hu Bo, the most famous phantom physicist on the planet."

Gao seemed unable to restrain his lips from momentarily curling upward. He glanced back at Thomas. "This must stop," he said to the youth. "Everything. Keep up the playacting and I will arrange for a sergeant the size of a yak to escort you back to Beijing." He bowed slightly to Abigail and Hostene. "If it is not inconvenient we will dine in thirty minutes. Enough time for a hot shower if you like," he added to Abigail. Then, still awkwardly keeping the gun out of sight, he gestured Thomas and Shan to the door.

■ ■ ■ ■

Abigail was radiant when she walked into the candlelit dining room, greeting her uncle with another long embrace and affectionate words in their tribal tongue, smiling at Shan, then asking a surprised Gao where the altar had been in the old dzong before it was converted since, as all Tibetans knew, such places had been garrisoned by warrior monks. She guided the conversation as if she were a hostess to old friends, expressing her regret at not meeting Thomas's German uncle, entrancing Gao by describing a workshop she had once attended on the cultural aspects of space travel — Russians always insisted on bringing some form of borscht into space, Americans always wanted more privacy in the living quarters. She looked forward to seeing what the Chinese would introduce to the mélange. Gao was fascinated by the theories behind Abigail's work on the mountain, though quick to point out what a simple thing it should be to compare the writings, the social structure, the dress, and even architecture of the two peoples.

"By definition, that is impossible," Abigail explained. "The Tibetans became a sedentary civilization long ago. For thousands of years my people were nomads, until only two centuries ago. What I am trying to reconstruct is the prototype, the people who existed before the split, then postulate what would happen once they split, one developing printing, colleges, the substantial social structure that is possible in a fixed and fertile geography while the other, nomadic for centuries, was unable to develop printed books or even a written language, unable to develop a substantial social structure beyond the family unit because they never stayed in one place long enough. It is as if a planet left the gravitational field of a solar system. How do you prove the lost planet once belonged to it?"

Gao seemed to be in his element, offering other analogies from the physical sciences, observing the coincidence that both peoples had settled on the highest plateaus of their respective continents.

"So you are building a model of the Tibetans ten or fifteen thousand years ago," Shan recapitulated.

"Exactly. Professor Ma and I were developing one. The original people were fierce soldiers. They were deeply philosophical. They were resourceful, adapting to severe environments, and not just in a physical sense. They interacted with earth and sky in a primal way."

"Spirit warriors," Shan suggested.

Abigail nodded. "You begin to understand," she said, and described the reasons she suspected the early Tibetans did not distinguish between physical and spiritual endurance.

Gao studied them both with an expression of curiosity, then excused himself for a moment, bringing back a small cardboard box. "I believe this belongs to you," he told Abigail.

It was the golden beetle. Abigail, unable to contain her gratitude, grabbed Gao's hand in both of hers and, as he blushed, pumped it up and down. She explained that it was a family heirloom, a protective charm made by a Spanish artisan for an ancestor who was one of her people's holy men in the eighteenth century, handed down to his daughter and the first daughter of each generation thereafter. To daughters, because the Navajo were a matriarchal society and the corn beetle was a symbol of fertility.

As Thomas asked to examine the beetle Abigail praised him as demonstrating the intellectual energy of a great scientist in the making. "I have no doubt he saved my life," she said.

"He's a student, Miss Natay," Gao said in a polite voice. "In China there are far too few universities of the first rank. If he engages in questionable conduct he will be banned. There are a thousand other qualified students waiting for his place."

"She says she can help me to qualify for university in America," Thomas blurted out.

Gao ignored his nephew. "Thomas has a great career ahead of him after he settles down. Heinz and I have conquered the mysteries of the earth. Thomas will conquer mysteries off the earth. I have decided to remove him from the temptations he has here. I am sending him to Beijing. I spoke to his parents this evening."

The color drained from Thomas's face as he stared at his uncle. "But you said you would give me another chance," he protested.

"I reconsidered. I began to realize how many lies you must have told us. You stood in front of us and lied about Miss Natay going to Tashtul. Your uncle Heinz has been put to a lot of trouble to find her."

"But it was to protect me," Abigail said.

Gao ignored her. "Thomas has been crossing over the mountain frequently, deceiving us, knowing we forbid it, telling me he is looking at wildlife."

Shan considered the words a moment. Gao must have spoken on the phone with Kohler, now in Tashtul. "Thomas could be useful here," Shan interjected. "He is helping us discover the murderers of Tashi and Dr. Ma."

"The truth stares you in the face." Gao's patience was wearing thin. "But you refuse to accept it because it is so mundane. The killers were miners. They are greedy, opportunistic creatures, rats that salivate as soon as a bell is rung. Was there ever any doubt as to what would become of wealthy strangers who stumbled into their lair? Every one of them is a criminal by definition. I am sorry, but the moment word spread that you were trespassers without protection, your party was doomed. Once they knew no one would miss you, no one would complain of your absence, your fate was sealed."

"We're not wealthy," Hostene interjected.

"To people like these, all foreigners are wealthy. You became a target the moment you set foot on the mountain. Your companions should have known better, and they paid for the mistake with their lives. Americans are notorious for not taking no for an answer. But it's finished. Go home. When you think of your tragedy in the future tell yourself it was an attack by wild animals. An accident of nature."

A brittle silence fell over the table.

Shan, who had been looking down, felt Gao's gaze.

"I see Inspector Shan disagrees," Gao observed.

"What you say could be true," Shan responded. "I don't know. What I do know is that one thing connecting the acts of violence on this mountain has been the kora. It is like a common thread in a long bloody fabric."

"That's nonsense," Gao said. "You've spent too many years locked up with old Tibetans."

Shan gazed at Abigail as he continued. "Every killing has been at a station of the pilgrim path. You have been studying the path, trying to find its upper terminus, as has the hermit Rapaki for forty years. It's like a three-way contest."

"Three-way?" Hostene asked.

"Abigail, Rapaki, and the killer have been converging."

Abigail stared at Shan, searching his face as if for an answer. Then she began making small talk like a good hostess, asking Thomas about his life in Beijing, about Chinese rock and roll.

Her uncle tossed the fragment of burned sweatshirt onto the table as Shan asked Abigail, "Did you meet a man named Bing?"

The American professor looked at her burned sweatshirt in confusion, then nodded. "Twice. The first time I found him sitting on a rock, watching me as I worked. Tashi came running up as if to protect me, but Bing seemed very polite, almost charming. They spoke for a few minutes and then Bing left." She fingered the charred fabric. "This was left in our camp that night. The last night."

"What did Tashi and Bing talk about?"

"I don't know, I didn't hear it all. The weather, the wolves. . . . Tashi told him I was Tibetan, from Lhasa. I don't know if Bing believed him."

"And about gold?"

"Of course not."

"Did Tashi seem to know Bing already?"

Abigail hesitated. "Tashi was from the village. I expected him to know people here. He was paid to be our guide. That included guiding us around the people. We couldn't afford to let anyone know what we were doing."

Bing was not native to the mountain. He had only arrived the year before. And Tashi had been away for several years.

"You said twice," Shan pointed out.

"I saw Bing again just a couple days ago. He was throwing things off a cliff when I came up the trail. He didn't notice me at first."

"What things?"

"They weren't new. They may have been washed down one of the streams after a storm. It happens." Abigail shrugged. "What do you do with them? It's awkward. Most people simply want to be rid of them."

Hostene leaned forward in his chair. "I don't understand, Abigail."

"Bones. I saw a tibia, a fibula, at least one femur." She spoke the words with such ease it almost seemed she was speaking about the weather. It took a moment before she noticed that everyone else had stopped eating.

"Bones, Miss Natay?" Gao asked.

"Bones. Old bones. It's to be expected. In my business I encounter them all the time. People have lived on this mountain for hundreds of years. He threw something else after the bones. I couldn't see it clearly because I'd hidden behind a rock. He scared me a little. It was something he could toss with one hand. When he had finished he came down the trail so quickly he was in front of me before I realized it."

"What did he do?"

"He hesitated, then came to shake my hand in a friendly way. He seemed to be in a hurry. I spoke in Tibetan, only Tibetan, like the first time. He smiled and bowed. He looked at my pack, at my cameras, then he waved goodbye and trotted down the trail. A few minutes later I saw him on the slope below, riding one of those red mountain bikes."

Shan asked Gao for the map Kohler had used, and Abigail pointed to each of the spots where she had seen Bing. One was near the old gold mine, the other near the ridge that the miners believed to be haunted.

"It will take a day to make arrangements," Gao informed them as he poured tea for his guests at the end of the meal.

"Arrangements?" Shan asked.

"By tomorrow night we will have transport lined up. Professor Natay and her uncle will be taken by helicopter to a quiet border post whose commander is a friend of mine. They will leave the country without undergoing a lot of uncomfortable questions from Public Security. On its return the helicopter will pick up you and Thomas."

Shan felt his stomach tighten.

"Thomas," Gao continued, "will be taken

to the airport in Lhasa for a flight to Beijing, with a soldier for his escort. The helicopter will stop at Drango village and soldiers will remove your friends from that man Chodron's custody." Gao folded the map and tucked it under his arm, then fixed Shan with a cool gaze. "Their orders will be to drop you and your Tibetan companions anywhere you say in Lhadrung County, where you came from. A high ledge miles from any town will not be objectionable."

"A generous offer," Shan admitted. "But there is still a murderer out there." He fought the temptation to embrace Gao's proposal. He and both his old friends could soon be far removed from the agonies of Sleeping Dragon Mountain if he accepted it.

"Wolves have a way of settling disputes within their own packs."

"I have my work still —" Thomas's protest was cut off by a glare from his uncle.

"Thomas! Feng Xi," Gao said, his voice growing heated. "You are like a son to me. That is why I am doing this. You must leave your childhood games behind. You will act like a responsible adult and return to your studies. Or you can return to Beijing and sell noodles on the street. Either way, you are going back tomorrow." Gao glanced at

Shan. "There will be a doctor in the helicopter. And there will be soldiers stationed across the passage to the other side of the mountain until we can find a more permanent way to seal it." He stood, blew out the candles, and left the room.

The housekeeper showed Abigail and Hostene to their quarters in the tower. Shan studied Abigail's videotapes again. When he reentered the sitting room Thomas was there, frowning.

Gao's nephew said in a desolate tone, "I read somewhere that when you are sent to the gulag you gradually forget everything about your life before, that none of it seems real anymore, that your memories become like a movie of someone else's life."

"Where you are going is a long way from the gulag."

"Living in a cage, living someone else's idea of your life, I think they're not much different."

"A gilded cage. There are scores of millions who would gladly trade places with you."

"So you agree with my uncle. I should just put my dreams on a shelf and let them gather dust." Thomas looked at the floor. "If you ever return to Beijing, you'll know where to find me. Just ask for the most highly educated noodle seller in the city."

"There are professors at the forensics academy who might still accept a letter from me. Give me your address in Beijing and I will write them. Perhaps they will give you special projects even if you are not officially enrolled."

Thomas quickly wrote out his address.

"How often did you see Professor Natay?" Shan asked as he tucked the paper in his pocket.

"You mean after the murders? Twice, before yesterday. The first time she was working and didn't mention the murders. She didn't think I knew about them, so she wasn't going to tell me. But she was so upset that she almost couldn't talk. She asked me if I could get her a gun. Then she asked me how tall a Tibetan would have been five hundred years ago. She said she had realized something important — that on a pilgrim trail a sinner could walk beside a saint, that maybe when people died on this mountain it was intended, as part of the kora, as if its true purpose was not to reach the end, but to attain something along the way, to help people reach their next incarnation." The words cast an odd chill over Shan. People reached their next incarnation by dying.

"I think she may have spoken that way because she was starving. I gave her all the food I had with me. The next time I saw her she was not so upset. She asked what kind of music I liked. We spoke about rock and roll. It was strange in a way that she never spoke about the thing on her hand."

"What thing?"

"The eye. She had painted a white eye on her hand. It was still there yesterday morning when I saw her. She rubbed it off later."

Shan gestured toward the bedrooms in the tower. "After a night's sleep," Shan said as they climbed the stone stairs, "we can both speak with her. I want to find out exactly what she saw when she returned to the campsite that morning."

But Shan could not sleep. He left his bedchamber, climbed to the top of the tower, and lay on the cold stone floor, facing the night sky. In another twenty-four hours he and his friends would be free. They could forget Chodron, forget the gruesome murders, go back to the restoration of old manuscripts and day-long meditation among the other secret monks of their hermitage. He began rehearsing the words he would use with Gendun and Lokesh: the violence on the mountain was not of their making, it only affected the miners, who

326

were outlaws themselves. Hostene and his niece were going to be safe. Gendun and Lokesh had a duty to remain safe as well.

But an internal voice grew in volume, intruding on his frail hopes. Gendun would never leave willingly, not with the people of Drango so spiritually distraught. Shan would have to ask Gao's soldiers to forcibly remove him, and that act would forever stand between them. The way to save Gendun was one that guaranteed Shan could no longer sit at his side.

Many of the monks who had once inhabited Tibet had followed an often terrifying meditation ritual called *chod.* They would spend a night in a charnel ground, with bloody remnants of human corpses and bird-gnawed bones all around them, as a way of underscoring the fragile, transient nature of living creatures. Shan had found his own form of chod. The tower, inhabited by the old Navajo dying of cancer, the young woman whose spirit was adrift, the boy whose hopes had shriveled before Shan's eyes, was a place where dreams died. Not far away in Drango village, Gendun was being tortured because of Shan and a few acts of reverence by the villagers. The village itself was being slowly strangled by Chodron. And he had no hope of helping any of them unless he found the killer.

He went to a dark, deep place within himself, not exactly meditating but not sleeping, visiting memories, remembering nightmares, unaware of time or place.

It was always damp inside the tool shed, and the burlap sacks they hung to block the light of their candle were stained with mildew, the scent sometimes mixing so strongly with that of the night soil in the rice paddies outside that he would become nauseous when he entered it. As usual, he sucked a pebble as a remedy for hunger as he waited, arranging and rearranging his shirt so his father would not see how his ribs poked out. Food was strictly rationed at the reeducation camp, and the inmates of the children's dormitory only received what was left when the field workers were finished. Sawdust was sometimes mixed with the rice gruel, which usually cramped his nine-year-old stomach so severely he had to lie on his bunk, unable to walk.

He passed the time silently repeating the Taoist verses his father had taught him the night before, struggling not to cringe at the small sounds of the night. If he was caught outside he would be caned until the bamboo came away bloody.

There was a rush of movement and the door was flung open and closed. There was a rustling of clothes, the flare of a match lighting a candle, and all hardships disappeared. His father was there, embracing his son, his gentle smile marred by the missing front tooth that had been knocked out in a tamzing. Officially, at the reeducation camp, parents and children were separated. Officially, the punishment for Shan's father, the professor, would be far worse than Shan's if he was found to have broken the rules of curfew, the rules against having unapproved books, the rules against candles.

They worked for an hour in the little shed at the back of the rice paddies, reciting the Taoist verses, reviewing another segment of European history then, the best always last, looking over a page torn from the book of poetry from the Sung Dynasty that Shan's father had secretly, illegally, brought from home. It was their favorite, Su Tung-po, the poet bureaucrat:

Grasses bury the riverbank, rain darkens
  the village.
The temple is lost in tall bamboo — I can't
  find the gate.

Together they wrote the words in chalk on

the plank wall of the shed, his father's hand sometimes guiding him in the strokes of the complicated old-style ideograms. Then they spoke of how they had spent their days, Shan trying not to take notice when his father's words were interrupted by long hacking coughs. His father let Shan lean on his shoulder as he spoke of older, happier times, so lost in their reverie that neither heard the sounds until too late. They were still sitting in the corner when the handlers burst in, lanterns in their faces, batons lashing out at his father. The last sight he had of his father for a month was of the professor stuffing the poem into his mouth. The next morning Shan had a bowl of real rice and vegetables, even shreds of chicken. Later that day, the political instructors praised his mother for having turned in his father for reactionary behavior. It took much longer for him to understand the bargain she had struck: she had done it in exchange for Shan's single square meal.

Suddenly he noticed the gibbous moon high overhead. Hours had passed. Inside, the tower was still, lit only by dim bulbs along the stairwell. Hostene's door, previously closed, was ajar. Shan pushed it open, confirming that the Navajo still slept soundly. But on top of one of his boots was a slip of paper.

Shan hesitated, then with a pang of guilt lifted the paper and took it to the stairwell, where he held it under one of the bulbs. He read it once, then again. He sat down, blinking at the words, confusion burning away his fatigue as he read them over and over:

In Beauty before me I walk
In Beauty all around me I walk
It is finished in Beauty.

It seemed to take a long time for him to cross the room toward Hostene's bed. He paused, listening to his friend's peaceful breathing, gazing at the objects he held in his hands. He had removed the large feather from inside his vest, the feather he had brought from home, found a short stick, and tied the feather to it with thread taken from the sheet, inserting several smaller colorful feathers around the base of the larger one. Clasped in his fingers at the base of the feather stick was the small leather pouch Shan had seen hidden inside his vest. Devout Navajos, Hostene had told him, carried with them a pouch of soil from the Navajo sacred mountains.

With another stab of guilt Shan retreated

into the stairwell. But then he read the note again, went back inside, and shook his friend's shoulder.

Hostene shot upright, squinting at Shan in the dim light.

"Get dressed," Shan said, handing him the verse. "Abigail has gone back to the kora, to the path of the murderer."

Outside, the motion detectors had been pushed over so that they faced the ground. The granary door had been left open. The pack that had contained Abigail's field equipment was gone. Several cartons of canned goods had been ripped open and some of their contents removed.

"She wouldn't steal," Hostene said in a worried voice.

"What do they mean," Shan asked, "the words she wrote?"

"They are from a prayer used by my people, for summoning the holy ones," Hostene replied.

They moved quietly, pausing at every outcropping that offered cover, aware that Gao had promised to put a guard at the passage, not knowing how far in front of them Abigail was, but knowing that she was not alone. Thomas's bedroom had been empty as well.

They waited for a cloud to cover the moon

before they ventured to the last outcropping before the summit, then watched, waiting. As the moon reappeared, Hostene uttered a hoarse gasp and pointed to a shape lying beneath the cartoonlike painting of the Buddha. Shan thought it could be a rock at first, then saw the glow of teeth near the ground.

Hostene rushed forward. "My God!" he moaned. "What have they done?"

Shan's stomach almost turned as he saw the small fleshy kernels oozing out of the soldier's hairline. But then he sniffed. As he took the man's pulse he noticed two cylinders lying on the ground. "It's not what you think," he explained to Hostene. "Someone threw cans of corn at him. One hit the rocks and exploded. He probably bent to investigate and was hit on the head with the second. But his pulse is strong."

Hostene helped Shan to clean the man's head and prop him up. Shan took the rifle that lay beside the soldier, removed the clip of bullets from the weapon, pulled the spare clips from the man's belt, and threw them all high overhead, out of sight. Hostene removed a small, high-power flashlight from the soldier's belt and switched it on. Together they entered the shadowy passage.

They moved quickly, both men stumbling frequently on the loose gravel underfoot,

Hostene pausing sometimes to shine the light behind them, certain he heard sounds of pursuit.

When they reached patches of soil, Shan took the flashlight and examined the ground. The first prints, of Abigail's boots, were single sets. A second set appeared later, often superimposed on the first. But after a mile the tracks proceeded side by side. Thomas had followed, then caught up with Abigail.

"He's running away from his uncle," Hostene said.

"Not exactly," Shan replied. "Running away is part of it. But he could have gone in any direction, all of which would have been safer than this one. He followed her to protect her. A brave thing, considering he has seen the killer's work up close." Shan paused. "What is it, Hostene?" he asked. "Why is it so urgent for Abigail to complete her work on the other side?"

But Hostene didn't answer as he passed Shan and entered the darkness.

The Navajo waited for Shan to cross the ladder bridge first, then began his transit, upright this time. He was nearly at the far end when he froze. An owl, the biggest Shan had yet seen on the mountain, came flying straight at him, nearly touching his scalp with its talons as it swooped by, then wheeled and returned in the direction from which it had come. Hostene began to lose his balance, his arms flailing the air, his body swaying, the flashlight flying out of his grip.

Shan darted back onto the ladder, grabbing Hostene's arm an instant before it seemed he would surely fall onto the sharp rocks below. But as he did so, the dry old wood began to crack under their combined weight. When they reached the end of the ladder Shan pushed Hostene forward and leaped onto the rocks.

Hostene soon assumed the lead again, moving more rapidly, as if he sensed a destination close ahead. When they emerged from the cleft in the rock wall, the sky had taken on a bright predawn blush, lighting three lanky shapes lurking at an outcropping fifty yards away. The wolves were hesitant to leave, not reacting to the first stone Shan threw at them, only trotting away when both men moved closer and began pelting them with gravel.

As Shan watched, the animals stopped and looked back with fear in their eyes, not at him, but at the shadows beyond the outcropping.

It wasn't fear Shan felt as he saw what lay

behind the rocks, it wasn't fear that sapped his strength so quickly that he fell to his knees. It was the black mood that had seized him the night before, his bleak despair now redoubled, hitting him like a club, roiling his stomach, numbing him.

Thomas had a slight grin on his face, frozen in place, as if he thought his assailant had been joking with him. His eyes stared vacantly into the dawn sky. A stream of blood trickled from his scalp, though it seemed unlikely the blow to the head had killed him, for the large pools of blood at the ends of his outstretched arms and the stains on the adjoining rocks showed that his heart had still been pumping when his hands were severed.

CHAPTER EIGHT

Shan meant to stop Hostene from entering the little rock-walled chamber but he was unable to make his body act. The old Navajo stood beside him uttering an anguished moan then, staggering, dropped onto a rock. When Shan was finally able to move, he looked up to see Hostene staring at the corpse, a single tear rolling down his cheek.

"Abigail," he said in a hoarse voice.

"This time," Shan said, "I think the killer did take her." He gestured into the shadows where a pack of hair ties, a small battery, and a toothbrush lay on the ground. Someone had tipped over Abigail's pack.

Hostene wiped his cheek. "We have to follow, quickly."

"There will be no trail. And if he wanted her dead, she would be lying here beside Thomas. Can you find that cave again, Rapaki's cave?" Hostene nodded. "Then you must go there and bring back Yangke, as fast as you can. But if you see any miners you must hide."

Hostene nodded again. Before he left the rock circle he picked up Abigail's toothbrush and pocketed it, then surveyed the sky, wary not of killers but of owls.

Swallowing his despair, Shan studied the scene, retracing the two sets of boot prints that led from the passage to the cluster of rocks. Abigail and Thomas had stopped, taken several small, shifting steps as if undecided about something, then walked straight to the rocks, as though someone had called them. While the killer was performing his grisly work, what had he done with Abigail? She owed Thomas a debt. Shan did not think she would have fled if she had seen him attacked. Had the killer knocked her unconscious, then bound and gagged her? Or had she been bound and gagged but awake, forced to watch as the killer stretched out each of Thomas's arms and butchered him?

Shan fought down another wave of nausea, then forced himself to study the bloody stumps at the end of Thomas's arms. The left had been taken off with one clean chop, the right with two, leaving an uneven line on the bone where the blade had stopped the first time. The edge of the blade had been chipped, which probably meant it was made of either cheap steel or old, brittle, forge-worked metal. The tight pattern of blood reached across the ground onto a rock five feet away, leaving no doubt that Thomas had been alive when his hands had been amputated. But even with such ghastly injuries, a youth in prime health might have survived. Shan bent over Thomas's head, noting for the first time the burst capillaries in his corneas, the discoloration around his mouth. With another chill Shan looked back at the hair ties and the battery on the ground. He remembered seeing them in the granary. They had been in a plastic bag. The killer had been patient, proceeding as if he had all the time in the world. He had covered Thomas's head with the bag and waited for the unconscious, bleeding youth to suffocate.

Shan's legs became weak twigs. He lowered himself onto the ground, staring, unfocused, at the boy. Thomas had been so alive, so full of defiance and ambition, much like Shan's own son. He had been beaten down, had reacted by fleeing, escorting his new American patron to the deadly side of the mountain. Only the day before his uncle had told him he was finished with his childhood.

When Shan finally found the strength to rise, he walked in ever-widening circles around the site of the murder, eventually finding the plastic bag tucked into a crack in a large boulder. Except for a few drops of blood in a line leading up the slope there were no tracks, no evidence of the direction the killer had taken, no sign at all of Abigail Natay. Thomas and Abigail had been doomed the moment they had stepped out of the narrow passage. But how did the killer know they were on their way through the passage? No one should have expected them, they were meant never to return to the western slope again. But the miners had been prowling, filled with blood lust. A miner from Little Moscow could have been there, waiting for Shan and Hostene. Thomas might have been his poor second choice, when his intended targets did not appear. But the hands! Even if a miner seeking revenge had severed the hands, surely he would not have taken them away.

The ledges of rock would have afforded an untraceable route for anyone leaving the scene. The short line of blood, probably drops from the severed hands, led upward toward the miles of rugged, undulating terrain that rose toward the summit.

Gravel rattled behind him. Shan spun about to see Yangke, slowing from a frantic pace, bent over, hands on knees, panting.

"You have to go to the village, to Chodron," Shan said.

"I'd rather seek a pack of wolves."

Shan's reply was to gesture toward the outcropping. "The bridge ladder is gone. Even if it were still there, we couldn't carry a body across it."

Yangke's eyes filled with pain. Shan did not follow him into the circle of boulders but waited, watching the slopes, wondering what reason a man could have for collecting human hands on Sleeping Dragon Mountain. When the Tibetan finally reappeared his face was drained of color. He walked as if the canque were on his neck once more. "It's him, isn't it? The Gao boy. This is the end of everything. The army will take over both sides of the mountain now."

"Go. Tell Chodron who the victim is. Tell him to send four men with a blanket and two poles, for a stretcher. Tell him to reach Professor Gao on his radio, but only Gao, no one from down below. Gao should bring a helicopter to Drango in" — Shan did some quick mental calculations — "six hours' time. I will go to the cave for Lokesh."

Yangke glanced forlornly back toward the body. "There's no point. You should run. Get your friends and flee. I remember hearing about a Chinese prince, centuries ago. He was murdered in a village somewhere. The emperor couldn't tell who was responsible so he had everyone in the village killed. Whoever murdered Thomas has killed us all." Yangke looked longingly toward the wild mountains to the south, where a man could lose himself, then back at Shan. He began to trot down the trail toward Drango village.

It was a slow, silent procession. Four men carried Thomas's body tied to the makeshift stretcher, Shan and Yangke alternately bearing Lokesh on their backs. Even Chodron was pale and subdued when he met them at the top of the fields. He ignored Shan who was walking beside the stretcher. He had arranged a plank table by one of the stone granaries and covered it with a piece of black felt.

The headman did not object when Shan and Lokesh headed toward the stall where Gendun remained under guard. The lama appeared to be reading the unbound sheets of a text propped before him on a milking stool. But he was not reading, only staring at them, unfocused, one hand trembling uncontrollably. He was propped up with rolled blankets, as Hostene had been when Shan first saw him. Shan had never seen Gendun look so frail. After an earlier dose of tamzing torture this sometimes happened. It had taken time for the damage to manifest itself.

Lokesh touched the lama on the knee. Gendun slowly came to his senses, raising his head with what seemed great effort. "Dolma visits me," he reported, his voice thin but steady. "Yesterday we polished the prayer wheels in the temple." Shan and Lokesh exchanged an alarmed glance.

"Rinpoche!" Shan cried, using the term for a revered teacher as he touched Gendun's hand. The lama did not respond, did not even seem to take notice when Shan pushed up his sleeve. Shan's heart lurched as he saw the marks — new bruises and electrical burns. He had thrown away the battery but Chodron still had his generator.

Lokesh fell into the quiet rhythm of a mantra to the Compassionate Buddha. Gendun's lips moved but his eyes were empty. Shan found his own lips mouthing the words as he fought to control the flood of emotion, first anger then deep helplessness. He could do nothing. The more he protested, the worse it would be for Gendun. He heard a dull, staccato rumble overhead. By the time he reached the landing circle the helicopter was on the ground and Gao stood before the makeshift bier. He examined his dead nephew without expression, then somberly studied those who had gathered around the table.

Shan did not move when Gao reached him, did not react when Gao, his face like a gray mask, raised his hand and slapped him. He stood still as a post when the scientist slapped him again harder, a third time still harder. Finally, Gao broke away and disappeared behind the granary. Chodron dispersed the crowd as Shan helped two soldiers wrap Thomas's body in the black cloth and carry it into the still-whining helicopter. When Shan descended another soldier was there, holding a set of manacles. Shan silently extended his hands and watched without expression as the soldier locked them around his wrists and walked away. The villagers stared at him, stepping fearfully aside when, like a dutiful prisoner, he followed the soldier with the key. No one met his eyes. He had been claimed by the government and, with the final snap of the steel bracelets, had become nobody. He was a number again, nothing more.

The soldier led him to Gao, now seated on the same flat rock Lokesh had been perched on when Shan first arrived in the village. Gao's face was gaunt, no expression, not even sadness in his eyes.

"When Public Security comes," Shan said, "they will sweep the slopes and arrest everyone. There will be forced confessions. A heavy price will be exacted."

"Listen to you." Though Gao's face seemed numb, his voice overflowed with bitterness. "Suddenly, the careful politician."

"Leave the village alone. These people suffer enough."

"But you told me before, they tortured your lama, they were going to kill Hostene. Why should you care?"

"Even so . . ." Shan didn't finish the sentence. He lowered himself onto the rock beside Gao. It was a quiet season for Public Security, and their Ax to Root campaign still needed to gain momentum. There was not a shadow of doubt that once senior officials outside Chodron's sphere caught scent of Drango, the village would be obliterated. There would be photographers, perhaps even a film crew, certainly speeches about progress and the twenty-first century. The inhabitants would be herded out, perhaps on two hours' notice, then a reconstruction brigade would arrive, possibly prisoners who were themselves Tibetan. Shan had seen it before, had been in such a brigade when it was ordered to such duty in the hills above their compound, had watched Lokesh and the other old Tibetan prisoners weep as the prison guards started the process by throwing torches into centuries-old wooden homes.

"Don't you realize that the man who did this is too clever to be caught by a sweep?" Gao said after a long silence.

"Criminal justice in China is an approximate thing. I didn't say he would be caught, I said a heavy price would be paid." Shan gazed out over the distant ranges. "If Thomas is looking down on us," he ventured at last, "there would be something more important to him than finding his killer."

"You mean the Navajo woman."

"She is up on the mountain. I think she is still alive. She crossed paths with the killer before and was spared. But this time I think he took her with him."

"Why would he do that?"

"I don't know exactly. He needs her for something."

"What are you trying to say?" Gao asked after another long silence.

"Hostene and I can find her. When we

find her we will know who the killer is."

"If I let you go, I will never see you again. That's what convicts do in Tibet. Disappear."

Shan lowered his head into his hands. His body was fatigued. But his spirit was beyond exhaustion. "How many years did it take," he asked, "to find the old dzong you live in?"

Gao did not reply.

"When they come," Shan continued, "they will also find out about the gold. Not even the army will be able to stop what will happen then. Maybe it could have twenty or thirty years ago, but not today. Economic development is Beijing's new mantra. The first year or two they will just send survey teams. There will be helicopters coming and going overhead. Geologists will drill and blast. After that, they will build roads, with bulldozers and more dynamite. They'll assign a gulag crew to do the work for a year or two, maybe three or four hundred prisoners, so they'll probably build a prison camp right here at the village site. A new town will go up, built of metal and concrete. A depot, a garage, dormitories. Then the real work will begin. Scores of miners. More dormitories. Huge trucks to move the material as it is blasted loose. After they deplete the seams and have sluiced the dust in the streams, they'll pick a small valley in which to heap the soil they strip from the slopes, then spray it with sodium cyanide to leach out the ore. They won't stop until there is nothing left but bare, sterile rock. Once they start, a Tibetan mountain lasts about a dozen years."

Shan never heard the angry words forming on Gao's lips. Chodron had appeared, accompanied by two of his men. The headman pointed at Shan. "He's mine. He has already been arrested by the civil authority. I released him on his parole, to assist me."

"Already arrested?" Gao asked, suppressing his rage. "On what charges?"

Chodron swallowed hard and pressed on. "Interfering with municipal government. Violations of the Ax to Root directive."

"Ax to Root is a campaign," Gao pointed out, "not a criminal law. A campaign against Tibetans. Shan is not Tibetan."

"He has no government registration. He is nothing, an escaped convict. Leave him with me and we will find the bastard who did this to your nephew. I have already started an investigation. I know what to do with men like Shan." Gao's silence was making Chodron nervous. "Do not blind yourself to the truth, sir."

"What particular truth am I missing, Comrade Chodron?" Gao asked.

"Your nephew would still be alive but for Shan. He may have been a Beijing investigator once, but not now. Once a criminal, always a criminal. People like you and me are his enemy. He stirs things up, he breeds instability. He cares nothing about the laws of Beijing anymore. He does not intend that the murderer be sent before a Chinese judge."

"Deny these things," Gao demanded of Shan.

Shan looked toward the distant mountains. "I am not your enemy," he said.

"Would my nephew still be alive if you had not gone up the mountain?"

"I don't know," Shan's voice dropped to a whisper. "Probably. I went up the mountain to find answers. The killer was feeling pressured. If Hostene and I don't go back, his niece will certainly die."

Chodron said, "Shan may have murdered your nephew." He leaned toward Gao. "I could easily write a report for Public Security. Shan was in the area, had access to heavy blades, had a simple motive. He had been found out. Was this killing an unreformed convict's last desperate attempt to keep from spending the rest of his life in prison? Was there a conspiracy between Shan and this Hostene? Perhaps Shan took a bribe to cover up the evidence that Hostene killed his two companions. Then he had to silence your nephew because he was conducting his own investigation and had discovered the terrible truth. A convict and an illegal foreigner — the kind of solution Public Security welcomes."

Chodron turned to Shan. "A simple confession will prevent unnecessary suffering by your two old goats."

Shan searched Chodron's face. He saw movement behind the stable. Two of the headman's men were carrying Gendun, who was limp as a sack of rice.

Shan took a step toward the lama.

"The other one, Lokesh," Chodron added, "his turn comes next. I recall that he was quite rude to me that night you arrived."

Shan was unable to speak. He jerked the chain tight between his manacled wrists, his fists clenching and unclenching. He had thought when he discovered Thomas's corpse that things could not get worse. But now he stood in chains as Chodron demanded that he confess to murder to save Lokesh and Gendun.

Someone moved between Shan and Chodron. Gao. "We will allow Shan and the

American to go up the mountain again," the scientist declared. "They can have seven days, no more. Put the manacles on the two old men who are his friends. Treat them as prisoners awaiting Public Security.

"If anything happens to me or to Kohler, or if they are found on the eastern side of the mountain again, or if Shan does not return in a week, the two old men are to be surrendered to Public Security. Major Ren is touring the district. He is responsible for Ax to Root in this region. He will know what to do with them."

"Ren," Chodron muttered with a grunt that seemed part satisfaction, part fear.

Gao did not look at Shan as he continued. "When Shan returns, he will be given a choice. He can surrender to me and I will send him to Beijing, where he belongs, to learn how to serve his government once again. Or he can surrender to you and return to prison."

Shan's throat went dry as a stone. "You won't call Public Security for a week?"

"Not unless Kohler or I am endangered." Gao exchanged a glance with the headman. "Or Chodron."

A delicate, treacherous bargain was being struck between Chodron and Gao. Shan was the prize.

"No," Shan said.

"No? It is not *your* decision!" Chodron said.

"I will not sign a confession. And I will not go after the killer unless Lokesh and Gendun are unchained and put under Dolma's care and provided with whatever she says they need. And no more tamzing."

Shan braced himself as Chodron swung back his open hand. But Gao caught the headman's arm. "It will take a criminal to catch this criminal," he said.

Chodron replied, "The manacles stay on the lama. A guard stays at the door. They may not leave Dolma's house." He glared at Shan, then accepted the key extended by Gao. "Three sessions of tamzing are sufficient for now," Chodron added with a satisfied air as he released Shan from the handcuffs. "Come back without the murderer and there will be three more sessions."

Shan gazed at Gendun. Three more sessions would kill the old lama.

Chodron announced in a suddenly cheerful voice, "In another week, we celebrate the annual harvest festival. This year's is our best harvest ever. We will also celebrate the solution of the murders. We will celebrate the compassionate power of our elders in Beijing."

■ ■ ■ ■

Gendun lay on a pallet, Lokesh at his side, as Dolma heated tea on a brazier by the open window. Gendun's cheeks were discolored in several spots, his forehead was creased, a sign of the lama's silent battle to control his pain. He seemed weak and fragile. He appeared, Shan realized, with a wrench of his gut, exactly like the Tibetan prisoners he had lived with in the gulag, the old lamas who had slowly withered before his eyes. He had buried so many of them he had lost count.

"Chodron found two shepherds counting prayer beads," Dolma reported in a tormented tone. "A family had mounted an old rusty prayer wheel at their front door. He was furious. He burned the beads, smashed the wheel, then dragged Gendun out into the street, saying it was all his fault."

As Shan lowered himself beside the lama his hand reached out of its own accord and cradled Gendun's, a chain around it now. He recalled with a numbing sense of defeat the way his father had lain dying after he had been beaten by the Red Guard. Shan had sat helplessly, squeezing his father's hand for hours, until with a terrible rattle that still echoed in his nightmares the professor had breathed his last.

"We are brewing teas used by the old healers," Dolma said with a nod toward Lokesh, who chanted a mantra for the medicine deity. The widow busied herself among the small crocks and jars that lined a shelf below the window. At first Shan thought her preoccupation was with the teas, then saw that she fidgeted with a cleaning rag, twisting it in her fingers, casting nervous glances out the window. Shan rose and stepped to Dolma's side. "I need to understand your nephew, Tashi," he said in a low voice. "What did he do when he left the village?"

She scrubbed her eyes with her apron. "He was a good boy, Yangke's best friend. Ten years ago, Yangke came back from the Chinese school Chodron had sent him to. He had many problems there, always being disciplined, refusing to respond to the Chinese name assigned to him, protesting when they punished him for speaking Tibetan. But he had the best grades in all his class, and they are always looking for Tibetans to go to the universities in China. Chodron announced that he had arranged for Yangke to attend university in Sichuan Province, that our village was honored to have one of its own selected by the government. But at the celebration Chodron held for him, Yangke announced he had already been accepted somewhere else, as a novice in a monastery near Lhasa. Chodron was furious but the next day Yangke left for the *gompa*. Only later did we discover that he had persuaded Tashi to go with him. But being a monk didn't suit Tashi. After a few months he left for a job in a factory."

"And he got into trouble there?"

"He was never happy. He loved drawing. He always kept his pen case with him. He would have become a great painter of tangkas if . . . if things had been different. When he left all he took with him was that old silver pen case. They say he committed a crime that had something to do with the black market, with shipping stuff across the border. He was found guilty of falsifying export documents and sentenced to three years in prison."

"What prison?"

"In the west, near Rutok," the old woman said. Rutok was the largest city in remote western Tibet, home to many hidden military bases and gulag prisons.

"And when was he released?"

"I don't know exactly. He sent us postcards once every few months to let us know he was still alive. He was driving trucks for a factory, he said. The last time I saw him was on the anniversary of his mother's death, two years ago. He brought me something from far away." Dolma rummaged for a moment on her shelf, pushing jars aside, finally producing a little porcelain reproduction of the Taj Mahal. Tashi had been in India. But as a convicted felon, he would never have been legally permitted to drive trucks in and out of the country.

"How well did he know the upper slopes?" Shan asked.

"It was his world, when he was young. He and Yangke tended the sheep there."

"Would he have spent time with your first son, Rapaki?" Shan asked.

"Rapaki was born a few months after the temple was destroyed. My sister was certain he was the reincarnation of one of the monks because of the way he would sit for hours in the bombed-out foundation, even as a young boy." When she looked up, tears filled Dolma's eyes. "He was a good boy. Some people sent their children to schools far away, long before Chodron required it. I wouldn't do it. I had lost my husband in the war and couldn't lose Rapaki too. It was hard because we had no real teachers. The monks had always taught our children. When he first put on a robe, people thought

Rapaki was playacting. They laughed at him. Day after day he would sit in one of the granaries, reading scraps of old scriptures we had saved from the flames. Finally the headman, Chodron's father, demanded that he stop. Monks were illegal and planes would come again if anyone heard. The next day Rapaki disappeared up the mountain. It was two years before we saw him again. By the time Yangke and Tashi were old enough to go up the slopes with the sheep, people were calling my son the saint of the mountain. When they got into mischief they said all they had to do was touch Rapaki to redeem their sins.

"Now he lives on the pilgrim's path, where men are being murdered. What do you know about the path?" Shan asked.

"Not enough. I always intended to learn more about it. I had begun helping at the temple. But then those Chinese airplanes came. I remember a lama speaking with some pilgrims who arrived at our village once seeking an escort to the path. He wouldn't let them follow the path. He said it wasn't what they thought, that it was the opposite of what they expected."

"What did he mean?"

"His words haunt me when I think about Rapaki. This kora was Bon, a remnant, very ancient. Not like other sacred paths constructed after our lamas adopted the way of Buddha. The Bon lived in a violent world. They were not reluctant to help the weak find a new incarnation."

"What does your heart tell you about it?"

"I don't know. You think I have not tried to understand? I wandered the slopes every summer for years, hoping for a glimpse of my son Rapaki, for a chance to talk him into coming home. Maybe it's a place where people must die. Maybe the mountain is killing them."

Shan turned to see Hostene, sitting cross-legged at Gendun's feet. Dolma gasped, and Shan opened his mouth to whisper an assurance that the Navajo would not harm Gendun when he saw the dim figure beyond, standing in the shadows of the ladder stair. Gao was there too, watching silently.

"In the old ways of my people," Hostene said when Shan approached, "it was necessary to summon deities for a healing."

"That is what Lokesh is doing," Shan explained.

"But we also worry about demons entering someone who has been weakened. When I was young I had rheumatic fever. My father brought a doctor but my mother painted my face with soot, to make me invisible to demons. Every door or window facing east — but only those — was kept open, because that is where the good deities live. All their lives my parents argued about which cured me, the white man's medicine or the Navajo prayers."

Hostene produced his feathered stick from inside his vest and stirred the air over Gendun.

Shan translated for Dolma. She cocked her head a moment, studying him with an expression of wonder. "My grandmother spoke of having her face painted in such a way when she was sick." She rose, retrieved a small, cold brazier from below the window shelf, then rubbed soot onto two fingers and began painting Gendun's face.

Shan rose to intercept Gao, who stepped forward.

"My nephew lies mutilated and murdered. I don't even have all his body to bury and you indulge in this — this sorcery session." Gao spoke in Chinese, thinking no one else could understand. "Chodron is right. At heart you are the worst kind of reactionary."

Lokesh halted his mantra. "He is wandering aimlessly right now, deeply afraid, unwilling to accept that he has crossed over so early, not mindful of the terrible dangers that lurk about him." Lokesh spoke in such a calm voice, in such perfectly articulated Chinese, that Gao looked about him, as if to identify the source of the unexpected words. Lokesh gazed at him inquisitively.

"What — who are you speaking of?" Gao asked hesitantly.

"The boy. Your nephew. I am very sorry he was taken away. But there are words that must be said or he may become an angry ghost, doomed to roam the slopes forever."

"He was a scientist," Gao rejoined. "From a family of scientists. We don't believe . . ." He paused, frowning, as if wondering why he was debating with the old Tibetan. "My nephew needs nothing now that a firing squad can't provide."

"You are speaking of the murderer," Lokesh said. "I am speaking of your nephew, and of you. I think being a scientist is something that is in the body. I am speaking of what happens to the kernel when it rises from that husk." The old Tibetan groped in his pocket a moment, then extracted a *tsa tsa,* a small clay tablet bearing the image of a deity. "Take this," he said, handing it to Gao. "There will come a time soon when you feel your nephew close by. Hold this in your hand when you do, and let him know we are working to help him find his way. When Gendun awakens we will recite the death rites for him for the next seven days."

Gao stared at the little clay image in confusion, as if trying to understand how it had appeared in his hand. Shan thought he was going to pocket the tsa tsa but then, with a look of revulsion, Gao threw it against the back wall, shattering it into a dozen shards.

"If you prefer," Lokesh offered in the same level tone, "I could teach you some of the words."

"Be quiet, you damned fool! It's this kind of nonsense that lured my nephew to his death."

Shan was about to protest, to point out that the lamas had never even met Thomas, when he realized Gao meant Abigail Natay's particular form of nonsense. Abigail had fled the safe side of the mountain to continue her work on the ancient shrines. Thomas had followed her.

"Your shining consciousness has no birth, no death." Lokesh spoke the opening words from the death rite facing the shadows, where the deity lay shattered on the floor.

Anger flared on Gao's face, followed by despair. He retreated. Shan followed him to the foot of the stairs. "I am only able to search the mountain," Shan said.

"What do you mean?"

"Something is finishing here. It didn't start here. There are men up there who are hiding things." Shan quickly wrote a name on a scrap of paper and handed it to Gao. "He was in Public Security and was stationed somewhere in Tibet, I think. I need to know where he served, what his duties were. And there's something else." He leaned forward, speaking close to Gao's ear. The scientist's frown grew deeper.

There was movement behind them. Hostene stood on the steps.

"I came here to offer to take you back to my house in the helicopter," Gao said to the Navajo. "There is plenty of room. You are in no condition to climb the mountain."

"Even if Shan wasn't going, I would go back. I won't let my niece die."

"When Shan finds her, he will let us know."

"He's right, Hostene," Shan interjected. "We're aware of your sickness. Don't make things worse."

Hostene, confused, searched their faces. "You mean my cough? I smoked for twenty years. It's the price I pay. Doctors say my lungs are good enough, for my age."

"The medicines," Gao said, "for cancer."

Hostene sank onto the step. "That's a private thing," he said.

"You'll do your niece no favors by getting sick on the mountain," Shan said.

Hostene was forced to explain. "An old family doctor put the prescriptions in my name, so no one would suspect that Abigail was ill. What you saw was the extras I was carrying." He looked up at Shan. "You asked once why completing her work is so urgent for her."

"What are you saying?" Shan asked, a chill spreading down his spine.

"It isn't me. It's Abigail who has cancer. They give her no more than a year to live."

CHAPTER NINE

Screams mingled with Shan's nightmare of Gendun in tamzing again, growing louder and louder, until he became aware that Lokesh was shaking him. The desperate shouts came from outside, spreading from one house to the next as Drango's inhabitants caught sight of the flames. The barley fields were on fire.

Few things are drier than a field of barley ripe for harvest. The flames swept inward as if famished, gorging on the paper-crisp stalks. Within minutes every man, woman, and child in the village were in the fields, battling with brooms, buckets, and shovels. Soon some collapsed onto their knees, breaking into helpless sobs. The barley was their life, their food supply for the brutal winter ahead. The tsampa, the gruel, the kernel-laden soup, the fodder that would keep them and their animals alive was disappearing in a wind-driven inferno. Cho-

dron shouted furious orders for more buckets, for a trench to be dug from the stream,
but no one seemed to hear him. Another
voice rose, younger and surprisingly calm.
Yangke was wielding a sickle. Soon a dozen
men were following his example, cutting a
swath to deprive the advancing fire of its
fuel, sealing off a small quadrant of the crop
with a fire break.

Shan paused at the edge of the field,
surveying the grim scene. The fire had
started at the top of the field, feeding on
the predawn downdraft from higher eleva-
tions, ignited at half a dozen places, probably by someone running with a torch. As
he gazed at the devastated village he caught
snippets of frantic conversations. Someone
said it must have been lightning. Someone
else said he had seen a flame suspended in
the air, magically moving along the top of
the fields, faster than any man could run.
Someone, pointing, said Chodron had
received an invitation from a demon. Shan
followed the gesture, walking toward the
granaries, stopping in the shadows when he
discovered the village headman standing in
the circle of pressed earth, staring at a dead
sheep. The animal had had its throat cut
and was propped on its haunches with sticks
so that its lifeless eyes seemed to be watch-

ing the house of the headman. Stuffed in its mouth was an ornate silver pen case. A case Shan had seen before. Tashi's pen case. He watched Chodron hesitantly open the case. It was empty.

Shan spotted Hostene and jogged to his side. The forlorn cries of the villagers rose in volume. They worked beside Yangke, pulling away the stalks as he cut them, stomping out embers as they landed on the cleared swath of earth. Shan watched as Chodron appeared, running upward. A new field caught with a sudden terrible swoosh of hot air as Shan darted behind the nearest structure.

Chodron's house was empty, the back door open. The office was still padlocked, but using a stone and a heavy nail he had taken from the stable the night before, Shan began working on the hinges. He quickly popped the pins and swung the door aside. Inside, he lit one of the candles on the desk. Wiping his hands clean of soot on his trouser legs, he began sifting through the papers on top of the compact desk, then searched the drawers and folders stacked on the table along the wall. This is what Shan had done best in his previous incarnation, finding and interpreting the secrets of the corrupt. He had once been feted as a

Hero Worker for deciphering the code in a ledger used by a Ministry of Energy deputy minister to send millions to bank accounts in Hong Kong. Chodron's files held reports about the harvest, medical care, party meetings, expenses for quarters in Tashtul town, everything but what Shan sought. He puzzled over how Chodron had managed to keep the village official for some purposes, like enrolling its children in government boarding schools, but unofficial for others, like keeping out watchful administrators, census takers, and tax collectors. He eyed the books on the high shelf over the table — Party scriptures, a collection of essays on socialist thought for agrarian communities, even a book dealing with the treatment of fungus in barley. Only one book showed any sign of use.

Chodron was not subtle, though Shan had to admire his daring. The headman had removed the contents of a hardcover copy of *The Quotations of Chairman Mao* and glued a ledger within the boards. He had hidden his secrets in plain sight. The sinner had disguised his transgressions with his bible.

It was an impressive volume, Shan had to admit. For over ten years, Chodron had recorded payments from miners, collected in early September as they passed through his makeshift tollgate on the trail above town. Each year's entry listed miners', changing slightly year to year, gradually lengthening until the past year showed payments from forty different names. Two names had been scratched out at the end of the past season, another a month earlier.

He leafed back and forth among the most recent annual accounts. Only the current year and the prior one had any names removed. All the previous years' entries appeared to have been completed on the same day, with the same pen and same ink, listing name and payment as received. But the last two lists were different. The names had been prepared in advance of the payment date, pursuant to a more organized system, utilizing a list of names provided in advance with payments registered on the payment date. Chodron had become Bing's partner.

Shan remounted the door on its hinges, tapped in the pins, and stepped outside into a swirl of smoke. He went toward Chodron's generator, unscrewed the gas cap, and dropped a handful of dirt into the tank. The smoke thickened, conveniently concealing his return to the fields. He located Hostene and took up a position beside him, pulling back the stalks as the men in front swung their sickles.

Shan did not notice when Hostene departed. He became aware that Yangke had paused. Shan followed the young Tibetan's gaze toward the nearest granary, where a smoke-stained figure stood with two packs in his hands. Shan realized the Navajo was right. They could ill afford to be within reach of Chodron's fury when the flames had run their course.

Yangke put a hand on Shan's shoulder. "I will try to find you," he said in a bone-weary voice. "Lha gyal lo."

By the time they reached the path above the village the sun had risen above the ridge, and they could see the full extent of the devastation. No more than a tenth of the crop survived. It was the end of life as the villagers had known it. They could not survive without appealing to the township authorities. Then the authorities would arrive to assess their plight. The end would come quickly.

"Who would do such a thing?" Hostene asked.

"Someone who wants Chodron to lose," Shan said.

"The murderer?"

Shan pointed to a set of bicycle tracks that veered off the trail along the top of the fields. The flame that ignited the barley had moved faster than a man could run.

"Murder," Shan replied, "is only part of the war being waged on this mountain." But in the short term, he knew murder would be Chodron's sole obsession. For if Chodron the harvest manager was deprived of his victory, then Chodron the village magistrate would need an even more spectacular success. Shan tightened the straps of his pack and with grim determination headed up the mountain.

Lightning began to strike an hour later, a single bolt at first, starting at the distant summit, then a dozen more, approaching in rapid succession, shaking the ground, singeing the air, emitting a metallic scent of ozone. A huge dark cloud, nearly black, settled over the mountain, creating an eerie twilight. Now the lighting began in earnest. Most of the bolts were concentrated near the summit but some struck much closer, one less than a hundred yards away. It was as if some angry deity had awakened and begun hammering the mountain.

Shan and Hostene ran for shelter under an overhanging ledge. Hail fell, marble-sized balls that were blown sideways by a sudden gust, slashing at them so hard they had to turn and face the stone, their backs to the onslaught. Then it stopped as abruptly as it had started. Except for the hail it had been a dry storm, the kind that made Tibetans believe in mountain gods.

As the sun emerged, they surveyed the now deceptively tranquil mountainside.

"Why does she lead her killer?" Shan was not even certain he had given tongue to his thought until he saw the old Navajo stare at him in alarm.

"Why do you say such a thing?"

"Each of them has a destination, up the mountain somewhere. They have discovered it is the same one. I think she knows more about how to find it than the killer does. And the killer knows it."

"You said *her* killer."

"I am sorry, Hostene, but whoever is doing this won't release her when they reach their goal. And I think she realizes this. Now I understand why she acts as if she has little to lose. If she's convinced she's dying," Shan continued, "if she truly believes she will be gone soon, then completing her work is everything."

"Her work," Hostene repeated. "It's not work anymore. It's all part of the same thing now. The guilt she feels toward her dead parents. The need to put things in balance. She came to me that night at Gao's, in tears.

371

She said something that kept me awake for hours. It was wrong that Tashi and Ma had died too, she told me. The more I thought about it, the more it alarmed me. She was saying she was the one who was meant to die."

In his mind Shan had been revisiting the videos of Abigail he had watched with Hostene, viewing them not as the work of a brilliant professor but of a troubled woman who knew she was dying. "That's what she's been doing all along," he said softly. "Connecting with lost gods." A minute passed before he spoke again. "The words she wrote you at Gao's house. 'In Beauty before me I walk.' What is their origin?"

"They're from our Blessing Way. Our chant to open dialogue with our holy ones." He gazed out over the tortuous terrain ahead of them and nodded. "She's become more of a Navajo in Tibet than she ever was as a girl in New Mexico. But no one kills for the old gods," Hostene observed in confusion.

This was a leap Shan was not prepared to make.

They turned onto the track that led to Little Moscow. The trail was blocked with lashed poles, tied together and jammed against rocks to form a gate. The poles bore patterns of colored stripes at the top, in different orders, as if the miners were sending a unified warning to all trespassers. Beyond the poles, on the trail, was the headless carcass of a sheep.

Shan followed Hostene's worried gaze back toward Drango village, where the smoke still spiraled high. Fire behind, vengeful miners ahead. It was time, as the Tao te Ching said, to block the passages and close the door. He turned back to Hostene. "I think we should pick some flowers," he announced.

Managing Director Bing was perched on a boulder at the mouth of the ravine watching the column of smoke from Drango when they approached Little Moscow.

"You have the balls of a water buffalo, Shan," he muttered as they arrived at his side. "Two days ago every miner on this mountain wanted both of you dead."

"Two days ago Thomas had not been murdered. That changes everything. With Dr. Gao watching, who will dare try to eliminate his investigators?"

"Dr. Gao can't tell the fox from the hens," Bing shot back. Then he gestured toward the smoke. "How bad?"

"The village stands. The crop is all but

destroyed."

Bing ran his hand through his thick hair, muttered a low curse.

"Not particularly well planned," Shan suggested. "How will Chodron keep the village fed without calling on the government for assistance? But why should a village need grants of food supplies when it never did before? That alone will set off an investigation. You and Chodron better forget the gold and start planting peas."

Bing glared at him. "You can't think *we* had anything to do with it."

"As you said," Shan observed, "Little Moscow exists in a bold new world. Where every man can live up to his full potential."

There was something different about the miners' town, Shan thought as he followed Bing into it. The photographs of family were stowed away, the little signs setting forth mileage to hometowns gone. The men had eradicated any evidence of who they were when off the mountain. They were growing suspicious of one another. A rooster stood tied to a pole by one lean-to, as vigilant as a dog. The birdcage he had seen on his former visit was gone, replaced by a plank upon which someone had inscribed an old-style charm against evil ghosts. The few miners who showed themselves glanced warily at

Shan and Hostene. Shan walked along the perimeter of the town's central square, pausing for a moment to study the crumbling fresco, noting the small oval shapes that had outlined some of the sacred objects depicted in the painting, squatting for a moment to examine the section that had fallen out and been placed by the entrance to Bing's quarters, a fragment showing the head of a fanged creature that appeared half human, half lion.

Bing directed them to the central fire, where he poured tea into metal mugs. "We are honored to entertain the ambassadors from the great court of Gao," he said mockingly. "But there's nothing more to find here about the murders."

"Murders?" Shan asked. "I have recognized my assumptions were faulty. I am now doing research into the creativity of entrepreneurs in the socialist market economy."

Bing raised his cup in salute, gesturing toward his community of miners who were assembling, forming a circle around them. "Here you see the future of China at its birthing."

Shan swallowed half the contents of his cup. Hostene began extracting items from his pack.

"The miner who was killed last year,"

Shan said abruptly. "What happened to him? Were there witnesses? Why did you conclude that his partner had killed him?"

"You said you weren't interested in murders anymore."

"On this particular mountain, corpses are but another resource determined by supply and demand. So much so that when you run out of murders you borrow a body and call it a murder."

Bing glared in silence at Shan, then glanced sharply at the Navajo. He made a small gesture to Hubei, his wiry, bulldog lieutenant, who fetched one of the shovel handles. "We don't believe in digging up old ghosts."

"But that's my job," Shan said. "Reviving old ghosts. Making them speak, tapping their wisdom."

Bing was disturbed. "Talk like that scares people. Every day they're more superstitious here. Look what they've done. Some hang charms outside their quarters. One man bought an old prayer box from a farmer, because he says the only gods here are Tibetan. Another put his rooster outside because his grandmother once told him they frighten off evil spirits."

Shan nodded at Hostene, who had now arranged certain of the contents of his pack on his brightly colored blanket — his feathered spirit stick, a bag of pollen they had collected from flowers picked on the trail, the leg bone of a yak they had found near the path.

A worried murmur swept through the onlookers. Each miner represented a separate mystery to Shan. The only thing he knew for certain was that they were all superstitious.

"What the hell is he doing?" demanded Bing.

"Hostene is frightened of ghosts too," Shan declared in a voice loud enough for all to hear. "He is going to perform a ceremony to speak with them, to ask them why they are so upset with Little Moscow, why they think someone is lying to them."

Bing's mouth opened in protest. "He's an American" was all he could manage.

"He's an American Indian. A shaman among his people. A ghost speaker."

"Sorcerer!" someone barked.

Shan studied the men. Half a dozen had lowered themselves to the ground, forming a wide circle around Hostene. Others had stepped out of their dug-out homes and anxiously watched from the shadows. The Navajo began murmuring in his native tongue, arms flying toward the heavens.

Hubei backed away several steps, then hurried off.

"I want him stopped," Bing muttered to Shan.

"He is speaking to the ghosts, asking them to tell us the truth. Surely the citizens of your bold new world have nothing to fear from old world ghosts. Or is it you who are scared of ghosts, Captain Bing?"

"What do you want?"

"The man who died last year. What exactly happened?"

"He was found with a chisel in his back and a bloody patch on his head where he had fallen against some rocks. A shopkeeper from Guangzhou had come here with him, his partner. But they were always arguing with each other, and with the rest of us. We confirmed it was his partner's chisel."

"We?"

"Hubei and I."

"And the killer?"

"No one knows how *he* died. All we found was his skeleton."

"Wearing his old ring. A skeleton with jewelry. Even the dead adapt here."

"That's when we organized ourselves. Signed articles governing Little Moscow, so it would be a safe harbor, a place to keep supplies."

"And that's when they elected you to lead them," Shan pointed out.

"The murder made it clear that someone had to do it. I had government experience. It was my duty to accept the nomination."

"Supply and demand again," Shan pointed out. "After all these years, a need for protection arose, and the perfect candidate was there to fill it."

Outside, Hostene was speaking in his tribal tongue, holding the bag of pollen up to the sky. "There are still some who consider him a killer," Bing ventured.

"Where's the body of the man who was killed last year?"

"I don't know. We left him under some rocks. But when the wolves get hungry enough —" Bing finished with a shrug.

"You're saying you haven't been back to the grave?"

"I had no reason to go there."

Shan considered Bing's calculated lack of interest. He decided not to ask the question that leapt to his tongue. Instead he said, "When I go to Tashtul town, where will I find the gold agency?"

"What are you talking about?"

"Where does one go to sell gold? Officially, only the government buys gold."

Bing replied, "You're not actually going to

Tashtul."

"A fascinating idea, though. The miners disperse all over China come autumn, they have black markets all over China to go to. But you and Chodron, you need to convert the share of gold paid to you by the miners somewhere much closer. It's against the law to exchange it without involving the government. The Ministry of Mines is the flaw in your business model. It restricts the upside potential of your enterprise. The worst possible partner in a conspiracy is a bureaucrat. You'd be surprised how quickly such officials can be made to sing. Investigators love to start with bureaucrats because they harbor no delusions about the criminal justice system. And this year," he added, "some of the miners have already converted some of their gold into cash, in the middle of the summer. As if there were a new gold dealer nearby. Or a bank."

Bing glared at him, then shrugged. "You have no way off this mountain. If you try to go to Tashtul, Chodron will make sure you're never seen again." He pushed the canvas flap aside, his anger building, as Hostene began sprinkling pollen on the miners' heads. Bing cursed under his breath and hastened back to the square.

Shan found Hubei packing a sack with

mining equipment near his lean-to.

"That last day Thomas was here, before I arrived, what was he speaking about? Who was he speaking with?"

"Everyone." Hubei did not stop his packing, but did not hesitate to answer. "Anyone who came along. One moment he was hawking his wares, the next bragging that he knew how to catch criminals."

"What did he say about catching criminals?"

"Forensics, he called it. He claimed he could tell what made a wound by examining the blood spatter, could tell if a man was dead or alive when he was stabbed or shot by whether blood had flowed out of the body. Bones. Bullets. Fingerprints."

"What about bones?"

The miner tied off the top of the pack. "Fractures. A skull fracture from a fall made a long crack. A skull fracture from a hammer might knock out a circle of bone. A leg fracture from a car accident was different from one where the leg was held down and smashed." The miner raised the pack onto his back.

Thomas had spoken of how a victim's bones could betray a murderer, and then Abigail had seen Bing tossing old bones from a cliff.

"Did you help bury the man who died last year?" When the man did not reply Shan blocked his exit from the shelter. "Did he still have his hands?"

Hubei lowered the pack and rubbed a hand over his face. "There was no need for the others to know about that. We rolled the body in a blanket before they could look."

"Which means you know his partner was *not* the murderer."

Hubei glanced toward the square, where Bing was putting Hostene's ritual instruments back into his pack even as Hostene continued dispensing pollen. "Maybe there are different murderers. New people came to the mountain this year. Last year, we softened the man's partner up with a couple of shovel handles, enough to scare him off the mountain. We borrowed his ring before he left," he admitted.

Shan nodded at the confirmation of his suspicion. "By my count that makes ten hands that have been severed and taken away. How many do you suppose this killer needs? An even dozen? A score? You're a brave man, going back to your claim alone. Be sure to get some of that pollen sprinkled on your head before you leave."

Hubei winced, rubbing at the tattooed numbers on his forearm, the nervous reaction of a former prisoner. Hubei was wise in the ways of the world. He, at least, understood that they were on the brink of disaster. His hand went to his belt. For the first time Shan saw an old military knife tucked in his waist.

"You aren't going mining," Shan observed.

"No one is to get past the claim Bing posted down the trail. Between patrols I'll push some rocks around and pan the streams."

"The problem with being in the middle of a war, Hubei, is that everyone eventually has to choose a side."

"I'm on the side of my family," Hubei said. "You should get out of the way. Leave the mountain, Shan, and the war ends."

Shan said, "I'm not leaving until the murderer is caught."

For a moment Hubei looked as if he meant to argue with Shan. Then his attention focused on the town square of Little Moscow, which had gone very quiet except for a voice chanting in Navajo. "He's had a message."

"Bing?"

Hubei nodded once more. "From that damned woman. He says she came to him yesterday when he was alone working his claim, asking him to give a note to her uncle. We should've stopped her the first day she arrived, and sent her away from the mountain. She's nothing but bad luck."

"He knows we are looking for her. Why didn't he give the message to me?"

"A man like Bing doesn't share secrets. He uses secrets."

"He told you. He told Chodron."

"Me, because he doesn't read English. Only me," the miner added pointedly.

Shan didn't wait for Bing to return to his makeshift house. He quickly slipped inside the shelter of rock and canvas, and began searching, starting at the entry from which he surveyed the entire chamber before examining each chink in the rock wall. When he finished with the wall, he searched under the pallet on the floor, then moved to the jacket hanging on a peg. The note was there, in an inside pocket sealed with a zipper. It was written on a page torn out of a journal, the same thick unlined paper she'd used for her note at Gao's house. It was the same handwriting. *"I am safe,* Abigail had written, *and on the way to Tashtul town. After what happened to Thomas I cannot bear to stay here. I have research to do in Lhasa and will wait for you there at the hotel we stayed at before."*

He put the paper into his own pocket and walked down the nearest of the little alley ravines to the square. Hostene was pacing around the circle of men still, blowing pollen onto them. No one was ridiculing the Navajo now. These were men who would take a blessing any way they could. Even Bing stood and let Hostene scatter the yellow spores on him, as did a new arrival who stood at the rear, watching with a curious, uneasy expression. Yangke had found them.

Shan retreated to consider Abigail's note. Bing was keeping her departure a secret even from his patron and partner, Chodron.

A sound came from behind him, a soft, summoning whistle from the shadows. He glanced back to confirm no one in the square had noticed. He did not see the heavy loading boom over his head or the flicker of movement until it was too late. The loop of rope, expertly thrown, cleared his shoulders and was tightened around his waist, pulling him off his feet as it was raised by the overhead pulley, suspending him six feet in the air, his arms pinned to his sides. A man came out of the shadows holding a pole. He wore a hooded black sweatshirt, the hood drawn so low that the man's face was obscured, even when he began to beat Shan.

By the time Shan tried to call out, he had no breath left with which to speak. His assailant concentrated on his ribs and abdomen, delivering no bone-breaking blows but inflicting maximum pain. The pole, Shan noted, was of juniper. A sacred wood should not be used for such a profane task, he thought.

And then he must have lost consciousness. He was aware only that he was in a storm, with the wind howling, men shouting in fear, deafening thunder and darkness directly overhead. With painful effort he twisted to look upward. If lightning was going to strike him he wanted to see it coming. Despite his pain and the swirling dust, he could see the great black thing. The dragon deity, the thunder maker, the mountain shaker? Then a pebble stung his cheek, awakening him. The dust was scoured away by a downdraft, the shape of the thing outlined by daylight. It was a different breed of demon entirely. It was an army helicopter.

Hands reached up. Knife blades cut the rope that bound him. Orders were shouted, by Bing, by someone in a uniform. Shan was on Hostene's blanket. Someone was washing his face with a wet cloth, a man with a yellow-streaked face was handing him tea. His shirt was being unbuttoned. Fingers pressed against the pulse in his wrist. He passed out.

Shan lay in a swirling, confused place of memory and fear, in a bed of a remote Public Security ward. The hospital was in the desert, and sand crept into everything, even the cold rice they served him three times a day. He was in a special section reserved for Party luminaries, staffed with special doctors trained in interrogation. They experimented on him, using sodium barbitol, injections of iodine solution, and electric wires and small needles.

"I can't find a pulse. Just like him, the son of a bitch."

"Look, he's vomiting."

"Excellent. Better than a pulse."

They tied him naked to a chair and two bald men entered, one with a single long syringe, the other holding a short piece of bamboo.

"No ribs broken," they confirmed before starting in again.

His handlers were artists. They took pride in never breaking a bone. He could feel the needle that went into his bicep but could not raise his arm to react to it, could only sense the heat oozing up into his shoulder.

All at once he was awake, heart pounding, no longer in his prison of five years earlier but propped against a rock in the central square of Little Moscow. Gao was loading a syringe from a small clear bottle. Over the professor's shoulder stood a soldier holding a medical kit, nervously eyeing the miners.

"Who was it?" Hostene asked. "Could you see them?"

Shan, unable to speak, shook his head. He leaned and retched, emptying his stomach, then retched again, and again, until nothing came up.

Gao hovered over him with the syringe. Shan held up his hand. "What is it?"

"A painkiller."

"No," Shan groaned and, with Hostene's help, he sat and surveyed the assembly. Bing was calm but the miners looked terrified.

From the lip of the ravine a ladder of small chain links and steel bars hung from the door of the helicopter that had landed. "You're late," he said to Gao.

"I'm sorry. The storm delayed me."

"For the first time in years I was actually happy to see a helicopter."

Shan pulled Abigail's note out of his

388

pocket, handed it to Hostene, and fixed Bing with a level stare. "When did she leave?"

Bing's eyes flashed as he recognized the paper in Hostene's hand. Before answering he snapped at the gathered miners, ordering them to disperse. Then he said, "I found her wandering, lost, that morning when Thomas was killed. I sent her on her way with a map on a fast mule. She was hysterical. She said she had been knocked unconscious and awakened to find Thomas lying dead beside her."

"You didn't try to stop her?"

"Good riddance as far as I could see. I told her how to find the herders' camps at the base of the first range. They will set her on the right trail to town. She could reach town by this afternoon."

"And from there?"

"There's a bus to Lhasa from Tashtul twice a day."

Shan turned to Gao. "Who else came with you?"

"The pilot, who's an old friend, and his mechanic, who knows better than to ask questions."

Shan stood up and took a step, fighting dizziness, then faced Bing again. "I want four gold nuggets. Say half an ounce each."

"Fuck you."

"For two men who need to be given a big incentive not to talk."

Bing eyed Gao, who listened with a curious expression. "It's a crime to bribe a soldier."

"Haven't you heard?" Shan asked. "In the new world order there are no bribes, only business expenses. A reasonable item for your municipal budget. Call it emergency repairs."

Bing cursed and stepped into the shadows of his shelter. Shan took a step toward the ladder but doubled over in pain. Hostene dropped the gear he was gathering and rushed to Shan's side. Shan's raised palm stopped him.

"Go," Shan said, "climb the ladder. We'll bring the packs."

"We?" Gao asked. "You're in no condition to travel."

Shan found a familiar face watching uncertainly from the edge of the clearing and gestured toward him. "Yangke will come with us."

The young Tibetan glanced nervously around the clearing, drawing an unhappy glare from Bing, then gathered up the remainder of the gear and went to the ladder. Shan took three steps before he had to stop, his head swimming.

Bing blocked his way. "No way," he said.

"There is a way," Shan said. "Send Hubei with us. You don't need him to watch the trails once we've left."

Bing stared without expression at his deputy, then slowly nodded. Hubei began retreating into the shadows, then froze as Bing beckoned him. Hubei came forward reluctantly and Bing bent to murmur in his ear, then extracted a folded paper from his pocket and handed it to him. His deputy brightened as he stuffed the pages into his own pocket.

Shan waited for Hubei to climb the ladder, then followed shakily. Gao leaned forward, syringe at the ready. But Shan grabbed the syringe and with an unsteady hand emptied out half its contents before jabbing it into his own arm. Then he headed to the ladder and began climbing.

Once they were on their way Gao asked for the gold nuggets Bing had surrendered to Shan.

"A bribe from you?" Shan said. "Not credible. It needs to come from an unrepentant criminal." He palmed the nuggets and went forward into the cockpit.

Five minutes later he settled into a small nest of military blankets built for him by

Hostene as the machine roared to life and began to rise. Hubei had already found another pile of blankets at the rear of the hold and appeared to be sleeping.

"Where is the pain?" Hostene asked.

With a forced grin Shan pointed to the bottom of a foot. "There is the only place it doesn't hurt. He was no expert. Professionals go for the soles of the feet."

The landscape began to roll past the narrow portholes.

Yangke rose to sit beside Shan. "I have no papers," he said anxiously. It was a crime in itself to be without citizen registration papers. They were the first thing police asked for when they encountered strangers.

"Nor do I. Nor does Hostene for that matter, not for this region. We won't stay in town long. Just overnight."

"It will take us days to make our way back on foot."

"I gave the pilots two nuggets today, one for each of them. They get the second installment when they pick us up in the morning." Together, the little yellow rocks represented at least half a year's pay for the officer, far more for the soldier.

"Why do you think I can help with —"

"You know Chodron," Shan interjected. "We need to find Abigail. But we also need to track Chodron's connections in town." He glanced at their companions. Gao had put on a set of headphones that allowed him to speak to the pilot. Hostene was looking out a window on the opposite side of the ship, as if searching for a woman on a mule. "But first we need to talk about your partnership with Tashi."

Yangke's face clouded. He began fidgeting with a cargo strap that hung along the side of the fuselage. "Tashi is dead."

"If you don't wish to speak of Tashi, then how about the explosion at the old mine?"

"I don't know what you mean."

"Chodron keeps very thorough records. Careful records of the miners, careful records of his village administration. But there is no record of your stealing anything from him. By my calculations, the day he locked the canque around your neck was the day after the old mine blew up. Tashi and you were friends. Tashi knew the miners."

Yangke absently ran his finger around the rim of the porthole. "He said he could get me to India, to start a new life. He knows . . . he knew a monastery in the south I could join. Otherwise, without his help, it takes a lot of money to cross the border when you have neither papers nor passport. I'm an outcast monk. What do I know about making money?"

"Why didn't you join the miners?"

"The gold on this mountain is not meant to be taken away. What Tashi was doing was different. He told me about the professors seeking old deities. I figured they could make better sense of the past than I could. He offered me a bargain. He knew I had a secret I had kept since I was a boy, even from him."

"You mean they didn't discover the old mine," Shan said after a moment. "You told them where it was."

"I told Tashi where it was. Tashi told the professors. None of the gold had ever been taken down the mountain. In exchange, Tashi promised to get me across to India. He said he had a foolproof way, that I could ride with gods all the way."

Shan closed his eyes a moment. He had been so blind. "It had never been taken down the mountain," he repeated in a hollow voice.

"I had searched when I was a boy, spoken with all the old ones, considered how poor our village had always been. They never used it in the temple, except for a couple small statues. Abigail and Professor Ma made rough calculations based on what they saw at the mine. Tashi told me they thought maybe two tons of gold had been mined. Two tons."

"But someone else found out about it?"

"Tashi got drunk. Sometimes with Bing. Thomas had started selling liquor. That boy had everything he could want but he had to come across and throw alcohol on our smoldering fires."

They gazed out at the landscape in silence.

"So Tashi told Bing, and then the mine blew up," Shan said. "Then Chodron put the canque on you. Because," he suggested after a long moment, "he was furious that you kept the secret from him all these years."

"No," Yangke said in a slow voice, "it wasn't like that. The explosion was huge. It shook the ground all the way to the village. Chodron came up the slope immediately, demanding an explanation. Bing was already on a bike, riding down to explain. He said that some of the miners' works had been blown up, had been sabotaged. And there was only one person who hated the miners and Chodron enough to destroy their claims. He told Chodron that someone had stolen explosives out of the stores at Little Moscow the night before. Chodron never goes to Little Moscow. He stays away from the miners, and only speaks with Bing. So, of course, he believed Bing."

Shan let the words sink in a moment. "Bing didn't want Chodron to know there were two tons of gold waiting to be found somewhere higher on the mountain. And he couldn't take the chance of someone finding the old mine and reaching the same conclusion." He looked at Yangke. "But didn't you deny blowing up the mine?"

More mountains sped by their window.

"You didn't," Shan concluded. "You didn't contradict Bing."

Why would Yangke protect Bing, he almost asked, then realized that for Yangke there was perhaps a more important question. "Why did you let Chodron put the canque on you and condemn you wrongly as a thief in front of the whole village? Why did you keep it on? You could have run, you could have hidden, you could have gone to Tashi or even Rapaki."

"At first, it was to protect Tashi and our plan. Because if I had run then, Chodron would have tried to find me and he would have discovered Tashi's secret camp," came Yangke's simple reply. "But later . . . I realized I deserved it. I should have understood that the only possible way to save the old things is to keep them away from the

396

new world. I knew that, but when Tashi said he could get me to India, where I could be a real monk, I was tempted and I succumbed," Yangke added.

Shan closed his eyes, letting the painkiller do its work. But he did not sleep. He had learned in the gulag that there was a part of the brain that drugs never reached, the part that kept repeating Yangke's words until, as the helicopter began to descend, he found himself looking at the young man again, understanding the full depth of his pain. Yangke had accepted the canque because he had betrayed the secret of the mine. He had worn it because he believed, as Shan now did, that the secret he had disclosed to Tashi was the reason his friend had been murdered.

Like most older communities in Tibet, Tashtul was two towns, the efficient concrete-and-steel construction Beijing had erected and the traditional Tibetan market town that survived. As they walked from the weed-thatched, crumbling soccer stadium where the helicopter deposited them, Shan found his eyes drawn not to the two- and three-story block structures that dominated the low skyline but to the diminutive, decaying buildings that dated from earlier centuries, a wooden stable here, a crumbling chorten there, a stone tower where Buddhist banners would have been displayed during festivals that had been banned decades earlier.

They stood for several minutes at a rusting war memorial by the entrance to the stadium, Beijing's monument to the fierce battles that had taken place in the region, Chinese divisions pitted against small brigades of Tibetan resistance fighters.

"I take it," Gao said reluctantly to Shan, "you are about to propose that I lead this fragile expedition." As he spoke he cocked his head toward the street. Hubei was running away.

"It would be suspicious for a man of your renown not to be," Shan suggested. "Not to mention that we have neither money nor friends here. Not even a street map."

"A street map," Gao replied, "is one thing you don't require in Tashtul." He pointed to the squat block structure two hundred yards away, in front of which a tire was being changed on a decrepit bus by means of a cable slung over a tree limb, pulled by a tractor. "The transportation center." He pointed to an open-air pavilion beside a row of buildings with glass storefront windows, then to a four-story building, the highest in town, that sported a Chinese flag and a dozen antennae. "The center for food and the center for authority."

They walked past half a dozen barracks that had been converted to school rooms, behind which were five or six blocks of residences, a mix of old wooden structures and stucco bungalows. Shan did not miss the way Gao, finished with his orientation lesson, gazed back at the flagpole on the government center. Below the flag waved a long red-and-black banner, an unfamiliar ornament, the kind traveling armies used to fly.

"Where should we —," Yangke began. Then Hostene decided the question for them. Without a word he began jogging toward the bus station. Shan clenched his jaw against the pain in his ribs and followed as quickly as he could. By the time he caught up, the Navajo was already in the station, extracting a photo of his niece from his wallet, gesturing toward it as he approached people waiting on benches, the sleepy vendor at the news kiosk, a wide-eyed girl selling dumplings from a steaming bucket.

As Shan reached his friend he caught several wary glances in his own direction. He had not changed his clothes since he'd been attacked. His pants were torn at the knee, his shirt mottled with dried blood. He drew Hostene into the shadows, calming him, hoping none of the Tibetans had paid attention to his urgent words in Chinese about an American woman.

Gao went out into the sparse crowd now, passing out small-denomination notes, asking softly about a woman who had become separated from a mountain-climbing party after an accident and might be seeking transport to Lhasa.

Too late Shan saw the gray uniforms among the throng of men at the disabled bus. The Public Security officers, often called knobs for the ornaments on their shoulders, were led by a man who, though middle-aged and overweight, had the sharp predatory eyes of every knob Shan had ever known. The officer's steely gaze fell on Yangke and Shan. With a hand on the radio at his belt he approached. Yangke sank helplessly onto a bench.

Suddenly, Gao was at Shan's side, thrusting a dark brown souvenir sweatshirt into his hands. XIZANG, it said in gold letters — Western Storehouse, the Chinese name for Tibet — arranged in an arc over overlapping images of a mountain, a yak, and a truck. Shan turned it inside out and pulled it over his soiled, torn shirt. He was heading for Yangke when he froze, every instinct sounding alarms. The station had nearly emptied. The dumpling vendor sat as if paralyzed, knuckles white on the rim of her bucket. The wall behind her began changing colors — dirty brown, then dirty blue, then brown, then blue. He overcame his paralysis to take another step as Hostene was guided by a knob to Yangke's side, then he felt a firm grip on his lower arm. He did not speak, could not speak, as another knob led him to a bench and pushed him down.

"You can't take them!" The words, meant as a shout, emerged from Shan's throat like a moan. With a patient, businesslike air the knob at his side withdrew a baton from his belt. The sight of the weapon sent a new ripple along Shan's ribs. He could not take another beating, not now, not without the risk of injuries that could force him off his feet for days.

Yangke and Hostene offered no resistance as they were manacled together and led into the prisoner wagon that waited, blue lights flashing, at the front of the station. Shan struggled to his feet, his wrists in front of him, to accept manacles. Then, when none were presented, he staggered toward the wagon. He had caused this. He had to be with them. But the knob at his side grabbed him again, pulling him back, as the doors of the van closed. The last thing Shan saw inside was Hostene, pressing his sacred feather against his forehead.

CHAPTER TEN

Shan collapsed onto a bench as the prisoner wagon sped away, disappearing in the direction of the government center. There would be holding cells in its basement — dim, damp places with insects and mold and dark, ominous stains on the walls. The two men had come to Tashtul because of Shan's wishes and now they would be photographed, fingerprinted, and sprayed with disinfectant. Then the knobs would begin their entertainment.

Gradually he became aware of his surroundings, of people filing back into the station, of the girl hawking her dumplings in an unsteady voice, of the first set of knobs who had been in the station going to their car, then driving slowly down the road, of Gao sitting on a bench across the street, calmly reading a copy of the *Lhasa Daily*.

"Yangke won't have a chance," he said as he lowered himself onto the bench beside

Gao. "Once they discover he was ejected from a monastery they will be like dogs fighting over fresh meat." Shan spied something at Gao's feet. Hostene's pack.

"They overlooked it," Gao said.

Shan unzipped the front pocket and saw the American's passport. "Without this they'll assume he is one of the old Tibetans. You know what that means." Hostene would become part of the Ax to Root campaign. They called the special reeducation camps for such men sausage grinders, for the way so many types of Tibetans were thrown into them, only to emerge two or three years later, unrecognizable, in neat homogeneous forms. "Or else he will start speaking Navajo and they'll declare him crazy. They'll feed him through a slot in a cell door for the rest of his life."

Gao gestured to a brown sedan that had pulled to a stop at the curb. A short, stout Chinese man in a blue cardigan sweater and white shirt climbed out of the driver's seat, offered Gao a quick bow, and opened the rear door. Gao rose and, taking Hostene's bag, stepped into the car then waited with the door open. It took nearly a minute for Shan to decide to join him.

For much of the drive Shan's eyes were fixed on the central structure of the town, its front clad in faux marble, as he made quick calculations. How fast could he reach the basement of the building if he leaped out of the car? How long would it take Yangke and Hostene to be processed before they were thrown into the cells and the torment began? Where could he flee with them if he could somehow effect their escape? He was responsible for them, and, blinded by everything except the need to help Abigail and Lokesh and Gendun, he had led them into a trap. He had trusted Gao and now Yangke and Hostene were paying for his mistake.

"On my very first day of training as a physicist," Gao declared, "my professor, an elderly Russian, told me, 'Never trust reality.' He wrote it on the chalkboard in Chinese and Russian. 'You will spend the next few years learning that the reality you have always experienced is a myth,' he said. 'You will spend the rest of your lives proving that all the important forces of the universe are unreal.'" Gao gazed from the car at the banner floating above the government center.

Shan studied the famed scientist, perplexed by Gao's interest in the black-and-red banner that fluttered over the government center. "I wasn't thinking about physics. I was thinking about birds," Shan said.

"Birds?"

"Your lammergeiers. Karl, Friedrich, Albert. Their names say it all."

Gao carefully folded the newspaper. "I don't understand."

"I think you do. Famous theoreticians. They never had to be accountable for the terrible effects of their words and their equations, never had to act in the real world. You're going to have to choose, Gao."

The scientist did not respond. He stared out the window for the rest of the ride.

They arrived at a tidy two-story building that consisted of two traditional Tibetan houses that had been joined together with stuccoed walls. SNOW LEOPARD CULTURAL NOVELTIES INC. proclaimed a small sign over the central entry.

"Kohler," Shan guessed.

"A joint enterprise," Gao explained. "He is managing director, but we are equal owners."

A sober well-dressed Chinese matron, introduced as the office manager, met them at the door and escorted them through a hallway lined with shelves full of figurines in porcelain, clay, bronze, and brass. Fat laughing Buddhas. Yaks, some wearing comical expressions. The Potola Palace. Camels. Mythical garuda birds. Tibetan goddesses.

They arrived at a simply furnished office in the front of one of the joined houses, where a tea tray awaited them. Shan poured out two cups as Gao conferred with the woman, who wiped tears from her eyes as she spoke. He studied the office. A framed certificate hung above a desk, testifying to the registration of the company ten years earlier. On another wall was a map with pins inserted in over thirty cities, inside and outside China, including half a dozen in India. Framed photographs stood on a small table. Kohler, with a dozen workers posed in front of the building, apparently at some kind of company celebration. Gao with Kohler, ceremonially shaking hands behind a table spread with two dozen different types of figurines. Kohler in front of the Taj Mahal. Kohler on a white sand beach with a woman in a very brief swimming suit. Several photos featured Thomas, spanning a period from when he was perhaps twelve years of age to the recent past. In one, the boy held four figurines of bronze in his hand.

"He designed those," Gao explained over his shoulder. "It was the first run out of the little foundry Heinz installed last year. Thomas would always spend a week or two here each summer."

Through the window Shan saw the woman trot to the car, where she spoke to the driver, then got in. A moment later the sedan sped away, back toward town.

"Where is Heinz?" Shan asked.

"Lhasa. When I called him on the satellite phone to say Abigail was with us in the mountains he was about to come back but he received word that there was some trouble with a shipment. He decided to take care of it before returning, to avoid the need for a trip later. We spoke again when . . . after Thomas left. Now he's also making arrangements for Thomas's body, which rests in the morgue here."

Shan poured himself more tea as Gao sorted through papers on the desk. Through the window, in the distance, dimly outlined against the cobalt sky, he could make out the low ranges that led to Sleeping Dragon Mountain. "Where does the trail emerge from the mountains?" he asked.

"It branches into three forks as it approaches the town, following different streams. There are farmers living along each fork. Abigail will be seen by someone."

"You need to speak with them," Shan

stated. "I am going to Public Security."

"The driver is asking the farmers now. And the worst thing you could do for your friends would be to go to the government center."

Shan searched Gao's face, trying to decide if his words were meant as a threat. "Then there is somewhere else we must visit," he announced, and bent near Gao's ear to speak in a low voice. Gao called for the office manager.

Shan expected Chodron's Tashtul home to be a small apartment, perhaps even an assigned room in a government guest quarters, not an ample bungalow at the edge of town. It was larger than the headman's home in Drango village, with well-tended flower gardens surrounding it. Two bicycles leaned against a railing of painted metal pipes that flanked the concrete walkway to the door.

Gao declined with a shake of his head as Shan got out of the car and gestured toward the house. Shan ventured up the walkway, studying the house, trying to assess what he would find inside, worried about the two bicycles. The house was of simple, new construction, a beige-painted block with brown metal shutters. The front windows were covered with curtains. The glass panes in the door displayed decals of flowers and panda bears.

There was no answer when he knocked. He tried the doorknob, found the door unlocked, and stepped inside.

The lining of Chodron's Tashtul nest was far more luxurious than its modest exterior. The spacious sitting room Shan stood in held four upholstered chairs and two sofas, arrayed around a lush sculptured carpet to face a unit on the wall holding a large television set and other electronic equipment, and shelves of videos and discs.

Fast-paced music came from a room down a dim corridor, a Western instrumental featuring saxophones, drums, and electric guitars. He should flee, a voice inside him shouted. He would be unable to help Hostene and Yangke if he were thrown into the same cell. Instead, he went farther, reaching a dining area with chrome-framed chairs surrounding a table rimmed with carved lotus flowers. The kitchen counter bore an array of small appliances he could not name. It was not the house of a Tibetan family. Behind the dining table, opposite the kitchen, was a half-open door that led to a room that seemed to be half office, half storage area. Along one wall were cardboard cartons bearing labels for various electronic devices. Beyond them was a desk on which stood a radio similar to that which he had seen Chodron use in Drango. Over the desk, pinned to the wall, was a collection of name tags bearing Chodron's name, with legends identifying Party gatherings, some with clips, some on lanyards.

Shan began opening drawers, quickly passing over one that contained office supplies, another brimming with personal items like disposable razors, skin cream, unused wallets, and packages of breath mints. He paused over one that was crammed with file folders and settled upon two files and a ledger book from the bottom drawer, whose separate lock yielded to the careful levering motion of a letter opener. When he had read through them he reentered the dining room and gazed upon the riches of the house. In his mind's eye he saw Gendun lying prostrate in Chodron's village, his limbs shaking from nerve damage. Shan started at a noise from the rear of the house. Through the kitchen window he saw an old Tibetan hoeing weeds in a bed along the wall.

At the kitchen sink Shan washed his hands and face. He quickly explored the closet by the front door, then grabbed a hanger that bore a dark suit and a gray shirt inside in a plastic cleaner's bag. In the office he stuffed the sweatshirt Gao had bought for him behind a box, threw on the shirt and the suit jacket, and pulled the trousers, far too loose to fit properly, over his own tattered pants, fastening them at the back with a spring clamp. He grabbed a lanyard from which a name tag was suspended, selected the thinnest of the wallets, and hastily worked with a rubber band and paper clips. Before leaving the office he retrieved the letter opener, unscrewed the back cover of the radio, and pried several components away from their fittings before replacing the cover.

She was in her midthirties, taller than Chodron, with the strong, full features of a Manchurian. Still dripping from her bath, she wore only white briefs, her long hair covering her breasts. She did not raise the towel she held, did not even seem to breathe when she discovered Shan sitting facing her at the end of the dining table, his hands folded over the ledger and files in front of him.

Shan had chosen the chair by window, with the glare of daylight behind him. Chodron's gray suit jacket was only slightly too large in the shoulders. He had blocked the

412

view of his feet with a briefcase, knowing his tattered boots would betray him in an instant. But he need not have worried for the woman's gaze remained on the little black leather folder hanging from the lanyard around his neck.

He opened the top file and lifted a pencil from the table. "Let's start with your name," he said in a level voice. He had spent twenty years on this side of the interrogator's table.

The woman's mouth opened and shut several times but no words came out.

"Get dressed," Shan instructed, the weary impatience of a senior official in his tone. "Get a glass of water. Get a chair."

Chodron's mistress was named Jiling. She worked in the municipal affairs office and was responsible for census data and the distribution of funds to the county's villages. Chodron had found the perfect partner. Now Shan understood how he was able to function in an official capacity in an unofficial village.

"I don't know you. Are you from Lhasa?" Jiling asked after his first quick round of questions. She had chosen to wear an austere dark blue suit. She took back her identity card when Shan finished with it and kept it in her hand. "I saw the banner," she said in a hoarse whisper.

"I am from Beijing."

The woman slumped.

"Cooperate now and you may not hear from us again."

"I don't know anything."

"You have already told me you are involved in the administration of the villages in this county."

Jiling looked down at her identity card. "It is a big county," she observed, beginning her defense.

"Surely you know the penalty for misappropriation and misallocation of public funds."

The color drained from her face. Executions were almost always public events in China, but the ones that were given the most publicity, that sometimes filled entire stadiums, were those of corrupt officials.

"I have over a hundred villages —"

Shan cut her off with a wave of his hand. "There is a saying in English — If a tree falls in the woods and no one is there to hear it, does it make a sound?"

"I don't — I don't understand."

"If villagers don't exist, are their tax payments considered public funds?" He gestured toward the opulent furnishings of the sitting room. "If we have to continue this after today's visit, you will be required to provide receipts for everything in this house, with the source of payment for each."

Jiling straightened in her chair. "I am merely a low-level official," she declared.

Good, thought Shan. The ones who crumbled immediately were usually the least helpful.

"Drango village is on the official list," she added.

"But what is its official population count?"

"Thirty," she admitted, her voice cracking.

Shan had seen more than double that number of people in the village. So Chodron could collect taxes from everyone and pocket the difference. The village might appear on the official rolls but half its taxes never reached the government. No one would have complained. The villagers who realized would have considered it protection money, a fee for keeping the government away. An antitax.

Shan studied the woman, refilled her glass for her, began casually asking about her office, about her superiors, about where she and Chodron kept their bank accounts, whether she traveled with Chodron at Party expense. These were tedious queries that Shan could propound by rote, and which any experienced bureaucrat would expect to be included in such an interview.

"Where do you sell the gold?" he asked abruptly.

"I don't know what you are talking about."

Shan gave an indifferent shrug. "If you won't speak about it then you just give him the opportunity to do so first, to use the information for negotiation. It will be an interesting dilemma for the prosecutors, who to make their primary target. The attractive, well-educated Chinese bureaucrat versus the Tibetan farmer. Except the farmer is a revered Party member."

Jiling no longer fidgeted with her identity card. She was squeezing it so hard it began to dig into her flesh, drawing a thin line of blood. She calmly stepped to the sink and washed her wound.

"Who are you if you are not with Major Ren?" she asked from the counter.

"Perhaps you should look outside."

Jiling studied him uncertainly, then went to the front window. She pulled the drapery cord, opening the curtain only a few inches. When she finally focused on the brown sedan parked outside she pressed a hand against her heart.

Shan approached the window. Gao was leaning against the car smoking, though Shan had never seen him with a cigarette before. The woman from the factory office now sat in the driver's seat, strangely transfixed, eyes forward, hands on the wheel.

"Some people said he was dying in his castle in the mountains." Jiling spoke in a whisper, as if fearful Gao might hear. "Others said he went back to Beijing to live in a palace. They call him the chairman's chief sorcerer."

"When Chodron is here, who is he exactly?" Shan asked.

There was another car, a black utility vehicle, parked fifty feet behind Gao's. "Do I need to invite him inside?" he continued when Jiling did not answer. Then his mouth went dry. Two men in gray uniforms got out of the utility vehicle and began walking toward Gao.

"Chodron has offices in the county Party administration," Jiling told him. "He used to be termed the chief Party representative for the rural proletariat. Now they call for ethnic diversity in the Party leadership. The last title they gave him was secretary for indigenous agrarian workers."

That explained how Chodron managed to come and go as he pleased, an official without portfolio, though if he spent too much time in town with his Chinese mistress he might jeopardize his standing.

Jiling had gone silent. She was looking at his feet. Shan had forgotten his tattered boots.

"Undercover work," he asserted. He motioned her toward the table. She hesitated, glanced from Shan to the men outside.

"If I need to summon them I will," Shan said. "But I assure you I will try not to involve you further. Write down what you have told me. When Dr. Gao comes to the door, hand him the statement."

"Where are you going?"

"To interview the groundskeeper," Shan ventured.

"He's nobody, some old Tibetan."

Shan pointed to the table. She looked at his boots, then at Gao and the knobs outside, then retreated to the table and began writing.

Shan quietly slipped through the rear door and scanned the yard. The groundskeeper was sleeping against a tree, his chin propped on his chest. Shan removed his lanyard, pushed it into the pile of plucked weeds near the man's feet, and entered the shadows at the back of the yard. The small strip of forest behind the row of houses gave him cover until he reached the street, two hundred yards from Chodron's house.

His eyes stayed on the town's tallest building but his feet, as if by an instinct all their own, went in the other direction. In a small park consisting of a derelict playground and a grove of trees, he settled onto a bench made of cinder blocks and weathered planks. His ribs were aching from his beating at Little Moscow. He lowered his head into his hands. He had not felt such despair since the early days of his exile and imprisonment in the gulag. His life was spiraling out of control. The lives of everyone close to him were threatened by dark destinies — prison, a firing squad, cancer. Murderers who hacked off hands were loose on Sleeping Dragon Mountain and he could protect no one. He needed to rest. He needed to meditate, to expunge the despair from his mind, to expel the pain from his body. He needed to do what Gendun called taking himself out of himself.

As if from a great distance he watched three children play on a broken swing, hanging on the side chains, chinning up the support poles. Once he would have been warmed by such a sight. He had spent years learning from the old Tibetans how to savor the simple joys of life. Now, after ten days with Chodron, Gao, and the faceless killer, the sight of the children only brought sorrow.

He did not know how long he stared at the cracked dirt at his feet, or when exactly he looked up at the children again. They had stopped playing and were gazing at a patch of sunlight in the trees in which a man stood. The man was at least twenty years older than Shan, a Tibetan, wearing clothes that were patched and threadbare. His legs and arms were in constant, though very slow, motion, his hands like the heads of two swans on long graceful necks. He was performing a combination of Tai Chi and Buddhist meditation exercises. Shan found himself walking toward the man. Loose threads hung from his frayed pants over his bare feet. His serene smile showed he was missing most of his teeth. His thin wispy hair was mostly gray. He was oblivious to Shan, oblivious to the children who watched. They shrank back, awe in their eyes, as the man began to jump in great arcs until one of his leaps placed him under the swingset. He grabbed the overhead pole and propelled himself upward. He kept his grip, working his legs to gain height, so that soon he swung in nearly a half circle, his face lit with joy.

Shan watched as if in a trance. Though he could not explain why, as the old man swung, his despair lifted. Finally, he turned his gaze toward the government tower and began walking to it. At the edge of the park he turned for a moment. The serene old Tibetan was still swinging.

When he reached the building he studied it, walking circuits around it, noting the unmarked Public Security vehicles behind it, the steps at the rear that descended to a heavy metal door, the small slits of windows just above ground level covered with thick wire. As he watched, the rear door opened and a man was carried out on a stretcher, his feet in chains. From behind a truck, Shan dared a glance at his contorted, swollen face. Too old for Yangke, not old enough for Hostene.

He ventured into the reception area, searching for video surveillance equipment. Seeing none, he went to the building elevator. Public Security had offices on the third floor. There was no listing for the basement.

Out front he noted three gray utility vehicles, bearing license plates for Lhasa. He circled the building. A dented, unwashed van pulled up in back of it. The driver, a plump, middle-aged man in a white shirt, opened the back doors and began lifting out shiny metal buckets and plastic containers. The instant Shan smelled the steamed rice he emerged from the shadows. Then he extended one of the remaining gold nuggets to the deliveryman.

He carried two buckets of steamed rice, walking one step behind the deliveryman. The guard inside the door, more interested in the food than its porters, waved them toward a sterile-looking room at the end of a row of cells. At a table in its center sat another guard, working on documents. Shan set a small container of soup onto the table too close to the edge. Some of its contents spilled onto the papers.

"Ta me de!" the guard yelled, then launched himself toward a shelf on the rear wall that held bedding and towels. The door guard ran over to gather up the papers. The nervous deliveryman, backing up, upended a bucket of rice Shan had set on the floor behind him.

As the cursing guards bent over this new mess, the deliveryman shouted for Shan to bring rags from the van. Instead, Shan darted down the dimly lit row of cells. A teenage boy sat in the first, his arm in a sling. In the next cell was a Chinese girl, lying on the cement floor, a vacant drug-induced grin on her face. An overweight man in a sweatsuit slept in the next. The remaining cells were empty, except for the last, its door open, where another guard lay

422

on a bunk, snoring. Then Shan saw the metal door at the end of the cell block and realized his mistake. As new prisoners, Yangke and Hostene would still be in the interrogation rooms. He opened the door and shut it behind him, leaning against it for a moment, gathering himself, bracing for the inevitable scents of urine, antiseptics, singed hair, and vomit.

Six more metal doors awaited him, three on each side of the corridor, each with small squares of wire-strengthened glass at eye level. The first two were open and empty. Shan flicked on the lights in the second, revealing a metal table, three metal chairs, and a large metal bucket. On the table were a pair of needle-nosed pliers, dental probes, a ball-peen hammer, and leather straps used for binding prisoners to chairs. In the air was a new odor, the faintest scent of cloves. The knot in his stomach tightened. It was an old trick from the gulag, one he had nearly forgotten. Pull out a tooth and offer oil of cloves to deaden the pain. Then pull out another and withhold the oil.

The next room was locked but lit, its sole occupant a man sitting on the floor in the shadows of the far corner, beating his head against the cement wall.

He found his friends in the last room. The

door was open. Yangke stood behind Hostene, who sat at a table opposite a young uniformed knob officer. There were paper and pencils on the table on which were written half a dozen simple words in the Roman alphabet. Hostene was teaching the man English. As Shan eased the door shut, Yangke awkwardly gestured toward a table bearing two large thermoses and mugs with domed porcelain caps. "There's tea."

His friends were unharmed. A dozen questions sprang to Shan's tongue but he choked them down, uncertain of the role he was to act in their little play. Strangely, he was more certain of how to address the knob officer. "Are you with the Lhasa team?" he asked.

The officer turned the papers over, then stood and retrieved his uniform hat. "Major Ren? Of course not. Those red-banner men are . . . He only comes when . . ." The young officer could not finish his thought.

"We have to go," Shan ventured.

"I haven't received instructions," the officer replied. Shan studied him. He had a careful, educated air about him. He relied on instructions, not orders. On his collar was a small brass star in a circle, an emblem unfamiliar to Shan.

Another knob entered the cell, glaring at

424

the younger officer, gesturing to someone in the corridor. A man in manacles, wearing a prisoner's hood, appeared, followed by an officer in his forties, who gave the prisoner an unnecessary shove. Without thinking Shan went to Hostene's side.

This officer had a cold, sleek countenance, his hair oiled and combed back, his thin, pockmarked face like a hatchet. Around his arm was a band of red and black. One side of his mouth curled upward as he examined first Yangke, then Hostene, and finally Shan.

"Where is he?" the officer snarled.

"Not — not here, Major," the younger officer stammered.

The notorious Ren finally had a face.

Blood leaked from the bottom of the prisoner's hood. The knob jerked the hood off. Hostene's head shot up. Yangke gasped. It was Hubei.

"You fool!" the major snapped at the young officer. "Don't you have sense enough to keep prisoners separate? Each man to his own interrogation room — now! No food or drink until I —" His words faded as he saw Hostene gaze over his shoulder.

"Surely," came a refined voice, "you would not deny a meal to my colleagues?" Gao glided into the room, an expression of studied ease on his face. Behind him came one of the guards, carrying a tray of bowls heaped with rice, which he set on the table before scurrying away.

"This is not Beijing," the major growled. "Nor one of your sacred research reservations. Here we are governed by the rules of Public Security."

Gao calmly went to the tea table and then extended a steaming cup to Shan. "It has been a long day for us, Major. There have been unforeseen logistical difficulties requiring us to stop over in Tashtul and pursue different tasks. But now" — he indicated Hostene and Yangke with a sweep of his free hand — "now with the help of Public Security we have been reunited."

Ren's eyes narrowed. "Public Security?" he growled. "You mean with the help of these sniveling, ignorant babysitters?"

Shan gazed at Gao with new respect. There were indeed separate units of the Public Security Bureau assigned to protect and assist special people with special secrets. Given the many secret installations in the area, a post of such officers in Tashtul, wearing brass stars in circles, was to be expected. He remembered Gao's worried reaction when he had seen the red banner that morning. He had known Yangke and Hostene would have no chance against Ren's visiting squad, so had called in a preemptive strike. Never trust reality, Gao had warned on the park bench.

"Some aspects of security, Major Ren, require more subtlety than a gun and a baton."

Ren seemed unconvinced. He gestured with one hand. His men sprang into action, stepping to either side of Hubei, dragging him to the end of the table and pushing him into a chair. In another few seconds they had produced leather straps and secured his arms to those of the chair.

Ren turned to Gao. "This man was found lurking about outside the bus station with a knife. He tried to flee when my men approached him. He can't decide who he is. We know he's a former prisoner from his tattoo. But he says he is a shepherd. Then, later, he said he arrived with your party. Imagine my surprise, a shepherd who knows of Gao. Your driver also paid three farmers to provide him with intelligence about a person coming from the mountains. One recognized his civic duty and came forward to confess. He waits in the next room. He has already spoken of mysterious caravans that head into the mountains in the spring."

"We have had this conversation before, Major Ren," Gao said, barely stifling his impatience.

"What were these men bringing to you?" Ren demanded.

Gao did not reply right away. He made a show of bringing tea for Yangke and Hostene before replying, "Your job is to protect state secrets, not to know them," he finally said.

Ren made another gesture. One of his men produced a black box with a small rod extending from it, one of Public Security's favorite imports from the West, a cattle prod.

Shan had to admire Hubei's grit. Other than clenching his jaw, he showed no reaction to the first jab of the device onto his bared forearm. Behind his back the officer adjusted the output and thrust the rod between the rails of the chair, into Hubei's spine. Hubei gasped, arching his back, lifting the chair off the ground.

"I have never seen this man before," Gao said.

Ren extracted a folded piece of paper from the pocket of his tunic. "This is your shopping list," he said to Hubei. "Medicine. A long bead necklace. A cardboard mailing box at least twelve inches long by ten inches. Small plastic sheeting in which to wrap the contents. Fifty renminbi postage." He looked up with a surprised expression, as if reading it for the first time. "A lot of postage. With it one could send something heavy to the other side of the world. You *shepherds* fascinate me. What kind of medicine?" He tossed the paper down on the table, then closed the door and nodded to one of his assistants, who lifted the prod again.

The miner, twitching, spittle hanging from his jaw, finally yielded. "I came on an errand," he said with a groan. "I was sent on an errand, that's all."

"What kind of medicine?" Ren repeated.

"Painkillers. And stomach medicine."

"Your big mistake, Gao," Ren declared, "was not claiming this man to be one of your own. Now he is mine."

Shan's protest started as a hoarse whisper but grew louder as he met Ren's gaze. "But he *is* with us," he began. "The professor can't be expected to know every porter at every work site."

"Making a false statement to me is a crime in itself. He said he was a shepherd. Was he lying?"

"We would be foolish not to have a cover story for all of our workers. More than foolish. Unpatriotic."

"Unpatriotic?" The word seemed to catch Ren off guard.

"Tell me, Major," Shan continued, "can

429

you imagine a project more important to the people of China than sending a rocket to the moon?"

Ren studied Shan.

"An electropulse relay transmitter must be repaired," Shan announced. "The part must be carefully packed, and a detailed description of the problem will be enclosed. The manufacturer is in Tianjin. If we handed it over to the army they would send it to their supply depot, fill out endless forms, and deliver it to the right place maybe four months from now. If it is shipped direct we can get it back in six weeks. There is a test launch in eight weeks. We must have a functioning transmitter by then. This man was bringing the packing material back to our camp. Until you stopped him." Shan scooped the paper off the table and pocketed it.

"And the necklace?"

"Surely a man can be forgiven for trying to buy a trinket for a woman."

Ren studied Shan with a cool, calculating expression. "Who are you?" he demanded.

Shan took a sip of his tea. "It was the Chairman himself who promised that the People's Republic will put a man on the moon."

"I asked for your name," Ren pressed.

"I want *your* names," Gao shot back. "And that of every man in your squad. Name, rank, and serial number. I want to be able to identify of all those responsible if the launch test fails." He turned to the young officer behind Hostene, who stepped forward with a pad of paper in his hand, nervous anticipation in his eye. "Do we list your office as Lhasa or Tashtul, Major?"

"Inner Mongolia perhaps?" Shan suggested.

Ren gripped the back of a chair. The raw fury in his eyes was aimed at Shan. A dozen thoughts raced through Shan's mind as he returned the stare, ending with one that almost caused him to break away. Chodron. If Chodron were to walk through the door, Shan's life wouldn't be worth ten fen.

Ren paced along the far side of the table, pausing to give a muttered order to one of his men, who darted out of the room. "It's peculiar, Comrade," he said to Shan as he began releasing the straps binding Hubei. "You are wearing two pairs of trousers." Something bright appeared in his hand, which he abruptly tossed across the table. As they watched, a flash erupted, and another. The second officer had returned with a camera, and by the time the object landed and rolled to a stop he had photographed each of their faces. They all stared at the object Ren had tossed onto the table. It was the gold nugget Shan had given to the deliveryman.

"I shall of course release your shepherd," Ren volunteered as he pocketed the little nugget. "No doubt you need him to pilot a rocket."

They were sober as they left the building and headed toward Gao's car. Shan handed the list to Hostene, who thrust it into a pocket. As they reached the car Yangke halted. They followed the Tibetan's gaze. Hubei was sprinting away.

"Shan is coming with me," Gao announced to the others as he waved them toward a decrepit sedan bearing a taxi sign. "We will meet you back at the factory."

Gao stayed in the taxi when they reached the bus station. Shan found Hubei sitting on a wooden crate in the shade of the cinderblock wall of the station, stricken with fear. He had no resistance left in him.

"If you had told us about your brother it might have been different," Shan said.

The miner's eyes flashed but then he sagged. "No family, not ever, that's Bing's rule. It makes for too much conflict on the mountain. But then my younger brother came to me in the winter. He had lost his job as a chef, but he had big plans. All we needed was some capital and he would get us to Hong Kong, where we would start a restaurant. He would cook, I would be the manager. We always spoke in secret. We met at out-of-the-way places like in front of those old paintings."

Shan thought back to the strange video that had so disturbed him. Abigail had told someone to think of his family and of the Eight Treasures in a Winter Melon, the classic gourmet dish. "Did he encounter Abigail at a painting site?"

"I told him to stay away, that foreigners were trouble. But he could speak some English. He began to help her with little things. Tashi didn't like it. He threatened to tell her uncle."

Shan studied Hubei. "Were you the one who found your brother's body?"

Hubei's voice trembled. "So much blood. At first I thought he must have been hunting for a goat for us to eat. But when I spoke to him, I saw something was wrong with his tongue. I kept talking to him, asking what was wrong, asking why he didn't answer. Then I saw a stick of wood with eyes painted on it was jammed into his mouth. It took me a long time to realize that he was dead. He couldn't be dead! We had plans, we were going to start new lives. I didn't know what to do. He had picked flowers and sprigs of juniper for an offering. I put them on his chest, and was going to cross his hands over them."

"That's when you saw he had no hands."

The miner nodded. "I would have had my vengeance by now, but you came along."

"It was you on the bicycle, with the club," Shan said, "You who hung me on the rope today and beat me. You lit the fires in the barley to punish Chodron for failing to punish Hostene."

Hubei said nothing.

"If you think Hostene killed your brother, why help his niece? Why undertake to do the shopping for the things on the list she gave to Bing?"

"Because it's the way to find her again. And when I have her, I will get her uncle."

"Where were your purchases to be taken?"

"Bing has a map. To a place with black sand, near the summit."

"Why did she have your brother put out those skeletons?"

"She wanted to keep people away from the old paintings."

"People?"

"Some of the other miners. There were legends about an ancient gold mine. I had told my brother about the skeletons Bing and I had set out, so he wouldn't be frightened. He must have told her."

There seemed to be a surplus of bones on the haunted ridge. "They were ancient bones, weren't they?"

"Very old, I think. Last week, they all disappeared, even the skeleton on the grave."

Right after Thomas had boasted of being able to tell old bones from new, Shan realized. But fortunately for Bing a new body had materialized, the corpse of the farmer who had been struck by lightning. Bing had staged his death as a murder to keep the miners frightened of the haunted ridge.

Gao was becoming impatient. Shan went to the car and spoke to him. "How do I find this black-sand place?" Shan asked Hubei when he returned.

"It's past the old shrines, near the top of the mountain. All summer she kept moving higher up the slope, looking for paintings with the little ovals. Watch for the crazy monk, if you want to find her. She could speak to him, calm him, and get him to help her."

"What do you mean, little ovals?"

"Tiny ovals, outlining shapes. She taught my brother to use her video camera, so he

435

could take pictures of them."

A siren blared. Hubei looked as if he were about to bolt.

"Do you know what reincarnation is, Hubei?" Shan asked.

"This is Tibet. Everyone knows."

"You have just been reincarnated, without going to the trouble of dying. Congratulations."

Hubei stared at a paper Shan had dropped into his lap.

"It's a ticket to Golmud, in the north. A big factory town. Lots of jobs. You're not going back up the mountain."

"Like hell."

"I'm saving your life. If you go back up the mountain you won't survive the summer. What do you think Chodron and Bing will do, once they find out you burned the barley fields?"

As they spoke a bus pulled up, northbound.

Hubei stared at the bus, stared at the ticket, then boarded the bus.

"There are sleeping quarters upstairs," Gao announced when they met the others at the company compound. "I will arrange for food."

They ate in the conference room, with the

driver perched at the window like a guard.

Hostene broke their weary silence. "She intended to trick us. Abigail never left the mountain. I don't understand."

"She intended to make you leave, to get you out of harm's way. She knew Thomas had been killed, and she knows the killer is close. But she is determined to reach the summit. Only two things are important to her now — your safety and reaching the end of the pilgrim's path."

"A cheap trick," Hostene said. "We came all this way because of that damned Bing."

"It was *her* trick," Shan pointed out. "Abigail wrote that note willingly."

Hostene nodded. "She doesn't want us to interfere. She asked us for a box and postage. She means to send her work home."

"It's as if she —" Gao did not finish his thought. As if she didn't expect to make it off the mountain.

"If the doctors are right, she has three or four months before her strength fails."

"If I went to Ren right now and explained, he would forget the rancor between us," Gao said. "This is the kind of thing he lives for. He could have a hundred men on the mountain tomorrow." He handed a folded paper to Shan.

"No," Hostene said, and it seemed to

settle the point. "It's between me and Abigail."

"And the killer," Shan added.

"And the killer," Hostene repeated. "But if we don't find the killer, what becomes of Lokesh and Gendun?" he asked Shan. This was the question that never left Shan's mind.

There were only three beds for visitors in the upstairs chamber. When Shan arranged a blanket for himself on the floor Yangke argued, saying he should take it, as the youngest, relenting only when Shan explained that after so many years in prison he was unable to sleep on a mattress.

As Gao began to draw the curtains Shan put a hand on his arm. "No. Don't give them any reason to think we are trying to hide."

"You think they are watching? Impossible."

"Some people feel impending rain in their joints," said Shan. "I can feel Public Security in my spine. They are out there, a team, at least two men, maybe four."

"What are we going to do?" asked Yangke in alarm.

"What we are going to do," Shan said as he removed his outerwear and stretched out on the floor, "is sleep." But he did not sleep right away, for he had read the folded paper from Gao. It was a record of Bing's assignments in the Public Security Bureau. For the five years immediately preceding his retirement, Bing had been commander of prison guards at a gulag camp near Rutok.

It was perhaps two hours past midnight when Shan awoke, trembling, from another recurring nightmare about Gendun and Chodron. Lifting his boots from the floor beside him, he tiptoed down the stairs, into the silent factory building.

There the gods awaited him. Lit by moonlight filtering through a high window, tiered rows of tiny Buddhas, Taras, and saints stood, waiting to be painted and packaged. An army of miniature Tibetans waiting for a signal. Lokesh would have said a prayer over each one.

He sat in a pool of light facing the little figures, like a lama facing his students. Or perhaps from another perspective, they were like a legion of lamas patiently abiding their single, faltering student.

He lowered his head, shamed by his earlier relapse into his Beijing incarnation. "I'm sorry," he heard himself say to the figurines. "I strive to become a shape like them." His audience of perfect little ceramic gods would know he meant Gendun and Lokesh.

"But the only clay I have to work with is that which I brought from the outside." He fought a chaos of thoughts, forming his fingers into a mudra, Diamond of the Mind, and focusing on it, letting the storm within him blow itself out. Eventually, for the first time in nearly two weeks, he found a quiet place, a meditative place, and worked to stay there. It was, as Gendun once told him, like balancing a smooth weathered rock on the tip of one finger.

His meditation ended abruptly, a long time later. Something was lurking at the edge of his consciousness. The words that sprang onto his tongue seemed to bypass his mind. *"On mani padme hum,"* for the Compassionate Buddha, then other words for each of the images he recognized among the little figures. Some were words he had not spoken since learning them on dark winter nights from very old Tibetans, risking the penalties of curfew to speak them. *"Om ah vajre gate hum,"* he finally added, and paused, wondering why something inside, unbidden, had offered up the words for the Green Tara, the Droljang Tara. Of all the manifestations of the Tara he might have chosen, something within him had settled on the aggressive protector form.

His mind became impossibly clear. He

heard an insect crawling on the window, a mouse scratching at the rear of the building. He began reviewing the events on Sleeping Dragon Mountain, starting with the moment he had set foot in Drango village, reconsidering every piece of the puzzle, changing their positions, twisting them like little pieces of colored glass, watching them transform in hue as he turned them this way and that. His fear receded, replaced by what some of the Old Ones would have called the mind of the warrior protector. By the time he rose, the moon was low in the sky and he had begun to grasp the pattern of the puzzle.

He bowed to the assembled deities in gratitude and went toward the front of the compound, pausing at the factory door as he reminded himself of what Yangke had said on the helicopter. Tashi had promised he would "ride with the gods" all the way to India.

Gao stood in the dark in the doorway. He spun about at Shan's approach, then relaxed. "You were right. There are two of them."

Shan stepped to his side. Gao was watching a shadow inside a shadow. But then the man drew on a cigarette, casting his face in a quick orange glow.

441

"I wish Heinz were here," Gao said. "He knows about such things."

"Have you spoken with him?"

"I called the hotel where he keeps an apartment. He checked in. But he had to drive to the airport. He'll phone tomorrow."

"But you'll be gone tomorrow."

"No. I can't leave on the same helicopter that brought us here. Ren would note the serial number and make the pilot talk. Then the mountain will be smothered with soldiers. You would never find the killer."

Gao was repeating Shan's own warning back to him. The scientist too must have been meditating in the dark. He seemed to have finally accepted that the only justice for his nephew would be unofficial justice.

Gao tapped a compact instrument on his belt. "My satellite phone. I called the pilot. He landed at a nearby base after arranging to have a mechanical problem. He will take the helicopter on a test flight and come at dawn, without lights." Gao reached into his pocket and handed Shan a wad of banknotes. "This will make up for the gold you used."

Shan went to the backpack they had left there earlier. He extracted the digital camera, fumbling until finally he discovered how to scroll through the stored photos. When

442

he found the one he wanted he extended the camera to Gao. "Can you print this here?" he asked.

Gao studied the photo. It was of Abigail Natay, cheerfully sitting on a rock, left foot under her body, right foot hanging over the edge. Her hair was upswept, adorned by flowers. After a moment Gao went to the computer on the desk and then pointed to the printer. A still image emerged. Shan retrieved the photo, placed it in his pocket, then checked the window again.

On the adjacent table, dimly lit by the street light, was the photo of Kohler, his arm around a woman's shoulder. They were on a beach. Shan held it up. "Where was this taken?"

"In the south of India. Heinz does a lot of business there and has made friends. The company owns a house and a warehouse in India."

"You must enjoy the contrast in climate."

When Gao did not reply Shan realized his mistake. "They won't let you out," he said. The government's lifeblood was secrets, and Gao was a walking vault containing the most dangerous secrets of all.

"If I want sun," Gao said, "they arrange for me to speak at a conference on the southern coast of China. With an escort."

Shan replaced the photo and rejoined Gao at the window.

"When you find Abigail Natay," Gao said wearily, "bring her back to my house. But first we must find a way to get the three of you out of here before sunrise."

Shan considered the problem only briefly. "What time do your workers arrive?" he asked.

An hour before dawn, Gao switched on the light in his office and walked purposefully to the window, pointing to the blush of pink in the eastern sky as Shan, then Hostene and Yangke appeared beside him. He gestured toward a table that had been positioned near the window, then closed shut the filmy inner curtain and sat with them. The office manager appeared with a tea tray.

They waited several minutes, talking and gesturing broadly before signaling for the first of three early-arriving workers who were squatting along the wall. Shan rose, approached the wall as if to look at a picture, then flattened himself against it and sidled out of the room. The first worker took his place at the table. Soon the three of them were outside.

Shan watched from the deep shadows until the nearest watcher lit a cigarette with a match, destroying his night vision. Shan motioned to his friends and they headed to the soccer stadium. Soon they were airborne. Shan was ready to wake the dragon.

CHAPTER ELEVEN

The fields that had fed the inhabitants of Drango village their entire lives were black and barren. In the charred fields, they crouched on their hands and knees to glean a few intact kernels, sometimes finding an entire seed head that had survived the flames. Their hands and faces were covered with soot, and with their desolate expressions they seemed to be wearing the masks Shan had seen used in ritual plays portraying fleshless puppets of the dead.

Yangke ventured into the village. He returned with a warning that Shan should not seek out Lokesh and Gendun. The villagers were still dazed by the catastrophe that had struck their village, and the only thing they knew for certain was that their troubles had started when Shan and the other outsiders arrived. Gendun was now under double guard because Lokesh and Dolma had tried to move him.

"To where?"

"I don't know. Away, out of the village," Yangke replied. "They had him on a litter, but weren't even able to carry him past the fields. If Dolma wasn't an elder, Chodron would have had her caned too."

"Was Lokesh caned?" The words seemed to choke Shan.

Yangke slowly nodded. "Thirty strokes of Chodron's bamboo rod. He demanded to know where you were." Yangke restrained Shan, who had taken a step toward the village. "He's not there. I couldn't find Lokesh or Dolma. But they said he is all right, that he hardly seemed to notice the cane, that he —"

"— recited a mantra and looked toward the sky as he took the beating," Shan finished in a hoarse whisper. How many times had he seen it before, in their prison camp? Forty? Fifty? At times Lokesh had difficulty bending, because of all the scar tissue.

"Chodron is furious. His generator is broken. He has no radio contact. He keeps hounding the man who is trying to fix it. Everyone is afraid of him and his men. They're hiding from him."

Shan had seen the headman observing when the helicopter left them on the slope above the fields. He must have thought Gao was still with them or he would have rounded them up.

"And Gendun?"

"He sits in Dolma's house, reciting the death rites when he has the strength. For Thomas. For Tashi. For Professor Ma. The villagers took the farmer who died to the fleshcutters. They asked Chodron who killed him. But he told them they must wait until the festival. No words have been recited by the dead farmer's family. They know if they perform any act of devotion, Chodron will punish Gendun."

Shan's throat was so dry he had trouble speaking. "You saw Lokesh?"

"No. He and Dolma must be locked inside too." Yangke recognized the furious expression that crossed Shan's face. "Dolma will have ointments for Lokesh's back. He will be safe. You can't go down there." Yangke scanned the slope above them with a worried expression.

"Hostene has started climbing," Shan explained. "He wants to be alone. He knows where to meet us." Shan stood, slung his pack over his shoulder, and starting walking. After half a dozen steps he paused and looked over his shoulder. Yangke had not moved.

"You are going to seek out ghosts," Yangke said.

"Someone once asked Lokesh what I do," Shan said. "He told the man I am a confessor of ghosts. It's the best description I have ever heard. In my experience the only people who can be relied upon always to tell the truth are the dead."

When they arrived at their destination it was late afternoon. The hermit Rapaki was not in his cave. There was no sign that he had been there since he'd fled during their first visit. Hostene had lit a small fire and balanced one of the hermit's battered saucepans on two rocks to boil water. Shan could see the Navajo scanning the mountainside. Every hour that passed brought his niece closer to death. He had urged that the helicopter drop them off as high up the mountain as possible. Shan had resisted, explaining that they could not risk being spotted by the miners in Little Moscow or spooking the killer.

Shan lowered himself against a rock at the mouth of the cave and found himself blinking away sleep. A warm southern breeze carried the scent of gentians. A bird warbled from a grove of junipers. When he awoke, less than an hour of daylight was left. Soup was cooking. Somewhere behind him, in the dim cave, Yangke was whispering the soft syllables of a mantra. Hostene sat on an outcropping, watching another of Abigail's videotapes.

When Shan entered the cave, Yangke ignored him. Had Rapaki returned? Shan lit a butter lamp and squeezed through the narrow opening that led to the chamber the hermit used for refuse. The chaos of trash and stores was gone. Someone had cleared the central part of the room, arranging the debris into piles in the two far corners. For the first time Shan saw that the floor had been painted, probably centuries earlier. There were faint broken lines of color, tiny staggered ovals that led from the eastern wall, defining a wide circle at first, then spiraling inward in a counterclockwise direction, making six — no, eight — ever smaller loops until it ended among images that had been recently ravaged. Since his last visit someone had destroyed the center, roughly hacking at the floor with chisel and hammer, leaving only a few colored shards that offered no clue as to what the focal images had been.

Ovals. Hubei's brother had learned how to use the video camera so he could film ovals on a fresco Abigail could not reach. Shan explored every inch remaining of the strange pattern, following it outward now, discovering that the outer lines of marks did not exactly form a circle. The outer ring of the circle was broken. Two lines bent and climbed the adjoining wall. With his dim light Shan followed the lines upward. They each ended over his head in jagged shapes that looked like lightning bolts. Here, on the wall in front of him, the oval shapes were best preserved. He held the lamp against the wall and realized the little marks weren't exactly ovals; they were more like plump figure eights. Footprints. The lines were made up of symbolic footprints. Abigail had been here, had probably helped clean the cave in order to study the old signs on the floor. She had found a map of the pilgrim's path. This was the place of beginning — for pilgrims, for Abigail, probably for the killer. And now for Shan and his friends.

He followed the ovals back down the wall, unable to make sense of them. Then he stepped back to survey the faded characters on the wall as a group. They were all demons, the most fearful members of the Tibetan pantheon — not protector demons but the devils that had been integral to Bon belief long before the Buddhist saints had reached Tibet. They were the flesh-eating, fanged devils who wore skulls around their necks. The style of the paintings was like none he had ever seen in Tibet, crude yet powerful. But if Abigail was correct in her hypothesis, he should expect to see images unlike any found elsewhere. He followed the spiraling footprints, pausing at each of the demons along the way. When he reached the ruined centerpiece he gazed up, as confused as ever. There was no correlation to the mountain, no connection to the geography outside. It was simply a map to hell.

He took out the tiny piece of plaster he had been carrying with him since his first visit to Little Moscow, when he had been thrust against the fresco. He laid it beside the rows of ovals and walked around it, considering the ever-shifting pieces of the puzzle of the Sleeping Dragon, then studied the lines that led to the images on the wall, trying to identify the demons depicted based on their similarities to more modern images. There was a black bull that no doubt signified the Lord of Death, another signified suffering, others delusion and the impermanence of life. It was a map of the kora, though not a literal map.

At the mouth of the cave Yangke was stirring the soup. Dried branches had been added to the fire. Hostene was gathering twigs. As Shan lowered himself beside the fire he saw that Yangke was now cleaning containers in which to serve the soup. He had three of Rapaki's empty cans beside him and was cleaning three others.

"There's no need —," Shan began, then broke off as Yangke nodded into the shadows.

"She wouldn't let me join them," Yangke said. "She still blames me for Tashi's death."

In an instant Shan was on his feet, the butter lamp raised as he walked along the wall of the outer cave, pausing every few steps, fingers extended to catch any moving air. He found a fold in the rock, barely big enough for a man to crawl through. After four feet it opened into a wide passage. Juniper smoke hung about the roof of the tunnel.

They were in a chamber near whose center was a cluster of four candles, and half a dozen butter lamps were scattered around. They sat facing a wall lined with old wicker chests and huge clay jars. Lokesh was gesturing, speaking in the soft, patient voice of a teacher. Dolma was learning a mantra. Lokesh was using his own method to help Gendun and save the people of Drango village.

Feeling like a trespasser, Shan extinguished his lamp. Dolma did not trust Yangke. If Lokesh had seen Yangke, he would have assumed Shan was nearby, but still his friend had remained hidden.

Lokesh paused in midsentence, raised his eyes toward the ceiling, then twisted slightly and without looking back extended an open, uplifted palm in Shan's direction.

Shan approached uncertainly, painfully aware that he had been disappointing his old friend ever since arriving on the mountain. He had been in many secret chambers since he had been released from prison, had thrilled with discovery as Gendun and Lokesh explained the significance of old relics in hidden shrines, often felt satisfaction that he could now explain much of their content on his own. But here he was just another intruder.

More objects came into view. Holes had been hand chiseled into the rock and pegs inserted to hold equipment. But not the equipment of worship Shan had often seen in such rooms, not robes, not the twenty different hats used to signify roles and functions in the big gompas, not symbolic offerings. On the wall were ropes and staffs of wood, short yak-tail whips, manacles with hand-forged links, ritual axes and iron goads, wooden collars that looked like shorter versions of the canque Yangke had worn, many old leather bags with long drawstrings, and, even more strangely, felt vests with many pockets.

Shan lowered himself to the floor beside Lokesh. His friend was in a state of reverence. Shan would no more interrupt him than he would have interrupted Gendun in a meditation, though the more he listened the more uneasy he felt. A chill crept down his back. Lokesh was going to the same unlikely place Shan had visited the night before in Tashtul, when the little deities had seemed to push him to where he would not have gone on his own.

"Om vajra krohda," Lokesh intoned. *"Om vajra krohda hayagriva."* Powerful, dangerous words, words that Shan had heard only once before, words that were almost never written, but handed down orally, in remote secret places. They invoked one of the most powerful protector demons, Hayagriva the Horseheaded, the terrifying prince of protectors who clad himself in the flayed skin of his enemies.

"Hum, hum phat!" Lokesh concluded.

Shan listened, strangely scared. This was not the patient, forgiving Lokesh he had known for so many years.

The old Tibetan chanted the mantra invoking emptiness, then with a flying bird gesture recited *Om ah hum* three times, then *Ha ho hrih,* followed by the iron hook gesture, then *Om sarva bhuta akarsaya.* They were the words for summoning all demons.

A bead of sweat rolled off Lokesh's cheek, his hand trembled. Fear began building in Shan's chest. His heart began rising up in his throat. There was indeed something in Lokesh he had never seen before. There was no gentleness now in the old man beside him, but rather a dark power, a raw emotion that came close to fury. Lokesh was secretly invoking fierce protective demons and barely tolerant of Shan's presence, as if Shan were part of what he was protecting against.

He studied the room again, trying to understand, frightened for all of them now. Was it possible that the biggest of the wicker chests was glowing? Lokesh began new mantras, calling upon the tiger-riding Mahakala, then three-eyed Shridevi and snakebodied Rahula. He wasn't merely trying to summon a deity to protect Gendun. It was as if he were trying to rip the world apart and start over.

Then the demon rose up. With a wrenching moan Shan threw himself backward.

It was the serpentine Rahula, and it rose from the largest of the wicker chests, one that was nearly four feet high and six long. The thing gazed at the two old Tibetans then seemed to notice Shan sprawled behind them. It cocked its scaly head to study him.

The mantras had finished. Dolma and Lokesh seemed pleased at their work, nodding to the creature as it climbed out of the chest. It had a human shape beneath its demon head, human hands floated along its sides. Beginning to regain his breath, Shan watched as it kneeled in front of Lokesh and bowed. Lokesh uttered a solemn greeting, then pulled off its head.

"It's only us," Dolma whispered to Shan. She was at his shoulder, helping him to his feet. "We were not able to explain. The words had to be finished. There is probably not a man in all Tibet who remembers them so well as Lokesh. We are truly blessed." She brushed off his sleeve, like a mother tidying a small son. "You remember our Trinle, the town carpenter."

The shadow under the headdress resolved itself into the countenance of the most senior of the elders who had sat with Shan and Lokesh their first night in Drango, the silent one with the wispy beard who kept looking into the sky, the father of the guard Dolma had summoned to her house.

"Trinle has been working on the old costumes. That one's straps had rotted away. He used some yak-hair cord to fix it."

The carpenter grinned shyly. "Lha gyal lo," he whispered.

Shan studied each of the old Tibetans. They too were addressing the violent mysteries of the mountain but they saw them in a completely different way, as disturbances in the natural harmony, as an imbalance among deities. There were no words he could use to reach them, no possibility he could bridge what he was doing and what they were doing. "Lha gyal lo," he repeated.

"He is the only one left," Dolma added.

"Left from what?"

"He knows about these things because he used to help store them away each autumn and attended the rituals in spring to awaken them."

"I thought all the monks at the village temple were killed."

"They were. They all ran to pray in the sanctuary when the bombs started falling. Trinle was the groundskeeper. He was up in the orchard that day when the Chinese planes came." Her voice dropped. "He is all we have left. He made a drawing of the old temple that he keeps hidden from Chodron. Sometimes we get it out in the night and sing the old songs." Her voice became barely audible. "Because we have forgotten most of the mantras."

Trinle was busy adjusting the headdress again. Lokesh still did not acknowledge Shan. He had formed the Diamond of the Mind mudra. His entire being seemed focused on the top of the spire formed by his two fingers.

Shan walked along the row of chests and boxes, not daring to open any, but seeing two more demon costumes within those that were open. He looked back at the strange objects on the adjoining wall. A dozen questions sprang to mind but he dared not attempt them. "There's soup," he finally declared.

Dolma nodded and leaned close to Trinle's ear. The former groundskeeper reverently laid the Rahula headdress on top of its wicker chest and joined them. Shan paused, looking awkwardly at his old friend.

"Lokesh is not eating today," Dolma said, and gently pulled Shan away. They rejoined the others.

Hostene's near frantic concern for his niece impelled him to ask blunt questions of Dolma and Trinle. "My niece said that early pilgrims — people searching for something — came here, long before the other pilgrim circuits in Tibet were constructed. But she told me there was no clear route, no way back for those who set out. You must know the way up and the way out. Where is it?"

Trinle and Dolma listened, then glanced at each other. Hostene's mistake was that he thought they had come to help him find his niece.

"Everything here is very old," Dolma offered. "From the time before the first Buddhists arrived in Tibet."

Hostene nodded. "That's the reason she came here. But where does the path lead? Why is it hidden? We will find her on the path." Pleading was in his tone now. "I must find her."

"This place, this cave, was meant to be an ending," Trinle said. "Here the lamas tried to convince the travelers to turn back. This was the place between the worlds. When we came here from the village we had to undergo purification rites before we could even enter. This is where the lamas prepared themselves to repair the trail each summer."

Hostene searched Shan's face, as if he might be able to explain the riddle of the old Tibetan's words.

460

"I think," Shan said, "we have to understand exactly what was destroyed at Drango village fifty years ago."

Yangke leaned forward in intense anticipation as Dolma began to speak.

"The temple had been part of the oldest sect of the Bon," she explained. "Its roots arose from a time before history. Its monks considered Drango to be more like a spiritual guardhouse than a temple."

"Guardhouse?"

Trinle glanced around the shadows as if for eavesdroppers, then leaned forward. "It guards the entrance to the hidden home of the old gods," he declared, "the ones from before time, led by the dragon god who protects the earth."

The announcement seemed to release a torrent of emotion, and memory. The old man spoke quickly now, not always coherently. "Look at this! Look at this!" he said with a gesture at Hostene. Trinle touched the Navajo, pushed his sleeve up, pointing now to the tattooed figure made of lightning bolts. "The Old Ones said this is where all the lightning in the world begins. This one understands!" he said, looking at Hostene as if he had never seen him before. "This one was summoned!"

When Hostene and Shan stared uncer-

461

tainly, Trinle exclaimed in a sober tone, "Your niece was called here by the first gods."

The first gods, Trinle continued, had confided to the early Tibetans the location of a special door to their *bayal,* the underground paradise where gods and saints lived in lush gardens and assumed the shape of rainbows whenever they chose.

Hostene pulled out his map of the mountain. "If that is where the path goes, show it to us. It can't be to the summit. The summit is surrounded by cliffs."

Trinle did not seem to understand the question.

"It's not like that," came a dry, weary voice from behind them. Lokesh stepped into the ring of light. He poured himself a cup of Yangke's tea, but did not touch the food. "The more you rely on such a map, the farther away you'll be."

"The path was never intended for the gentle Buddhist pilgrims," Yangke said, "I know that much. It was more of a spiritual obstacle course."

Trinle nodded. "The Bon pilgrims led a harder existence. Many had been warriors. Salvation was to be won, like victory in war. The path was an ordeal, meant to be terrifying. It wasn't a reward, but a judgment.

They hoped the pilgrims would turn away here. People died on the kora, or else they were transformed into rainbow bodies to become saints. Start as a worm, end as a god, that's what the oldest lamas used to say. It was said there were certain reincarnates, special messengers of the deities, who would be born with the knowledge of how to find the path." The old man said apologetically, "The only ones who knew more died in the bombing. Even they rarely used the old path. It's been over seventy years since anyone tried."

"Was the equipment I saw inside intended for the pilgrims?" Shan asked. He quickly explained to Hostene and Yangke what lay in the chamber deeper in the cave.

"It was to help them achieve humility," Trinle confirmed. "To discourage them, to weaken them with doubt. Even the most devout were begged to turn back so they could see their families again."

"What do you mean?"

"Sometimes the devout made it to the top, to the end of the trail. *But none of them came back.*"

Shan remembered Rapaki's letter to his uncle, who had set out to find the gods over thirty years before.

"So," Yangke summarized, "the ones who

failed came back as corpses and the ones who succeeded were never seen on earth again. And that was before there was a murderer on the mountain."

The words seemed to take everyone's breath away. They ate in silence, watching the stars, stirring the embers.

"It is not the way of things," Lokesh said. And though Lokesh was staring at the fire, Shan knew the words were meant for him. "It is not worth it. You are simply re-arranging stones in a stream."

It was a lesson often repeated to Shan by Lokesh and Gendun and the other monks they lived with. What point was there in trying to manipulate events in the outer world, they would ask. The stream of destiny would not change. No matter how many rocks you rearranged in the stream, the water would always replace them and continue its fated course.

"We cannot simply wait below," Shan said, also to the embers.

"You must stay below," his friend said. "This kora is very old, almost totally unconnected to humans." His words, even his voice, had an otherworldly quality. "It could be the last one on earth. This *druk* god, this dragon god, could be the only hope for our people. You can't go up the path to chase a criminal, you can't ascend like animals following a trail of blood or this last god will give up and abandon humans altogether."

Despair settled over Shan. "I don't know how to stop searching," he said.

Without another word, Lokesh stood and hobbled away.

"There are bags here, in the chamber below," Trinle said later. "Those who refused to turn back here were given a pilgrim's sack, a blanket, and a staff, and told these were the things needed on the trail. Sometimes, if a lama was going on, he would ask to have a wooden collar or manacles put on as well."

"Tell me, Trinle," Shan said. "Is any equipment missing?"

"Some bags, though I can't say how many. And some things kept in one of the baskets."

"What things?"

Trinle stroked his grizzled jaw. "Ornaments for the Green Tara. A golden headdress, a green vestment, golden bracelets. Sometimes they evoked her by having a nun wear those things at the altar."

"I don't understand," Yangke said. "Is Abigail accompanying a pilgrim or a killer? It must be a killer, for he always flees, always hides, always expresses himself in blood. It must be a pilgrim, for who else would be

465

interested in the old path? But either way, why should he care if Abigail lives?"

"Because she can read the old symbols," Hostene ventured.

"There's another reason," Shan said, and extracted the photo Gao had printed for him in Tashtul.

Yangke took it from him, holding a lamp over it, studying it. Then his eyes widened in surprise. "Buddha's Breath!" he gasped. He handed the picture to Lokesh, who gazed at it a few moments, then began to nod.

Shan took the photo and explained it to the others. He pointed to Abigail's extended leg first. "It's called the position of royal repose, one of the customary symbols in the old paintings." He pointed to her upswept hair, her golden earrings, the flowers in her hair, her hand resting on one knee, her green sweater.

"I don't understand," Hostene said. "This was taken on our afternoon off. I insisted she have some rest. We picnicked."

Shan pointed to a tiny detail in the upper corner of the photo. "That is the back of a wild goat on the ledge above the rock she sat on. Look at the way it juts out. The goat could not have seen her. He was spooked by something on the opposite slope, someone who was watching you from above. Rapaki was up there. There is a prophesy that the Green Tara will come back to help Tibetans."

"Abigail," Hostene uttered in a hoarse voice. "He thinks Abigail is the Green Tara."

"The one thing of Tara's she doesn't have," Shan observed, "was the long beaded necklace Hubei was to buy in town."

"So she is safe," Hostene said.

"Safe from the pilgrim," Shan said, "but not from the killer."

Later, he found Hostene on a high rock, gazing toward the dark silhouette of the summit.

"When I was young, just a teenager," the Navajo said as Shan settled beside him, "my mother's uncle, a famous chanter, took me on a quest to meet the gods. He was planning to teach me what he knew, so my generation could keep the sacred knowledge alive. He brought me to one of our sacred mountains, gave me a rope, a flint, a feather, and a twisted piece of fragrant wood he had found on his own quest when he was a boy, and told me to climb to the top and stay up there for five days, fasting, and the gods would come to me. I climbed along a path with sacred symbols painted on rocks, guides, painted a long, long time ago. There were pieces of bone and feathers and red cloth jammed in rock cracks or on thorn-bushes, left by those who had gone before me. I reached the top and sang for a while, some simple words he had taught me. I sat and threw stones and watched birds. I started to sing rock-and-roll songs. After three days I climbed down the other side and hitchhiked to a town to see a girl I knew.

"My uncle came for me. He waited for two days at the bottom, saying prayers for me. He said a coyote had finally told him what I had done. He wasn't angry. Just sad the gods had not shown themselves to me. Later I got a motorcycle and rode all over the American West, taking odd jobs, hanging out in bars, and worse. I had my arm tattooed to mock my old relatives. My uncle kept trying to contact me because he was dying. He told my mother I had the makings of a great chanter, that I was one of those who were needed to keep the important things alive. I never answered his letters or returned his phone calls. He died before I returned."

Hostene stared into the heavens. "This is how the world ends, my wife said once, how great civilizations fall to pieces. The old things meant to be passed down, they are the best things distilled out of thousands of years of experience. But somehow in the last century we decided our own lives were too important, that fast cars covered with chrome, and television, and computers made us better than our ancestors. That's the lie that kills the great things."

"When I finally settled down and learned my two chants, I was going to have the tattoo removed but then I decided to keep it, to remind me of my shame." Hostene stared at the summit again. "Now that she needs me, what do I know about being a pilgrim? What do I know about gods?"

"People here aren't dying because of gods," Shan said. "They're dying because of gold."

Shan was alone before the little fire when a hand reached out of the shadows for him. Yangke gestured him into the cave. Then, lifting a butter lamp from the floor, he silently led him down the corridor Shan had taken before, to the chamber with the pilgrim's equipment. But they continued until they reached what appeared to be the end of the tunnel, a chamber smelling of old incense, whose ceiling was blackened with the soot of butter lamps.

Old Trinle sat near the center of the room,

gazing up at another painting, his eyes filled with tears.

"He won't speak to Dolma about this," Yangke explained. "He said he never came here before, that it was only for the senior lamas."

Another fierce protector was depicted, Shan thought at first, though the image was unlike any he had seen before. The god in the center was dragon-headed. Two dozen small demons surrounded it along the sides and bottom.

"It is the druk deity, god of the mountain, the earth god," Trinle declared in a raspy voice. "This is where the lamas started and finished each pilgrim season. He is the one the fortunate ones meet at the top."

Yangke said, "All these years, Rapaki didn't know why, despite his years of meditation, he wasn't shown the Kora. I think he decided he didn't have something the god wanted. He kept looking, trying to understand what that thing might be. He had no teachers," he reminded Shan.

"You must not tell Dolma," Trinle told Shan.

Shan stepped closer to the painting, not yet comprehending. Yangke handed him the butter lamp. Then he saw.

He had seen paintings of old gods with

necklaces and bracelets of human skulls. He had seen images of gods adorned with human skins. Until now he had never seen a god wearing a necklace made of human hands.

"After so many years alone," Yangke said in an anguished voice, "the mind might go to places . . ." He didn't finish the sentence. "I don't think he is exactly a murderer, not the way most people think of murderers."

Shan said, "Perhaps. But if one has an appetite for hands," he said, "someone else who *is* a murderer might find it convenient to feed that craving."

They lingered in silence, unable to break the spell of the deity before them. Yangke lowered himself beside Trinle. Shan found himself staring at the unsettling dragon-headed image.

"I could have learned its secrets," came a cracking voice, full of remorse. "I could have saved Rapaki," Trinle said.

In the quiet that followed only the occasional crackling of the lamp could be heard and a sound that Shan had begun to detect in all of Tibet's deep caves, a strange low resonance that was sound and not sound, something that made him feel small and meaningless, an intruder into a place not meant for mere humans. Lokesh had a name for it — mountain speaking.

"My uncle was the abbot," Trinle continued. "I was sent to the monks when I was ten, as had been the tradition of our family for centuries. But when I was seventeen I fell in love with a girl who tended the sheep. I would say I was meditating out on the mountain but it was not meditation I sought. We became like man and wife. When my uncle found out he banished me from the temple and took my robe away, saying the only way I could stay near the temple would be if I was digging its holes and tending its gardens. A year later, when the Chinese were advancing, my woman went down to Tashtul, to look for her mother. I never saw her again, never heard from her.

"I think it is true, that this is where the first gods started," Trinle declared after a long time. "A thousand thousand seasons ago. Once there were more gods than people. People were just made, like artwork, the way later people made paintings of gods." The old groundskeeper seemed about to weep. "Then there came to be too many people for the gods to tend, too many people who forgot the nature of prayer. The world could no longer be relied upon. And now," he pronounced in a thin, anguished voice, "I think there may be only one earth

472

god left, a frail old dragon at the top of this kora. When he finds the strength, he prays."

"What does he pray for?" Shan asked.

The answer came not from Trinle or Yangke, but from a lean, weary figure standing at the entrance to the chamber. Shan had no idea how long Lokesh had been there.

"That," his old friend said, "is the most important question in all the world."

Yangke began a whispered mantra. Trinle rose and brushed the dust from the deity's painted eyes. When Shan turned again Lokesh was gone.

He found Lokesh in the equipment chamber, at the wicker chests, gazing at the old masks. He lifted the headdress of a horned bull god and set it on an adjoining chest. "Trinle and Yangke tried to learn, but they had no proper guidance."

Shan noted the heavy-bladed instruments beside the yak-tail whips — ritual axes with curving steel at the top, a four-inch blade in the center. An outline in the dust showed one was missing.

"You must return with me," Lokesh said. "Now that we know what is here, the entire village will surely understand. Gendun says he needs to speak with Chodron, that if he can just sit and meditate with him, Chodron will see the error of his ways."

Shan could find no answer that Lokesh would comprehend.

"Then you are going up that kora tomorrow. Tell me that by doing so you will not beget more violence and more suffering." Death did not upset Lokesh for to him it was but a stage before rebirth. It was violence, which fed the imbalance he sought to heal, that he feared.

"I wish I could find such a way," was all Shan could say.

Lokesh stroked the golden nose of the horned bull headdress. "Return with me. Gendun and I will find a way. When he is healed, the three of us can climb to the summit together."

"If I return without discovering an answer to the killings, Gendun will be tortured again. To Chodron he is only a weapon to use against me."

"You know that is unimportant to Gendun."

"It is important to me." Shan's heart felt as if it were in a vise.

Lokesh tilted the bull up so that it seemed to be looking him in the eyes, and spoke to its golden face. "It is a season for killing, Dolma says. She says it is like a storm, that it needs to blow itself out so we can get on with life."

In the morning, outside the cave, Lokesh would not speak to Shan, would not look him in the eye.

Dolma transferred some apples and apricots from her own bag to Shan's pack, handed him one of the pilgrim bags Trinle had brought from the cave. "He says this is not what the track to the gods is for," she said in a strained voice, "that you must stop this, that you cannot turn it into some sort of contest between predator and prey."

"We have no choice." Shan lifted one of the pilgrim staffs and looked at his old friend, who stood on a rock, facing the sunrise.

"He says," Dolma continued, "that he wished they had taught you better. He says you know that if you follow the upper kora more people will die than if you did not. He says if he has a chance to remove Gendun he will do so. He says he does not know if the old hermitage is safe now, that he will not be able to leave word of where they are going."

A wave of tremendous sadness surged inside Shan. Was this how he would leave his Tibetan friends, the two men who had become like family to him? They had given him life when he had none. Now it felt as if he was betraying their teaching. He remembered a dream he'd had days earlier in which a phantom saint had told him his life would end on this mountain.

He and Yangke and Hostene had started up the trail, eyes on the summit, when Shan was stopped by the sound of hurried footsteps behind him. It was Lokesh, looking strangely frail. The old Tibetan lifted his beloved gau from his neck, the amulet that contained a prayer signed by the Dalai Lama, and placed it around Shan's neck. Then he went back to the camp.

They walked for a while before Shan stopped to spread the map out on a rock. Shan had marked each of the pilgrim's stations they knew of. "It's a puzzle laid out five hundred years ago," he said. "One station must point to a spur that goes upward."

Yangke fixed his gaze on the summit. It had been ringed with clouds all morning, the crooked pinnacle at times protruding from the top like an island floating in the sky. "You heard Trinle. The only ones who survived were the ones who failed."

"You forget the lamas," Shan said. "The lamas went up and down."

"We're no lamas," Hostene muttered. He

had emptied his leather pilgrim bag and was examining its contents. It held only a flint, an odd Y-shaped piece of wood, a butter lamp, and a coil of yak-hair rope.

Shan studied the maze of ravines before them. "Abigail recorded half a dozen pilgrim stations at this level. Once there would have been more. The most important one would have been the most difficult to find." He pointed to a clump of trees half a mile away on the table of rock that hung over the ravines.

Yangke's face darkened. "You must have a death wish," he said. But then he lifted his pack and began walking toward the trees.

"Why do you think this is the one?" Hostene asked as they halted near the lip of the ravines, directly above Little Moscow. Shan had taken out Abigail's video camera and was manipulating its controls.

"A pilgrim could get lost for hours, even days, in the ravines. The lamas wanted to make it difficult. They wanted to discourage as many as possible." He stepped into a shadow near the lip of the ravine, instructing Yangke to warn him if any miners became aware of the intruders above them. When he brought the faded painting beside Bing's cave into focus, the first thing he saw was a caricature of Chairman Mao someone had painted over the fresco. He began filming, zooming in and out, ducking as two miners lingered in conversation in front of the rock, then filming the empty place where the piece had fallen out of the painting, finally the piece itself, braced against Bing's front door.

"But you are only guessing this is the key," Hostene protested. "We should be climbing."

"It was you who made me understand."

"Me?"

"Your stick figures. The old gods you went to meet as a boy. The earliest Buddhists in Tibet were followers of the Thunderbolt. That's what this place was about: the thunder gods, finding the mouth of the thunder gods. If you want to find thunder what do you look for?"

Hostene knotted his brow. "Lightning."

Shan nodded as he squatted by a tree, out of sight of the ravine now, and replayed the film he had just shot. There had been another video, among those now missing, taken by Hubei's brother, who could venture into Little Moscow when Abigail could not. He stopped when he reached a frame that displayed the entire painting. The saint in the middle was surrounded by a dragon with a ball-shaped object in its claws.

Several sacred signs, including the ritual umbrella at the top left corner, composed of tiny oval marks, could be made out. "The images at a kora station had many purposes," Shan explained. "One was to provoke contemplation, perhaps create fear. Another, sometimes, was to explain where the pilgrim was to go next. At most stations I think the mantra was for the pilgrim's soul. This one was for his feet."

"You lost me."

Shan pointed to the beast. "When I was young my father taught me twenty different traditional words for dragon in Chinese. But in Tibetan there is only one term, druk. It is also the sound of thunder. Thunder comes from dragons. The druk is also the guardian of treasure." He pointed to the sphere in the dragon's claws. "The pearl is the seed of thunder, which is fertilized by the druk." Here he pointed to the strange shape that appeared as an upside-down mountain on which a miniature demon sat. "These are called *vajra* rocks, like floating islands. Vajra means lightning. The summit of this mountain is like them, cut off from the world, physically inaccessible."

"So far as we are concerned, clearly," Hostene said, his impatience mounting.

"Impossible to get to without an umbrella." Shan traced the dotted lines of the umbrella. "If you draw a line through the center of the pearl, the eye of the dragon, and the single demon, they point directly to the summit of the mountain." He demonstrated by freezing a wide shot of the painting with the summit in the background, then pointed to the umbrella. "At first I thought it was a primitive image of a white parasol, one of the sacred offerings. But it is more. It points the way." He pulled out the piece of plaster he had carried since it had fallen on his first visit to Little Moscow and handed it to Yangke. "The ovals that make up the lines are footprints." He paused at the look of wonder on Hostene's face.

"We use them, much like this," the Navajo said. "The path of our holy people — this is how we depict it in our sandpaintings, with little footprints."

Shan quickly counted under his breath. "Taking into account the pieces of plaster that have fallen out, I estimate the shaft of the parasol is composed of thirty-five to forty ovals, or footprints. The arcs joining it at the top each contain ten prints. It's an index, a scale. Each of the footprints on the shaft equals ten steps."

"To where?"

"The umbrella points the way," Shan said

again. On the video screen, directly beside the fresco was a series of small shadows, alternating up the ravine wall, though several had been destroyed by miners' chisels. "Climbing holes. Start directly over those holes and walk in a straight line for, say, four hundred paces."

"A pilgrim was supposed to comprehend this?" Yangke asked.

"Only a few. The most persistent. A pilgrim might spend weeks on a kora. Some would sit at a painting like this for days."

"The most contrite," Yangke suggested.

"The most desperate."

Shan followed his gaze, then quickly stowed the camera away. Hostene was moving along the rim of the ravine at a steady trot.

It took them a long time to find the second marker. They crept to the opposite side of the rim, above the painting, taking care not to be seen by those below, then walked three hundred fifty paces, debating the length of a Tibetan's stride centuries earlier. They fanned out, each man counting off another fifty paces. Finally, they discovered another painting, nearly faded to oblivion, this one depicting the thirteen possessions of an ordained monk, with the monk's staff drawn in tiny footprints pointed almost directly up the slope. The painting map called for another six hundred paces, toward a now familiar grove of trees. They found themselves in front of the ruined fresco with the ancient painting underneath. The footprints were tiny along the border surrounding the serpentine god, but Shan found them, and understood finally why the larger fresco had been constructed over the painting. No one had made it to the upper path for seventy years. The lamas had hidden the way by blocking the ancient explanation from view. In the early twentieth century more than a few oracles had predicted calamity for Tibetan Buddhists, and begged that their treasures be safeguarded. The lamas had tried to protect the mountain in their own way. But the person who had hammered away the plaster had not been interested in protecting anything.

"Abigail knew," Shan said to Hostene. "She kept coming back here."

The Navajo nodded. "She suspected. But she would never destroy the fresco."

"No," Shan agreed as he bent over the details of the little demon panels along the side of the painting. He pointed in turn to the tiny swords in four little hands, all pointing in exactly the same direction, and began counting the ovals. "Five hundred paces," he said a few minutes later, and pointed in the direction indicated by the swords.

They soon found themselves in one of the gorges at the foot of the summit and began passing small ravines with narrow, snaking walls that sprang out like fingers from the base of the summit. Shan began noticing black smudges near the entry to each ravine. He squatted and touched one. Soot.

"What does it mean?" Yangke asked.

"Someone made it this far but didn't know where to go next. He tested each ravine, then marked it with scrapings from a butter lamp."

Lichen was chipped away from the corners of several rocks, some with new growth appearing. They had been stripped a year or more before, no doubt by someone in search of another painting. Yangke pointed out small piles of ashes at regular intervals, and held some under his nose. Someone had been burning incense to attract the help of the deities.

"Look for fresh tracks," Hostene suggested.

After twenty minutes Yangke gave a low whistle. They found him before an undulating, wind-carved rock. "A self-actuated demon," the Tibetan declared. It took a moment for Shan to recognize in the ridges of the stone the shape of one of the tiger demons used by the Bon monks, even longer to notice that the colorations below the stone were not patterns of lichen.

Yangke knelt and began pointing to the barely readable letters. "Worm," he said, then "god."

"Becomes," Shan made out, then stumbled over vague markings that were too far gone to read.

"Worm. Becomes god," Yangke said in a puzzled voice. "Trinle said something about that."

The words echoed in some dusty chamber in Shan's mind. "Even the lowly worm eventually becomes a god," he announced. "It's a saying the oldest lamas use in teaching."

The three men exchanged perplexed glances, then began searching the two ravines closest to the faded message.

"Nothing," Yangke reported after several minutes.

Shan bent to the Tibetan's boot and touched it. His finger came away with grains of black sand. "There are no sand deposits up here," he observed.

"You're wrong," Yangke said, and led them down the passage to a small sand-filled depression.

Shan kneeled, running the sand through his fingers. "This was brought here."

"What does it mean?" Yangke asked once more.

Shan removed his pack and rolled up his sleeves. "It means we become worms."

Using their hands as shovels, they soon exposed a low hollow in the stone below ground level, then a narrow tunnel running through it filled with sand, a tunnel that, oddly, seemed to have been carved not by chisel but by water. Shan offered encouragement to a hesitant Hostene by explaining that this had been where Abigail had asked for her supplies from town to be left.

"But Abigail can't have come through here. The sand hadn't been disturbed," Hostene pointed out.

As he spoke, a sharp back draft of wind shot off the face of the mountain. In seconds it had refilled their excavation by several inches, answering his question.

When they reached the other side, they scraped the sand from their clothes. Directly opposite them on the rock wall was an image of another demon, his yellow eyes still vivid enough to be unsettling. Shan silently gestured them onward and a moment later they were at the base of the unattainable summit, looking up with disbelief into a fold in the cliff face. The builders of the path had indeed shown worms how to meet gods.

The color began draining from Hostene's face. Yangke paced nervously back and forth, shaking his head.

A chain of huge hand-forged iron links, each as long as Shan's forearm, hung in a long channel that seemed to have been gouged out of the rock wall. The chain was anchored to the rock near their feet by a thick iron staple and to the side of the mountain by long iron pins, which held it steady sixteen inches from the rock face.

"There's no end to it," Yangke said, looking up.

"It's just in shadow," Shan said, struggling to keep his voice calm. The end of the chain vanished into blackness nearly two hundred feet above them, where there might be an overhanging cave.

"It's so old," Hostene said. "The chain can't be safe."

"It's survived from the age of Tibet's great bridge builders," Shan suggested. "Special forges turned out chains like these for suspension bridges. Most of them lasted for centuries." He studied the big, uneven links uncertainly. They showed little evidence of corrosion or rust. "This one has been mostly protected from the elements."

"How old do you think it is?"

"Three, maybe four hundred years."

Hostene stared at the shadows above with a bleak expression, then lowered his pack. "We can't take everything."

"We are meant to carry what the pilgrims carried," Yangke said. "A blanket, a staff, our bags."

"Abigail would have carried more," Hostene remarked.

"Perhaps not much more," Shan said, gesturing toward the deeper shadows at the very base of the summit, where there was a small patch of color. Under a blue nylon parka they found a small mound of objects. A handful of ballpoint pens bound by a rubber band. A small cooking kit. A sweatshirt. A water bottle. Hostene opened his pack and began making his own pile, including the video camera. Shan watched for a moment, then began sorting through his own possessions.

Helping each other, the three soon had rolled their leather bags into their blankets and fashioned carrying straps out of the yak-hair rope. Hostene and Shan stared at the staffs, so awkward for a climb up the chain, then followed Yangke's example, securing them in the carrying straps around their necks.

They stood, gazing up, realizing how easy it would be for any of them to fall to his death. Seeing the fear on Hostene's face, Shan was about to suggest they reconsider when Yangke set a foot into the first of the links and began climbing.

At first they seemed to totter between heaven and hell, one moment reaching upward for the uncertain shadows above, the next slipping, fearfully clutching the metal to keep from falling onto the sharp rocks below. The links were rough and misshapen but wide enough for a foot or, when fatigue struck, for an elbow to be pushed through so that, locking arms, they could safely hang long enough to catch their breath. The old chain bore their combined weight without complaint.

As they climbed Shan began seeing a pattern in the clumps of vegetation that clung to the wall beside the chain, interspersed with open holes chipped in the rock, several of which contained bird nests. This kora was much older than three or four centuries. Before the chain's construction, holes had been chiseled in the rock as handholds to help pilgrims climb the wall.

They climbed together into the high channel of smooth rock. It had once been a waterfall, Shan realized, as he entered the vertical tunnel, a watercourse inside the mountain that had, by the hand of man or nature, been diverted, leaving the tunnel and a smooth vertical track for the chain, which reached its upper terminus alongside an open ledge. They had found the bed of the old stream. The rock wall of its bank sloped away at the top, leaving a five-foot gap between it and the side of the mountain. Hostene and Shan climbed upward, overlapping themselves on the upper chain. Yangke, who had preceded the older men, tried to reach the trail leading up the mountain with an extended foot.

"I cannot jump that," Hostene said anxiously as he gazed down at the rocks far below.

Shan, with his head at Hostene's ankles, studied the rock wall. Then he took the staff from his back and began probing a small patch of shadow that was darker than the rest, inches below the path. The end of the staff sank in nearly a foot. Shan threaded the staff through the opposite link in the chain and thrust it back into the wall.

Yangke, watching from above, announced that he had located another hole, four feet above the first. They soon had a precarious but firm walkway, with a rail to hold onto for the crossing. After some energetic coaxing of Hostene by the young Tibetan, they all made it across. Yangke lit his butter lamp with his flint and began walking up a gently sloping tunnel.

They had left the world behind, below. They were following Abigail and the killer into another world. The vertical gap they had bridged on the ancient chain felt as if it had been miles in length. There were acrid scents unfamiliar to Shan here, and images on the walls that he had never seen before of vengeful demons given movement by the flickering light. This was the land of deities, where men were outsiders, where men were playthings, their bones used to construct altars.

Their pace hastened as they approached the daylight at the end of the tunnel. Finally, they reached an opening framed in well-worked, sun-bleached cedar wood, carved with the signs of paradise. A short railing extended down one side. Yangke uttered a sigh of relief, handed his lamp to Hostene, and darted toward the outside stairs just as Shan recognized words written on the side wall of the cave that had recently been underlined in white chalk. The opening lines of the death rites. Shan shouted in alarm and leaped forward as Yangke fell off the side of the mountain.

CHAPTER TWELVE

With a terrified cry Yangke twisted about, his arms thrashing, desperately grabbing at the narrow rail with one hand but inexorably sliding downward. There was only one stair step past the end of the tunnel, though the rail extended another two feet to give the illusion of a flight of stairs. For four hundred feet down there was only air.

Shan thrust his staff forward. A firm hand closed around his belt at the small of his back. As Hostene gripped him from behind, Shan reached out for Yangke with the pole. The younger man seized it and Shan pulled. Then a downdraft hit Yangke and pushed him outward. It was as if the mountain were wrestling Shan for him. Shan and Hostene pulled together, Yangke got a foot on the single step, and with a final heave they managed to pull him inside.

The three men sat on the floor of the tunnel, gasping. "I — I lost it, I lost the bag,"

Yangke confessed when he had regained his breath.

It took Shan a moment to understand. Yangke's bag had slipped off his shoulder, his staff had fallen out of his hand. He had lost the kit that every pilgrim needed to survive on the mountain.

"You're with us," Shan said, hoping he was conveying more confidence than he felt. "We have enough to share."

He held the lamp high as he retraced their steps, chiding himself for not having noticed how the rock walls and floors had changed in the last hundred feet. The rock had been chipped away, not worn by water. Shan pointed to the fresh white chalk marks that highlighted the words from the death ritual.

"Abigail!" Hostene exclaimed.

Shan walked to the point where the floor changed and began tapping the walls with the end of his staff. He discovered a section that was hollow. A wooden panel had been painted to look like rock. Hostene found an edge and starting pushing. The dry iron pintles hidden inside the panel's edge groaned and it swung open. They were back in the course of the waterway.

As the panel swung closed behind them they lit the other two lamps and began following a twisting passage where the water had once followed a seam of softer mineral. But where, Shan wondered, was the snow-melt that had once rushed through the tunnel?

They emerged onto a small plain, surprisingly flat, sheltered by low ridges of rock, with smaller rocks scattered across the open ground, the dark summit looming above, closer now. Shan pointed to a nearby shelf of rock that overlooked the plain. "We should rest and study the slopes above while it is still light," he suggested. He heard no argument from his exhausted friends nor a syllable of surprise when they discovered another painting on a sheltered wall behind the shelf.

Yangke, suddenly full of energy, paced along the width of the painting. "This one is different," he declared and looked up at Shan. "Astrologers have painted this."

The central figure was called the astrological tortoise, its head that of a fiery demon, its clawed feet holding ritual implements. At the top was a cluster of flames — to the right an iron sword, to the left a tree, at the bottom waves, indicating water. In the belly of the tortoise was a circle divided into nine spaces by two pairs of perpendicular lines, each space with a number.

"Looks like a word game," Hostene said

over Shan's shoulder.

"It's called a *mewa* square," Shan said, then explained its significance to the Tibetans, beginning by translating the numbers in the nine spaces. Four, nine, two were the numbers in the top row, then three, five, seven, and finally eight, one, six at the bottom. Whether added up horizontally, vertically, or diagonally each row totaled fifteen. "It's used to tell the future," he said. "It depicts perfect symmetry. The base of three times the central five equals fifteen. The central five is midway between the numbers on either side and above and below it. But nine is its most important number. The central five times nine yields forty-five, which is the total sum of all the digits in the square. Nine is the perfect number. Any number multiplied by nine creates a number the sum of whose digits is invariably a multiple of nine. The square is used to calculate horoscopes."

"Which must be why there are nine segments," Hostene remarked.

Shan followed the Navajo's gaze. He saw what had drawn Hostene's eye. The smaller rocks that seemed scattered from the lower perspective could now be seen to have been arranged deliberately. There were not a lot of them, so their placement was not obvi-

495

ous, but from where the three men stood now the stones clearly defined nine separate squares.

Shan and Hostene stared from the plain to the painting, examining the tortoise again, watching as Yangke climbed down and began walking among the squares.

"The Emperor Yu," Shan murmured as Yangke wove an erratic course through the stones.

"Emperor?"

"It's an old story, from before history. The Tibetans borrowed many things from India and China, where the early astrologers wrote on tortoiseshells and bones. The mythical Emperor Yu received a tortoiseshell from the deities, inscribed with the magic square. He then traveled the nine provinces of his kingdom in the sequence of the numbers." Shan traced a finger over the tortoise's belly to demonstrate, pointing to the script that looked like an Arabic number three leaning to the right, then to another Tibetan digit that resembled a three with a tail. One, then two. It's called the Nine Paces of Emperor Yu. My father told me the pattern is used in the West also, but there it is called the Seal of Saturn."

"But we can see what's before us. It's obvious we have to keep climbing to the summit," Hostene said, leaning on his staff. "And there is only one trail up," he added, pointing to a long thread of shadow on the ridge to the east of the plain. "Why waste time walking zigzags on these squares?"

"Because the devout do not question their prescribed fate," Shan replied as he started to climb down to the plain. "Because all life is a zigzag."

"Abigail is up there," Hostene said to his back but his protest had no energy.

"A teacher of ancient religions would recognize the square, and she would have done what was intended," Shan countered.

Hostene followed Shan out onto the plain.

Assuming that the top of the square would lie to the north, Yangke led them to the section corresponding to the number one. He dropped to his knees, extended his arms, and lowered his body to the ground, then pulled forward as he folded his body up.

"I don't understand," Hostene said.

Shan watched the Tibetan and gave a hesitant nod. "Yangke is right. We must be pilgrims in all respects. The pilgrim would proceed by prostrations." He saw the frustration on Hostene's face. "Some pilgrims still travel hundreds of miles this way, taking months to reach a shrine. We," he said as he dropped to his knees, "only need repeat the Nine Paces of Emperor Yu."

It was a slow, laborious process. On the third square, Yangke sneezed as he inched up from the dust of the reddish gravel that was scattered about the square. On the fifth square Shan paused for a moment to look at the white dust that suddenly appeared on his hand. At the edge of the last square, where their prostrations finished, there was an small overhanging shelf of rock that, from the perspective of someone walking by, would have obscured the words painted on the flat wall underneath. But they were prostrate pilgrims, and saw it. *Om nidhi ghata praticcha svaha,* they read.

"A mantra used in offering rituals," Yangke said. "It refers to the sacred treasure flask."

"But we could have just come here directly. It is the only way," Hostene complained as they joined the short steep path that led to a bulging rock formation in the broad shape of a treasure flask.

"No," Shan said, "there was a reason." He halted and studied the squares again, the colored stains on his hand, the discolorations on all their knees. "It is the colors." To Hostene's obvious chagrin he walked back onto the squares. Some — but not all of them — bore faintly colored soil or fine gravel, noticeable to the pilgrim with his face on the ground but so subtle as not to be obvious to the casual glance. "A sequence," Shan observed, "red, white, and green."

"Why?" Yangke asked.

"I don't know," Shan admitted. "The treasure flask will tell us," he suggested, and led them back to the trail.

The climb to the flask rock was arduous. They were reaching an altitude where the thinness of the oxygen might affect them. Hostene had to pause often, leaning on his knees, and seemed about to collapse onto a rock at the side of the trail when he uttered a cry of glee. As Shan ran back to him Hostene pointed to a white chalk mark on the rock. Drawn hurriedly, in the shape of the Emperor Yu's paces, it showed that Abigail had been there.

What they found under the wide overhanging rock behind the flask tower was not an homage to the gods but a memorial to the frailty of man. Men had labored there, for there was a blackened, shaped hole in the rock wall that appeared to have been a small furnace. There were bits of cast iron on the ground, a lichen-covered iron shape on a stone pillar that proved to be an anvil with an iron ring attached to its base, a few feet from a weathered juniper post in the ground holding fragments of what had been a large bellows. But Shan's companions' attention was focused elsewhere.

On a large slab beyond the furnace lay a dozen skeletons arranged like the spokes of a wheel, skulls at the hub. On a small, narrow shelf beyond, deeper in shadow, were twenty separate skulls. On a lower shelf, five feet off the ground, lay skeleton hands and arms, mixed with the weathered hands and paws of protector demons from ritual costumes.

Hostene, who shied away from owls and even from talk of death, stood as if petrified in front of the display. Yangke, however, seemed fascinated. "Pilgrims," he declared in an awed whisper as he leaned his staff against the wall and pointed to the hands. "From centuries of following the path. Can you feel their —" His sentence ended in a terrified gasp as one of the demon hands reached out, grabbed his wrist, and jerked him toward the wall. His head struck the rock and he slumped against the wall, then slid lifelessly to the ground. Breaking out of his trance, Hostene darted to his side. Yangke's staff rose and slammed against the Navajo's back, knocking him off his feet.

Shan leaped forward, then froze. A pistol had materialized in the floating demon

500

hand, aimed directly at him.

Shan said, fighting to keep his voice level, "Those who built this place, Captain, would have told you that bringing a weapon here would damage your spirit."

"It wasn't to enrich my soul that I followed you up here." Bing stepped into view. The hands, Shan realized, were not arrayed on a shelf carved into the rock but atop a squared-off boulder whose back was totally obscured in shadow. One of Bing's arms was covered by the costume of a demon, a long black glove-like device with bones of white-washed wood affixed to it over the hand. Switching the pistol to his bare hand, the mayor of Little Moscow pulled off the glove with his teeth and tossed it into the shadows.

"Damn, you're slow," Bing said. "Performing all that mumbo jumbo below, when any fool could see you had to come this way."

"Is that when you passed us?" Shan asked. From a position of prostration they would have seen nothing. "You made it from the chain without a staff?"

"I have the legs of a frog, my mother used to say."

"I did not see you at Little Moscow this morning," Shan observed.

"I was waiting at the painting."

Shan understood. "You destroyed it, but

you still did not understand what lay beneath."

"When I saw you up on the rim above the town this morning, I knew you'd get to the painting sooner or later."

"Like Abigail Natay."

"Like the American woman," Bing agreed.

Shan bent over his friends. Hostene was still conscious, although he'd had the wind knocked out of him. Yangke, who was beginning to stir, had a jagged cut on his forehead.

Shan rose and paced around the skeletons, ignoring Bing's gun. "This is what happens," he said.

"Happens to whom?"

"You should go back, Captain. You should go back now, or else promise to help us find the Navajo woman. The people who built this path intended the wrong minded to stay on it forever."

"You make it sound like I'll encounter three-hundred-year-old pilgrims still wandering about," Bing sneered.

Shan gestured to the skeletons. "Something like that."

Bing kicked the nearest of the pilgrim bags that lay on the ground before kneeling and upending it, without taking his eyes off his prisoners. "And what about you, Comrade

Shan? Are you so saintly that you need not worry?" He picked up an apricot and took a bite, the juice running down his chin.

A small ache rose in Shan's heart. "Me? I am beginning to realize I can only live between worlds. I'm not sure the deities take much notice of me." The words had been uttered without conscious thought, as if something in the shrine had pushed them from his heart directly to his tongue.

Bing laughed derisively. "As much as I'd like to stay and hear the contrite confession of another prisoner," he said in a mocking tone, "I haven't got time. Where are the other packs?"

"There's only one more. We lost one." Shan pointed to his own bag by the old anvil. Bing kicked it toward the one he had already emptied and upended its contents. He drained one of their two remaining water bottles, then began filling his pockets with their meager rations.

"Abigail!" Hostene shouted, as if she might be near. Then he called again, and again, his last word like a cry of pain.

Bing grinned. "Is it really true, old man, that you came all the way from America for this?" he said.

"Is it really true," Hostene shot back, "that you could kill so many in cold blood?"

"I am nothing compared to him," Bing said, and pointed to Shan. "This is the man who has killed an entire mountain. If we had women and children on board we should have sent them away in boats the second we saw his face." He stood, his task finished. "It was Shan who unleashed the real destruction. That son-of-a-bitch Ren never studied economics. He doesn't know shit about the market economy. The miners have kept out of his sight for all these years. But now that Shan has him so fired up, he'll make arrests, interrogate people, turn over every stone on the mountain. Ren will destroy a thriving enterprise that supports scores of people, then call himself a hero and return to his one-room apartment with a certificate from a grateful bureaucracy to hang on his wall."

Shan's chest tightened. Chodron must have repaired his sabotaged generator. "What is the major doing?"

"It's what he's not doing. Not leaving Tashtul when he was scheduled to. Not allowing the helicopter he summoned from Lhasa to depart. Not letting any of his men take leave. Not allowing anyone onto the trails into the mountains. Not letting anyone know the responses he is getting to your photographs that he e-mailed to every army and security office in Tibet. He is methodical and deadly."

"Let him come," Yangke said. He was rubbing his head now. "Let him arrest you as a killer."

"When Ren comes, nothing on the mountain will continue as before. Not in Little Moscow. Not in your village. Just remember, it was Shan who brought him down upon you. It will start in earnest when Ren finds an illegal lama in shackles. Ever see a shark when it tastes fresh blood?" Bing bent over Hostene and Yangke, expertly patting them down. "Empty them," he said to Hostene, pointing to his pants pockets. Then lightly pressing his pistol barrel against Shan's chin, he patted down Shan as well. "And that one," he said, pointing to one of Shan's pockets. He quickly sorted through the little pile they'd made, tossing Hostene's pocket-knife over his shoulder, taking all their matches, pausing over Shan's shard of plaster before dropping it onto the ground.

"All Tashi wanted was his freedom," Yangke said.

Bing shrugged. "I liked Tashi. I miss Tashi. The drunken artist, like a character in some old play. He always told jokes. No one jokes anymore. I'll have to pay for my entertainment now. Tashi will be hard to replace."

He glanced back at Shan and grimaced. Sometimes birds too were surprised by the songs they sang.

"One thing I don't understand," Shan said. "Tashi was going to smuggle the gold over the border. But how was he going to get it off the mountain without Chodron finding out?"

"I know your type so well, Shan," Bing said. "God, how well I know you. I was responsible for ten barracks of prisoners like you — pathetic, morose creatures with no vision, only bitterness about the past. They would sit in reeducation classes and copy out slogans from little red books like robots, praising the Chairman, reading aloud apologies printed in other books, using someone else's words. Never a one among them with the balls to stand up and say, Fuck the Chairman, screw the Party secretaries, and screw the limo drivers who brought them to town."

"I tried at first," Shan replied in a weary voice. "They sent me to a special hospital for the criminally insane."

"Unfortunately," Bing said soberly, "you are the sanest person I have ever met."

Hostene picked himself up and began refilling his bag. "I'm going after Abigail," he said. "You'd better shoot me now if you mean to stop me."

"I like this old fool," Bing said, gesturing at Hostene with his pistol. "He reminds me of the old Tibetans. In the town by my prison barracks there were some monks who had resigned their robes. You know, they'd been forced to marry, forced to break their vows. They made the best drinking companions. They'd bet on which lower animal forms they would attain in the next life."

Bing glanced up toward the summit, then eyed his prisoners. "Here's my dilemma," he said to Shan. "We had a celebration in the early summer, got drunk, and shot at cans and at pikas. Like a fool, I used every bullet for this gun except the five left in this clip. Tell your friend to forgive me, but I am unable to waste a bullet on him." He kicked one of the ropes to Shan. "Tie them back to back to that post. Then I'll do you." He glanced toward the summit again.

He paused, stepped to Hostene, and held the pistol barrel before his chest. "Do not even think of following. If I see you again, I will shoot her. As much as I like her, I will shoot her, and for the rest of your life you will know you caused her death."

"You don't know the route, Bing," Shan warned as he was tied to the iron ring below the anvil. "It's too dangerous. The path punishes those who don't respect it."

"You have it bad, Shan. You wouldn't stand up to those who ruined your life, and now you want to kowtow to a bunch of monks who died five hundred years ago." He pointed to a line of shadow that ascended along the nearest wall toward the summit. "Look close and you can see there are smudges of color along that trail. There's no secret to the path those monks laid out. Only follow the paintings and don't step off a cliff." He draped one of their blankets over his shoulder.

Before he departed, Bing checked the tightness of the ropes. "Here's a plan," he said, mocking them again. "One of you must die. Then he comes back as a rat and chews the ropes through to free the others." He was still laughing as he disappeared around the end of the rock formation.

They sat, bound by ropes, seeming to drift on a tide of fear and helplessness.

Hostene said, after a long silence, "Colors may represent directions. For the Navajo, white is east."

"To the Tibetans too they signify direction," Yangke observed with surprise.

"But also elements," Shan said. "Red meant fire, white meant metal, green meant wood. And it is wood you must focus on.

The post," he explained. "If you can pry it out of the ground you can slide the rope over the end and have enough slack to free yourself."

With Shan's coaching, Hostene and Yangke learned how to coordinate their movements in order to pull the old post out of the ground. Minutes later they were all three free.

No one seemed willing to speak about their next step. Yangke stared at the skeletons. Hostene repacked and shouldered his bag with a determined expression, then seemed to reconsider. Shan began mentally cataloging the reasons for turning back, starting with Bing and his five bullets, followed closely by the likelihood that Ren's helicopter would soon appear. While he was silently composing a speech to persuade his companions to retreat, Yangke began studying the skeletons' arrangement, lifting some skulls as if looking for old friends.

Hostene, sensing Shan's gaze, upended his bag. Its sole contents were a coil of rope, a flint, his prayer-stick feather, and a piece of wood. A look of wonder appeared on his face. There had been an earlier pilgrimage he had failed to complete on which his long-dead uncle had given him a rope, a flint, a feather, and a piece of wood, then asked him to go meet the gods. Hostene slowly repacked his bag, then stood, retrieved his staff, and began to walk in the direction Bing had taken. The sun was beginning to set. The little plain below was already in shadow.

"No," Yangke called out. "You cannot leave yet. We have to spend the night here. We have to understand what the message of the colors means, and sleep with the skeletons. It's what the pilgrims were meant to do."

For a moment it seemed Hostene might bolt but he lowered his bag and grimly nodded.

Using one of the iron scraps as a striker they lit a fire, though a small one, for they felt like intruders. With nothing to cook, nothing to eat or drink except their single bottle of water, they stared at the flames in silence, each man lost in thought. At last Yangke rose, holding one of the burning sticks of juniper. Shan thought he was using it as a torch but instead he extended it at arm's length, first low, then high, as he walked around the wheel of skeletons. He was spreading the juniper smoke to attract the deities.

Hostene began studying the ground around them, stepping out into the fading sunlight, pausing to examine scraps of wood. Shan joined the search, studying the collection of skeleton hands, finding footprints in many directions as well as several stripped leaves of fragrant herbs. He was collecting the leaves when Yangke gave an excited cry.

Hostene was already at Yangke's side when Shan reached them, pointing at white marks on the stone wall overhang. At the top was a jagged streak of lightning, then two of the stick-figure gods, then a row of Tibetan sacred objects. Leaning against the wall were two eight-inch-long pieces of juniper, scraped flat, decorated with black-and-white patterns. Shan picked up one of the sticks. It had been lightly coated with white chalk, then a jagged black line running its length had been inscribed with a charred stick. The other stick held the same pattern but instead of black on white the pattern was white on black.

"Prayer sticks," Hostene explained. "Thunder prayer sticks." Lifting the second stick to examine it more closely, he exposed a final sign in chalk on the rock behind it, an oval with eight appendages with a smaller flat oval for a head. A beetle. Beside it was the chalk image of a sacred lotus blossom. It was as if Abigail were introducing the two worlds, Navajo and Tibetan, to each other.

Shan extended the leaves in his hand toward Hostene, dropping them into the Navajo's palm. "Medicine herbs."

The Navajo sniffed the leaves, then stared at them. "Some days she has pain in her abdomen. Once I found her doubled up behind a rock. She said it was nothing, told me to leave."

Yangke showed Shan that under the skulls at the hub of the skeleton wheel was a pattern of colored marks. Red, white, green. They were working to keep their small fire alight when an eerie humming sound rose from nearby. Yangke braced himself, looking wide-eyed at the skulls as if to see which of them was speaking. Shan rose and followed the sound.

In the light of the early moon Hostene was standing on a flat boulder, whirling a piece of wood tied to a length of the yak-hair rope over his head. It made a low ululating roar that varied in pitch as it moved through the air, reminding Shan uncannily of a Tibetan throat chant. He became aware of Yangke at his side, and the two of them sat and listened until the Navajo stopped.

"It's called a bull roarer in English," Hostene explained as he showed them the flat piece of wood, triangular at one end, that he had fashioned with his knife. His voice was somber and low, that of a monk in a temple. "In my people's tongue it is called the thunder speaker. It's used in many of our ceremonies. Thunder drives away evil. It summons the Thunder People."

"But the Thunder People," Yangke whispered, "they are dangerous."

Hostene looked out at the stars. "They are like your protector demons. The Thunder People have the power to find lost things. They know every inch of the sky."

Hostene showed Yangke and Shan how to propel the bull roarer over their heads, letting its weight carry it around in a circle. Hostene did not enter the alcove with the bones. He stayed by Abigail's chalk marks, a blanket wrapped around him. Three times an owl called, and each time Hostene rose and used the bull roarer as if in defiant reply.

Shan settled against a rock near the fire and, despite a terrible feeling of foreboding, drifted into a fitful sleep. An hour later he woke up shaking from a nightmare. He had been falling down a seemingly endless hole, passing skeletons on ledges that cringed in fear as he floated by.

As he walked out into the moonlight Hostene spoke from his vigil by the chalk marks.

"I had a dream too," the Navajo said in a haunted tone. "Abigail was a ghost and was gliding over the mountain in the arms of an ancient lama who was explaining the old ways to her. I kept calling to her but she ignored me. When they swooped close I jumped and grabbed the lama by his robe. She turned to me. 'You need to accept it, Uncle,' she said. 'This is the way I was meant to learn. This is how I walk in beauty.'" He looked up at Shan, moonlight lighting his melancholy features. "When I pulled the lama ghost around to face me, it was Gendun."

In the morning Shan arranged his friends according to what he called the pattern of the colors, the only solution that made sense to him of the dozen he had considered in the night. They erected the wood post and Hostene stood beside it. Green for wood, in the tradition of Tibetan ritual. Yangke stood at the anvil. White for metal. Shan stood at the furnace. Red for fire. Extended, the line they made intersected a thin, sharp shadow perhaps one third of the way up the trail that climbed the slope above them, the trail Bing had taken the evening before. They retrieved their bags and staffs and started walking.

Half an hour later they reached the

shadow, a cleft that could easily have gone unnoticed by someone watching his footing on the precarious trail. They entered the shadow and followed a passage through a spine of rock into a small garden on the other side, a bowl where a spring formed a pool surrounded by ferns.

They relaxed in this oasis, drinking and washing, cautiously sampling the little berries growing on low vines, then they followed the path up the spine of rock, realizing that the arch they had seen from below was yet another passage through the rock, though not one intended for the pilgrims.

When their path finally intersected with the end of the arched passage they found themselves on the final flat plain before the summit itself. Outside the arch, on the near side, was a now familiar painting of a dragon deity. On the other side, Bing waited for them.

The former Public Security officer leaned against a rock, the blanket he had stolen from them draped around him. He looked strangely weak, greeting them with only a sour grimace. He made no effort to reach for the pistol that lay at his side. Several feet beyond lay the pilgrim bag in which he had carried away their food supply.

Shan took a step toward Bing, his eyes on the gun. It was the kind of game Bing would play, to see how close you could come before he flipped open the blanket and drew the pistol, perhaps even pulling the trigger. Shan was ready to play, ready to advance close enough to attempt to kick the food bag toward his friends. But then with a chill he saw the blood, still wet, in a circle of stones behind Bing. Bing must have used the gun already.

Shan looked futilely for bodies. Then he feinted toward the bag and darted to the weapon. As he reached it, Bing lashed out with his foot, hooking Shan's leg, pulling Shan on top of him, squeezing him, at first with a savage strength, as if to break Shan's ribs, but then steadily, quickly, weakening. Shan fought his grip, squirming, realizing in terror that Bing must have stabbed him, for there was suddenly a spate of blood — on Shan, on the blanket, on Bing's face. Then there were hands pulling Shan away. As he stood upright, he saw his friends' faces first. They were drained of color. The blanket had fallen in Bing's struggle with Shan, revealing why he had not reached for his pistol. He had no hands.

CHAPTER THIRTEEN

Shan did what he could for the mayor of Little Moscow, offering him water from the bottle Yangke refilled from the spring below, wiping the blood from his face as he slipped in and out of consciousness. A quick scan of the clearing behind him showed two nearly identical blood patterns, sprays with the force of spurting arteries behind them, at each end of a low mound of heavy rocks.

"Tell me what happened," Shan said as he wiped Bing's brow. Hostene had ripped two strips from his shirttail and wrapped them around the stumps of Bing's arms.

"When it happens," Bing murmured with a dreamy gaze, "you're not real anymore."

Shan considered the words, trying to understand if Bing was speaking of himself or of the one who had severed his hands. "Was Abigail here?" he asked.

Bing's mouth twitched. Had he any strength left, he would have grinned mockingly. "She watches," he said in a hoarse whisper. "She doesn't care. Living with the gods, it's all playacting."

Shan shot a worried glance toward Hostene.

"How did this happen to you?"

"I was exhausted. I fell asleep. I woke to find him standing over me, grinning, singing one of his damned songs. Before I could speak, something hit me on the back of the head. When I came to there were rocks on my arms, so I couldn't move them. He had already cut off my left hand when . . ." Bing drifted off.

Shan stepped into the little clearing behind him. It seemed like Bing had lost gallons of blood. Even at this altitude, small flies had located it.

He dripped water into Bing's half-open mouth. "The young miner, earlier this summer," Shan said as Bing opened his eyes. "Did you kill him, too?"

Bing struggled for his answer. "Define kill," he whispered.

"Let's define it this way. Last year you killed a miner, then put his partner's chisel in his back to show to Hubei, your witness. The miner had been threatening to undermine Chodron's business structure, and you had to show you were worthy of becoming the miners' leader. The perfect answer was to kill him and blame his partner, the man you chased away. Placing the skeleton on the grave wearing the partner's ring was truly inspired. But then Thomas started telling everyone that he could tell the cause of any death, even what caused a skull fracture. And you must have inflicted such a hard blow to the miner's head that the weapon would have been obvious as soon as Thomas saw the skull. A hammer leaves a distinctive round indentation when there's a lot of force behind it. You had to dig up the bones of the man you killed and dispose of them."

"No miner would go onto that ridge. It was haunted," Bing said, with a low whistling sound as he inhaled.

"But Thomas was ready to study every bone on the mountain for his project, especially if it might belong to a murder victim."

"You never tried to go up there," Bing added. "Why? I was hoping, watching. I could have killed you a dozen ways up there and everyone would have blamed the ghosts."

"I didn't need to," Shan explained. "I've seen old burial caves before. I've seen what people like you do to them. One man had already died up there. Chodron was so suspicious he sent that farmer to follow you. No doubt he would have been one of your victims too, if the lightning hadn't killed him first."

"I was going to show them the skull of some old saint and say it was you. Push a leg bone into one of your old boots. They would have believed me, after everything else that's happened."

"A burial cave," Shan said, "contains lots of old bones. And it's a perfect hiding place for treasures, like the gold you had begun to buy from the miners without Chodron's knowledge."

"How was I supposed to guess she'd go up there looking for her damned gods? There is no evidence left," Bing added in an oddly defiant tone.

"Because even those old bones became liabilities when Thomas announced he could tell the old from the new. He would have proven your story about the revenge of the ghost was wrong."

"The little prick. One of those teacher's pets who always has to show off how much he knows.

"They have artificial hands for amputees," Bing said with sudden malice. "I'll get ones with electric choppers. I'll come looking for you, Shan."

"You could have just sent Tashi away," Shan continued. "None of this had to happen."

"Tashi was the reason it all started. It would have been ungrateful to simply order him off the mountain. Worse, it would have been untidy."

Shan paused, trying to understand. Bing's breath began to rasp. He coughed. His breath came in short, shallow gasps. His lungs were beginning to fill with fluid.

"Tashi hadn't a clue about keeping secrets." Bing's throat rattled. "The moment the fool appeared on the mountain, I knew there would be trouble. His services had already been bought and paid for. I gave him a chance, but he couldn't stay away from vodka. We did him a favor, considering what might have happened."

"Like the gratitude Rapaki showed you?"

"Too many years with those old Buddhist books, I guess. Nothing was real to him anymore. Everything was a symbol. He would hallucinate sometimes, talk to the paintings, stop suddenly and start speaking to a rock." Bing's breathing became labored. "He decided I became . . . one . . . in the end."

"A demon," Shan said, filling in for him. "Even though it was you who explained about demons to him last year."

"He was like a damned cat, appearing out of nowhere, never making a sound unless he was telling his beads. I had no idea he was there, watching last year when I killed the miner. I had to think fast. The man was down but still breathing. I told Rapaki, Quick, help me get him to the painting of the old saint. I knew there was one close by. I said I had a prayer, given me by a saint, which had special powers near the old paintings, a way to identify a demon in human form. If I said the magic words, and the man was actually one of the demons who opposed the gods, then a red eye would appear on the man's hand."

"Your laser pointer," Shan said with a sigh. "Ni shi sha gua."

Bing gave a hoarse laugh, which triggered a fit of coughing. "I hid it in my hand and said the magic words in Chinese. You should have seen his face that first time, when that miner's hand lit up with a demon's eye. Rapaki was terrified. But then he began to smile. He ran away, and I thought that was the end of it. A few minutes later he showed up with that old ritual ax."

"And now someone has borrowed your laser pointer."

"Go any further and it will happen to

you," Bing vowed. "Soon everyone you know will have no hands."

Shan ignored him. "It's the new age indeed, Bing. High-tech demons. And thieves no longer know the meaning of honor. No loyalty. No gratitude," Shan added, with a gesture to Yangke.

Bing weakly raised his brows in query.

"You never thanked Tashi's friend. He didn't tell Chodron about your lie. He didn't tell him that you knew where two tons of gold, mined centuries ago, lay near the top of the mountain."

Bing made an effort to push himself up. He rolled on top of Shan, who fought for a moment, then grew still as he realized Bing no longer resisted, realized the sour breath no longer came from Bing's mouth, inches away from his head.

"He's dead," Hostene declared, and with Yangke's help lifted the body from Shan.

They helped him to a nearby stream, where he thrust his face into the frigid water. Then, with gravel from the bed, he cleansed his hands and arms until the skin stung. When he was clean, to his surprise, Shan found he was hungry. As they ate, they debated what to do with Bing's body. Yangke favored leaving Bing spread out by the gateway, to become a skeleton on the pilgrim's trail. Hostene was inclined to shroud him in the blanket and heave him over the cliff. In the end they wrapped him in the blanket and covered him with rocks in the blood-soaked clearing, though not before Shan had studied the stumps of his arms. Each hand had been severed with two strikes. Each had left the same small nick in the bone.

They removed Bing's shirt after Shan searched the pockets, ripping it into squares that Yangke inscribed, using a stick and Bing's own blood, then left the prayer flags anchored with the burial stones. One more shrine to a demon.

"If he had followed the pilgrim's path," Yangke declared in a hushed voice, as he and Hostene pushed up the trail, "he would have seen who was lying in wait on this side of the passage." It was Bing's only epitaph.

"We can't leave like this, Hostene," Shan called to the Navajo's back.

Hostene halted. Only Yangke turned, confused.

"We can't go forward like killers," Shan said.

Hostene leaned heavily on his staff. "You sound like Lokesh now."

"We can't go forward," Shan repeated.

"You saw what happened to Bing," Hostene said. "I don't know what to expect now. One person alone could not have done that to him. Someone knocked him out from behind."

He was afraid that Abigail was involved.

"I don't know what to expect either," admitted Shan. "But we know what to expect of ourselves."

Hostene closed his eyes a moment then walked forward without bothering to see if the others followed him. Their silent procession reached the cliff and he lowered his bag and staff, reached inside his shirt, and pulled out Bing's gun. "My uncle once told me some of the sacred mountains felt empty to him, as if the gods had left them, because so many men came with firearms to hunt the animals there." With a long underhand throw he launched the pistol into the air. They watched it fall and get lost in the shadows at the base of the cliff.

They climbed now with grim, silent determination, up steep trails, bracing themselves against powerful downdrafts. They paused at every painting, twice following directions set out in the form of the little footprints and the outlines of sacred objects. Shan and Yangke had to pull Hostene away from a painting surrounded by chalk marks, whose deity, he insisted, resembled one of the

Navajo holy people.

When they reached a ten-foot-wide chasm over which two thick yak-hair ropes had been tightly strung overhead, they hesitated.

"I'm not trusting my life to a four-hundred-year-old rope," Hostene protested.

"It's not that old. The lamas maintained the kora until they died. And it's made of yak hair, which lasts despite the weather." With a businesslike air, Yangke extracted the Y-shaped stick from the bag he carried, straddled the rope with it, grabbed each end in a hand, and slid across, dangling over several hundred feet of emptiness. He tossed the stick back to Shan as Hostene extracted the stick from his own bag. In another minute, both Shan and Hostene were across.

They halted at a narrow canyon intersected by half a dozen trails, each with a small painting of a demon at its entrance.

"Which one?" Yangke asked in a chagrined voice. "We could lose hours going down false trails."

But Hostene pointed to the flat face of a boulder on which images had recently been drawn in chalk. He dropped to his knees in front of the drawings. "She has done the work for us," he said. He began to explain how his niece had been trying to correlate Navajo symbols with the primitive symbols on the paintings at the trailheads.

"But what does it mean?" Yangke asked.

"Hunchback God," Hostene said, and looked up. "The mountain goat god, that was the last one she drew, as if that was the explanation she sought."

Shan walked in a semicircle along the trailheads. "Only one of these shows goat tracks," he reported. Taking that trail, they soon reached another pilgrim station, with a small waterfall and beds of moss marked recently by boots.

Where the trail was obvious ahead Hostene pressed forward alone. On a sun-bleached rock with a view of the surrounding ranges for dozens of miles, they found him sitting cross-legged, stripped to the waist, his skin rubbed with dust, in his hand the little leather bag that contained his sacred soil. Yangke clutched his beads and lowered himself into the lotus position. Shan realized they had barely spoken above a whisper all day. It was as if, having left the gateway where Bing died, they had entered a temple where voices should not be raised.

But Shan, gnawed by his ever-present worry for Lokesh and Gendun, could not find a prayer within himself. He sat apart and arranged bits of gravel before him to randomly construct a number for the Tao te

Ching. But for the first time in his life, he kept losing count, trying and failing, as if the book in his mind had closed. Instead, he was visited by memories of Gendun in chains, of Bing squeezing him without hands. He kept remembering a note left by an aged lama whom Shan had discovered sitting on a high ledge by a work site the first year of his imprisonment. Shan had gone after the lama after seeing him slip away, hoping to find him before the guards did. He had found the lama — naked, smiling, but dead, having written words with a charred stick on the rock beside him. His death poem read, *All I have left behind is the water that has washed my skin.*

When they emerged later onto a high windswept ledge where several poles were anchored by cairns of heavy stones, Yangke pointed out the threads attached to each, still whipping in the wind. Once they had been prayer flags.

"There!" Hostene said, and trotted to the last of the poles, Shan following behind. It bore a new flag, a red bandanna with flowers printed on it. Written over the printed pattern, in black ink, was a prayer to the Compassionate Buddha. He eagerly scanned the mountain above. "She's still safe!" he called out, and pointed to a small solitary figure on an exposed shelf of rock high above. It could have been anyone but Hostene was convinced it was his niece.

"It doesn't matter now," said a downcast voice. Yangke had arrived at their side. The figure in the distance darted from view. Shan gazed at Yangke in confusion. A rumbling in the distance grew in volume. Shan's heart sank. By the time he gathered his senses and started pulling Hostene toward the shadows a helicopter was already there, screaming past them, hovering as if searching for a landing place, then shooting around the head of the rock.

A full armored squad could fit in the helicopter, and Ren was unlikely to arrive with less. They would have automatic weapons, grenades, sophisticated detection devices, Shan explained. The sound of the machine diminished, then sharply increased, indicating it had deposited its load somewhere nearby and ascended again. At least the knobs would take Hostene and Abigail off the mountain quickly. There would be doctors. Yangke, without papers, should try to hide, retreat, and reach Lokesh and Gendun. Shan might be a sufficient meal to satisfy Ren's appetite for a day or two. But Drango village was doomed. Shan knew how to resist interrogators, might hold out for maybe a week or even two. But eventually, whether they resorted to drugs, electricity, or just batons, he would be forced to speak. He was the one Ren sought. And if Shan did not fall into his trap, Ren would ferry more loads of soldiers to the mountain.

But when Shan reached the clearing where the helicopter had landed, he found only a solitary figure in black with a pack at his feet. Dr. Gao was inspecting a painting of a protector demon.

"I haven't sent his body back," the scientist announced in a flat voice. "It still lies in that morgue in Tashtul. I sat with it before I left. Every day I write a different letter to Thomas's parents. Every day I rip it up. 'I regret to inform you that your only son was laid out on a stone and butchered.' 'I am saddened to report that our plans to land a family member on the moon have been canceled.' 'I am sorry but the outlaws who run the far side of the mountain have taken our young prince.' "

"I supposed you would phone them."

"I can't. Heinz will do it when he returns. Heinz is good at such things."

"How did you know to come to the summit?"

"You told me, before. If the American woman was still alive she would keep going up the mountain, you said. This has always been about that American woman, hasn't it? Abigail. It started with her." Gao's voice was that of a rational scientist speaking about a colleague's expedition.

But it wasn't about Abigail, not for Gao. It was about Thomas, and the utter failure of a man who, in all his esteemed career, had never known failure.

"I don't know what you expect, Gao."

"My expectations," Gao sighed, "have meant very little lately." He pointed to the demon, and a chalk drawing of a thunder snake beside it. "Explain this."

Before Shan could do so, a low, steady voice rose from behind them. Hostene and Yangke had joined them. "The world begins with thunder," Hostene said. "The early Tibetans said so. The Navajo said so. Abigail came to confirm this with the deity that lives inside the mountain." Gao cast a worried glance at Shan. Hostene was beginning to sound like a lama.

Gao turned to the Navajo. "The altitude is affecting your brain, Hostene. I brought medicine for that." Then he faced the painting. "And where exactly does this earth deity live?" He seemed to fear the answer.

"In the paradise at the top of the mountain," interjected Yangke.

Gao looked up, not toward the summit but to the east, as if wondering if he might summon his helicopter back. Shan set off up the trail.

As they walked, Gao quizzed Shan relentlessly about his experiences on the mountain, making him repeat the puzzles they had encountered before he heard their solutions, then falling silent as Shan told him about Bing's death.

"Did he know my nephew?"

"He did."

Gao nodded. "Thomas would not have been drawn into a trap by a total stranger."

"Your nephew knew more people on the mountain than you might think."

"I keep reminding myself," Gao observed in a brittle voice, "that I live a fairy-tale life in a make-believe castle, unconnected to the world."

"When I said that," Shan offered, "I did not intend to hurt you."

"You are an escaped prisoner with a meaningless life," Gao replied in a hollow tone. "How could you hurt me?"

"I meant —"

Gao interrupted with a raised hand. "No more."

"No more of that," Shan agreed. "But now I have a question for you. Did you bring your satellite phone?"

As Hostene and Yangke ate some of the grain bars Gao produced from his pack, Shan and Gao sat on a rock and tried the number for Heinz Kohler. Gao held the earpiece so Shan could hear. An automated reply reported that the receiving phone was switched off.

"Where does Heinz stay when he goes to Lhasa?"

"Always with an old colleague who retired there. They discuss new reports in the scientific journals."

"Do you have that number?"

"Our satellite phones have always been sufficient."

"Except today. Call your office in Tashtul," Shan said. "Your office manager probably has some way to contact him in emergencies."

Gao frowned, then pressed a number on the phone's memory and handed it to Shan. The conversation was short. Kohler's emergency number was that of the most expensive hotel in Lhasa.

"Mr. Kohler has gone to the border on business," came the soft female voice at the hotel's reception desk.

"Did he leave a forwarding number?" Shan asked.

"He will be back in a few days," the woman said. "Is there a message?"

"How often does Heinz go to Lhasa?" Shan asked Gao.

"Once every month in the warm weather. There are always details of shipments to be arranged."

"That night in Tashtul when you said Heinz knew about Public Security," Shan asked, "what did you mean?"

Gao stood and fidgeted with the zipper on his jacket. "We always referred to it as his vacation. It was nothing really. A misunderstanding. He was pronounced rehabilitated, the record wiped clean." Gao began walking up the trail.

Shan followed. "You mean he had been in a Public Security prison."

"Half the great men in Beijing have had such episodes. A rite of passage." Gao stopped. "A foreigner like that, trying to succeed in Beijing, surpassing nearly all his colleagues. What do you expect? Jealousy was inevitable."

"I need to borrow your phone," Shan declared.

"Impossible. It holds many secret numbers."

"Just one call, to the colonel who runs Lhadrung County. You can sit beside me.

And I need the name of the scientist you said Heinz stays with."

Gao did not reply, did not even look in Shan's direction, as he reached into his pocket and handed Shan the phone before stepping to the edge of a nearby ledge.

Shan was gripped by the cold fear he always felt when he heard the voice on the other end of the line. They weren't friends, they weren't allies, merely two men who had been chewed up and spit out by Beijing. After a difficult opening, during which the colonel threatened to hang up, then warned Shan that his photo was being distributed by one of the most rabid Public Security officers in all of Tibet, it took less than five minutes to explain what he desired and another five minutes before a much friendlier, female voice returned with the information he had sought. The colonel's matronly assistant relayed the requested information, then recited the phone number twice. Shan gestured for a pen and wrote it on a slip of paper. "Have a wonderful day," she called out as he disconnected.

He went to Gao's side and held the phone as Gao had before, so both could hear. Shan asked for Heinz Kohler. "Mr. Kohler has gone to the border on business. He will be back in a few days. Is there a message?"

They were not only the same words but it was the same young female voice they had heard on their first call to Lhasa.

"I don't understand," Gao said after Shan had hung up.

"I asked about his scientific colleague. Then I asked if there was a private, confidential listing for a Heinz Kohler residence in Lhasa. His old colleague moved to a retirement home on the southern coast over a year ago. The number the colonel gave me was the private line of the Kohler apartment in Lhasa. Only nothing is private to a man like the colonel. Heinz has an apartment at the top of the hotel. The woman who spoke to you wasn't working for the hotel, she has an arrangement with the switchboard. She's living in Kohler's apartment."

Gao snatched the phone from Shan's hand and without a word marched up the trail, which was turning into a wide causeway leading to another tunnel near the top of a high cliff.

Shan followed at a distance, recalling the words of the old groundskeeper, Trinle. The mountain sought people out. It was true. Here before him was the mystery of the murders, the mystery of Abigail Natay, the mystery of the lost gold, the mystery of Gao.

The mountain had already dealt with the mystery of Bing. Shan looked up at the summit, surrounded by patches of snow. They were nearing the end of the climb. Somewhere between where he stood and the top, all mysteries would end.

The station at the top of the windblown section of trail might have been constructed as a classroom for Abigail. The walls of the high rectangular cavern, sealed at the far end, were smooth, covered with paintings, though only along the top of the walls, ending nearly eight feet above the ground. Below the paintings were more of Abigail's own drawings, though not only Abigail's. At least one other hand, which had written nearly illegible passages in Tibetan, was evident. Halfway down the cavern a rope hung from the ceiling. Yangke pulled it, producing the pleasing peal of a heavy bell chime.

"It's a dead end," Hostene declared. "A deception. We missed a hidden turnoff." But he seemed in no hurry to leave as he paced along the walls, perplexed. Had his niece also been deceived?

Oddly, Abigail's chalk marks looked faded, as if they had been there for years. As Yangke began reading the Tibetan words out loud, Shan fought mounting unease.

Several cavities punctuated the upper walls, some like small bowls, others holes without visible ends. Light filtered through a perfect circle chiseled at the top of the rear wall, which displayed no paintings. Below it was a dark shelf, an opening that ran the width of the cave, nearly two feet high. Shan pointed to a chalk mark he had never seen before, a circle divided by a horizontal line through the center, vertical lines running down from the center line to the edges.

"It's an old sign," Hostene said, "seldom used. I think it means House of Water." He looked at Shan and shrugged.

Shan studied the way the living rock had been carved to make two pillars at either side of the narrow entrance, the stone around them chiseled away to make two high concave hollows in the entrance wall. He picked up two pieces of gravel and tossed one into each of the hollows. The one on the south side bounced back, the other disappeared without a sound. He looked up to see Gao standing outside the chamber on the entry path, which for fifty feet had been laid with flat, tight-fitting pavers. Gao stared over one edge, where the low wall that lined the paved portion of the path had crumbled away.

"What are those?" Gao asked, pointing to

a heap at the bottom of the high wall they stood on.

"Sticks," Shan suggested. "When a tree gets blown off the slope above it ends up down there eventually. They tumble to the bottom and the sun bleaches the sticks white like that."

"Except we have climbed above the tree line," Gao said in a worried tone.

The wind began to pick up, bending the sparse clumps of grass that grew between the stones.

The moan came abruptly, starting as a low humming sound, then quickly elevated in pitch and volume to an unsettling noise that seemed to come from the rock wall at the end of the chamber.

"A throat chant!" Yangke gasped. "It's as if the mountain is chanting!"

It did seem as though the rock itself were speaking, like the beginning of one of the eerie prayer chants practiced by some of the old monks. Gao pointed to the circular hole at the end of the chamber that Shan had noticed earlier. Shan spoke into Yangke's ear and a moment later Hostene and Gao were helping him up onto Yangke's shoulders. When he straightened, his head was level with the hole above the long shadowed shelf. The sound grew so intense that he put one hand over an ear, using the other to steady himself as he studied the hole. Then he signaled for his friends to lower him.

"There's a wooden sleeve fitted inside the hole, with thin slats like reeds in it," he reported. "The hole widens past the sleeve. It's a sound funnel, and its been tuned to make this sound."

"But what is the sound?" Gao asked. "Why that sound?"

Yangke and Shan concentrated on listening.

Yangke's eyes lit with realization. "A seed sound," he said, referring to one of the root sounds used in Tibetan ritual. *Vam!* he said. "It is the seed sound Vam."

Shan cocked his head, telling himself it was not possible. But the sound was unmistakable now. Each gust renewed the syllable. The sound mesmerized the four men. The monks of five centuries past were speaking to them.

Hostene, his expression of wonder growing, clamped his hands over his ears. Gao stared not at the hole above now, but at the entryway. Shan pulled Yangke into a corner, where the sound was less intense.

He asked, "What does it signify?"

"The color blue," Yangke said, "And the direction north. And —" The sound grew louder now, accompanied by something new, a low rushing rumble.

The image of the white sticks below flashed through Shan's mind. "Run!" he shouted, pushing Hostene and Gao forward, pointing Yangke toward the entry. They were halfway down the chamber when the shelf below the hole erupted. There was indeed one more meaning to the seed syllable. Water.

It burst out of the wall with the force of a tsunami. As the makers of the chamber intended, they would not have time to run down the path to safety below. Shan pushed Yangke into the shadow behind the north pillar. The Tibetan understood instantly, and pulled Hostene into the narrow cleft before the wall of water reached them. Shan grabbed the collar of Gao's jacket as the scientist was swept off his feet, then braced himself in the opening of the cleft. He had to extract Gao from the torrent, he had to get them both higher, for the water was rapidly rising and would not stop, he knew now, until it reached a level just below the old paintings, eight feet from the floor of the chamber.

He pulled on Gao's collar, not daring to use both arms for fear of losing his balance. By the time he had pulled Gao inside the cleft, their heads were under water. Blind in the swirling blackness, Shan let his feet lead him. They found a narrow step, then another, and another. He slipped, almost losing Gao. Then hands reached down and tugged him upward.

He found himself lying on the floor of another cave. He struggled to his hands and knees, his stomach heaving up the water he had swallowed, Gao beside him coughing up water too as Hostene slapped his back.

"They weren't white sticks," Gao said once he regained his breath.

"No," Shan agreed. They were the flotsam of centuries of pilgrims who had not been so fortunate, the bones of what had been perhaps twenty or thirty bodies.

They spoke hurriedly, in tones of disbelief, comparing theories, until at last they understood what the ancient monk engineers had done. The bell. The bell rope would always be pulled by a pilgrim, for bells drove away evil spirits. But the rope not only tipped the bell, it activated a mechanism, releasing a cover over the wind funnel and then something else above, releasing a gravity-activated gate on a dam that connected to the wide opening at the end of the cave. The path had been paved at the top to endure the occasional floods without being washed away. The sidewall had not crumbled away but had deliberately been built that way, to make a death trap for those who were unlucky enough to be washed out of the cavern. They had found the missing spring melt, the water that had been diverted from the passageway they had used to enter the summit kora.

The excitement of their discovery, and of their survival, was soon replaced by the grim realization that all of their equipment, including that brought by Gao, had been swept away by the water. They had no food, no pilgrim bags, not even a butter lamp. A staff that Hostene had clutched during the ordeal and the contents of their pockets were all that remained. They took inventory. Gao's phone. A flint. Two pocketknifes. A few pencil stubs. Several feathers Hostene had collected along the way. And, Shan knew, the secrets secured inside Hostene's vest. Yangke, in his soaked clothes, started to shiver, rubbed his arms, and looked at Shan expectantly.

Hostene gazed toward the narrow stairs that had saved their lives. He had no way of knowing whether Abigail had been so lucky. He rose, then began walking toward the light at the end of the passage.

They clambered up trails fit only for goats.

As the day faded, they made a fire of goat dung under a deep overhang, surrounded by rocks blackened by lightning strikes, beside the painting of a dragon god. "When we capture this crazed monk," Gao asked as he stared at the vivid painting, "what will happen to him?"

"I don't know," Shan replied. "That depends on you."

"You mean because of Thomas."

"Because you are the only one among us who might report him to the authorities."

"If I don't, what then?"

"We take him back to Drango village, to save the life of Gendun."

This was the impossible dilemma that had been gnawing at Shan since they had begun their strange pilgrimage. Gendun would never forgive Shan for saving his life by sacrificing that of the hermit, however deranged Rapaki might be.

"I don't think it matters what I do," Gao said. "Major Ren is involved now."

The words quieted them. There were no pilgrims on this mountain, Shan realized. There were only fugitives. Their pasts had overtaken each of them, and their lives were changing. Every man there, including Shan, was beginning to glimpse the hollow shape of his future.

"Why did you do that?" Gao asked Hostene, and pointed to an object Hostene clutched between his hands. The Navajo had gleaned a splinter of wood from an old prayer flag stand and, with thread unwound from his shirt, had fastened some feathers to it.

"We've run out of mountain," Hostene said. "In the morning there will be an end to it. It is time to call on the deities." He had stripped off his shirt, wore only his vest, and had coated his bare arms with dust again.

Gao stirred the fire. "You have to understand," he said in a patient voice, "I am a man of science."

"And I used to be a judge," Hostene replied earnestly. "But I learned something on this mountain. Here it isn't about what we have put into our heads, it is about what we have put into our hearts." He rose and took a new seat fifty feet away, where he had a better view of the sun setting over a hundred miles of horizon.

"Perhaps Heinz had to cross the border to fix his problems," Shan offered a moment later. "You said the firm does a lot of business in India."

Gao, his head cocked, was watching Hostene. "This is where you play the part of the clever detective trying to trick me into tell-ing secrets. Didn't you hear what Hostene just said?"

"I'll tell you a secret, Doctor. Thomas may have presented many complex challenges but the reason he died was simple. He was trying to find the truth." Shan explained Thomas's fastidious work at the murder scene.

"There is a warehouse, in Bengal some-where," Gao finally said, "and that house on the ocean, in the south. Beautiful beaches. You saw the photo."

"Who arranges the schedules and cargo of the trucks going south?"

"I don't know. Heinz would know. He takes care of details. He's probably in Tash-tul now, taking care of Thomas's body for me."

"Only one more thing. Where did Heinz go, that year he was away?"

Gao did not reply. The fire died away. Soon Shan could see nothing but two dim eyes staring at the stars.

The end of the world came after midnight. There was no warning by wind or rain, only a massive bone-shaking clap of thunder that physically pushed Shan and his friends toward the back wall of the overhang, then a blinding explosion of light. They had come to the place where lightning was born. They had come to the home of the lightning god.

The bolts came one after another, with a deep rending force that seemed about to split not only the sky but the mountain as well. The air seemed to boil, churning in and out of their little cavity with the rhythm of the bolts, like the breath of some huge beast.

"Your eyes!" Shan shouted above the din, waving his hands. "Cover your eyes!" They looked at him in mute confusion, and he suddenly understood why. He was deaf, and, judging by their expressions, so were his friends. He crawled to each of them, pushing their forearms over their eyes, gesturing for them to face the wall, away from the flashes.

It seemed it would never stop. They could die so easily. One tongue of the lightning could leap into their confined space and leave them as bent, charred artifacts for some future pilgrim to consult as he passed by.

On it went, the explosions numbing not just his ears but his entire body, the light so intense that even facing the wall, the air smelling of metal, his arm over his eyes, Shan could sometimes see the crimson tinge of his flesh. He found himself slipping toward a place he had never been before, a destination perhaps intended by the path's builders. He had no body left, no mystery left, no *him* left. There were only explosions and light and shuddering air, and one question that would assure that when they found his remains there would be a look of wonder on his face — was this how it felt to be a deity?

CHAPTER FOURTEEN

His friends were all dead. When the storm finally stopped he crawled desolately from man to man, probing them, touching their backs as they lay curled against the wall. They did not move. Their flesh was so hard and cramped it seemed they had been baked alive.

Shan fell back against the wall, his heart and body ravaged, then eventually took stock of his own senses. He could see the stars and moon, could feel the wind on his face, but could hear nothing. His arms and legs ached, the hair on the back of his neck and arms was singed. His shirt was stiff and brittle at the cuffs.

He curled up on the ledge, facing outward this time, still so numb he couldn't even feel despair, only think about how painful it would be when it came. He glanced back at his companions. Each man's hands were balled up in fists, tucked under their chins.

In corpses this was called the boxer's posture, the effect of prolonged heat, which caused the muscles to contract. His eyes welled with moisture as he gazed out over the moonlit ranges.

Suddenly a foot kicked him. Someone was testing to see if *he* were alive.

It was as if they had been frozen and were slowly thawing out. He could not see whose foot it was but he helped the struggling figure straighten his limbs, then dragged him into the moonlight. The man worked himself into a sitting position, trembling, squeezing Shan's hand. It was Gao.

Shan sat with him, each man explaining with gestures to the other that he could not hear. Then he returned to the deeper shadows, leaving the scientist pondering the blackened edges of his clothing. He found the two remaining forms against the wall and felt each for a pulse. Hostene and Yangke were also coming back to life.

Half an hour later all four sat in the moonlight, Shan cradling Yangke's head in his lap, Hostene holding one of the Tibetan's hands. They were all deaf but Yangke was also blind.

No one argued when Shan took the lead in the morning, no one disputed their direction, still upward. After climbing for a while,

Hostene leading Yangke by his hand, they reached a wide sheltered shelf that held not only small clumps of heather but also a few pools of water. They guided Yangke to a pool and after he had drunk his fill they sluiced it over his head and over his closed eyes, then let him roll onto sun-warmed moss and sleep. They washed themselves. Hostene found some small waxy blue berries that, though tart, provided a makeshift breakfast. They sat, still partially in shock, staring at each other, rubbing their ears, casting fearful glances toward the summit, within an hour's reach now. If she had survived, Abigail could be up there, as deaf and blind as Yangke. But they were weary to the bone from the night's ordeal. The warmth of the little hollow soon had them sprawled against the rocks, drifting into slumber.

A bird was calling in the distance when Shan awoke, perhaps two hours later. He saw it only ten feet away, languidly watched it eating some of the blue berries. Why did it sound so far away? Shan sat up as the welcome realization hit him. His hearing was returning. He turned to see Hostene bending over Yangke, whose face had turned yellow.

The Navajo had opened his precious

sacred pollen from home. He had spread some on Yangke's hands, and more on his cheeks and brow, and was bent over the Tibetan, speaking toward the crown of his head, waving his spirit feather in the air. The unintelligible words, which seemed to filter down a long pipe, made Shan worry again about his senses until he realized Hostene was speaking in his native tongue.

Shan stretched, stood, explored the beginning of the trail to the summit, then began picking more berries for Yangke, soon joined by Gao, who confirmed that his hearing was also beginning to return. When they brought the berries back, Yangke was sitting upright, cross-legged, moving his hand back and forth across his lap. "I see shadows," he said in a hopeful tone. He could hear perfectly now, he explained, then ravenously consumed the berries they dropped into his palm.

Having passed through a corridor of natural stone covered with the most fearful paintings they had yet seen, they looked down on a quarter-mile-wide bowl directly beneath the summit. It seemed to be filled with debris, a jumble of jagged, lightning-scorched slabs that had sloughed off the pinnacle. In the center, at its lowest point, was an opening — not a crater but a jagged tear in the fabric of the peak, a crevasse perhaps a hundred feet long and thirty wide. All except the largest of the rock slabs had been cleared from around it. Its perimeter was outlined with tall cairns, some bearing the last threads of prayer flags from another century.

A wide pathway at one end of the fissure connected it to a shallow cave at the base of the summit, a twenty-foot-high indentation where a great piece of stone appeared to have been scooped out of the peak. Halfway between the cavern and the fissure were two figures, one in an oft-patched red robe who was prostrating himself as he advanced toward the hole. The other, wearing a long green vest with many golden bracelets and a tiered headdress, trudged behind him.

Hostene ran forward.

"No!" Shan shouted in vain. They had lost the benefit of surprise, lost all chance of comprehension before confronting those below. Gao hurried past, holding one of Yangke's hands. The scientist was supposed to be leading the blind Tibetan but Gao appeared to be dragged by Yangke.

Shan lingered, trying to see the place as Lokesh might, as the builders had intended. They had experienced the end of the world the night before, and now had reached the home of the deities. For one who believed the supreme deities were lightning gods, such a place would be the gateway to heaven, and the proper final home for a wandering Tara. He studied the fissure, the prostrating monk, the strangely submissive Navajo woman, then ran to Gao's side.

"Don't," he said, surprised to find himself panting for breath, reminding himself of the thinness of the air.

"Don't what?" Gao asked.

"I don't know," Shan said, a terrible premonition building inside him. "Don't believe anything is as it seems."

"Tell *him*," Gao said, pointing to Hostene, who walked beside his niece now, trying to get her attention.

Abigail Natay appeared to have aged ten years. Her skin was chalky, her eyes hollow, her hair dull and tangled under the old headdress of the Tara costume. She had been sprinkled with pollen. On one hand was a daub of white paint, tapered at the ends. She had acquired a third eye. Hostene seemed to be unable to touch his niece. As Shan halted a dozen feet away the Navajo extended his hand to within a few inches of her, withdrew it, then repeated the motion. She gave no sign of seeing him, staring straight ahead at the bobbing head of the pilgrim she followed.

Rapaki, moving at the snail's pace of the prostrating pilgrim, seemed to be heading for a stone altar at the rim of the fissure, beside a long heavy slab that had fallen so it extended perhaps eight feet over the hole.

Shan turned to see Gao guiding Yangke to a ring of flat stones arranged like seats in front of the cavern. As he watched, Gao paused, his expression rigid as he looked at something on the floor of the cave. Shan took a step closer, and another, trying to see, then broke into a run. The leg of a man sprawled from behind a rock in the cave.

He sped past Gao. A moment later he reached the prostrate form, which was bound with rope.

"How could —," Gao began as he saw the color of the man's hair. "What have they done?" he groaned.

Shan pulled the man onto his back. It was Heinz Kohler.

The German's temple was bleeding from a jagged cut. His arms were tied against his sides with yak-hair rope that had been wound around his body a dozen times. Gao bent over his unconscious friend, examining one arm, then the other. Satisfied that

Kohler's hands were intact, he began untying him. Leaning against the rock beside him was a short ceremonial ax, its four-inch blade stained brown. Shan lifted the blade. It matched the outline he had seen on the wall of the storage chamber at the hermit's cave. At the center of the blade the metal was nicked.

They laid Kohler in the sunlight, Shan cupping rainwater from another of the natural bowls in the rock and splashing it over the German's face as Gao hovered over him, wiping the blood from Kohler's check with his handkerchief. The German's eyes fluttered open and he gazed at Gao for a long moment before recognizing him. "They tied me up," he explained in a weak voice. "Rapaki. He's insane. He has her under some kind of spell." Then his eyes came into focus and he sat up. "Abigail!" Kohler shouted, then he staggered to his feet and ran toward her.

He did not hesitate to touch her but grabbed her and thrust her toward Hostene, then ran toward Rapaki.

The hermit was nearly at the edge of the fissure now, before the little altar. Shan reached him first but hesitated.

"Anything from your old lamas about disturbing a lunatic killer who is pretending to be a pilgrim?" Kohler asked in a bitter voice.

For the first time, Shan saw that Rapaki carried a leather bag, a pilgrim's bag, strapped to his belt.

"Rapaki," Shan called softly. The hermit did not react.

Abigail was moving again, in tandem with Rapaki, as if bound to him by some invisible cord. Kohler, blood still trickling down his face, cast an impatient glance at Hostene, then charged toward Abigail, scooping her up onto his shoulder and carrying her back to the cavern.

The mantra Rapaki chanted grew louder, and oddly joyful.

"I don't understand," Hostene said. He had taken several steps toward his niece, now seemingly out of harm's way, then paused, his troubled gaze on the hermit.

"He has an offering to make," Shan said, gesturing toward the altar.

"To what?"

"To all the gods and saints who live below."

"Below?"

"He's been looking for it all his life. Abigail showed him the way. The bayal, the home of the gods."

They looked back. Gao was with Kohler

now, wiping Abigail's face as the German covered her with a blanket.

"What are you waiting for?" Hostene called out. "He is the killer!"

"Let him finish," Shan said. "After he's come all this way, after all these years, let him touch the altar and make his offering."

"He has to be brought to justice," Hostene said. "We must take him back to the village. You have to think of Gendun and Lokesh."

That, Shan did not say, is exactly what I am doing.

Shan advanced toward the altar, and lowered himself to the ground. Rapaki touched the altar, his face radiant, then stood and bowed his head. His pilgrim's bag was heavy, with several bulky objects inside. From inside his robe he produced a small cloth pouch from which he extracted several ceremonial offerings, laying each on the stone altar. He absently glanced at Shan, went back to his work of stripping things from his belt, then paused and looked at Shan. He extended a single finger and pressed it against Shan's chest, glanced at Abigail, now at the cave, then gazed uncertainly at Shan again.

Shan brought Lokesh's old amulet box out of his shirt. Rapaki reacted with a smile, touching the box, nodding now as if he knew this much was real. He then stripped off his tattered shoes and robe, so that he wore nothing but a swath of cloth around his loins, a string of beads on his wrist, and a small silver gau around his neck. The hermit squatted for a moment, writing in the dirt below the altar, beginning the mantra for the Compassionate Buddha. He paused, touched Lokesh's gau again, then resumed writing with his other hand. Rapaki had never gone to formal schools. He had taught himself to write with either hand. He was both right-handed, and left-handed.

"What is he doing?" Shan saw that Hostene had gone to Abigail's side and been replaced by Gao.

Rapaki folded his tattered robe carefully. Advancing halfway down the slab that extended over the fissure, he dropped it into the hole. The robe fell only a little way down, then was lifted in an updraft, floating in the air fifteen feet, then twenty feet above them, rising, unfolding, appearing like a phantom monk hovering above them.

"The rope," Shan said quietly to Gao. "Perhaps he could be tied." The scientist offered a hesitant nod, looking uneasily at the still-hovering robe, and jogged toward the cavern.

As Gao retreated, Rapaki produced a scrap of folded leather from his waistband, unfolded it, and poured its contents into his hand. Pollen. The hermit was sprinkling pollen on his head. Shan reached into his pocket and lifted the little piece of gold he had found below, extending it on his palm. Rapaki saw it, glanced back and forth from the fissure to Shan, then stepped forward and with a small nod accepted the gold from Shan.

"Lha gyal lo," Shan whispered. He raised his left hand to a forty-five-degree angle, his palm downward, his forefinger down, tucked under his thumb.

Rapaki looked more serene than Shan had ever seen him. "Lha gyal lo," the hermit repeated in a scratchy voice as he studied Shan's hand and nodded again. He dropped Shan's gold into the pilgrim's bag, then stepped to the end of the slab. As he did so, the wind ebbed and the robe slowly floated down. Rapaki held out the bag at arm's length, speaking words Shan could not hear, and dropped it into the fissure.

Shan saw no actual movement by the hermit. It was as if the wind simply reached out for him. One moment he was on the slab, watching his bag drop, the next he was in the void, following it, passing his robe as it fluttered downward. His mantra seemed to grow louder as he fell. Shan could still hear it after he dropped from sight, leaving only his robe, empty, floating gently into the shadows.

He did not know how long he stared into the fissure. When he turned, Gao and Hostene were at the altar, anger on their faces, as if Shan had cheated them of something.

"What was that you did with your hand?" Gao asked.

"It was nothing," Shan said. But it was something. Shan had finally understood everything, and the only thing he could offer was the *abhaya* mudra, the hand gesture known as Bestowing Refuge.

"He had a bag," Hostene said. "Why did he take that old bag?"

Shan looked at the Navajo. He could see in his eyes that Hostene understood but needed to hear it said aloud. "His offering. The deity he prayed to seemed to favor necklaces of body parts."

"The hands," Gao murmured.

"I tried to stop him, tried to get the evidence," a new voice said from behind them — Kohler. "But he hit me and tied me up."

Shan studied the items Rapaki had left on

the altar. An agate *dzi* bead, a traditional good-luck charm. A small silver incense case. And, still in the cloth pouch, something hard and lumpy that Shan recognized from its feel. He handed the pouch to Hostene.

"The beetle!" Hostene exclaimed. It was Abigail's golden beetle.

Hostene followed as Shan moved to the end of the slab where the hermit had jumped. The Navajo pointed to a small ledge fifty feet below, then another deeper, and another to the side. The first held a rag, a piece of clothing caught in a crack in the rock. The other two held small yellow rocks.

"It's where the gold went, isn't it?" Hostene said, "the missing gold. All these centuries, they just brought it up to the bayal."

Shan nodded as Gao and Kohler approached. "It's the best use of gold, the old Tibetans always thought. To praise the deities."

Hostene offered a sad, reverent nod. "It's over. He'll kill no more."

"Not in this world," Kohler said. Then, remembering Abigail, he turned and jogged back to the cavern.

Gao watched the German for a moment. "Heinz returned yesterday," he explained to

Shan. "He had the helicopter leave him here when he discovered I had been dropped near the summit. He was already here when Rapaki arrived with Abigail, and quickly understood what had happened." The physicist studied the altar a moment, then gazed into the blackness below. "How does it happen? How does a holy man become deranged?"

"Perhaps the real miracle of modern Tibet," Shan replied, "is that they are not all like that."

They were reluctant to move Abigail immediately, and decided to make camp inside the shallow cavern. There was no wood for a fire but the goat trails around the summit were littered with dried dung. Kohler and Hostene set off to gather fuel in a bandanna as Yangke sat with Abigail, a makeshift blindfold over his eyes, his hand cradling Abigail's as she slept. Probing the back of the cavern, Shan gleaned from the shadows a small iron bowl and two cracked ceramic jars with dried grease inside, butter lamps abandoned long ago.

Soon they had a bowl filled with rainwater simmering with leaf tips. As the tea brewed, Hostene investigated the contents of his niece's pack. There were four feathered spirit sticks, two little ketaan figures, even some flower heads stuffed into a plastic bag for their pollen. Hostene held up her journal, pointing out several new pages of writing, describing newly discovered shrines but nothing more, nothing about their ascent of the summit, nothing from the days since Thomas had been killed. But then her uncle pointed to where the writing stopped. A dozen pages had been torn out of her precious book.

As she drank her tea, Abigail stirred from her trance slowly, finally holding the warm bowl in both hands herself, rocking back and forth in front of the little fire, staring into her tea. Hostene sat beside her, watching with worried eyes.

"Lha gyal lo," she said, looking only at Shan, then leaned against her uncle's shoulder, looking now like a tired and frightened schoolgirl.

"It's altitude sickness," Kohler explained. "I've seen it many times. The symptoms vary. Sometimes, when the brain swells, the victim loses all sense of reality. He or she might be capable of anything, I guess." He turned to Gao. "I will go to bring back help."

"No, Heinz," Gao said. He had hardly taken his gaze from the chasm since Rapaki had flung himself into it. "We are a blind man, an injured woman, and two old men. We need you and Shan with us for the descent. Only two of the staffs are left. We'll need them both for the final climb down that chain."

"Old? You and Hostene? Men of iron don't get old, even if they corrode around the edges."

Gao was not interested in glib rejoinders. "We need rest. As you have reminded us, the altitude alone can kill if we are not careful. As for the monk who died, I can't help but wonder if words should be said."

"Words?" Kohler shot back. "For a bloodthirsty killer? What do you think he had in that damned bag? He wasn't taking sweets to his heathen gods. Whatever Thomas was missing was —" The sentence faded as the German saw Gao's brittle expression. "OK," he said. "Right. I'll stay."

"You don't understand Rapaki," came a low, dry voice. It was Yangke, blindfolded, speaking. "He tried hard at first to understand what being a monk meant, but he had no teachers. It is as if he had been asleep for years, fighting through nightmares, and this was the day he finally woke up."

No one replied. A single tear rolled down Abigail's cheek. She did not speak, did not offer any explanation, did not look up from her tea again. Hostene hovered near her, his face dark with worry and foreboding.

In the afternoon they tried to sleep. Shan, knowing he would never find slumber, helped Yangke to Hostene's side, and left the camp with the bandanna to gather more fuel. They weren't going anywhere that day and it would be a long cold night. He probed each goat trail, many of which petered out into tiny ledges, inches wide, along rock faces impassable for humans. He climbed toward the summit, noting for the first time a small shelf that overlooked both the east and west slopes. Something on it flashed in the sunlight, and he ducked for cover for a moment before warily advancing. He was perhaps two hundred feet away when he recognized it for what it was, and shrank back. Two small shiny solar panels were attached to a metal box with two six-foot poles rising out of it, all camoflauged with gray paint to blend with the rocks. He had stumbled upon a radio relay station for the army base below.

Half an hour later, the bandanna full and tied shut, he found another ledge with an open view to the south and east. He stepped to the edge, resisting the temptation to sit with crossed legs for an hour and let the wind scour him. But he did not dare leave the camp for so long. The army's secret installation below was in plain sight, no more than two miles away. Above the base was a huge steeply slanting wall of rock, with a strange pattern of pockmarks. He knelt, shielding his eyes, as he studied it. Not pockmarks. Steps had been constructed along ancient goat paths, and the army had used howitzers to destroy them. The devout had not all died at the top. For centuries they had had a way to descend after visiting the mountain god into the lush, fertile valley below, which would have seemed like a paradise to a pilgrim who had navigated the old Bon kora. For a brief moment he was buoyed with the hope that there still might be a safe way down. But no, the army had shown its usual thoroughness. Great slabs had been blown away by artillery shells in a dozen places. Not even a goat could make it down.

"I can see why the gods decided to live here." The smooth, confident voice came from directly behind Shan.

Shan let the cloth slide through his fingers, catching it by the loose gathered ends. A red flowered bandanna loaded with dung, the perfect weapon for the battle he had been drawn into. He did not face Kohler, but turned sideways, to maximize the force of his swing. "The lost gold, Heinz," he said in a conversational tone, "it all went down that hole long ago."

"Lost gold?"

"The gold Bing died trying to find."

"Bing? Was he one of those miners?"

"We called Lhasa, looking for you." He raised the bag of dung from his side. "Your old friend moved away over a year ago. That woman in your apartment, the one who has the hotel calls routed to her, does she go to India too?"

"You must be giddy, Shan. I warned you about the altitude."

Kohler advanced in small steps toward Shan. Behind Shan, inches away, was a five-hundred-foot drop. Shan pulled out the slip of paper with the private number he had obtained through Lhadrung. Kohler, perplexed for the moment, took it.

"Gao knows you lied, though he won't admit it yet. He knows if he called that number right now she would give him the same message. It's only a little lie, but with a man like Gao, once doubt begins it can't be stopped."

Shan dashed past him. Kohler grinned, opened his hand, and let the wind seize the paper on his open palm. "Gao knows I have business in India. Gao knows I have girlfriends."

"You dispatch trucks from Tashtul to India. It would take a special driver, and special papers. There would be fees to pay, bribes even. Customs officials are notorious. A lot of trouble for some little trinkets."

"It's the new world order. Converting Western appetites into Eastern cash."

Kohler did not follow when Shan started down the trail. After ten steps Shan looked back. The German was astride one of the high boulders, looking toward the smudge of color on the southern horizon, the distant Himalayas, the white sands of India beyond.

In Shan's absence Hostene had used the spirit feathers, placing them in a semicircle against the rock to encircle the place where he sat with Abigail. Abigail had begun a transformation back to the woman Shan had first met at Gao's storehouse, washing away her third eye, removing the jewelry and ceremonial vestment that had covered her denims. Gao was sleeping. Yangke, his blindfold bandage still in place, was working his beads with a low murmur.

Kohler said nothing when he returned. He helped with the camp work, then sat on a rock beside Gao when the older scientist awoke, speaking of the weather, their company business, of arrangements for Thom-

569

as's burial, of suggestions for the boy's funeral service. He had made a bowl of tea for the older man, offering some of his spare clothes to cushion Gao's seat on the rocks.

"Heinz, look!" Gao suddenly exclaimed with ridiculous hope in his voice as he pointed upward. "It's Albert and his father! The young one is flying!"

The announcement seemed to jar Kohler. He paused, then raised a hand, squinting, pointing like an eager boy as the two birds disappeared toward the western slope. "It would take days for us, but they can get home in five minutes," he said. He exchanged an awkward smile with Gao. But something seemed to have broken inside him.

Their strange, otherworldly day was coming to a close. They were finishing their domestic chores, stacking fuel for the night fire, arranging what blankets they had around Abigail and Yangke, when Shan saw a solitary figure pacing around the fissure. He caught up with Gao, and walked with him silently for several minutes.

"You never did answer my question," Shan said eventually. "About where Kohler spent his time in rehabilitation."

Gao paused, bent, and picked up a tiny yellow stone that had fallen at the edge of the fissure. He held it between his fingers, examining it intently for a moment. "It's just a bunch of molecules that were randomly arranged this way because they happened to be in the right place at the right time in some pool of magma four billion years ago."

"Maybe that's what's at the bottom of the abyss," Shan observed. "A pool of magma, to give the gold a chance to become something useful, like iron."

"In Tibet, even molecules can be reincarnated to a higher form," Gao said with a sad smile, and tossed the little nugget into the hole. They walked along the edge. Stars were coming out.

"It was a misunderstanding," Gao said suddenly. "Heinz attended a symposium in Japan. His expenses were submitted for reimbursement twice. There was an investigation, which found half a million dollars missing from laboratory funds. There could have been many explanations, we had a large staff. But he was responsible for the ledgers, so he was accountable. The clerk who worked for him was killed in an accident early in the investigation so there was no hard evidence. But someone had to pay.

Heinz was sent to a reeducation labor camp."

A reeducation camp was the softest form of punishment. Which meant that Gao must have interceded.

"His first month there he had a misunderstanding with a Public Security officer, who had to be hospitalized. Before I knew about it they had shipped him away. It took me a month to locate him."

"A hard-labor prison," Shan suggested. "A gulag camp."

"It never should have happened. You know how it goes. A man like Heinz attracted abuse in the gulag."

"He was sent to western Tibet," Shan ventured. "To Rutok."

In the dim light Shan could barely see Gao's stiff nod. They walked in silence, continuing around the fissure. Two of the cairns they passed had human bones lying before them.

"What did the hermit think he was going to find?" Gao asked eventually. "Where exactly did he think he was going?"

"The bayal? It's always warm there. He would land on a soft rainbow, surrounded by flowers and birds. Fountains of sweet water. Compassion and wisdom. His uncle went there forty years ago. He has gone to join him."

"Ah," Gao said, as if understanding now. Shan realized that Gao too had had a nephew in search of something.

"My father used to write to his grandfather and send him letters in smoke." It was an ancient Chinese practice, to write letters to the dead, burn them, and let the smoke carry the message to the heavens. "My father died when I was a boy," Shan said. "But sometimes, in the old tradition, I write to him."

Gao and Shan watched the moon rise, then began speaking of gold, and India, and of three men who met at a Tibetan prison camp near Rutok, each with his particular skill. Tashi, the artist forger. Bing, with his military training. The third with his command of a small but conveniently placed company. Eventually Shan left, returning with a piece of paper torn from Abigail's journal, one of her ink pens, and one of the old butter lamps that Shan had lit.

"I don't know what to say to him," Gao said in a hoarse whisper.

"When I write my father, sometimes I just speak of my life," Shan confided. "Sometimes I say I am sorry for not being all that he would have expected of me. Sometimes I explain that once in a while I can still sense

573

him walking beside me. Once," he said, his voice cracking, "I confessed that of all the mysteries that are sent my way, the ones I know I will never solve are those of the human heart."

Shan left Gao then, and wandered up the trail they had arrived on that morning. He watched the camp from a distance, then retrieved two leg bones from one of the cairns, and set to work. When he finished he found a perch a short distance from where Gao still sat, writing. Shan looked into the blackness of the fissure, then at the sky. A dark shape fluttered across the face of the moon. It could have been a cloud. It could have been a dragon.

The explosions came in rapid sequence, jolting Shan from a fog that was almost sleep. Lightning, shouted a panicked voice in the back of his mind. No, worse, he realized. Gunshots. Three closely spaced gunshots, from the place where he had left his three companions.

CHAPTER FIFTEEN

Gao had already taken several unsteady steps toward the shots when Shan grabbed him, pointed in the opposite direction, and ran.

His quarry was moving slowly, far less confident about rushing through the night landscape than Shan. The ghost on the trail stopped him. Shan, watching from the shadows, tossed a pebble against the ghost to make it move. It had been a rushed job, building a four-foot cairn in a shadowed section of the trail, joining the two bones into a rough cross frame with the yak-hair rope, then arranging his white undershirt on it, topped by a face made from another sheet of paper from Abigail's journal, pierced by two round eyeholes. But on this mountain, on this night, it was enough to make anyone pause.

Shan made no attempt to conceal his presence as he approached. Kohler spun around at the sound of his boots. The German let one of the two staffs he carried drop against the tall rock beside him as his hand went to the small of his back. He turned sideways so as to be able to see both Shan and the ghost. More gravel rattled on the path behind Shan.

"Did you hear the shots?" Kohler blurted out as he saw Gao. "She's crazy. She talks to herself half the time. She helped the lunatic monk tie me up yesterday. We can't wait to go down together. I have to get help right away. God knows what she's done."

"Then we need you here more than ever," Shan suggested, inching forward.

Kohler edged toward the ghost cairn, seeming to recognize what it was. "You made this," he growled at Shan. "Take it down."

"It's a monument to dead hermits," Shan rejoined.

The hand behind Kohler's back re-appeared, holding a small black gun. "Take it down," he ordered. When Shan did not move, the German thrust the gun forward, then swung the staff in his other hand upward, a blow that was meant to break ribs. As Shan jerked sideways, a rock flew through the air, connecting squarely with Kohler's brow. The German crumpled to the ground.

A familiar face appeared in the moonlight, wearing a surprised grin, the cloth blindfold hanging around his neck. Yangke could see again.

"He wasn't going to kill you," Gao offered in a taut voice.

"On that slender thread," Shan said, "I was betting my life."

Shan handed the gun to Gao. Then, with Yangke, he half carried, half dragged Kohler back to camp.

They laid Kohler by the fire and bound his arms and legs. There was no sign of Abigail or Hostene.

"I don't know where he took them," the Tibetan stated in an anxious tone. "My vision returned in the afternoon but I made some holes in the bandage and put it back on. I saw him lead Hostene and Abigail into the rocks above. He came back, tossed some pebbles in the fire, and ran toward the trail. They exploded three times. They were bullets, I guess, not pebbles." Yangke looked toward the summit. "I don't understand. It's as if the mountain makes everyone crazy. Up there are only cliffs and crevasses, no place to be at night." Yangke looked from the fire to the unconscious man, then ran up the slope, one step ahead of Shan. Gao sat on the ground beside Kohler, his head buried in his hands.

The German had done his work well. They found Hostene and his niece, gagged and tied back to back, abandoned on the narrow ledge where Kohler had confronted Shan earlier that day. They had been left twelve inches from a drop of five hundred feet. Abigail was slumped against Hostene, unconscious. Her uncle was staring so intensely into the night sky that Shan had to shake him before Hostene noticed him.

As Shan kneeled and untied the ropes, Abigail rolled into his arms. Hostene checked her pulse. She responded by pulling her hand away, then stretching. A sigh of relief escaped Hostene's lips. She had been sleeping.

They kept Kohler against the stone wall, behind the fire, watching him in shifts. Only Hostene chose to keep the pistol in his belt during his shift, Shan and Yangke selecting one of the long staffs as a weapon. Yangke, who seemed to be brimming over with questions, sensed that his queries needed to wait. Just one mystery was entirely explained that night when Shan approached Hostene, who sat at the opposite side of the fire, and handed him a brown plastic vial he had discovered when searching Kohler's pack.

"Kohler was right," Shan said. "Altitude sickness can have many symptoms. And he was prepared for them all." He showed Hostene three other similar containers he had taken from the pack, each with printed Chinese and English labels. "Acetazolamide," he said, lifting the first jar, "is taken to prevent the sickness, and to relieve early symptoms." He pointed to the other two. "Furosemide is for edema, promethazine for nausea. And what you are holding is morphine. Two or three of those and anyone will act the way she did this afternoon with Rapaki. And if this bottle was full, then she's been drugged for the last couple of days."

Hostene extended an arm as if to throw the little jar away, then glanced toward his sleeping niece and tucked it into his pocket.

"Once, at my old temple," Yangke declared after a moment, "a teacher said you can't have a god without a devil. The sinner defines the saint."

"I stopped making excuses for sinners long ago," Hostene rejoined, and walked back toward Kohler. Shan followed, watching as Hostene paced around the German, whose eyes were still closed. "The difference between you and me, Shan, is that you were an investigator. You just find facts and arrange them in the correct sequence. But

579

I," Hostene said, "I was a judge. You defined the messes. I had to clean them up."

"He's not exactly a killer," Shan said.

"That's what Yangke said about Rapaki. What do you mean?" Hostene demanded.

"He's a physicist turned businessman, the real managing director of Little Moscow. He had a business plan: Eliminate Chodron by discrediting him and making Bing a better offer. Take the miners' gold and pay them directly, eliminating most of their risks."

A new disdainful voice joined the conversation. "It was never planned to end this way," Kohler said, twisting himself until he was leaning against a rock. "I never intended any killings."

"No," Shan agreed. "The only planned murder took place last year, when Bing and Chodron decided to murder the dissenting miner and accuse his partner. Bing proved he could protect the miners so they elected him their head, just as he and Chodron intended. But that was before you cemented your alliance with Bing, before the three comrades from prison camp realized all the money they could make if each applied his particular skills to the business. Before you installed the new smelting equipment in Tashtul."

"It was Tashi," Kohler said, looking into the fire now. "He was the catalyst. He offered to make fraudulent customs forms for me so I could avoid paying duties. He was an amazing forger, a true artist. He practiced in prison by duplicating Buddhist scriptures. Bing discovered him faking passes for the guards at the gulag. Bing knew real talent when he saw it. And then Tashi told him about his magic mountain. Imagine my surprise when Bing asked if I had ever heard of the Sleeping Dragon."

"But it was you who saw the bigger possibilities," Shan pointed out. "Ship the gold in trucks to India. At the end of the summer you could convert the gold into Tibetan deities and yaks, the gold painted over to look like a cheaper metal in your little foundry in Tashtul. Then Tashi would take the souvenirs across the border with forged papers. Chodron's scheme of simply charging the miners a secret tax to was nothing compared to this." Shan glanced up at Yangke, who listened intently. Tashi had made him a promise, that he would ride all the way to India with the gods. "Heinz thinks on a global scale. He reversed Chodron's business structure. Instead of taking a percentage from the miners, he would take the gold and pay them a percentage. He assumed the risk in transporting the gold out of China and converting it somewhere else. That's why some of the miners had so much cash." He turned to Kohler. "You had already begun to build your market."

The German offered Shan a respectful nod. "If you want to predict the price of gold, count the number of wars being waged in the world. It's a bull market."

"An entrepreneurial miracle," Shan said in a flat voice. "Except your driver and forger was too entrepreneurial."

"Driving was merely a sideline for Tashi. Artwork was his passion. You're on a roll, Shan. Don't stop now. Except you forgot to point out that no one is hurt by my scheme except Chodron, whom everyone hates anyway."

"That changed when Tashi violated your rules. He was supposed to stay away from the mountain, wasn't he?"

"A great kid," Kohler said. "Except when he got drunk. He had a sweet job at our warehouse in Chamba. I arranged sleeping quarters, a television. All he had to do was stay there until I sent for him in the autumn."

"But he got bored," Shan suggested. "He missed his mountain. Maybe he heard Yangke was back and wanted to see his old friend. The secret expedition Professor Ma proposed was too good to pass up. It wouldn't affect your plan. He'd be back in time to help you run the foundry in Tashtul at the end of the summer, then drive to India. But he was a social creature, and when he saw some miners with Thomas's vodka he couldn't resist approaching them."

"Technically," Kohler inserted, "it was my vodka. Never in a thousand years would I have guessed Thomas would steal my liquor to sell. Christ, that's how it all started. My pepper vodka."

"When Tashi drank," Yangke whispered, "he would sing old songs of the saints."

"When Tashi got drunk," Shan added, "he sang everything. He wasn't much of a criminal, he just wanted to have friends."

"But why kill Professor Ma?" Hostene asked in a hollow voice. "Why kill Bing himself?"

"Tashi was out of control. He had to be dealt with, he had to be silenced. I was the chief executive. Bing was in charge of dealing with details," Kohler said in a matter-of-fact tone. "Bing had Rapaki waiting in the circle of stones that night. He was going to bring only Tashi to him. But the professor woke up. And Bing might have lived if he hadn't followed us up here. It spun out of my control. You have to take your losses and move on, I told Bing. It had become too risky. But he wouldn't listen."

"Because he had a whole new plan," Shan suggested, "for which he needed no partner."

Kohler slowly nodded. "Apparently. After Rapaki started working on him he became obsessed with the lost gold. Bing said there was more than enough for both of us."

"But you had already borrowed the laser pointer," Shan said. "And you had learned Rapaki's magic words."

"Ni shi sha gua, ni shi sha gua . . ." Kohler's mocking mantra faded away. Gao had returned, and had been listening.

The German seemed to shrink under Gao's gaze.

They left Yangke watching Kohler and lay down in the little alcove at the rear of the cavern, though Shan could tell from the sound of their breathing that his companions were also unable to sleep.

"I don't understand." Hostene's voice floated through the darkness. "Kohler was going to get all the gold he could need. Why did he need the monks' gold?"

"He wasn't coming for the monks' gold," Shan said.

"That was all Bing's idea," a new voice

interjected. For the first time Abigail seemed free of the effects of the morphine. "He was waiting when Thomas and I came through the passage that morning. He hit Thomas, then tied me up and blindfolded me, and took me away to some other rocks. I was grateful when Kohler finally appeared. He said he had not been able to get to town, that he knew I might need help, that we had to hide until Shan caught up with Bing. He suggested we go up the kora, he'd always wanted to go follow the path and this was the perfect time to take Rapaki and finish my research.

"He helped me with my work, held the camera and carried my pack when I was tired. He didn't object when I said I had to let Rapaki dress me as Tara, to win his trust. I still thought he was helping, and that his intentions were good when he told me I was showing signs of altitude sickness and gave me medicine. By the time Bing caught up with us, my mind was affected by the drugs. I watched from a distance, in some kind of fog. I hated Bing for hitting Thomas and taking him away. Kohler told me Bing had also been there when Professor Ma and Tashi were killed. He sat me on a rock and told me to stay there. I didn't say anything, I didn't run away. I wanted Bing punished but I thought they were going to tie him up, to take him prisoner. Then Rapaki began reciting his mantras about demons. Heinz stood there with the laser pointer as if he were directing a play. I closed my eyes when I saw the ax. A few minutes later they came up the trail. Rapaki was serenely singing one of his songs. Maybe I hadn't seen what I thought I did, I kept telling myself. Maybe it was the drugs."

"Heinz came here to tidy up," Shan said, "To get rid of any witnesses. The three surviving people who could do him harm were on this mountaintop. He meant to go down alone. He would have reappeared from his business trip to India and mourned Thomas, maybe even helped us look for you, Abigail."

"I'm not sure what happens now," Abigail said. "If he goes to the authorities he will try to bargain for his life by telling them about the miners, about the village, about your friends. I don't want the Tibetans to be hurt, Shan," she said. "Tell me how to save the Tibetans."

But Shan pretended to be asleep.

In the gray light of dawn an owl interceded as Shan, rising from an hour's rest, approached the fire. Hostene had stayed several feet from Kohler but as Yangke exclaimed and pointed at the bird, Hostene, distracted and anxious, came too close. In a blur of movement Kohler leaped, kicking the remains of the fire with his bound feet, sending a shower of sparks into the air. His arms free, he pulled the gun from the belt of his surprised guard. Then he quickly untied his feet, herding his former captors into the back of the cave. He took Abigail's pack and his own, swinging the last two staffs onto his shoulder.

"Heinz," Gao said in a wooden voice. "It doesn't matter. He's on the way."

"What are you talking about?"

"Major Ren. With Public Security troops." Gao extracted his satellite phone from his pocket and held it up for Kohler to see. "You never searched me. I called them. Reception is remarkable from this altitude. It won't be long. This is the easiest place to find for fifty miles."

Kohler's face sagged. "I want everyone on that ledge," he ordered, "that high one that looks east. Now." He gestured with the pistol. "Yangke in front."

They walked in a solemn column. As the others entered the narrow gap in the rocks that opened onto the ledge, Kohler grabbed Shan's shirt and pulled him back. "Shan and I are going to speak for a while. Anyone who comes through this gap before I say so will be shot."

But Kohler was not really interested in conversation. He pushed Shan forward roughly, down the trail to the camp, onto the path toward the altar where Rapaki had prostrated himself.

Kohler said as they reached the edge of the fissure, "At the trial, you would be the one to tie it all together. No one else could. I started out thinking of you as a research scientist, drawing lines between disconnected facts. But that's not what you do. You're more like an artist. The barest touch of the brush, that's your style." Kohler's tone became whimsical. He tossed the staffs into the abyss. "Every paradise needs more artists." Shan tried to retreat from the rim. Kohler pushed him forward with the pistol against his spine.

"Two more months and I'll be in India — a new man, a new life, in a villa like a castle by the sea. I can still run the company from there. Gao will be lonely, but we can talk on the phone."

They reached the altar. Shan wondered how it would come. A violent shove? Or perhaps a blow from the pistol first? He remembered his nightmare of falling through bottomless darkness, passing skeletons who cringed when they saw him.

"He always had Thomas. He was going to spend more time in Beijing anyway, to be the boy's mentor. We could have talked on the phone," Kohler repeated, changing the tense of his words. "Nobody had to get hurt."

Kohler set his pistol on the altar. He began unbuttoning his shirt. "You're the only one who has any idea of what it's like," the German said. "The electric shocks. The batons. The pliers to the fingernails. We had a foreigner, a murderer, arrive in the winter, some poor fool from Pakistan. Outsiders who killed Chinese were always singled out for special treatment. They tied him naked to a pole out in the yard. He lived through the night but lost half a foot and six fingers to frostbite. Once he recovered, they beat him regularly and knocked out all his teeth. He ate worms when he could find them. Worms and rice gruel, that's all he could eat. Most of his hair fell out. He was thirty-five when he arrived. After six months he looked seventy." Kohler folded the shirt neatly, placed it at the foot of the altar, and glanced back at Shan. "You're the only one who understands what I mean. Someday, somehow, you must make him understand."

Shan took a step back, and another. "It

doesn't have to be like this, Heinz."

Kohler slipped off his shoes, carefully rolled his socks into them. "I kept thinking the damned kid couldn't possibly lift fingerprints from the rocks. He was just an amateur, after all. But he had to keep at it."

"Like sending fibers for analysis taken from cloth stuffed in the victim's mouth," Shan said.

Kohler gazed toward a passing cloud. "Like sending the fibers," the German agreed.

"From one of your scarves."

"We trained him to be persistent in his quest for knowledge."

"The price of fashion," Shan said. "No one on the mountain but you wears cashmere."

That message had sealed Thomas's fate, Shan knew now. Kohler had ascribed a distant, almost abstract role to himself in the killings the night before. Shan knew that the reality was much more direct. Kohler had stuffed his bloody scarf into Tashi's mouth and, later, when he was supposed to be hunting, helped Bing carry away severed body parts.

"Don't tell him," Kohler said in a whisper.

"There's no need for Gao to know," Shan agreed. "About that. Or about Thomas."

It wasn't simply that Kohler had been there when Thomas had died. He had summoned Bing and Rapaki to kill him.

Kohler pushed his shoes under the altar, his refined, assured voice returning. "You're supposed to be unburdened, right? Like Rapaki." He stepped forward. Along his naked back were the paired scars, familiar to Shan, where electric clamps had once been fastened. From his pocket he produced a small pouch, dumped some of its contents onto his palm, then sprinkled the yellow particles over his head. Not pollen. Gold dust. He paused for a moment, then poured the rest of the pouch over his shoulders.

"It's going to be an adventure, this bayal. Rapaki and I will probably be bunk mates. I'll debate physics with the gods who make lightning." Kohler stepped to the end of the overhanging slab and carefully placed his toes over the edge, extending his arms out from his sides. Bare-chested, barefoot, glittering, he was like a graceful diver preparing for a championship performance. He leaned forward, keeping perfect balance as he fell, his golden head raised, arms outstretched, until he disappeared into the blackness below.

When Shan turned, Gao was there, watching, his face ravaged with emotion.

Abigail ran down the path. "He could have shot you," she blurted out as she reached Shan.

"He could have shot me," Shan agreed.

Abigail looked from Shan to Gao in confusion, then over the side of the fissure. "He had to act before the helicopter arrived. He talked about the gulag one night. He couldn't face Public Security again."

Gao held up his phone. "There is no helicopter," he said. "The battery has been dead since that lightning storm."

Abigail was trembling. Hostene put his arms around her.

"We'll never make it down, not without staffs," Yangke said.

Shan peered into the surviving pack. He pulled out Kohler's folding knife, tossed it to Yangke, picked up a sharp, heavy stone, and pointed toward the summit. "You and I will go call our ride," he said.

It took them a quarter hour to reach the radio relay station, another ten minutes to remove its power supply. An hour later the army sent a helicopter to investigate.

CHAPTER SIXTEEN

Chodron avoided Shan and his friends after they returned to the village. When he saw Abigail he glared, then looked up the trail behind her, as if waiting for Bing to make an appearance. He seemed to be satisfied with asserting his authority by posting a guard at Dolma's house to keep Gendun, Lokesh, and the two Navajos inside. He did not object when they sent for food, did not seem to notice when ever-increasing numbers of villagers began visiting, often staying for hours, not even when his wife joined them. Several times a day he started his generator. More than once Shan saw him walking alone in the blackened fields.

The day before August 1, the headman and his lieutenants began erecting decorations for his festival day, though few others joined in to help fasten the paper flags and faded red and yellow streamers to doorways. An hour after dawn on his long-awaited day, he began playing patriotic anthems over a portable stereo connected to his generator, then stood in front of it in dress clothes, waving his arm as if conducting a chorus while his men set off strings of firecrackers. Shan sat on a bench with Yangke, watching and waiting.

Chodron did not immediately hear the approach of the helicopter that landed in the fields above. He kept waving his imaginary baton, calling irately to the villagers who were ignoring him, watching the slope. Then his arm froze in midair and his forced smile evaporated. He had noticed the two men coming down through the fields.

"There are refreshments," Chodron called to Gao as soon as they were in earshot. "Such an honor to have you and" — he looked uncertainly at the young Public Security officer who had helped Gao in Tashtul — "the military join us." He gestured toward his house.

Gao ignored him. He turned to Shan. "Do you have a preference as to where we do this?"

"I do," Shan said, and pointed to the empty granary where Chodron had carried on his tamzing sessions.

The headman looked about for his deputies, who had disappeared. The officer stepped forward and pulled him by the elbow.

"There is a relocation program," the young officer announced when they were inside. The hesitation he had shown in Tashtul was gone. He was all business. "This is your one-hour notice."

Chodron's mouth opened, his jaw moved up and down, but no sound came out. The color slowly drained from his face. "My village!" he finally blurted out. "We can't . . . I am secretary of the . . ." He looked to Gao, as if for help. But Gao stood silent, hands folded in front of him.

"I made no mention of the village," replied the officer. "The honor is all yours."

Chodron's eyes narrowed as they studied the officer, then Gao, and finally Shan. Color began returning to his face. "I am the secretary of the —," he began again in a louder voice.

The officer sighed impatiently, then extracted a folded letter from his pocket and extended it to Chodron. "You will see more than enough signatures." He made a show of looking at his watch. "You now have fifty-five minutes."

"Impossible!" the headman hissed. "We can't begin to —" His voice faded away as he scanned the letter.

"Your wife," came a soft voice from the shadows, "has chosen not to make the journey." Dolma took a step forward, into the light. She looked radiant, a freshly polished silver-and-turquoise prayer amulet hanging over her simple black dress. "She is going to live with me. Your house is going to become the village school."

Chodron fixed Shan with a spiteful glare. "I have many things to move to Tashtul."

"Just your clothes," declared the officer. "Your new home is nowhere near Tashtul."

"But I have a house there!" Chodron protested. "I have a . . ." He glanced at Dolma, and chose not to finish the sentence.

"Miss Jiling?" the officer replied. "I fear she left rather suddenly. Something about family trouble in Manchuria. And your house and all its contents are being sold."

"Sold? You can't just —"

"It should pay for the lost crop," Dolma interjected. "That should feed us through the winter. With the money left over, we will begin rebuilding the old temple."

"You!" Chodron spat at Shan.

"We're not sure if we can find all your accounts," Shan said in a level voice. "But no doubt Jiling knows where they are. She has probably already made withdrawals. She will have a lot of expenses in Manchuria."

Chodron looked as if he was about to strike Shan. The officer stepped closer. "We asked Gendun what should be done with you," Shan continued. "You owe your life to his compassion. We have arranged for your reincarnation. Without the inconvenience of a firing squad."

The officer explained quickly now, permitting no more interruption. Professor Gao had been kind enough to arrange for a posting for Chodron as head of civil affairs for a military installation in Xinjiang. It was deep in the desert, but the dry climate was said to be quite good for the health.

Chodron seemed to shrink before their eyes. "You can't do this," he said, though his voice had lost all strength. "There are people I can call."

"Your people," Shan observed, "won't return your phone calls. They've seen the letter, with the signatures from Beijing."

"You!" Chodron snarled again. "You have no idea what I can —"

"Perhaps you haven't read the final paragraph."

Chodron's gaze returned to the paper and the color drained from his face. The last paragraph reported that Chodron had been stripped of his Party membership. For the rest of his life he would be nothing more than a tiny cog among the vast wheels of the Chinese bureaucracy.

"If you wish to resist," Shan said in a weary voice, "the ledgers will be in safe hands. Before she left, Miss Jiling surrendered the one from Tashtul along with an explanatory statement about census figures, government allocations, and your secret accounts. And the other as well."

"There is no other," Chodron said in a hollow voice.

"A loyal Party member such as you would no doubt be pleased if the entire village read *The Quotations of Chairman Mao*," Shan suggested. "A clever touch. Your wife retrieved it for me."

Chodron's mouth opened and shut but no words came out.

"Fifty minutes," the officer announced.

Before the headman left the chamber Dolma handed him a letter, ready for his signature. It was being sent as his last official act. The census numbers were being revised to reflect that, due to the relocation of their families, the children in boarding school would have to rejoin their parents, and the village would have no more school-age children to send to the school. This had been Dolma's idea. She was bringing the children home and assuring that no more would be sent away. Yangke had decided to stay and become the first teacher in the new school. Chodron glared at Shan, then silently scrawled his name at the bottom.

No one bid the headman goodbye. The gathered villagers watched in silence by a small mound of boxes. While Chodron had been packing, Yangke, Shan, and two soldiers had been carrying the boxes from the helicopter. Gao had sent food, many crates of food, the likes of which some of the villagers had never seen. As they began opening the containers, Lokesh and Dolma appeared, helping Gendun to a nearby bench. When the roar of the helicopter faded into the distance, the old lama began to sing in a frail voice brimming with joy. His song grew stronger as the yellow and red flags were replaced with prayer flags prepared the night before in Dolma's house. One figure stood apart until a small girl in a bright red apron stepped forward and put her hand in his. Gao had arranged to be picked up the following day.

The afternoon was spent in busy, near frantic preparation, following the careful instructions of Hostene and Lokesh, who had been consulting for days, with Gendun as mediator. They had settled on the second of the old granaries as the site because, Hostene explained, the circular stone structure most resembled the hogans of his people.

Shepherds had left their flocks to collect colored sands and pollen, returning with reports that many of the miners were fleeing the mountain. Several of the village women had helped Abigail make feathered spirit sticks and improvise jewelry to wear. Hostene had passed the previous day with Lokesh in an improvised sweat lodge. Shan had helped to carry hot rocks and water as they were needed for the Navajo purification ceremony.

Shan was watching, vaguely smiling, from one of the flat rocks above the village when he heard a rustle of gravel. Gao did not speak as he settled beside him. The scientist seemed older but also somehow more human. Below them, the children were helping Gendun walk to the bottom of the fields, where Trinle was staking out the dimensions of their new temple.

"I saw you put that pack in the rocks above," Gao observed.

Since returning to the village Shan had spent hours alone every night, seated on the ledge above the village. He had finally reached a decision. There would be a day, not this day or the next, but soon, when he would slip away into the shadows. He loved the old Tibetans like blood relations but he could not bear the thought of causing them further harm. His life on the mountain was coming to an end. Lokesh understood, though no words had been spoken about it. His old friend had found him one night on the rock, had accepted the return of his prayer amulet, then sat with Shan in a silence that communicated far more than words. He had taken Shan's hand, cupping it, joining it at the fingertips to his own cupped hand. It was the Treasure Flask mudra. What they had done together had been a great treasure, Lokesh was saying. Then he had pulled his hand away and walked into the shadows.

"Once," Shan declared in a quiet voice, "the traveling beggar followed an honored profession in Tibet."

"I have to go back to Beijing for the funeral," Gao said. "But I will return before the cold weather. I have many empty rooms. Even a wandering beggar may pause under a roof, maybe even take up residence in a burrow for the winter. We could read the old poets as the snow falls."

"I would like that," was Shan's reply.

As purple remnants of the day lingered on the western horizon, Lokesh and Hostene

601

commenced. The Navajo healing ceremony usually took nine days, Lokesh's rites at least three. With Gendun's counsel they had settled on a ceremony of seven days, a marriage of Hostene's Mountainway chant and Lokesh's Invocation of the Medicine Buddha. Faces would be smeared with pollen, Hostene warned, and long nights would be spent chanting. Long-sleeping deities would be awakened, Lokesh had countered, and there would be frequent pauses to check the pulse of their subject at her neck, wrist, and ankle. On the first night, Hostene would begin a Navajo sandpainting with Lokesh's help. When that was finished Lokesh would start a Tibetan sand mandala, with Hostene's help. The old Tibetans spoke with Abigail in soft, murmuring tones, assuring her that they had often seen even the worst of illnesses cured by the old ways.

As Shan settled onto the ground in the place saved for him between Gendun and Lokesh, Abigail smiled at him serenely. Shan had asked her why she had stopped writing in her journal. She had admitted that scientific evidence of links between their peoples would always be incomplete. Abigail had explained that her weeks on the mountain had taught her the difference between truth and mere fact. She had at last learned the truth about herself, and as for the rest, this mountain, these people, this ceremony would be proof enough for her.

AUTHOR'S NOTE

The notion that two peoples separated by more than ten thousand miles and easily as many years could share common roots may at first seem but a romantic fancy, but the evidence has given pause to more than a few experts. The common elements between the Tibetans and the Navajo-Dine peoples set forth in these pages are, like all the themes in my books, based upon fact. Long before I considered weaving them into one of my mysteries I had been fascinated not just by the physical similarities between Tibetans and the native peoples of the American Southwest but also by the many common cultural and religious aspects appearing in such disparate geographies. Sandpaintings, thunder gods, and religious swastikas are only some of the more readily apparent indicators of possible links. Whether your particular interests lean toward linguistics, medicine, ice age geology, genetics, cosmology, or earwax, you can find fragments of evidence supporting an ancient connection.

While it seems unlikely that such fragments from conventional science will ever combine for unequivocal proof, I side with my ever-intuitive characters in concluding that the most compelling similarities have not so much to do with the artifacts of everyday existence but the overlapping remnants of the spiritual life of the two peoples. Over fifty years ago anthropologist Frank Waters, in his book *The Masked Gods,* noted the parallels between the death rituals of Tibetans and the Navajo and Pueblo Indians. More recently anthropologist Peter Gold expanded this premise in his fascinating book *Navajo and Tibetan Sacred Wisdom,* which masterfully probes parallels in the inner teachings of both peoples. As the debate over both ethereal and empirical evidence continues, the Tibetans and Southwestern Indians have dealt something of a preemptive strike: with the expansion of the modernday Tibetan diaspora, the traditional homeland of those Indians is becoming a significant relocation site for dispossessed Tibetan families.

Ultimately the real reward of the riddles about Tibetans and the peoples of the

American Southwest may lie in the telling, not in the answering. The most important lessons emerging from this exercise perhaps are not about whom they may be but whom the rest of us are. Years ago I hung over my desk Carl Jung's epitaph for contemporary man. Modern humanity, Jung wrote, "has sold its soul for a mass of disconnected facts." If we want to glimpse the way things might have been before we struck this hollow bargain we have but to look to the traditional Tibetans and Navajo, who, as they have for centuries, live lives of deep purpose, closely connected to the primal world.

However elusive may be the proof of prehistoric links, these people without question share a modern reality: they have both been under siege by outside political and economic forces. The Navajo, Pueblo, and Hopi tribes have long struggled with mineral exploitation on their sacred lands. The degree of environmental damage inflicted by mining on the Tibetan lands is of epic proportions. Entire mountains have been destroyed by mining, including a number that were considered sacred by the Tibetans, leading to destruction of adjoining watersheds and their accompanying ecosystems. While the largest of these projects have been organized by the government of China, outlaw miners, unaccountable to anyone, are rampant in several mineral rich districts of Tibet, particularly the traditional Tibetan province of Kham.

In some areas such miners are as much a part of the modern Tibetan landscape as the defrocked monks represented by Yangke in this novel. For many years the primary "illegal" monks in Tibet were those who had survived the wholesale destruction of temples and monasteries during the early years of the Chinese occupation. Now a new generation of orphaned monks is emerging out of the monasteries that Beijing's Bureau of Religious Affairs has permitted to reopen under its close regulation. Monks deemed politically undesirable, or who decline to submit to loyalty oaths, are ejected, prohibited from wearing robes again. Some make the often dangerous crossing to India to find monasteries outside their homeland. Others retreat to remote villages and do their best as monks without teachers, joining the ranks of the many unsung heroes in Tibet who struggle to maintain their ethnic and spiritual identity in the face of sometimes overwhelming adversity.

ELIOT PATTISON

GLOSSARY OF FOREIGN
LANGUAGE TERMS

Terms that are used only once and defined in adjoining text are not included in this glossary.

bayal. Tibetan. Traditionally, a "hidden land," where deities and other sacred beings reside.

Bon. Tibetan. An ancient spiritual tradition indigenous to Tibet which far predated the rise of Buddhism. The Bon pantheon of deities and rich array of Bon ritual practices were in many respects assimilated by Tibetan Buddhism.

canque. Tibetan-Mandarin. A heavy wooden collar, generally extending past the shoulders, clamped onto the necks of criminals as punishment.

druk. Tibetan. A dragon.

dzong. Tibetan. Traditionally used to describe a Tibetan fortress or castle. Today the term is also applied to local administrative units in Tibet.

gau. Tibetan. A "portable shrine," typically a small hinged metal box, often made of silver, carried around the neck or waist, into which a prayer and/or a relic has been inserted.

genpo. Tibetan. A village headman.

gompa. Tibetan. A monastery, literally a "place of meditation."

ketaan. Navajo. A small wooden cylinder cut from a branch growing on the east side of a tree, typically crudely carved with head and legs to indicate a human figure, with the head always carved from the growing end of the stick. Used as a ceremonial offering, the ketaan is traditionally painted according to the colors of the four directions and laid in pairs on a bed of cornmeal in a ritual basket.

kora. Tibetan. A pilgrim's circuit, typically a circumambulation around a sacred site.

lama. Tibetan. The Tibetan translation of the Sanskrit "guru," traditionally used for a fully ordained senior monk who has become a master teacher.

lha gyal lo. Tibetan. A traditional phrase of celebration or rejoicing, literally "victory to the gods."

mala. Tibetan. A Buddhist rosary, typically consisting of one hundred eight beads.

mani stone. Tibetan. A stone inscribed, by

painting or carving, with a Buddhist prayer for compassion, invoking the mantra Om Mani Padme Hum.

Milarepa. Tibetan. The great poet saint of Tibet who lived from 1040 to 1123.

mudra. Tibetan. A symbolic gesture made by arranging the hands and fingers in prescribed patterns to represent a specific prayer or offering.

ni shi sha gua. Mandarin. Literally "you stupid melon," more commonly used as a slur, connoting "you retard" or "you damned imbecile."

peche. Tibetan. A traditional Tibetan book of scripture, traditionally unbound, in long, narrow loose leafs which are wrapped in cloth, often tied with carved wooden end pieces.

ragyapa. Tibetan. Corpse cutters, the people who perform the dismemberment of bodies that is part of the Tibetan sky burial tradition.

tamzing. Mandarin. A "struggle session," typically a public criticism of an individual in which humiliation and verbal and/or physical abuse is utilized to achieve political education. The practice was widespread during the Cultural Revolution period.

tangka. Tibetan. A painting on cloth, typically of a religious nature and generally considered sacred, traditionally painted as a portable scroll on fine cotton.

Tara. Tibetan. A female meditational deity, revered for her compassion and considered a special protectress of the Tibetan people. Tara has many forms, each of which has specific ritual application. She is sometimes referred to as the Mother of Buddhas.

torma. Tibetan. A ritual offering made primarily of butter and barley flour, shaped and often dyed in many shapes and sizes in homage to Buddhist deities.

tsampa. Tibetan. Roasted barley flour, a traditional staple food of Tibet.

ABOUT THE AUTHOR

Eliot Pattison is the author of *The Skull Mantra,* which won the Edgar Award, as well as *Water Touching Stone, Bone Mountain* and *Beautiful Ghosts.* A lawyer, he is a world traveler and a frequent visitor to China. He lives in Pennsylvania.

The employees of Thorndike Press hope you have enjoyed this Large Print book. All our Thorndike and Wheeler Large Print titles are designed for easy reading, and all our books are made to last. Other Thorndike Press Large Print books are available at your library, through selected bookstores, or directly from us.

For information about titles, please call:
(800) 223-1244

or visit our Web site at:
http://gale.cengage.com/thorndike

To share your comments, please write:
Publisher
Thorndike Press
295 Kennedy Memorial Drive
Waterville, ME 04901